A Matter of Conscience

Fergal Nally

Order this book online at www.trafford.com/07-2770
or email orders@trafford.com

Most Trafford titles are also available at major online book retailers.

Note for Librarians: A cataloguing record for this book is available from Library and Archives Canada at www.collectionscanada.ca/amicus/index-e.html

Cover Design/Artwork: Fergal Nally
courtesy of Combridge Fine Arts Ltd, Dublin 2 www.cfa.ie

Printed in Victoria, BC, Canada.

ISBN: 978-1-4251-6095-1

We at Trafford believe that it is the responsibility of us all, as both individuals and corporations, to make choices that are environmentally and socially sound. You, in turn, are supporting this responsible conduct each time you purchase a Trafford book, or make use of our publishing services. To find out how you are helping, please visit www.trafford.com/responsiblepublishing.html

Our mission is to efficiently provide the world's finest, most comprehensive book publishing service, enabling every author to experience success. To find out how to publish your book, your way, and have it available worldwide, visit us online at www.trafford.com/10510

Trafford PUBLISHING™ **www.trafford.com**

North America & international
toll-free: 1 888 232 4444 (USA & Canada)
phone: 250 383 6864 • fax: 250 383 6804 • email: info@trafford.com

The United Kingdom & Europe
phone: +44 (0)1865 722 113 • local rate: 0845 230 9601
facsimile: +44 (0)1865 722 868 • email: info.uk@trafford.com

10 9 8 7 6 5 4 3

Born in Dublin Fergal Nally is a doctor of medicine, M.D.
For many years he was Head of a clinical department in the University of London and Consultant in several London hospitals.
Pain and cancer research formed a large part of his work and resulted in many publications in the scientific and medical literature.
He is also a Fellow of the Royal Society of Arts.

Dedicated to Maeve Binchy for her
encouragement, wise counselling and example
without which this book would not have been written

Part One

CHAPTER 1

She lies there on the floor, dying. The stench of burning flesh is hideous. Flames leap up at the end of the room and noise from the falling roof is terrifying. She's petrified. If she moves forward she'll go straight into the fire; a solid wall is behind and on each side filing cabinets, machines and computers block her escape. There's nowhere to go. No way out. Just has to lie down and accept fate. She closes her eyes and waits.

To her left a crashing sound is heard and a door collapses. A friend rushes in with fire extinguisher and attacks the flames.

She remains on the ground unable to move. Vaguely she's aware of the friend taking her in his arms and speaking softly. In the background the screams of others go on. It's horrendous. Smoke begins to suffocate, making it difficult to breath. Everything's an effort and is getting worse. She loses consciousness.

John is the first on the scene. Units One and Two are completely destroyed, although there are survivors in Unit Three. He approaches the beagle that's badly burned; it can only whine. Speaking softly he takes her in his arms. She responds in her usual way, the only way she can—with affection. There's a show of friendliness—flapping ears adoring eyes and stroking tail. Then only a whimper. He talks gently as the head is lowered and eyes are closed. He feels for the carotid. Nothing. She has died from sheer terror and others are in shock.

'The alarm's been inactivated,' the chief fire officer says with resignation. 'Looks bad.'

'Deliberate?' John asks angrily.

'Seems likely.'

'Bloody bastards!' He bangs a fist on the charred remains of his laboratory desk. Repulsion goes deep as he counts survivors. Eventually nausea overcomes him and he has to be helped from the building.

Soon after midnight the skies darken, snow falls and white covers everything. An hour later all is quiet. Trees are black under a shroud and the church spire rises in silent authority.

Next morning John Nicholson slowly walks to his office. Several times he stops in the hospital courtyard overcome with emotion. He's defeated by misery piled on misery; what he wants is to help, to work for a better life for all. Also, there's Linda's illness to cope with—an appalling burden. Will she be able to manage without him today? Constant monitoring is required with her new treatment. Now the fire. Trouble never ending!

Eventually he reaches his makeshift office and collapses into a chair. Twisting and turning he aimlessly arranges papers. Already exhausted he stretches his arms on the desk and bows his head.

Letters are delivered, many from countries congratulating him on new papers on chemotherapy. He opens one containing a scribbled message and smelling of smoke stating the animals were killed before the fire 'as a humane gesture to put them out of their misery.'

He shoves it in his pocket and rushes to Professor Wainwright's office. Without knocking he enters.

He flings his white coat across an adjacent chair.

'How did it happen?'

'We don't know,' Wainwright says calmly with a military bearing, 'although the Gardai are working on it.'

'I've my suspicions. And the damage is enormous.' His voice trembles. 'Data that's taken years to accumulate—gone! It could've saved lives, especially children. Now lost. Irretrievable. I even wonder if I can go on.'

'You can't give up now.' Wainwright's response is swift.

John bombards him with questions.

Days later a typewritten letter arrives addressed to Dr John Nicholson. It's from the Secretary of the Dublin Branch of the International Animal Liberation Front. A meeting is requested. First reaction is to throw it away. Then—there may be something to gain. He replies that he'd be prepared for a short meeting and it's decided their representative will call to the Institute.

Even though the sun's shining Tom Nolan's wearing his old raincoat. He pauses, staring at the building—ominous and menacing. Does he have to go through with it? He could turn away and go home. Yet, that'd mean he'd no courage and had given up. No, he has to keep the appointment. Matter's too important.

Noise from his hob-nailed boots is difficult to miss as he arrives at Dr Nicholson's door. He knocks hard and loud.

'Come in.' John's soft voice responds.

The office is a chaos of salvaged papers, boxes and books—some soaked in water others half destroyed by fire—and the smell of smoke is everywhere. It's not going to prevent Tom Nolan having his say. The matter's too important, too bloody important altogether.

'Dr Nicholson.' Tom glances around the room and offers his hand. John holds back and then reluctantly accepts. The man's grip almost mangles his fingers.

'Tom Nolan's my name and I've come to talk about your work. May I sit down?'

John shrugs indifferently.

'You've heard what happened?'

'We saw it in the newspapers.' Tom announces in his deep positive voice. He sits down and crosses his legs.

'Don't suppose you can tell us who did it?' John's question goes straight to the point. I bet he does know sensing the worst.

'No. But I can tell you why,' Tom says deliberately evading the other's eyes.

John waves a gesture of invitation.

'Please do.'

The man hesitates, then placing his big hands on the desk and looking straight at John. 'We detest abuse of animals including research—as you probably know.'

John nods and his expression changes. 'You use the words abuse and research to imply the same thing. Please go on.'

'Dr Nicholson.' Uncrossing his legs Tom leans forward. 'Animals are not inferior to us, not underlings. They're our distant cousins and yet we abuse them cruelly. Do they do the same to us? They can be agreeable if only we let them. Think of the simple dog—a wonderful and faithful companion.'

For a moment, John senses compassion, feeling the intensity of the man's argument. Yes, he's right to say what he's saying. He certainly believes it. And yet and yet, my work has to have priority. Its purpose is to relieve suffering in humans and in animals. God, what conflict, what a choice to have to make —status quo or progress!

Slowly and impassively he replies. 'It can be, although that's beside the point.'

'It's not Dr Nicholson.' Tom persists loudly.

John's irritation rises; his next sentence loaded.

'But you eat meat and yet you won't use animals to save lives.'

Tom dismisses the suggestion with a fist on the desk.

'I don't eat animals.'

'Well they eat each other, don't they?'

'Some do,' Tom concedes with a sigh. He's heard this all before. 'And look what's happened to others, such as the humble cow when she's forced to do so. Now we have the BSE crisis.'

Almost everyday John sees children dying in hospital. Usually it's a slow and painful death; yet he's unable to help. All he can hope for is that the inevitable is not drawn out so much it becomes unbearable. His current work could help stop this suffering.

What the hell was this man talking about? If only he could take him on a tour of the children's ward. That would open his eyes to what research was trying to achieve. My one hope is that you, Tom Nolan, or your family will never need our help for any of these illnesses.

'On the other hand, Mr Nolan, by research we can make our burdens—human and animal—all the lighter.' Anger is apparent as he asks another question. 'Can your people not see that?'

'We don't agree.' Again misunderstanding between them. 'There are other ways.'

John stares in surprise. 'Such as? I don't know these other ways.'

Tom takes time to answer. He's not prepared for this.

'I'm not an expert and … '

'… And we're trying to find a cure for cancer,' John interrupts passionately. 'In this Institute we'd almost reached a breakthrough in a form of blood cancer. That's until some of your friends destroyed our work.'

Tom gives a mocking smile. 'This is not the reason why I came.'

'Why have you come?' John asks blandly.

'My committee wants you to stop experiments on animals,' was the blunt reply.

'By what authority?' John shouts at him.

'By no civil authority, only compassionate grounds. More as an appeal on moral, ethical or even religious grounds.'

John is weary and irritable. This person is becoming impossible.

'Is man not a noble animal?'

'Far from it!' Disdain is written on Tom's face. 'Animals we call wild we treat with contempt and people who consider themselves well-bred and educated shoot them for sport to kill their own boredom.'

'You don't regard man very highly then?' John asks sarcastically turning away and not expecting an answer.

Tom declares in a ponderous voice. 'I would prefer animals as companions. They don't complain. Not one bows its head or genuflects to another or to one who may've lived thousands of years ago and … '

' … I must interrupt Mr Nolan.'

This is enough! This is too much! Nolan had asked for a discussion. This was ridiculous, overblown, like an hysterical speech from a zealous preacher. It was a display of intolerance, a diatribe. John is shocked, struggling with emotion,

Silence is like a brick wall.

A telephone rings. Briefly John speaks to Sister Agnes in ward 4 and replaces the dead receiver.

'Mr Nolan I'll have to leave you now. One of my patients has taken a turn for the worse. I must go and do what I can.'

'All right doctor. But remember what I say—when eyes are shut they don't cry. In the meantime, I'll give you our new address should you wish to contact us.'

Tom scribbles something.

'That won't be necessary. What I can say is we all must choose.' There's pride in his words. 'Apparently you have chosen. I know what my choice is. Goodbye!'

Noisily, Tom Nolan hurries from the building and gets into his old yellow van. Traffic is heavy as he drives across the city centre and gives him time to reflect on the meeting. He'd put his case well, yet there were many things left unsaid, such as the worldwide abuse of fellow creatures. He'd researched this problem for years. Unfortunately, cruelty was getting worse with pharmaceutical companies sponsoring more research and promising huge financial returns. Greed, pure greed it was! Many companies were multinational who knew how to influence politicians and legislators. A complex business. A difficult, almost impossible job to stop, but he wouldn't give up. Arriving home to his house beside the harbour later that evening, with Patsie, his faithful Labrador, first to greet him, eagerly followed by Annette, his ten-year old daughter and, of course, his loving wife, Ruth.

John goes to ward 4. A crowd of faces are waiting, children's faces, sad, happy and terrified. Nowhere, but nowhere, on earth is more pathetic than a ward full of sick children. They're so different to adults, always willing to tell the truth, but it's their loneliness and fear of the unknown that causes him greatest distress. Some find it hard to complain, others are beyond it—they've already given up.

He returns to his office having seen two children die, after attempting to comfort parents and answer their questions, after discussing future strategies, and after preparing detailed reports. Exasperation and disillusionment overcome him.

He notices a sheet of paper on his desk. Suddenly the handwriting. Anger sweeps over him. Yes of course! It's unmistakable. He writes with all the passionate intensity he's capable of. The letter is addressed to the President of the Animal Liberation Front. Putting his pen down he feels all emotion drained out of him. Then home to Linda who's getting weaker by the day.

Weeks pass. There is no reply to his letter. Only silence.

These events take place in Dublin during November 1981.

To understand the reason why, one has to travel back some years in the career of Dr John Francis Nicholson.

CHAPTER 2

Back to an April morning in Dublin when winds tore at trees and rain pounded St Mary's Hospital. At the entrance a black car stopped. Two figures emerged; it was winds of another kind that tore their hearts as they struggled up the steps. Even though it was warmer inside Catherine Kennedy shivered at the pungent smell of disinfectant and added to her alarm.

Sister Agnes smiled indifferently as they arrived in ward 3 A. They were expected. Catherine tightened her grip on her mother's hand.

'This is yours Catherine,' sister said, thinking another spoilt brat. 'It's the nicest bed in the ward and beside the window too.'

Ward 3 A was a drafty place with a high ceiling and six beds on either side. From one end a curved floor-to-ceiling window collected light. Children, mostly staring at nothing, occupied each bed. They seemed to have reached a stage of being unable to react to illness and treatment—anymore. Acceptance was a common denominator and tears were useless.

'I want to go home.' Catherine, only ten-years, buried her head in mother's coat frightened of something she did not know. All her life she was frightened, her home a perpetual battlefield, with parents clashing over things she didn't understand. Contact with her mother was the only security left—her loving caring mother. She must not let go of this only possession. She trembled, protested and cried bitterly, with knuckles as white as her tear-stained face.

Mrs Kennedy said there was nothing to worry about, and sister told her they were only there to make her better—she must realize that! Sister also said—in a low but firm voice—others were listening and impatiently pulled curtains around the bed. She looked at her watch.

'Mrs Kennedy, please help your daughter undress. I'll tell the doctor she's here.' She moved into the corridor ignoring the small faces following her.

Droplets of rain staggered downwards on the window. As they crowded together they fell in streaks. Catherine watched carefully. The more they accumulated the greater the chance they had of disappearing or resting on the window sash. She was so tired and exhausted—all she wanted was to rest.

'I'll be brave.' She had given in. Her hands shook as she attempted to undo the buttons on her dress. A new nightie was produced, pretty with red flowers and lace collar.

Her mother insisted she looked her best for the doctor; silently she wondered why they'd to go through with this.

Catherine touched her ankle. 'It really hurts. Hope they'll make it better.'

No point in undressing as Dr Nicholson left instructions to be called for an urgent admission. Because of staff shortages he'd to cover more wards than usual. Night-duty was taking its toll along with day duties.

Four years ago he graduated in medicine with honours from Dublin University and was now in surgical training in St Mary's. Life he took seriously, he was introspective and, yet, a relentless arrogance smouldered, which could arouse a range of feelings in others.

The phone gave a sharp ring. Without taking his head from the pillow he reached for it. 'Nicholson here.'

The new patient had arrived.

Patricia Kennedy hurried through the courtyard with blonde hair blowing across her eyes—eyes which saw, but did not notice, an old man and dog, shouting youths interested in nothing, a woman pushing a pram, even the barren trees offering no shelter from rain. She did notice however the small face pressed against the window.

She happily remembered walks with her daughter, and Sam, in the countryside. Delight of discovery was everywhere, smallest things had to be examined and explained. Catherine marvelled at the changing colours of seasons. She loved animals and hoped to devote her life to them when she grew up—that's provided music didn't get in the way. Anyway, Patricia Kennedy thrilled at the sheer joy of her daughter's childhood and shared every moment—perhaps too much according to her husband.

Later she drew the curtains in her gleaming sitting room so traffic would become a distraction. Light darted from her watch, like a gold arrow, reminding her of a husband who took pride in success wishing it to be seen. It was not the time on watches, however, that troubled her, more its fickleness. Long distance messages reinforced a determination to protect the only child that doctors—and husband—told her she could never have.

The phone startled her. Immediately she recognized his voice and her heart missed a beat. He'd that confident tone with a reassuring quality he used with business people. She was getting the professional treatment. Yet, there was an indifference she alone could detect and it went through her like a sword.

'How's Catherine?'

'She's fine, just fine.'

With lower lip pressed between her teeth she asked.

'Kevin, could we talk to one of the doctors this evening?' They'd already spoken to the consultant last week, he sighed, and there was a fair chance. What more did she want—for heaven's sake?

His voice became slow and deliberate as it did when he was angry. On and on he spoke, and she looked in the mirror. Her face was gaunt and haggard, even though she was extra careful with her make-up. What she saw almost made her ill. Recently she'd seen much of this face. Anxieties were all there. Her husband had developed a blind spot for these things. There was never a mention of her looks or inquiry about how she felt. She was left to battle and to suffer alone with no support.

'To hell with it Kevin. I want to know everything!'

Tears—controlled for too long—overflowed. Again she saw the small face framed in lace, against the window, a picture that was to remain for a long time.

'We'll speak to the doctor this evening. You'll make out a list of questions.'

There was nothing else to be said so he hung up abruptly. Some labelled him selfish and cruel, but words had no effect. Not going to influence his way of life. He was too busy. The impression he wanted to give was of a man standing back, half interested in others, who could only make time for the more serious and substantial things in life. He was too important for anything else.

For a minute she looked in disbelief at the dead receiver, and then silently replaced it as if she wished to prevent doing it any harm.

Kevin and Patricia Kennedy arrived at the hospital early that evening and asked sister was it possible to speak to the doctor-in-charge? Sister said it wasn't usual but as this was a special occasion she would ask the registrar on duty if he would oblige. They thanked her and waited in one of the corridors.

John Nicholson agreed although he knew that Mr Murphy, the consultant, would have spoken to them many times. He would be over in ten minutes.

'Good evening.' He greeted them extending a hand. 'I'm Dr Nicholson, Mr Murphy's registrar. I understand you'd like to talk about Catherine.'

'We would,' Mrs Kennedy said immediately, 'and we're grateful for the opportunity.'

'Indeed.' Her husband nodded, wishing to get on with it.

'Let's see if the consultants' room is free,' John said leading them to the end of the corridor. 'It's too public here.'

He pushed a door open and switched on a light exposing a Spartan room with an ornate fireplace and a fire still lighting, an empty table with five bentwood chairs and a bare light bulb above the centre of the room.

'It may be possible to have a cup of tea. Would you like that?' John asked.

'That would be lovely,' Mrs Kennedy said sitting with her back to the fire. She was cold and it would help.

John was busy in the corner while speaking. 'I must say you have a lovely daughter.' He prepared cups and saucers and poured milk. 'We've had long chats and I got to know her quite well.'

'Good to hear that doctor.' Again it was Mrs Kennedy who was the spokesperson for the couple. She was aware of John's gangling height, the pale face with anxious eyes, and black hair, which had a habit of falling over his forehead. Most noticeable, however, was the hushed and hesitant voice.

He placed cups on the table along with biscuits and sat opposite. The father was more than medium height with fresh complexion, dark hair and a ready smile. The smile intrigued John, especially under these circumstances; it revealed an almost perfect set of teeth any Hollywood star would be proud of. Perhaps, there was more than one reason to smile—perhaps this was a professional smile. He was dressed in a single-breasted striped dark suit and wore an expensive watch, which was referred to frequently. He stared directly at John and, even through the smile, a degree of impatience and hostility could be detected.

Patricia Kennedy was a tallish woman with blonde hair swept back over the ears. The expression was fixed in a frown, where every aspect from the moist eyes, the gentle ridges below the eyes and the tilt of the head—gave a picture of dejection. When she tried to smile, it was only with her mouth.

'Dr Nicholson,' she said slowly, 'can you tell us Catherine's chances of getting through the operation?'

'That's difficult.' John hesitated. 'We'll have a better idea during and immediately after the operation. I'm sure Mr Murphy has explained things to you.'

'He's done his best doctor,' Mr Kennedy said hastily, 'but there are always the dreaded unknowns when something can go wrong and … '

John interrupted him. ' … I know what you're saying Mr Kennedy and it's only natural your wife and you want to find out as much as possible. If it's any help, Mr Murphy's one of the top surgeons in the country and Catherine couldn't be in better hands. I must assure you.'

'But what are her chances?' Mrs Kennedy looked so anxious John's heart went out to her. It was like watching the effects of a wind on fragile leaves stripped from a tree.

'About fifty-fifty in a case like this. We can't say much more than that. If she has no treatment then the outlook would be black indeed. Do you understand?'

'We do. We've really no option,' Mr Kennedy said.

He turned to his wife.

'I think, Patricia, we've kept the doctor long enough and we should leave.'

Instantly she was persistent.

'But I want to know she'll be all right.'

Slowly John stood up and looked down at them.

'You can both be assured she's getting the best possible treatment anywhere.'

'Thanks doctor,' Patricia Kennedy said, obviously relaxing for the first time. 'I suppose that's what we really wanted to hear more than anything else.'

They stood up and shook hands. It was time to go.

Each week John made time to visit a maiden aunt who lived alone in an apartment in the city centre. When he entered he felt the place embracing him—it was so small. A delicious smell of cooking was always present. No matter what or how simple, she had sandwiches and a cake spread out. The living room was that lovely green colour in his old home and a brown sofa almost filled the room. It was old and difficult to get out of again. The ornate clock on the mantelpiece, Victorian pictures, and marble fireplace now filled with an electric fire, were familiar and gave him a sense of home. One cold afternoon he was concerned about her health and arranged for her doctor to call which he did. She made progress with regular visits from the practice nurse. Having lunch in the staff cafeteria one day he overheard a conversation between the practice nurse and several hospital nurses including Sister Agnes.

'I went to this old spinster's apartment some weeks ago,' the practice nurse was saying loudly, 'she had pneumonia, you know. But, Christ, the place was so small. No room to swing a cat—not that she had a cat, mind you. The kitchen was filthy and always had something burning. The smell was awful. And there was a horrible couch in the sitting room. I refused to sit in it because I might tear my uniform. And the green walls were the end! They made me sick. Fortunately, she's making a good recovery. I'm glad as I never liked visiting that Victorian stage-set.'

CHAPTER 3

'Nurse Sutton attend to your duties and stop nattering.' Sister Agnes stormed into the records office with the intention of humiliating the nurse. 'All you do is talk. If this continues I'll have to report you.'

Diane Sutton, transferred to ward 3 A, was discussing work schedules with junior nurses. Although tempted she didn't reply—this was her final year. A tall nineteen-year old with auburn hair and green eyes she was, in spite of a convent education, possessed with a reckless impatience that shone through her refined beauty.

Sister was gone as swiftly as she'd appeared. Diane rushed into the corridor with a load of papers as John Nicholson reached the top of the stairs on his way to the children's ward. As he turned the corner they collided and papers fell over the place.

'Nurse can't you look where you're going?' He exploded and immediately regretted saying it. Why can't he keep his bloody mouth shut?

'Sorry doctor. I didn't see you. I'm so clumsy.'

He walked on.

She salvaged the shambles with the help of two juniors, again embarrassed and crushed.

'Isn't he awful—who is he?' One whispered.

'That's Dr Nicholson Mr Murphy's registrar. He's a brute!' The other replied more loudly for Diane's benefit.

Her second rebuff that morning. Oh hell! Ward 3 A is a terrible place—worse than intensive care. How am I going to survive here?

Sister, striding towards the children's ward, spotted her trying to cope. A fleeting smile appeared.

As John raced along the corridor he didn't know why he was always in a hurry—it had become a way of life.

'Dr Nicholson.' It was Sister Agnes. 'A word with you please.'

She moved a hand towards her office and he followed. 'I suppose you've come to see that Kennedy girl admitted today.'

'Right,' he replied a little breathless. 'I have to examine her and check out some details.'

'I must warn you doctor.' She continued, raising a finger advisedly. 'I found her a strange child. I spoke to her but she refused to answer—point blank.'

He sat on the chair, pushing back hair and giving a sigh. Another problem looming! 'I wonder why.'

'I suppose she's plain spoilt.' She dismissed the incident with a gesture.

It seemed too easy to him.

'I'll see what I can do. Thanks for putting me in the picture.'

'I tried to speak to the mother.' Folding her arms to emphasize the next sentence and keep him listening. 'The cause lies preciously there! A real hysteric if you ask me.'

'Why do you say that sister?' He began to feel sorry for the family. It was a harsh judgement to pass on any family and especially on a first admission.

'The girl refused to get undressed when told. The mother had no control over her. She cried, and the mother let her carry on. If she were my daughter I'd give her a piece of my mind.'

'I'm sure you would.' John agreed openly. 'It's the only way to keep order in a ward like this. All the other children are quiet and no trouble. That's all credit to you sister.'

She smiled, grateful for the compliment.

'That's right, doctor. It takes discipline. But it pays in the end.'

Sitting sat back in the chair he was prepared for a lecture on the rules, regulations and discipline involved in running a ward; even felt he was going to enjoy it when suddenly, she looked at her watch.

'Dr Nicholson I mustn't keep you in idle chat. You're very busy. The other children in the ward are well and there's nothing urgent to report. I only wanted to alert you to the new patient in the corner by the window. That's Catherine Kennedy.'

'I'll be careful sister.' He lowered his voice. 'But we mustn't forget the reason why Catherine's here and what her family are going through.'

She had no answer. Her expression was serious, manner fractious, with an air of forced servility, and a reluctance to manage where she didn't want to manage. She'd an assurance of one who knew what she was doing and where she was going.

Entering the ward, examining day charts he made his way around the patients. He'd a word for each and some extended a hand inviting him to stay a while. Once or twice, he accepted and before he left gentle laughter could be heard. Catherine Kennedy's eyes were on him all the time. Eventually he arrived at her bedside with a junior nurse in attendance; sister guessed it was wiser not to be present and sent an emissary instead.

He said nothing as he approached; instead he smiled his best good morning smile and put out a hand. To his surprise she accepted and he asked her permission to sit on the edge of the bed. She nodded.

'Catherine. I'd like to tell you who I am and why I've come.'

There was no response. She maintained a clear gaze at him hardly blinking.

'My name is John Nicholson,' he continued pleasantly, 'I'm a doctor and I work with Mr Murphy, the consultant.'

She nodded slowly, yet remained silent.

'I want to ask a few questions, then a short examination, with the help of Brigid, our nurse here. Nothing to worry about. Do you understand Catherine?' He grinned at her.

She nodded again and said nothing.

'I suppose Mr Murphy has explained things. But, Catherine, before we begin I want you to know you can ask any questions you wish. Would you like to do that?'

She nodded again and spoke in a hushed voice.

'Doctor. Please can I ask a question?'

'Of course.'

She weighed her question for a moment and then shrugged.

'Why are you a doctor and your boss is only a mister?'

He put a hand to his mouth to stifle a smile. He said nothing and then broke out in a laugh. Brigid, the junior, glanced at him and giggled, and others around the ward looked towards the bed in the corner.

'Catherine,' he said at last, 'you're a funny girl. Aren't you?'

'Doctor I don't mean to be funny.' She was still serious, a frown on her forehead. Then she grinned.

'The answer Catherine is quite simple,' he explained. 'At College and Medical School you study hard, and when you qualify you become a doctor. Then, if you study harder still wishing to specialize and obtain a higher degree you become a mister again. Hence Mr Murphy used to be a doctor. Understand?'

She looked puzzled, the frown disappeared gradually and her eyes brightened. She thought for a moment and gave a little shrug.

'It doesn't sound funny to me. I think it silly to study so hard and end up a plain mister again after all that work.'

'I agree. It's silly. But that's the way the system works.' He gave another laugh and some of the other children joined in although they didn't know why. Sister Agnes appeared at the entrance and clapped her hands.

'That's enough of that!' She shouted for all to hear. 'Please be quiet. Some people are trying to rest and others have work to do.' She glared at the bed in the corner, turned on her heal and left quickly.

Catherine gazed at John and hid a smile with her hand. Shrewdly she looked at him as if they knew each other a long time.

'Sorry doctor. I don't want to get you into trouble. That'd be awful and I couldn't forgive myself.'

'Don't worry Catherine,' he reassured her. 'You're not to worry about me. Now down to more important things. And that means you.'

Questions were answered pleasantly, the examination went smoothly and John Catherine and Brigid ended up best of friends.

When formalities were completed Catherine was eager to continue talking and he was reluctant to leave. They chatted about school, friends, games and parties.

'That's all for the moment Catherine,' he said eventually and stood up. Again she looked at him, her new friend, in a conspiratorial way. 'There are one or two tests to be done this afternoon. Nothing to worry about.'

She tried to smile again although anxiety was coming back.

'And will the operation take long doctor?'

'Not long.'

'And can I leave hospital soon afterwards?'

'We'll have to see.' He warmed to her matter-of-factness. 'Why do you ask?'

'Well doctor I'm preparing for Grade Five Piano in three months.' She was now sitting up laughing openly and happily. 'And there's still a lot to be done.'

He nodded. 'You know Catherine I love music too. You must be very good.'

Again he was aware of large blue eyes and long blonde hair. Normally he'd no time to study the finer features of patients; life was too busy. Now he gazed on a face that had the makings of a remarkable beauty; the potential was there. Bone structure promised a symmetrical oval face and complexion, even though pale, was arresting. He was reminded of John Singer Sargent's paintings of children in satin dresses surrounded by opulence and wealth.

He'd compassion for this fragile creature and a premonition lurked in the background. Life was unfair. No satin or opulence for Catherine but a special radiance glowed when she stared at him—this she did a lot, trying to decide whether to ask a hundred questions, yet afraid to let herself go.

'Would you like to see photographs of me and Sam?' She asked with a generous smile. Few people she'd share her memories.

He sat down again. 'Yes Catherine. That would be lovely.'

Other pressing engagements could wait. This was more important. A large blue album was produced. Pictures were selected and offered with delicacy and pride. He was shown a world of make-believe, of innocence and childish appreciation of the good things of life—if only we'd time.

'These are my dearest treasures doctor.' She lovingly closed the album. 'I'll keep them close to me always.'

She looked away with a sigh.

'When I grow up I'm going to be a pianist and maybe a vet. Will you come back when you've time and we can talk some more?'

She'd a warm feeling inside her talking to this tall stranger, a man who listened, and listened carefully, and who'd time to listen—not like her dad who never listened; he was only interested in business and sport.

She wondered if John had children, if so, she'd love to meet them.

He gave her his sunniest smile.

'I'll try.'

'That's good and doctor ... 'He stopped at the end of the bed. 'Some day I will play music for you.'

Reluctantly, he left the bedside of Catherine Kennedy. He'd experienced an unusual—no—an emotional encounter, talking to this ten-year old who'd a blend of magical innocence and flashes of wisdom beyond her years. She believed in fairy tales, in wizards and witches, the terrible powers of nature, and was certain there were forces for good and evil. One had to be constantly on the look out for people who could trap you into something you could not escape from—ever! She'd read about them and even though she read more and more, she became more terrified.

He'd asked why she persisted.

'We can be less afraid of the things we know about, than the things we don't; it's a kind of preparation for growing up, and I want to grow up a good person and help people less fortunate than I am.'

Once she got going on her hopes and ambitions for the future, he couldn't stop her. Not that he wanted to. He was unsure if he'd ever met such an intelligent, sensible, yet modest young human being before in his life. There was a bond between them; each feeling they could say exactly what they liked knowing it would be accepted gracefully and fully. In spite of the difference in years, they were two of a kind—or kindred spirits.

Catherine's parents stayed a long time that evening. The operation was rarely mentioned. When it was time to leave Mrs Kennedy put an arm around her daughter's shoulder.

'Come home soon Catherine. There's a surprise waiting.' She hadn't intended to let out the secret, yet it was impossible not to. Catherine held out her arms to her father. She was near to tears.

'Daddy did you get it already? I know what it is—don't I?' She hugged him, clinging tightly, not wanting to let go. Eventually he managed to untangle himself. A longing in her eyes between the tears was so evident.

'I'm dying to see it.'

The Kennedys left the ward for home.

Darkness crept through the window filling the ward and stillness compelled Catherine to listen to her troubled heart. Memory came back like the darkness. The night was occupied by a dream of gifts life had given her. In it she drifted back to those sun drenched days when she lived in open spaces, where only wind and trees and great bright clouds mattered. Their voices were happy and free in the air as they laughed and ran in the fields. Sam was her constant and trusted companion. She was dazzled by the knowledge he loved and adored and worshipped her. He shared her secrets; her troubles and always listened. This was his greatest asset. The previous night he'd listened closely as she poured her heart out. Speaking with wise black eyes he was able to answer her more clearly than anyone else. He didn't use words as he rested in his small neat basket in the corner of the kitchen.

That same night Dr John Nicholson sat at his desk in his bedroom. He was on night-duty again. Medical and surgical books were strewn all over the place, open at references on surgery. He knew it all anyway, yet something drove him. Perhaps, a remote paper he hadn't covered, which threw a different light on procedure. A technique he'd used for years, with success, but, unfortunately, there had been some failures such as infection, haemorrhage, shock and drug reactions. Occasionally, no reason could be found why a patient gave up; perhaps, he or she had no real support or love to fall back on, maybe felt unwanted, and the best way for everyone was to just curl up and die. There were a lot of references on socio-economic factors, long psychological names where experts wrote about their clients—new word—as if they had no feelings of their own. Any worthwhile views should be implanted into them whether the client liked it or not. If there was resistance in the client, they were labelled a difficult case that needed group therapy to break it down.

He slammed the book closed; it was filled with claptrap. Why couldn't we sit back and listen to the poor suffering patients? We'd then hear them saying exactly what was wrong. This psychological mumbo-jumbo made him angry. He'd no time for cover up and obfuscation. And this stuff and nonsense was no earthly use to Catherine Kennedy now.

CHAPTER 4

John Nicholson woke early. The day ahead included an amputation—Catherine Kennedy, that lovely but tragic girl. She'd a rare bone cancer and surgery was imperative. After breakfast he visited the ward and found her asleep in a world of silent thoughts, tears and touches of joy and protected, for a while, with a teddy beside her. Her transparent beauty was delicate—as if painted. She opened her eyes.

'I'm too sleepy for a chat.' She tried to smile in spite of the pre-medication. A hand was extended.

'Don't worry. I haven't come to talk.' He gently touched her hand. 'I only wanted to check you were all right.'

'That's nice.' Her gaze moved about the ward unsteadily, her voice trembled on the verge of coherence. The glow faded as she looked into the darkness of her mind. Her arm went limp and he replaced it under the clothes.

The operating theatre was full of activity; increasingly John felt the atmosphere here unreal—light washed everything intensely white, sounds of instruments lacerated his ears and the reek of anaesthetic added to his distress. As he closed his eyes a vine of veins clawed at his thoughts.

'You all right Nicholson?' Colm Murphy the consultant surgeon asked.

'Yes. Fine.' He gave half a smile.

As all right as can be although what about the futility of this procedure? The chances of success are low, the post-operative complications and the long-term effects can be awful. There has to be a better way!

Colm Murphy also detested this operation in anyone, especially children, although it was the only option. With osteosarcoma only one thing was certain—no surgery, no survival. Glancing at Nicholson, a long strip of misery this morning, he wondered what was on his mind. Maybe, he'd a late night or something was bothering him. Recently he'd to shout at him to get a move on. This was unusual, most unusual. The lad had a bright future in surgery, bursting with brains and talent and had a terrific pair of hands. If only he'd apply himself. Yet he'd a feeling Nicholson's heart was not in it. Bloody hell! He wasn't going to get involved unless he had to or was asked. Enough of this nonsense. Let's get on with saving lives!

Incision made and major bleeding points coagulated in rapid succession. This was the only way to save the child.

'Blood pressure's dropping Mr Murphy,' the anaesthetist said. 'We'll have to step up the transfusion rate.'

Murphy looked up. 'All right but be quick. She hasn't much time to spare'.

The operation took one and a half hours and what John saw appalled him.

'Any questions?' Murphy's voice startled the students.

'Yes,' one said hesitatingly. 'What are her chances?'

Murphy shrugged as he removed his gloves. 'I don't know. But without surgery this child will be dead within six months, or sooner, having suffered a great deal. Incidentally, you should all go to Dr Whelan's lecture this afternoon.'

Later that evening, the reflection of a street lamp in a mirror grew brighter. John Nicholson sat beneath it pretending to read. Usually words raced across the page. Not this night. Outside a young moon stepped on her path of darkness. An open window framed trees touching through the soft light. Below, sparks—full of anxiety—shimmered and sparkled on surface water.

Gazing at the light he reflected on the time he was Catherine's age. He was an only child. School days were difficult and he kept to himself in most things. Attempts were made to 'take him down a peg or two'—whatever that meant—by self-appointed class leaders. They subjected him to horrendous torments aimed at humiliating him—to break him.

One in particular took pleasure in bullying him, usually verbal abuse that occasionally became violent. Eventually John confronted him, asking why he was so cruel? The bully said it was because John, the runt, was blocking his light and was in his space. John didn't understand, whereupon the bully grabbed him by the lapels, spat in his face.

'Even a dog, or a rat, casts a shadow,' he said. 'If that shadow comes near my boot I'll kick it to smithereens.'

That night the Kennedys were called to the hospital and stayed with Catherine in Intensive Care for about two hours. They witnessed the dedicated work of the staff including Dr Nicholson who was in control of procedures. Emotional outbursts came from Patricia Kennedy and her joy was overwhelming when Catherine woke and was able to speak, clearly and calmly, to everyone. After a while she tired and went into a deep sleep.

John advised them to go home and await developments. He'd stay another hour and if everything was satisfactory he'd return to his room. The parents went home, collapsed into bed and were asleep within minutes.

A phone rang. Again it was staff nurse in intensive care.

Catherine Kennedy had deteriorated suddenly. John rushed to the unit and battled to keep her condition stable. She rallied and at one stage regained consciousness. He spoke about music and dogs and anything and everything; all the while she wanted to hold his hand. She appeared to fall into a natural sleep.

Much later, when the moon had completed her journey, and the very air gave no breath, he turned out the bedside light. Darkness switched on within and he was gripped in grief. He was physically sick. Fatigue finally released him. Without knowing it he'd suffered more that night than ever before.

About eight o'clock next morning he telephoned Mr Kennedy. Tragically, Catherine had slipped away about an hour ago, peacefully and in no pain. Mr Kennedy thanked him, hung up and went to the sleeping Patricia with the news. At first she couldn't take it in. She thought everything was going well—the doctor said so.

Catherine would be all right. What went wrong? For God's sake, what went wrong?

That same morning John Nicholson's mind was limp and clear, his body an empty shell.

He knew what had to be done.

CHAPTER 5

John Nicholson faced a crossroad and Colm Murphy was asked for advice. Murphy, who lived a few miles south of Dublin, invited him to his home the following Saturday afternoon.

That morning John decided to get the car cleaned. After surviving coloured lights, soapy blizzards, hammering of cylindrical sea monsters and, finally, the scream of vacuum cleaners he drove into a bright new world feeling like a million dollars.

Bach's The Art of Fugue on the radio helped his thoughts as he travelled along the north side of the Liffey. The river was like a slender lady moving with reflected sunshine in sinuous curves. Walls of glass, put up by progressive architects to uglify this once gracious town, dismayed him—or perhaps he was just old fashioned.

He was old fashioned. Was that a fault? Moral judgement, keeping one's word, admiring character and courage and making the world a better place. Anyway the journey to Killiney—an important one occupied him—maybe life changing. Up to now he'd worked hard and yet derived little satisfaction. Workloads were increasing because bureaucrats collected information—clinical audits they were called —to 'improve' the work of clinicians. They invented Performance Indicators to measure them. If information was not forthcoming clinicians were haunted by repeated demands to know why and were accused of shroud waving if they did not get their way. The relationship between staff and bureaucracy was not a happy one. John thought more about good patient management than good paper management.

Through Dalkey Village and on to the Vico Road and Killiney Hill, the winding road led past elegant buildings. Eventually, he reached a hollow below the obelisk, which rose like a dark spearhead into a smoking sky. His car came to rest beside a black Mercedes and Murphy's elegant daughter showed him into the lounge, a spacious room relishing in effortless comfort.

It was his first visit to Murphy's home. The house was built in the eighteenth century to accommodate a big family when there was an easy supply of servants. Murphy had kept up the standard of děcor and finish. Cream walls created a neutral backdrop for works of art and above was the most delicate stuccowork. Over the fireplace an oval guilt mirror reflected the world. Floor to ceiling matching curtains framed the Georgian windows and a cherry wood sofa decorated with loose cushions was covered in red silk. Everywhere there was the rich flamboyance of the house's roots.

Could he ever aspire to this?

Murphy, a Corkman, who's every movement was a masterpiece of self-confidence, strutted into the room, his steps loud on the wooden floor. Reddish hair, rugged complexion and a persistent frown gave the appearance of one who contested life; and he breathed wealth power and success.

John said he wished to devote more time to cancer research—if that were possible. Current biochemical techniques he was familiar with and he was inadequate dealing with patients, even angry at times. The more he learned about surgery the more its limitations became apparent; yet people expected miracles. When these didn't happen the surgeon was often blamed—he was no good! Lawyers fuelled this; the blame and shame culture resulted in appalling stress for many surgeons.

'I know the feeling,' Murphy said, 'but this is most unusual. Now you've the Fellowship I thought you'd make surgery your career.' He'd hoped for this all along. The hooded eyes were like a predator's ready to strike. Then they became dull and his voice querulous.

'This way I may have something to contribute.' John said quietly.

'Perhaps you have. You're an idealist, a bloody idealist.'

Silence pulled different ways for a while.

'There'll be sacrifices and the financial rewards will be limited.' Murphy continued.

Instantly John was on the defensive. 'There could be others.'

'You're bloody serious. Sit down John. You make me nervous standing there.'

John pushed back hair and sat as instructed. Murphy remained standing; he preferred to strut about if there was something serious to be worked out relishing the feeling of looking down on any adversary.

'You relax now and tell me again about this nonsense of leaving surgery.'

'As I say, I wish to devote more time to cancer research.'

'You what?' Murphy shouted indignantly. 'Joining the backroom boys plugging away with test tubes and cultures and all that. Really dull stuff! I assure you. Don't tell me it's to help one's fellow beings and all that crap!'

'I may have something to contribute.' He could only repeat.

'Rubbish!'

Murphy rubbed his forehead in exasperation trying to think of something, anything, to save a sinking ship. He sat down.

'You're too bloody high-minded. Why can't you continue to do what you're good at? I mean surgery. You'll go places if you finish your training and you've an original mind.'

His voice was emotional. Not unexpected. They nearly came to blows but matters resolved slowly when he saw the resolute look in John's eyes. He gave up and walked to the window.

'I'll speak to Wainwright who's head of Oncology in Trinity. Know him?'

John shook his head.

'Not personally.'

'The number of fellowships is limited and the competition formidable.'

However, he'd write a letter of introduction. He was once tempted to go the academic path, and nearly did so, but money—or lack of it—changed his mind.

'Wonderful,' John said. 'Thanks for your encouragement.'

Murphy pulled away and stood up again.

'Encouragement! Balderdash, I'm not encouraging you.' He made a gesture of resignation. 'You may collect the letter from my secretary on Monday. Incidentally, you should avoid Pickford if you know what's good for you—he's well known to go deeply into the surface of things,' he said with a wry smile. 'Now let's eat. We've had enough of this sad business,'

Later, as John drove back to Dublin, the city's shape swelled into the sky and helped by its own light drowned the star-splashed night.

A baby grand gathered dust in a not so gleaming room in a large empty house. Kevin Kennedy continued to prosper losing himself in work and sport; of his wife no one knew or cared.

Patricia Kennedy was inconsolable. Initially, complete disbelief and denial. It's not true. Catherine's all right. She knew it. She could feel it. They don't know what there're saying. Surely they were talking to her recently and she was smiling. No, she cannot be dead.

Then she remembered something she'd heard from her parents. 'You lose a parent you lose your past, you lose a child you lose your future!' Catherine's death had proved the existence of a mocking God. Yet, she prayed to this God but what she prayed for she knew not. Her life was empty with no future. Hopelessness and loneliness were burdens she'd have to carry for God only knows how long.

Kevin Kennedy was calmer. After all, for months he was prepared for the worst. Especially when he'd listened to the advice of Mr Murphy who hadn't held out much hope. He'd anticipated an outcome like this. His accountant's mind had decided to work on the figures available. All pointers were not good. So he was prepared emotionally and intellectually. Yet he made no effort to prepare his wife for the true nature of their daughter's illness. She didn't want to know or to listen anyway; there was total resistance. Reluctantly, he'd to leave her to her own devices.

And Sam, the mongrel, wandered over the sun drenched grass with the morning air around him hushed, the sky vacant and everything bright with shadow. Even the birds went unheard and the laughter was gone. He was alone and lost. His feelings given so freely were useless now, his suffering a kind of silence known only to him. Above, the branches touched indifferent to any passer-by.

The funeral was arranged. A big affair it was because Kevin Kennedy was an important businessman and the undertakers were given instructions to spare no expense. Word got round that the family were so shocked and traumatized, they wished their grief to be shared. Removal of the remains to the Church of the Assumption the evening before was a pious and social occasion. Hundreds gathered in the church and, after the short ceremony, friends, relatives and business associates collected outside discussing the tragedy and offering condolences. The resting place for the coffin overnight could not accommodate all the flowers, cards and wreaths.

Three priests concelebrated the funeral mass at ten o'clock the following morning and a soprano from the School of Music was commissioned to sing. Well-wishers, including girls from Catherine's school and staff members, packed the church.

John knew of these arrangements. It was the policy of the hospital not to attend, as a routine, the funeral services of any patient. However, feeling amongst staff involved in Catherine's care indicated they would like to be present. This was passed on to John by Colm Murphy but with the understanding that there was no obligation.

He decided to attend and arrived in good time to sit, unnoticed, towards the back of the congregation. He'd time to reflect on the occasion and circumstances surrounding it. He mourned equally amongst many.

Beside her in Intensive Care he'd wept internally. No emotion was shown. When the struggle was over, he'd bent down and fleetingly kissed her on the still warm forehead, not caring what others thought. He'd whispered farewell into her ears; she might still just hear it. Who knows? Others stood and waited so that the important business of keeping other critical patients alive could continue. The Kennedy case was now closed. Finished. What others said when he was gone he did not know, nor did he care.

In church, hers was the great death, with a large demonstration of grief. Catherine would probably have preferred a quiet, simple ceremony with a few, true friends. He sensed the grief of parting, the tragedy and regret of never again, the never to be glad and happy and a future never fulfilled.

And yet Catherine probably was happy now, perhaps, happier than ever. This gave him some relief. No more pain or suffering. His was a profession primarily concerned with saving lives, and not preparing for death, although it was part of the picture. In his young days he foolishly believed in immortality. This is where Catherine had shocked him, and he was badly shocked. Death could come at any time, uninvited and unannounced. The grim reaper could creep up in a sleep or violently and suddenly. There was no way of knowing.

He looked around at people coming into the church. Did they think of the things on his mind? Somehow he doubted, because most were looking at each other, seeing how many they recognized.

He thought back on Catherine's case. The reports, radiographs and other tests leading to the prognosis. All his working life he'd to confront others about the truth, the present, the future and found it harrowing. He had been less inclined to say much to Catherine. It would've been cruel, and he detested anything that was cruel to children. Besides, a doctor must preserve a clinical detachment, in case he might give away too much of himself. He'd to be constantly on his guard; but this morning was one exception—a simple prayer to send the lovely Catherine on her journey into eternity.

The service took about forty-five minutes and the final procession proceeded down the aisle after the coffin. He joined the queue of mourners. When his turn came to offer condolences he put out his hand to Mr Kennedy. The hand was ignored. Instead, looking straight at John, Mr Kennedy said in a loud and clearly audible voice.

'Why bother Dr Nicholson? You know this was not necessary, not the right thing to do. Goodbye to you!'

CHAPTER 6

Reluctantly Sister Agnes Lynch made her way home. Although she lived several miles from the hospital she preferred to walk; she had to think of ways to cut down on expenses. After all she was the only one bringing income into the home. Her face was hard and determined as she headed northwards in the drizzling rain. Even though traffic was heavy she ignored it; her mind was elsewhere.

She'd been closely involved in the fight to keep Catherine Kennedy alive, and the tragic outcome disturbed her. Normally, she would take it in her stride. This time she'd also to deal with the parents who were unable to handle such a tragedy like most parents she'd known. There was something profoundly different here and she couldn't understand what it was.

She felt blood rushing to her face and nausea in her stomach. Her hands trembled as she thought of the day her husband, Bill, walked out on her. Then, she was furious, but what could she do? She was trapped. Everyone said she was too good for him, except, of course, her mother who was anxious to get the spoilt brat of a daughter off her hands. Growing up, Agnes had always caused trouble; she had her own mind, and was determined to do exactly what she wanted, in spite of plenty of advice from her mother. Take nursing, for example. Mother was against it as a career because of years of training and the pay was not good, not good at all. Agnes shouldn't be wasting time studying books; she could earn decent money as a secretary.

Then Agnes met Bill and fell in love with him when in training. Charming he was and apparently had a good job in the construction industry. He had a light and swaggering sort of way about him, short dark hair, full of loud talk and bravado, and with the head well set back indicating he was willing to take anyone on in an argument, and usually intended to win it by fair means or foul.

Quickly he learned the domestic situation whereby Agnes looked after her ageing mother. But that was no problem to him. The mother was the sole owner of the house and he made sure of being especially nice to her. The marriage had lasted a few years and young Stephen was born, a healthy and happy baby and things went well.

Until the accident.

Agnes reached the house with her clothes dripping wet. It didn't matter anyway; she was well used to it. She opened the front door to find Margaret Doyle ready to go.

'Was everything all right Margaret?' She was a little breathless as she took her coat off. 'No trouble I hope.'

'Not really.' Margaret smiled benevolently and gave a little frown. 'Your mother's been her usual cantankerous self. I ignore her most of the time.'

'And Stephen?' She asked with apprehension.

'Oh Stephen's a pet.' Margaret laughed gently. 'He's no trouble at all. Never is really. And he tried to smile several times.'

Agnes opened the hall door. 'I won't keep you Margaret. I'm sure you're anxious to get home. See you same time tomorrow.' What a blessing Margaret was; she didn't know how she could cope without her.

Agnes went into the front room where Stephen was sitting in his wheelchair, looking at television. Although it was an effort he smiled slightly when he saw his mother. She'd made the room as comfortable as her modest salary would allow. After all, it was Stephen's complete world and he deserved the best.

Everything was cosy, comfortable and at peace.

Stephen had been disabled since the car accident two years age when he was ten-years old. Doctors said he was lucky to be alive but he'd have to manage in a wheelchair for the rest of his life. The court settlement was some help yet it would never compensate for the human wreckage that resulted.

She bent down and kissed him on the forehead.

'Hello, Stephen.' Her words sounded like a sigh. 'I'm home at last and I'll have tea ready when I change out of these wet things.'

Stephen nodded. She went upstairs to change. As she reached the landing a rasping voice came from one of the bedrooms.

'Is that Agnes out there?'

She turned around to stare at the open door.

'Yes mum. I'm just in.'

'What kept you?' The voice demanded. 'You're late again. What kept you this time?'

Agnes sighed. She removed her wet clothes as she spoke.

'I walked home and it was raining'

The old woman raised her voice in anger. 'Excuses. Excuses. Always excuses. Now get me my tea at once. Do you hear me? At once.'

'Yes mum.'

After mother's tea was delivered, she went downstairs to sit with Stephen, for a while. The boy's face was masked as if in a sleep. She sat watching for a while; occasionally intense fear or horror crossed his face. Then his clear eyes opened and he saw her. Immediately, he uttered strange, inarticulate sounds, which she translated as joy and happiness. She held his hand soothing him for about an hour. All was quiet and she was deathly tired. The stress of the past days in the hospital along with looking after a bed-ridden mother and disabled son was enormous. And things were getting worse. Or were they?

With her eyes closed she went back to when Bill lived in the house. Lived in was hardly correct as he merely used the place as a bed and breakfast. Each day he disappeared somewhere and not always to work; in fact, his notorious temper relieved him from that burden at regular intervals. In the evenings he'd come home, his manner harsh to Agnes and Stephen, although charming to his mother-in-law. After all!

Things came to a head one evening when he was full of com plaints and other things. Everyone else was to blame for the way he was, nobody understood him. His work mates were fed up hearing how he'd to bend over backwards to do everything to please his demanding wife who nagged him accusing him of things he'd never done. Also he'd to cope with a vindictive mother-in-law whose obnoxious ways sickened him. He complained about Stephen saying he was a useless brat and used other colourful words; a son he could never be proud of—and even ashamed of.

Dark anger entered her voice, her eyes blazing.

'Stop right there Bill. You're not getting away with that.'

'With what?' He sneered. 'The truth, for Christ sake!'

'Insulting our only son who cannot defend himself.' His words shocked her to the core.

'How could you be so callous and cruel?'

'Look whose calling me callous and cruel,' he mocked, 'the kettle calling the pot black! And, there's no chance of us having another child. Whose fault is that?'

'How twisted can you get?' She screamed at him. 'You know damn well that's a crazy thing to say.'

His manner was totally hostile. 'Don't you dare talk to me like that, you … '

He raised his hand to beat her, but held back. Completely overcome, she glared at him, managing to utter two words.

'Get out!'

He turned on his heal, grabbed his coat and burst out of the room, banging the hall door after him.

Then more shouting, high pitched and sharp, came from the bedroom upstairs. It was her mother demanding to know what was going on.

At this memory, she collapsed on the sofa and was out of control, hands shaking, her body gripped with great racking sobs. She cried bitterly. Yet, life had to go on. Yes things were awful when Bill lived here. She was better off now. Only two crosses to bear and not three. At least that's an improvement! Then Catherine Kennedy and her parents. Through her own suffering she was able to understand, to pity more, the two unfortunate people who'd lost their child. At least Agnes could count her blessings. Things could be worse.

Stephen watched her cry, watched every movement. He'd so little time in her presence. Out at work all day, then her brief evening rest in the sitting room with him. She'd talk gently, telling him events that happened in the hospital, the joys, the arguments and tragedies. It was his only contact with her and, through her, the outside world. Although he was unable to respond adequately he did his best by facial expressions; there was no other part of him that could communicate. As for speech, he could only manage grunts, and occasional words. These, combined with eyebrow movements were sufficient for her to understand. There was little else he could do to make his teeming brain heard; his burden resulted in enormous frustration and loneliness. Maybe, some day that would change.

He loved these precious moments, after tea, when she sat with him, holding his hand. If there was an exciting programme on television they watched it. As she laughed he followed her, perhaps looking more at her rather than the screen. These were his happiest times—she communicating and he listening. It could not get better!

Good things had to come to an end. She wheeled him into his small bedroom on the ground floor, specially adapted by the Health Authority. His physical needs had been well catered for by a system of moving his lifeless body from one position to the next. Again, for this he was thankful.

Then in his special orthopaedic bed. She sat with him for as long as she could, holding herself straight as she fought tiredness. Still, he could not utter a word of thanks, or love or anything. Oh, my Jesus, he said to himself, please let me talk to people properly again. Please. Please. It will make such a difference. The doctors told me some day, with new research, there was a possibility I'd improve, be able to talk, move my limbs. That would be fantastic!

All I can do now is talk to myself and listen to my mother. She's reading a short story by William Trevor, her favourite author;

sometimes they're hard to understand but I try. At this moment I'm probably the happiest twelve-year old in the world!

A time of quiet reflection. No danger of going to sleep for another three or four hours. He'd to occupy his mind with other things to prevent those awful nightmares, which would leave him terrified for days. And he could tell nobody about them.

Then the accident two years ago. It was not his fault. He was playing football with his friends on the road outside his home, normally a quiet road, one Sunday afternoon. After scoring a goal he ran back acknowledging the imaginary applause when a Land Rover screamed around the corner and went straight into him. He was brought to hospital with great care because of suspected spinal injuries. All he could remember was the paramedics complaining about the stupid ramps on the road leading directly to the hospital. Then everything went blank.

Before sleep he thought about his grandma. How could she, persistently, demand errands to be done, which were usually not necessary; who never had a kind word to say about anyone, and didn't know the meaning of 'Please' and 'Thanks.' Also he remembered his father's violent reaction to the accident, which hurt Stephen more than any physical injury ever could. His father was so angry. But it was not his fault. No.

It was not his fault at all!

Next morning Agnes Lynch left the two blessings in the hands of Margaret Doyle, for another day. She made for St Mary's on foot wondering how long this frantic life-style could go on. There had to come a time when something would give.

Then what chaos!

CHAPTER 7

Simon Pickford questioned a junior was Nurse Sutton on duty. She was, although she was with one of Professor Wainwright's patients at present. Then he would just have to wait. In the meantime she was ordered to make tea and toast for him.

'Yes doctor. Certainly,' was the breathless reply.

The tray arrived. 'You must tell her it's urgent,' he said loudly.

A moment later Diane Sutton appeared flustered. 'You sent for me. I'm told it's urgent.'

He stood, hesitated and invited her to dinner.

'That's not urgent!' Her eyes widened with anger.

He straightened and raised his head.

'It is to me.'

'Did you realize I was assisting the registrar?' She glared at him.

'I don't give a damn about him.' He dismissed her comments. 'Will you come?

Her eyes flashed and face flushed.

'I won't. What answer would you expect?'

She turned her back and left. How could he be so thoughtless and bigheaded? No need to interrupt a clinical procedure for a social nicety. The arrogance of it, the conceit! Still, a thrill went through her at the invitation.

Professor Walter Wainwright was head of Oncology in Trinity College, Dublin and physician to St Mary's and the Cancer Institute. A difficult man, being possessed of little patience, who regarded it as a disguised form of despair. Brilliant ideas on research made him an international figure, even before he left Addenbrook's Hospital in Cambridge. The Chair in Oncology was advertised and he was undecided to apply or wait for advancement in the UK. Marriage to Gillian Fitzgerald, a scholar and celebrated beauty he met in Cambridge clinched the matter. Her stunning looks, auburn hair, sparkling green eyes—her most striking feature—were his lasting impressions. She'd love to return to Dublin, where she was born and her family were there. The advertisement was a special message from fate and he'd no objection to moving.

The city's location on the sea he loved. Dublin was then a place of simple pleasures, the church still played a major role in the nation's affairs and country roads were comparatively traffic free. A certain decaying morality, especially in those who were chronologically advantaged, was evident. They were easily shocked by the nefarious ways of Britain, and yet, seemed to travel there in droves for a vacation from virtue.

Miss O'Sullivan, his secretary, knocked on his door saying a Dr John Nicholson had arrived.

'Please show him in.'

He waved a hand impatiently towards a chair as John entered.

'Dr Nicholson what's on your mind? There's a meeting at three o'clock.' It was now two-thirty. Murphy's letter of introduction was taken and read with a gathering frown.

John took a deep breath. 'To study under you would be an honour.'

Wainwright's expression changed to a scowl. 'Don't be presumptuous, young man!'

'I wish to apply for a position in the Institute.' John pressed on.

He explained his background and research proposals. At first, Wainwright interrupted him abruptly with comments and questions; then allowed him to unfold his knowledge and aspirations. Minutes passed. Eventually Wainwright raised a hand.

'We can pursue your ideas another time. Ask Miss O'Sullivan for an application form on your way out. Good afternoon doctor.' Wainwright looked at his watch, walked briskly to the door and held it open.

John sent the form with curriculum vitae to the administration office. Within days a letter arrived inviting him to attend for interview. Seven were short-listed and shown into the senior staff room by the Institute Secretary, Mr McCormack, a small bespectacled man full of good humour. The room was long and faced the front of the building with its constant traffic. John glanced at the others; one was busily removing imaginary fluff from his clothes, another was staring into space. Simon Pickford had an air of assurance. Each interview took about ten minutes.

'Dr Nicholson.' McCormack was standing at the door with an arm extended. John was shown into a large room where portraits gazed down unseeingly. The assembled also stared and the walk to the empty chair was an eternity. The committee consisted of Mr Edward Corrigan, a large bald-headed man who wore a red carnation, Professors Wainwright and Pickford, Dr Whelan the immunologist and one representative each from University College, the Royal College of Surgeons and the Department of Health.

'Good afternoon, Dr Nicholson, please be seated.'

Mr Corrigan moved a hand towards an empty chair. 'I'm the chairman of this committee and I'd like to introduce the other members.' He spoke calmly with a smile. John nodded as he sat down. A clump of hair fell across his forehead and was immediately replaced. 'Is there anything you would like to add to your application, doctor, before we proceed?' Continued Corrigan, leaning forward.

'Thank you. No.'

'Professor Wainwright, would you like to ask the candidate some questions?'

Wainwright, more relaxed and benevolent this time, turned to John.

'Dr Nicholson, Huxley once said. "The great tragedy of science is having the slaying of a beautiful hypothesis by an ugly fact." I would like to hear your views on this statement.'

John didn't know what hit him and was nonplussed. To start by accepting—or rejecting—a famous philosopher's statement was quite a different matter. What was Wainwright up to? He remained silent and the tension mounted.

He cleared his throat.

'Well, sir, it's a beautiful and romantic statement but one I don't accept on its face value and I think Huxley wouldn't really accept it.'

Wainwright raised his eyebrows nodded but made no comment.

John continued groping for words.

'To progress we depend on those before us. In many instances we can only extend the boundaries of knowledge by trial and error.'

Wainwright asked incisively.

'Even in medicine doctor? I mean trial and error on patients.'

'In as much as using substances that have been thoroughly tested in animals and perhaps by other methods.'

Wainwright hesitated staring at John and then looked away. 'Was that always the case doctor?'

'Certainly not professor. One has only to think of the work of Jenner and Pasteur for example.'

'But they were brave men—were they not?'

John began to relax and felt a touch of enjoyment. 'Brave yes, and also men of genius.'

Wainwright held papers in front of him and gazed out the window behind John. As he formulated the next question he let them fall gently on the table for emphasis.

'Dr Nicholson do you think we'll ever have a situation where human trial and error, as you put it, will be undertaken especially with all the safeguards?'

'I do professor.'

There was a pause.

'Go on doctor explain yourself.' Wainwright said impatiently.

'An occasion might arise in the management of some forms of cancer.' John, at long last, sat back in his chair and waited for the next question.

A smile passed over Wainwright's face as he turned to the chairman.

'Thank you. I have no further questions.'

Professor Pickford was next. Always ponderous and cynical, he'd recently become invested with a pseudo-profundity and one could see it in his appearance; thin face, white hair brushed, with great care, to one side. Brows were thick, making the eyes deep set in which low cunning floated. A bowtie completed the air of superiority.

'Dr Nicholson I would very much like you to give this committee your considered comments on the legal implications of an incorrect or wrong diagnosis.'

John knew this was a trap.

It was almost impossible to answer the question.

'I'd leave the problem in the hands of lawyers.'

Pickford's voice was cold as steel.

'There is little doubt in my mind that that is not a satisfactory answer, Dr Nicholson—what you have said is, frankly, a cop out. And you know it!'

'No matter what answer I give, Professor Pickford, it would not satisfy everyone,' John replied, immediately regretting it. 'However, as a doctor I'd always be guided by my conscience.'

There was a palpable silence. No one moved, only heads nodded gently here and there. Pickford's colour brightened. He seemed disturbed, confused. His plan had collapsed and he looked for a way out. With great effort he conquered his indignation and turned to the chairman.

'Notwithstanding the fact that I got an unsatisfactory and evasive answer to my question I'm afraid I have finished with this candidate,' he said with injured dignity, slamming the folder in front of him.

Paper shuffling occurred as Corrigan turned to his left.

'Perhaps Dr Whelan would like to ask some questions.'

'Thank you Mr Chairman.' Whelan imparted a feeling of reassurance as he spoke. Half glancing in Pickford's direction he continued. 'So far, you have answered well. Now tell us, doctor, what do you want to do most urgently in your career?'

John explained the projects he hoped to undertake.

'To come back to the original question and Huxley's quotation,' John concluded at length, 'even though failures are discouraging, they should urge us on to further efforts. Perhaps the original quotation should be forgotten. In other words, with deference to Huxley, we could say the great joy of science is to slay an ugly hypothesis with a beautiful fact.'

A silence! For a moment no one spoke. Then the chairman remarked benevolently. 'I must say, Dr Nicholson, you're quite a philosophical young man.'

Having invited other representatives to participate, the chairman said. 'There are no more questions, doctor, would you kindly wait outside?'

'You took your bloody time in there, Nicholson,' Simon Pickford remarked sarcastically.

John looked through him. Time dragged by. The things he should have said, but did not. An ambulance screamed outside.

'Dr Pickford would you come this way please?' McCormack suddenly appeared, beaming as usual. 'The rest of you may go except Dr Nicholson.'

John's pulse quickened; he knew Simon Pickford was their choice.

Presently McCormack reappeared seeming subdued.

'Please go in Dr Nicholson. The committee are waiting.'

Again he was obliged to make the journey to the empty chair; this time it was much longer.

'Doctor, we've asked to see you again for two reasons,' the chairman began as John sat down. 'Firstly, I have to tell you we've decided to offer the position to Dr Pickford and he's accepted. It will be renewable on an annual basis for up to three years. Even though there will be clinical duties in the hospital Dr Pickford will work mainly in the Biochemistry Department and we hope he'll do well under the guidance of Professor Pickford. The other reason, Dr Nicholson, concerns your behaviour during the interview this morning.'

John bowed his head feeling weak, wishing he could walk away as the chairman went on. 'We have to tell you most of us were impressed by the way you conducted yourself. We considered this fact together with your curriculum vitae and references and we've asked ourselves whether there was any position available to accommodate you here. Even though money is limited, Professor Wainwright informs us he has some funds in his department and could offer you a position of Assistant Research Fellow for one year. The position would also carry an attachment to St Mary's entailing certain clinical duties and responsibilities. The salary would be less than Dr Pickford's but I should point out, if you accept, your main duties would be in Oncology and you'd be responsible directly to Professor Wainwright. Now tell us, what's your response?'

Corrigan was smiling and the others looked at him anxiously.

'I should add that as Chairman of the Board I've the power to offer you the position without the necessity for a further interview. Well now, what's your answer?'

He knew the offer was considerable. Suddenly there was no

difficulty.

'I'll regard it a privilege to work with Professor Wainwright.'

CHAPTER 8

Another gruelling day for Agnes Lynch and, on top of this, was the forthcoming investigation into Catherine Kennedy's death. Kevin Kennedy was taking an action for negligence and looking for compensation from the hospital. She could not believe it—for negligence—after all the care and attention young Catherine had received. No one could have been better looked after, anywhere. She especially remembered the dedication of Dr Nicholson in Intensive Care. Now the hospital was been sued for negligence! She was furious just thinking about it. But thinking was useless.

She had to get home and was already late; the manager insisted on hearing her evidence in the case. Walking through the fog she thought about Stephen again; the child bothered even exasperated her. She was impatient for something she knew not what. Maybe, horribly responsible for him as if she were guilty for his every breath. And this was agony to Stephen and everyone else.

How was it going to end?

Fatigue hit her like a hammer as she put the latchkey in the door. The house was silent, although the table lamp was on in the hall. Beside it there was a note from Margaret Doyle saying she had to go, but not to worry, everything was all right. Agnes rested at the bottom of the stairs for a few minutes.

'Is that you Agnes? I hear you. You're late again.' Nothing wrong with her mother's hearing. 'Get my tea at once. You ungrateful daughter.'

'Yes mum,' was all she could manage.

She went into the front room and smiled at Stephen in his wheelchair. Kissing him on the forehead she was guilty for the impatience she had on her way home. Here was her treasure and blessing.

The Kennedys had lost theirs! She carried her burden gratefully and acknowledged her role with stoicism few possessed. She would care for him forever, if needs be!

The mother's tea was prepared. She left it aside momentarily to go through the mail, nearly all bills, electricity, telephone and some reminders. She struggled upstairs with the tray when the thumping of the walking stick became unbearable.

'Here's your tea mum. See I have everthing as you like it.'

'Show me.' The mother said with an air of hostility. 'You'll have to get rid of that Doyle girl. She's hopeless. Do you hear me? Hopeless. She won't do anything I ask her.'

'But mum. She's so good. She does all the housework and looks after Stephen.' I've heard this so often. Will she ever stop moaning?

'Of course she does,' the mother hissed, 'but she doesn't look after me one bit. I tell you, you'll have to sack her. Do you hear me? Sack her.'

'Don't shout mum.' Agnes was getting impatient. 'I can hear you all right.'

'I'll say whatever I like to in my own house.' She yelled. 'You ungrateful woman.'

'No mum. Be reasonable,' Agnes pleaded and her voice was rising, 'please be reasonable. Life is hard enough as it is. I can barely manage. And if you shout at me any more you'll upset Stephen.'

'I don't give a damn about that rascal.' She gave the floor an almighty thump with her stick. 'He's no good. Good for nothing. Sitting there all day.' She was screaming now making sure her voice carried downstairs.

Agnes stared in horror at her mother, whose dilated eyes, nearly all black seemed to be looking at something wild and despicable.

'No. Mum. No.'

'I will. You'll see I'll say what I like.' She couldn't bear to be thwarted. The tray was thrown on the floor, as she reached for her walking stick and quickly got out of bed.

Agnes saw what was coming, turned on her heal, and hurried on to the landing. She leant over the banisters, weeping uncontrollably. Out of the corner of her eye she saw her mother approaching with the stick raised. A lightning flash of pain exploded on her head again, and again. She rushed to the top of the stairs and felt a dig in the small of her back. Then she rolled, tumbled and crashed down the stairs coming to rest beside the table with the lamp still alight.

She closed her eyes and let consciousness drift away. Gradually darkness filtered through, pain lessened and she lapsed away from the sick abandonment of life within her. A jangled echo of something left undone came back for seconds. But it was useless. She had to let go.

Stephen heard the noise, the words and the shouting. All that was left was the screaming upstairs.

'You wicked, wicket woman. Agnes.' He could still hear the old woman ranting and raving. 'You were never any good. Now who's going to look after me? You gone and done it now. It's all your fault.'

Stephen was desperate. He tried to cry out but couldn't; trapped in his useless body. Now, above everything he was needed, but could not move. He saw the telephone on the hall table. How was he to reach it?

He rocked to and fro, to and fro. Useless. He tried again. This made the wheelchair fall sideways on the ground, his left shoulder crashing on the carpet and he was thrown free of the chair. He tried to roll over and over. It worked. He rolled again, and then, in agony, inch-by-inch, he moved towards his mother. It took an eternity. Eventually he made it.

'Mama wake up,' he heard himself whispering. She responded with a moan. He tried again. The same response. He saw the telephone and pulled it to the floor. The receiver lay on its side and the dialling face looked up at him. He struggled towards it. With great effort he slowly pressed 999 with his chin.

Immediately a clear female voice came over.

'What service do you require?'

He couldn't answer straight away. He moved his head nearer the receiver.

'My mother is dying. Please come.'

The voice said more slowly and clearly.

'I cannot hear you. Please speak up.'

It was such an effort. 'Mother is dying. Come quickly.'

'Where are you?' She asked desperately.

'Help please. Help.'

'Where are you now?' She repeated more loudly.

'29 Liffey Cottages.'

Immediately the line went dead. Stephen rolled over on his back, closed his eyes and mind. He lay there for what seemed ages and thoughts went through him …

Still the shouting and screaming went on upstairs, with occasional thumps on the floor.

'Agnes you selfish wicked woman. Where are you? You're never here when I need you. You wicked, wicked woman.'

Still he waited and waited. Was this the way it was going to end? Bedlam upstairs and Mama dead in the hall. He wished he could be beside her; that would be the right way to give up. He was going to try if it was the last thing he would ever do. He'd to make a start, inch-by-inch, he could move, another inch. He was getting nearer. She was so far away. It was sheer agony. He must persevere; everything depended on it. He must not give up.

She lay there motionless beside him. The light from the lamp fell on her hair making it glisten and shine like a tussled wig on some ragdoll. He saw the fine down on the nape of her neck with wisps of gold fragments straggling across the skin. She was still breathing, lightly. He could see that. He watched her, hoping against hope it would not stop. All he had, all he was, ever will be, was there. Anguish for his mother was tightening around him, he was afraid almost to destruction. Afraid to think what was slowly happening to her.

Grief seized him like physical pain. He placed his head on her chest, whispering to wake her up, to move, to do anything. There was nothing. Attacks came in bouts and he knew she was in pain; her moans told him so. The tide of his grief gathered in strength, heaving and forcing him onward towards its breaking, bringing him farther away from his meagre reality than he'd ever known.

He stretched as much as possible and kissed her on the neck—all the while suffering those nearly insane bursts of grief and gradually losing contact with reality. A nightmare, life had burst its bounds, and he was lost in a great, and suffocating flood. He could only breath, irregularly and in silence. A hopeless rage came on again but didn't last. It was followed by a strange and blessed calm, as he looked at his beloved mother, friend, and lifeblood. He closed his eyes. It would be so easy, maybe even enjoyable to step out, with her, in imagination, and leave behind the cold damp days that never changed, to walk freely into the glorious sunshine of an eternal morning.

No one could avoid his or her hour. Maybe, this was theirs. He hoped it was.

On the mantelpiece the clock ticked away rapidly.

Suddenly there was banging on the front door. Then a crashing sound as the door was forced open. In rushed the emergency services and paramedics. One of them bent down to a twelve-year old child weeping over an unconscious woman lying at the bottom of the stairs. He felt for the carotid pulse—feeble action. She was still alive but there was loss of blood from the head.

He looked at the pupils' reaction to light— sluggish response.

He shouted to the others.

'This one is still alive. Get stretchers with spinal injury gear ready. Jim, you see to the child. And Sarah, search the house. There may be someone upstairs.'

Sarah rushed up to the bedroom and found an old lady, looking at her with wild pathetic eyes in which reason was already dead.

She asked.

'Is my tea ready yet?'

The whole recovery operation went smoothly and all three occupants of number 29 Liffey Cottages were rushed to hospital.

Chapter 9

Diane Sutton smiling at Andrew Baker tucked in bedclothes that didn't need it.

'How's the patient today?'

'Not too bad nurse.' Speaking was not easy and his paleness was made worse by sandy hair and abundant moustache.

'We'll soon have you on your feet,' she said. 'Dr Nicholson will be along shortly to take another sample.' He winced. It was becoming difficult to obtain blood because of fibrosed veins.

'Why so often?'

'I don't know. Although he's doing research into your condition.'

'And what is my condition?'

Andrew waited in silence. Looking at her watch she tried to skate around the answer.

'I can't discuss such matters. Ask Dr Nicholson or Professor Wainwright.'

'I already have.'

'And?'

'I've some abnormal blood cells and there are medicines to control them.' His voice was a murmur. 'They didn't say they could cure me.'

'Please excuse me Andrew.' She drew the curtains back and rushed to the phone in sister's office.

Andrew tried to walk around the ward to test his strength. It was a struggle; his reserves were gradually disappearing and he felt like a walking corpse. He shuffled like an old man. Enough of this, I'd better return to bed before I faint. Then sitting up, a cold finger probed his heartstrings as his mind drifted back to childhood.

He was the only child of Sydney Baker, the vicar of Rathmoy in County Kildare. Initially, the vicar toiled with generous reserves of self-pity but the flock—a vulgar throng—did not appreciate his superior qualities.

Also, he couldn't forget his mother. Her reserves were more generous never accepting insolence. Deference she demanded everywhere, yet indifference was her only thanks. With injured pride she turned her glare inwards. Only then she discovered a husband who'd abandoned any duty to her, to himself or anyone else. She retreated into silent rages. Bitterness settled around her giving some warmth from a thankless world. Delight she took in her misfortune and endowed her son with a wretched childhood.

He tried to analyse how things were between them. They didn't speak; communication was nil. They didn't openly find fault; that is, not in front of him. Still, they lived in the same house all his childhood years, no hint of leaving from either of them. A silent agreement must have been made with neither giving an inch. In the house there was nothing—no stimulation, no friends and no visitors. Nothing for years—except silence. They were cruel, not trusting the other, always aware of the possibility of some planned treachery. His mother hating a man she'd once loved, his father ignoring her. Many times he sat in the living room on a winter's evening, the air oppressed with a heavy silence.

By the end of school he was diffident, withdrawn and unapproachable. Eventually he finished his studies and left home to pursue a career in third level education. As there was a great deal of arrears in living to make up for he grabbed life with both hands.

John Nicholson settled into the Oncology Department receiving valuable advice from Wainwright. His interest was leukaemia and he'd learned the technique of culturing cells. He was attempting to identify substances that would inhibit the growth of malignant cells and yet have no serious effects on normal ones. Progress was reported to Wainwright at one of their research meetings.

'Good news—I think.' He said sitting opposite Wainwright. 'The results are variable when the one agent is used. Even though the same diagnosis is made in a group of patients, yet, the same agent can produce different results in their blood cultures.'

Wainwright had liked Nicholson from the first day. There was something forthright and honest about the young doctor. He reached for pen and paper. 'Remarkable,' he said thoughtfully. 'What next?'

'There's one culture that's behaving strangely.' John enjoyed these daily challenges. 'From a twenty-five year old male with a strange type of leukaemia.'

'Yes. Baker's one of those who's not responding to drugs or radiotherapy.'

'His cells have a remarkable sensitivity to chlor 10-6A. I've used it on all cultures, malignant and controls, and Baker's die rapidly even in high dilutions. If only chlor 10-6A could be conjugated with human gamma globulin it'd probably be safer.'

'It's quite toxic. What about its clinical application?' Wainwright asked.

'I knew you'd ask that,' was the quick reply, 'I've tested normal tissue cultures with the same dilution as with Baker's?'

'And?'

'The majority showed no significant change.'

'What about the minority?' Wainwright gave a suspicious glance.

'The cells were destroyed,' was the frank reply. John felt uncomfortable.

A pause.

'I see. Suppression of all cells in a patient might occur.'

'There's a risk. We've no way of telling unless … '

Wainwright hastily reminded him. ' … You'll have to test it on animals, of course! I need hardly say that.'

'I know professor, but ... '

Wainwright's anger was instantly apparent. 'Nicholson, you're not suggesting we use it on Baker. It's unthinkable and completely unethical.'

Slowly John lowered his head and looked at the floor.

'The patient is dying.'

'It could kill him in twenty-four hours.' Wainwright was implacable as he turned on John. 'As he is now, he may live for four or five months and, who knows, may even go into remission, although that's unlikely.'

'Professor can Baker wait for that to happen?' John was pleading now.

Wainwright banged his fist on the desk.

'Damn your impertinence Nicholson!'

Immediately he stood up and walked to the window looking out with unseeing eyes. A silence followed. He was not angry with Nicholson. It was the futility of having one's hands tied by rules, regulations, planning strategies, performance indicators coming from remote committees that were unheard of when he was Nicholson's age. He'd always believed in freedom—freedom in teaching, discussion and inquiry. Today, most were afraid of doing something wrong, afraid of making a decision. Was it wrong to save a patient's life when it was almost extinguished? If he allowed Nicholson to give chlor 10-6A, and the patient died, he could visualize the committees of inquiry; the fuss and nonsense coming from bureaucrats whose minds would take the breath of life from the most vital subject, whose concept of reorganizing their files was to make a copy of everyone before destroying them!

But that was only his opinion.

CHAPTER 10

'Damn it! Hold the retractor steady.' John Nicholson said to Diane. He was edgy as he surgically exposed a vein for a blood sample. Also, a drip had to be set up before he went off duty and he insisted on doing it himself. They worked quietly for a while—a hand tremor was visible—and then an instrument slipped piercing Diane's surgical glove. 'I'm sorry doctor. I'll change my gloves.'

John tried to soothe the patient.

'I'm almost finished now Andrew. Everything's fine.'

When the procedure was completed Andrew forced himself up. 'Dr Nicholson, may I ask a question?'

'Of course.' John sat on the bed as Diane cleared the instruments.

'I'd like to know my chances of getting better.'

John glanced at Diane; the question caught him off guard.

'There is a chance Andrew.' He tried to dismiss it with a smile.

Andrew waited in silence.

'I'm sure you've been asked this question many times.' He said eventually.

John had, and yet didn't know the answer. Telling the whole truth was always a dilemma and was becoming a bigger problem in medicine. How much do you tell, can you tell, how should you tell? A little truth could be good for the patient but the complete truth—not sparing the gory details—could do damage to a vulnerable person who was already finding it difficult to cope. Perhaps, they were better left alone for their own protection and peace of mind, letting them have the comfort of false hope. Unfortunately lawyers would not agree. Their attitude was the truth must come out otherwise the patient should be encouraged to sue for compensation.

'Everyone's telling me how pleased they are with my progress including Nurse Sutton here.' Andrew continued. 'They mean well and yet as the days turn into weeks I get weaker and weaker.'

Diane made a gesture as if to go.

John looked up and shook his head. 'Please stay nurse. I'd like you to hear what I have to say.' He turned to Andrew and his next words tasted like sawdust.

'The latest tests show you probably have a rare form of leukaemia.'

Andrew was transfixed. One could see the blood draining from his face and the eyes dilated. An abyss opened beneath him—confirmation of his fear. 'I see. What you're saying is the outlook's hopeless.'

'I wouldn't put it like that,' he said gently. 'There's a gradual deterioration and could account for the nausea and weakness.'

'Doctor is there any hope?'

'Indeed there is.' John was subdued but quite firm on the matter. 'In some, the condition may suddenly disappear—we call it a remission. We can't explain why, and it could happen in your case.' A pang of cruelty rose in him as he recalled Wainwright's prognosis.

'Doctor. We can always hope.' His words were empty.

Diane said. 'Doctor I've heard you're doing research into this condition.'

'I've also heard about your work.' Andrew took the lead with enthusiasm as he sat up. 'Would it be all right to ask about it?'

John was trapped. What was he to do—dare he mention chlor 10-6A? He knew he shouldn't, but against his better judgement, the words flowed out.

'The investigation, Andrew, concerns a substance that has an effect on some cells, called abnormal lymphocytes, in that they are destroyed. The evidence only comes from laboratory experiments.' He paused for emphasis. Diane soaked up every word. 'However, the dose required to kill them is so high—dangerously high in most instances—that it also damages normal cells.'

Andrew was hesitant with his next question. There was a rising expectation in his face. 'You say "most instances"—but not in every case?'

'That's right—not every case. There are abnormal lymphocytes that are sensitive to small doses that do not appear to affect normal cells.'

Feeling he'd gone too far he stood up. Diane remained motionless. There was no escaping the next question. Andrew went straight to the point.

'Doctor, are my cells sensitive to this chemical?'

A desperate pause. He had to extricate himself.

'I know what you're thinking—and you must not. This chemical is highly toxic and must be tested in animals before it is considered fit for humans. These are the rules.'

'The rules and regulations,' Andrew repeated, almost inaudibly.

'We must follow ethical procedures.' John's tone was sombre. 'We are also attempting to combine this chemical with a protein to make it less harmful to normal cells, that is, if we're going to use it. All this takes time Andrew.'

There was no stopping Andrew. He came out with it immediately looking straight and hard at John.

'How much time have I got?'

John looked away.

'I cannot say. Maybe three months, maybe six. We really do not know.'

Andrew's voice seemed untroubled, even remote as he extended a hand. 'Thank you for being so frank doctor. It hasn't been easy. I appreciate it.'

Slowly John turned away feeling defeated. Oh God, how difficult it is. A horrible position to be in. Another person's future, to know what's ahead, suffering, pain, battles with depression, even despair, Andrew would have to endure. It would be a matter of months. He'd seen it all too often, witnessing the slow, inevitable decline of a progressive disease was one of the most harrowing experiences any doctor could have.

John's compassion was stretched to the limit. What frustrated most was the inability to stop progress of some illnesses, especially in his field. What use was his work to Andrew Baker? No use at all, he was going to die a slow and painful death.

Yet this was why his research was so important. It was uncanny how Wainwright could detect pitfalls and direct him to those areas that could lead to valuable results. It was a slow process. Too damned slow and a heavy burden! The main concern must be to give maximum support to Andrew and to reply to his questions in cautious terms.

'You could use a coffee.' Diane felt his distress and suggested coffee as they reached the corridor.

'Sounds like a good idea.' He replied weakly.

Her heart melted towards this young doctor—no he wasn't that young; there was probably eight years in the difference. Yet he'd some of the qualities she admired in her father—stubbornness, introspection, almost self—imposed isolation. She knew how to get around her father—to get her own way. Now she was confused, even at a loss for words.

'Poor Andrew—he's quite right. The outlook is hopeless.' John said eventually.

CHAPTER 11

Andrew Baker's voice was little more than a whisper.

'Diane nice to see you again.'

She gave a humourless laugh.

'You were nearly not going to see me this evening.'

'Why?' He asked suddenly serious.

She sat on the visitor's chair and lowered her head.

'Feeling a bit low—that's all.'

'I'm sorry to hear that,' he said in a courteous voice. 'Diane there's a question I want to ask. It's about Dr Nicholson.'

Her heart missed a beat.

'Yes?'

'He doesn't visit me very often. Do you think he's avoiding me?' He turned his eyes away. 'Perhaps I might've upset him.'

'No Andrew.' She tried to reassure him. 'You've every right to see him or anyone else for that matter. Have you spoken to Professor Wainwright? You couldn't be in better hands'.

His next question was gentle as if pleading.

'Diane is there any way I could be put in Dr Nicholson's hands?'

She felt sorry for him—then the final straw—at the mention of John's name a tear came to her eyes. Andrew was not looking at her.

'When he explained his work it was the first time hope returned to me.'

Yes, Andrew, some say where there's life there's hope—a bit silly in medicine, especially hospital medicine. It is rather meaningless. Here, life is in short supply—its greatest export is death! We must distinguish between hope and expectation—but she didn't have the courage to say so.

Andrew's eyes, fixed at a distance, drank in a vision of the future, a future running out as time spilled a swifter sand each day.

'I felt there was something seriously wrong after coming into hospital,' he continued in the same tone, 'because of the way people spoke to me—including you Diane.'

She wiped her eyes and forced a smile.

'What do you mean?'

'I knew I'd never be well again. You even had me playing the deception game.'

She laughed nervously and shook her head.

'What else can we do except encourage? To give hope.'

Andrew closed his eyes and lay back on the pillows. He felt lost.

'Where there's none Diane?' His eyes were still closed.

'That's not fair,' she said weakly. This was salt in a wound. 'We try our best.'

After a moment he opened his eyes and lowered his head.

'I know. Please forgive me.'

'There's nothing to forgive.'

'There is,' he insisted, feeling ashamed. 'My ingratitude.'

He was tired and it was late. Others were settling for the night.

She stood up brushing invisible dust from her uniform.

'I'll see you tomorrow Andrew.'

Desperation was in his voice as he struggled to say. 'Diane, one thing before you go. Would you ever talk to Dr Nicholson and say I'd like to speak to him again.'

Suddenly Diane was her old self. 'I will of course. I'm sure he'll see you. He's very conscientious and clever.'

Andrew smiled and his face lit up. 'He's handsome too. Isn't he?'

She took the question in her stride. 'Why do you ask?'

'One can sense things.'

She nodded, smiled and didn't feel embarrassed. Yes, she would try to find him first thing tomorrow. She said goodnight, left the ward and made for the staff quarters. Sitting alone in the large room, she sensed a depression hanging over the hospital courtyard; some of her friends had rushed out to a few hours freedom. It had rained incessantly. Now the last of the sun broke through mist and smeared a pallid hand across the walls, its fingers reaching into the room. Was it a sign? She wished it were.

Recently there developed an unfulfilled dream consuming her very being and resulting in restless nights and lethargic days. She just couldn't understand why she felt so tired and exhausted. The influenza was taking such a long time to shake off.

She always wanted to be a nurse as her father was a doctor. Because of training schemes he'd to work in different locations—Wicklow, Dublin, where Diane was born, a spell in England, returning to the midlands before settling in his home town of Westport. He'd always longed to live permanently in this lovely Mayo place beside Clew Bay.

However, this didn't satisfy everyone, especially his wife Maud. She, being from south Dublin expected more out of life than a large village. Intense conflict resulted. Mother wanted to go back to Dublin; it was the least she could expect from a loving husband who wanted to carry out her every wish. They did move—again—when a practice became available. For Maud, it was still wrong. But it had to be.

Domestic friction and experience in a local school prompted Diane to ask her father: 'Please dad, would you ever send me to a boarding school. I'd love to go.' He was full of understanding, even her mother agreed. So it was settled.

Then Andrew Baker. She admired him in a way she couldn't understand. After school, he'd told her, he went to the United States where he lived, for a while, in the fast lane. Returning to Dublin he qualified as a teacher. His friends were many, admirers he had and life was good. High ideals he burned to pass on to his colleagues and pupils—the younger the better. Mounting opposition faced him and life became so difficult he was afraid his mind would snap. He even looked old. And he became ill.

He was in hospital. And now he'd no visitors, no friends. Yet he didn't complain, not much anyway, which was in contrast to some people she knew. Diane had been reluctant to visit him because she couldn't endure the gradual defeat by his illness, an illness she or others could not comprehend. It was destroying someone as young as herself.

Andrew was alone again, with his familiar silence. And it was getting late—bedside lights had been switched off. The conversation with Diane set his mind turning. He'd enjoyed the States but was glad to be back. Now this illness. What was it—a rare form of leukaemia? Why wasn't he started on any treatment yet? Did the doctors know what they were doing?

He worried about the future. The possibility of death kept intruding into his conscience ever since entering hospital. Was it a feeling most get when they go into hospital? However, he did feel strongly he would continue to exist somehow after he had drawn his last breath. Perhaps, existence would be like a dream in a sleep that never ends.

Walking across the courtyard Diane noticed lights blazing in Wainwright's laboratory—the rest of the research wing was in darkness. It wasn't the Professor. He was in Cambridge. Arriving back in her room—her own space—she'd time to reflect on recent happenings. She'd always wanted to do nursing. All her life she'd heard about patients, good ones, bad ones, and difficult ones and, of course, the hypochondriacs who could drive a doctor crazy. They were the greatest cause of stress for her father in practice.

Still the awful tiredness prevented her from enjoying life, as she should, as she wanted to. Everyone else was able for it. Why couldn't she? For some reason she cried herself to sleep.

CHAPTER 12

It was one of those summer days when the air glittered with the sun's brilliance. Wisps of cloud hung over Cambridge but now a warm wind sprang up and brushed them aside; it fluttered along the lawns and gardens known as the 'Backs', sloped towards the river, and moved south to King's Bridge where it circled a solitary figure, which stood looking east towards King's College Chapel. Wind and figure moved forward to the west face of the building whose beauty—as always—was extreme.

Darkness and solitude accompanied Walter Wainwright as he entered. The interior, with its lofty ceiling—a perfect example of petrified music—had always given him joy. He'd come here often, not for religion or piety, but to saturate himself in the peace of the place that had encouraged the relentless enthusiasm of his youth. At school in Winchester he was fiercely individualistic. There, he found the system geared, not to impart knowledge, but to mould, to socialize and to conform. It was one of the unhappiest times of his life. Defiant by nature, he found it difficult to control his temper and his tongue; at times, they landed him in trouble with superiors.

In spite of this, by hard work, and sheer determination he succeeded in passing the requirements for university, and wishing to emulate his father—a distinguished physician to St Bart's in London—he enrolled in Cambridge University Medical School when he was eighteen. These same qualities helped him through undergraduate medical school, but it was in the years after qualifying his undisciplined tongue really got the better of him. A lot of lessons were learnt. In the closed ranks of the medical profession these qualities were bound to impede advancement. He slipped into despondency, a kind of frustration felt by those who are never stretched to the full potential of their powers. This was a critical time in his academic life—the tough years preparing for the Doctorate in Medicine in Oncology. He felt he was surrounded by intellectual snobs and fools whose only ambition was to place obstacles in the way of others.

Gillian Fitzgerald he had met and his world changed. She'd much to teach him, including the cultivation of friends and, perhaps, the hardest lesson of all, how to swallow his pride. She had made him listen more carefully, to criticize less, and to defer to those who earned deferment. Simply, to give credit where it was due. This eventually paid off in his success by obtaining his Doctorate. He had her to thank for it.

At the thought of Gillian he sat down remaining motionless with a fixed expression. Clear-cut lines were on his face, the mouth was set in a scowl and the hair, now almost completely grey, was brushed straight back. His eyes were deep-set and blue—a blue that could dazzle—but now sad. If time had cut deep grooves in his face it had chiselled deeper ones in his mind because sadness became a permanent fixture.

Gustav Isselherg, a postgraduate from Sweden and close friend had tried to console him. Both were now in Cambridge for the annual symposium of the International Association for Cancer Research and Isselherg was due to present an important paper.

'Walter, my friend, how are you after all these years?' Isselherg recognized him leaving the main auditorium in Addenbrooke's Hospital.

'I'm fine, Gustav, just fine. And you've changed little except for the beard. The years have treated you kindly.' He was genuinely glad to see his old friend from student days.

Gustav laughed heartily. 'It must be all the clean air in Sweden.'

'Perhaps, although I'm sure there's more to it than that. How's Rachel?'

Isselherg was a big round man and a typical extrovert. He was obviously enjoying himself. 'She's well. And, of course, she looks after me. Sometimes too well I feel. What with her fussing and the three daughters I've no excuse. Let's take a walk and see some of the old places again.'

They walked slowly up Hills Road, turned left into Bateman Street and made for the Botanical Gardens, which are amongst the finest in England. They sat before a silent choir of roses in the late afternoon and reminisced about times long past, about days of dreamy softness and things that might have been.

Eventually, Isselherg said in a gentle voice and with the best intentions. 'You know, I often think it was a great pity you didn't remarry after Gillian died.'

Wainwright didn't reply but his silence was loud.

'I'm sorry Walter—perhaps I shouldn't have said that.' Isselherg added almost under his breath. 'Leukaemia is a terrible thing.'

It his latter years in Cambridge Wainwright married Gillian Fitzgerald, an Irish philosophy student doing postgraduate work. Her stunning beauty, auburn hair, sparkling green eyes and vivid mouth glistening in passions of laughter everyone remembered. They first met in the Rockingham Tennis Club. He was listed to partner her in one of the College tournaments and the match was the result of a random draw.

They won. He then invited her to a College dance to celebrate and she accepted. They danced and talked—each finding out things about the other.

She was from Dublin, a town she adored because of the excitement of the people and there was always plenty to do. She'd been successful with her Doctorate in English Literature and was anxious to pursue her studies in the best possible place, she announced proudly to him, and that was in Cambridge. Who was he to disagree?

Wainwright found her fascinating not only to look at—which, of course was a splendid experience for a young college lecturer, but to listen to her about philosophy and language. She had a wonderfully incisive mind that carried a wealth of knowledge and a huge amount of common sense; the latter appealed to him immensely because it was all too often lacking in other acquaintances. Her joie de vivre was almost infectious—he sensed she'd a lot to teach him. And so she did.

Gillian thought Walter was quite nice, under all the hustle and bustle. He was full of surprises. She was impressed with his six foot four inches height, underweight and possibly undernourished figure, restless hands, thatch of straight blond hair and always-reluctant smile. His aloofness and arrogance in avoiding her eyes when he told her something important things intrigued her. She promised herself she would, come hell or high water, make him look at her.

In the weeks that followed he certainly did look. She found the attention flattering but wouldn't admit it. A struggle ensued. He would telephone about another match. Would she be available? No, she wouldn't, because of another engagement. Yes, another engagement. This excuse was offered several times and he thought enough is enough. What was this other engagement?

He knew where she lived. Gillian Fitzgerald was not just a second fiddle to anyone; she was a member of the local Vivaldi Quartet. He looked out for their next performance.

The evening of the concert arrived, which was to be held in the Chapel of Saint John's. He managed to get a seat near the front. Beethoven's last two string quartets were on the programme.

The experience was extraordinary. From that time he avowed to learn as much about classical music as he could and the effort was to make all the difference in winning the hand of his beloved Gillian.

And because everyone can overcome grief except the one that has it, he never completely recovered from her death, which occurred soon after his success with the MD. This left him bitter and agnostic.

Wainwright smiled gently. Before Isselherg could say anything he said.

'Please don't apologize. It was a natural thing to say. A good memory may be a blessing but the ability to forget is probably a greater gift.'

The smile disappeared on Walter's face.

'Let's have supper this evening. There's something we should discuss.'

The breeze had grown tired as the two men stopped after supper to admire the picturesque 'Backs' from the Garrett Hostel Bridge. Isselherg said goodnight to his friend and went on his way.

Wainwright walked alone on the path beside the river. He came across a wooden seat and sat facing the fading light. The water hardly disturbed the blue and gold reflections. The sky was speckled white and yellow, then pink; orange and crimson stole into the horizon. Magical dusk was all about as nature made that enigmatic transition from day to night. He closed his eyes and luxuriated in the coolness. Why had he no time to relax like this anymore, not a minute or two, but the whole evening? It was strange to sit in elegant surroundings and meditate on anything, anything at all. At a time like this he wouldn't resist getting on in years, getting old. He might welcome it.

Even though he lacked tolerance, and was almost proud of his brusqueness, ambition made him unable to sympathize without a feeling of degradation. He could not pity what he hadn't experienced himself, the gift given but not received.

Yet, he was not a coarse man. He was glad to be alone. It was eerie how these surroundings flooded Gillian's memory back. One could not thread the fields of human pathology and medicine without a small well of tears stored secretly and only become evident at certain times. Tears were rising now as she gave him a warm smile and a hand's touch of welcome. She whispered her thanks for the flowers he'd left that very day. She was gracious about the life she had shared with him and, before leaving, she wished him better things than he could ever hope for. Then she was gone.

He stood upright, sturdy as an oak in a storm and made his way home.

CHAPTER 13

The Oncology Department was located on the third floor of the new science block in Trinity; a large and active department with people coming and going all the time. Data was collected from tissue sampling, blood analysis, studying behavioural problems and other clinical findings on animal models. White-coated individuals hovered over excited centrifuges, humming beta-counters and elaborate microscopes. Wainwright and Nicholson's work was closely tied into day-to-day activities and already led to many important publications.

A telephone rang in the Department. Peter McKenna, one of the senior technicians, answered.

'Diane Sutton here. Could I speak to John Nicholson please?'

'I'll try Diane,' he hesitated, 'he's been so irritable recently. He was in the lab this morning when I came in and was probably up all night. He was exhausted and there was glass on the floor.'

'Poor John.' She was shocked. 'He shouldn't drive himself. Peter please see if he's available.'

She waited trying to visualize the scene.

'Hello.' A voice startled her.

'John. I'm sorry to disturb you.' She stopped, hoping for a response. There was none. 'Andrew Baker's asked to see you.'

Again a pause. She didn't know if he'd heard her.

'How is he?'

'Getting worse. He didn't say what he wanted, but … ' She was reluctant to proceed. John desperately wanted to talk to someone who would listen—Wainwright was in Cambridge. This was going to be awkward.

'I'll see him of course, but Diane, could we discuss things beforehand?'

'I'm on duty until six o'clock,' she said simply.

He vacillated trying to make up his mind.

'Would you be good enough to have a meal with me?'

'I'd love to,' she whispered urging him on.

'Good. I'll wait at the main entrance at seven o'clock.'

He'd no plans to get involved—his work was all-important. Nothing must interfere; there was little time to prove himself. It was imperative he should produce convincing results if he was to be granted an extension.

He was at the gates at seven o'clock, punctual and expectant, his face thin and pale and sporting an old-fashioned cap and raincoat that seemed out of place.

Still, Diane was delighted to see him. Close up, he was younger than she thought; or perhaps, it was the insecure look in his eyes, which made her feel sorry for him. His expression was one of regret, almost an apology for dragging her out in the evening like this. There was a sense of expectancy everywhere.

His heart missed a beat when he saw her out of uniform. The

wide green eyes were like the centre of some lovely flower, hair glinting the colour of a freshly opened chestnut. Up to this, nurses looked the same, each in identical white regulation dress. There were plenty milling about; they were like automatons. It was unfair of him to think like this. Everyone is different; own personality, aura and body language, no matter what type uniform.

Now the young creature walking beside him took him aback. The effect was stunning. She was much taller than he'd imagined. Beside him was a dark-haired young lady that would take any full-blooded male's breath away. All completely new.

Then the onslaught of colour. A red silk scarf was tucked around her neck and almost up to the chin. She wore a gorgeous lightweight tweed half-coat with twin pockets at breast and waist level with a matching belt around the narrow waist. The skirt was ankle length but didn't hide exquisite ankles above black-lace shoes. Perhaps, she wore the high shoes to compete with him.

'You've been working too hard.' She laughed nervously and shook her head. 'Is it worth it?'

'It is,' he said with a frown. 'If this work is not done by someone we're just going to stagnate and achieve nothing.'

'But why you?' She was persistent, determined not to let him away with anything.

'I don't know what drives me Diane. Some might call it ambition but there must be something else.'

His careful nature told him he could less afford error, so he sighed himself to a close. 'Someday I may be able to tell you.'

The Bay View restaurant in Dalkey was about half-full when they arrived by taxi. Outside was a lovely elegy from a robin, singing farewell to the day, each note pure, high and rounded like a flowing fountain. Inside Genaro was pleased to welcome them.

'Dr Nicholson, how nice to see you again and what a beautiful signorina we have tonight.'

He ushered them to a secluded part of the room. A rose was placed on a table; music and lighting were warm and intimate. A mural created the illusion of an Italian loggia with inspiring vistas and wisps of real plants escaped from the wall emphasizing the trompe-l'oeil effect. Genaro explained that, as the room was converted into a work of art, he intended to feed body and soul together.

'A noble thought,' John replied and Diane smiled approval.

'An aperitif to begin with Signor?' The headwaiter asked as he set two places.

'Diane what would you like?'

'Dry sherry please.'

'And later Signor?'

'A bottle of your best Lacrima Christie.'

Two menus arrived but they studied one. 'I'll leave the choice to you John.'

'That could be risky.'

As the meal progressed they talked with increasing ease.

'A little more wine?' He suggested mischievously, as he peered over the tip of his glass. 'Although it can make one mistake words for thoughts.'

'Don't be silly. It makes people more interesting.'

'Perhaps it does,' he smiled, and then his eyes narrowed.

She felt awkward; the ice still cold between them. A little thawing was necessary. She spoke of the trials and tribulations her father had in practice before settling down in Westport, although it was not her mother's scene.

'And here I am now,' she said throwing caution to the wind, 'out with a handsome doctor, wining and dining, and thoroughly enjoying myself.'

Recklessness and impatience were in her nature; if she wanted to say something, no matter, she would do just that, and leave the thinking to another time. Tonight was no exception. She was a girl in a hurry with no time for extended overtures in getting to know you. She'd expect a quick response; if none came, it would be abandoned and on to the next. She deplored how time could be wasted on trivialities and how people dispensed niceties with their smiles.

'That's good, Diane.' He sat back beginning to relax. 'You're fond of your father then?'

'Oh yes.' Eyes bright with memories. 'I love him dearly.'

'Then why did you run away from home to boarding school?'

She looked uncomfortable, trying to find the right words.

'I suppose it's because the failings of parents compel a child to seek comfort and solace elsewhere in the big world.'

'Your father must be a remarkable man, but you should remember he won't always be there for you. We're all mortal.'

'Don't I know John? Don't I know?' She looked at him wistfully.

'Enough of this philosophising,' he dismissed the thought with a gesture and was suddenly serious. 'We've something to discuss.'

She'd almost forgotten—Andrew Baker was anxious to talk to John. She felt sorry for him since he was told the diagnosis.

'He asked me,' he said, immediately on the defensive.

'I know. What little hope he had, he now realizes there's none. He was getting weaker physically and now he's mentally shattered.'

'Stop Diane!' His tone was peremptory. 'Anyone would think you were blaming me.'

She set her glass down carefully.

'That's not true. At least you could talk to him. Don't you agree?'

'I'll do my best.' He put his elbows on the table and looked at her.

'Diane I don't think you realize the implications.'

She nodded. As far as she saw it, Andrew needed to be told his case was not hopeless and research was making progress.

'When you say that you make it sound simple. But it's not. Diane, it's not easy! Cancer chemotherapy is one the most complicated fields in medicine.'

She noticed how pale and thin he was, the weary eyes—deprived of sleep—that saw too much misery in the human condition. She'd seen him in the wards talking to patients and noticed his compassion. There was the time he was late for a meeting because he listened to an old lady's lament for the good old days. Also, the times he missed lunch-breaks because a sick child, lonely and neglected, suddenly found there was one adult that'd listen to her woes and he would tell wonderful stories about the little folk in the west of Ireland. Then she'd notice an improvement in the child's condition—he had this lovely magical touch!

She asked eagerly. 'John could you explain your work? Perhaps I'll understand a little better.'

'Difficult to know where to begin,' he said looking into the distance. 'Most visualize cancer as a tumour that spreads and sets up multiple growths, which eventually kill. That's the clinical picture, but there're over one million cells in one gram of a tumour. It breaks all the rules controlling normal cells. It becomes unique. When cells divide the process begins but the patient appears healthy.'

'I suppose it's at a later stage a lot of patients are first diagnosed.'

'And then it can be too late. The cells must have a selective advantage, because they're able to avoid the fate of normal cells to age and die.'

'Surely the body can fight back.'

'Yes. In 1970 Burnett suggested cancer cells arise in normal people, but are rejected by an immune response—in the same way we recover from measles.'

'By the production of antibodies you mean?'

He took a sip of coffee.

'That's right and the antibodies will normally destroy the malignant cells so that there's a constant battle going on. Chemotherapy is one of the methods we're hoping to devise in eradicating some tumours.' Initial results suggested significant advances would be made in treatment, especially in leukaemia, in the next few years.

There was surprise, even a little anger in her tone.

'How about more immediately? I'm thinking of Andrew.'

He didn't know what to say. It was the question he'd most dreaded, but he had to try and answer it somehow. He gave a sigh.

'I hope signor and his lovely signorina have enjoyed themselves this evening.' Genaro interrupted good-naturedly. It was just the wrong moment as John had intended to ask Diane not to discuss the research with anyone.

'A most enjoyable evening Genaro. Everything was perfect.'

'Then you must come again signor and bring the young lady.' He turned to Diane. 'Look after your young man, my dear. He's been looking tired recently.'

'I'll try Genaro but will he listen?' She answered.

They prepared to leave. Genaro followed, held the door open and looked crossly at John.

'Dr Nicholson you forgot something.'

He couldn't think what. The proprietor produced a rose and gave it to Diane.

She laughed openly. 'Thank you Genaro. How romantic!'

'Tell me, my young friends, have you ever been to Italy, to Roma?'

They looked at each other and both said 'no' almost together.

Genaro was full of enthusiasm.

'Then you haven't lived. You must. It'll be the experience of a lifetime.'

'You never know,' she said, 'you just never know what's in store.'

They talked about Rome on the way home. He'd never been there but it would be a priority on his list of places. Before saying 'good-night' they both lingered, both wishing it would not end—perhaps should not end. And a cheek kiss was given gracefully, and accepted hopefully.

CHAPTER 14

A portrait in oils was placed on the wall behind Professor Pickford. Visitors remarked how good it was, giving him endless pleasure and feeding a certain need. It emphasized positive features—deep-set intelligent eyes, elegantly curved nose and firm strong mouth—all under a dramatic shock of white hair. His expression suggested an acquaintance with the highest moral principles together with a hint of suffering.

Also the academic robes were superb and splendid.

Otherwise, his office was sparsely furnished with visitors' chairs—lower than his of course—behind the desk. Some found him fastidious; this was apparent by the way they behaved. Still he liked being fastidious; it had an assured quality that appealed.

Faults in others he was quick to detect and had no hesitation in pointing them out. It was his duty, a guiding principle he lived by and it would help improve the unfortunate he picked on. After all, he was trying to help—even though the other might take offence.

Obviously, that was his or her problem!

Cultured and well bred he was; his tastes in clothes, food and wine were impeccable. Some resented these qualities at university and other gatherings. Again, he couldn't help their unhappy shortcomings—their unfortunate failings.

No doubt, to some he was handsome although the thick horn-rimmed glasses were a detraction. The grey eyes seemed to be looking at nothing, nothing at all, the white hair, heavily oiled, was brushed back from a low brow. The voice was charming and cultured, although the more discerning traced a falsity, which could be the result of the R A D A course some years ago. Be that as it may, the words were well formed, articulate, resonant, maybe too many at times and this fondness for circumlocution could make the listener confused. Then perhaps, that was the intention.

He'd been married for only ten years and had a son, Simon. His wife was unable to appreciate his good breeding and high standards. In a storm she left him to his own devices. It was a good riddance. She was so careless, always wanting to go out and be entertained. This was intolerable, even though in most things he was a very generous person.

Simon was different. The mother tried to instil beliefs and morals in him with little help from the father. The only contribution he'd volunteer, and usually repeatedly, was to say if Simon wanted to learn how to do things correctly, all he had to do was to observe his father. If so, the child couldn't go wrong. Thus Simon's early years were filled with conflicting signals that only made him a rebel. Eventually, he couldn't care less.

Professor Pickford was tolerant in keeping Miss Telford as his secretary. She was a good worker and non-confrontational, but her hair was thin and needed grooming, her face was blemished and she was perpetually anxious and worried. Qualities he hoped would contrast nicely with his own elegant appearance and fine manners.

This morning he'd requested his son to come to his office.

'Please tell me how your work is progressing Simon.' He said with an air of superiority.

'Coming along fine.' Simon's tone was off-hand.

'In spite of what you say I find that hard to believe.' His father was more than a little sarcastic. 'What have you achieved?'

Simon had to face this regularly. 'At present I'm collecting data in the wards. So far I've twenty-five patients under observation.' He said avoiding his father's eyes.

'Good. But you will need at least a hundred cases to provide a satisfactory contribution to your eventual thesis.'

'Should be no problem here.' Simon affected indifference.

'In view of the fact that Nicholson's research is making good progress ... '

' ... That's different to my work,' Simon replied with calculated casualness.

'I beg to differ.' His father was sarcastic again. 'If only you would work half as hard.'

Simon's nonchalance was all too apparent. He'd no interest in reviewing the literature and was disorganized in planning a scientific proposal. All the help was there, available for the asking. But no! No enthusiasm, no interest, just a complete waste of time. A blow to his father who had high hopes for him and even spoke in glowing terms at the selection committee. What a waste, a terrible waste of good talent. How could he get Simon to change his ways and get down to proper work, which everyone knew he was capable of?

Simon didn't answer. For the present, he was content to look aggressively on the world and enjoy himself. He'd been brought up in an atmosphere of domestic suffocation, intolerance and rigidity—and he was always wrong!

The meeting ended abruptly. Simon decided to see patients in his programme. Two were in ward 3. When he arrived he spotted Diane.

'Nurse Sutton, please assist me with Mr Bedford and Mr Jones and get their records now.'

'All right doctor. I'll be with you in a few minutes.' Diane replied modestly.

'Nurse Sutton you'll do as Dr Pickford asks immediately.' Sister rasped. 'Leave those blood pressures.'

'Nurse Sutton I'd like to speak to you in the staff room.' Simon said.

Inside his attitude changed.

Again he asked for an evening out.

'Simon we all know you're a lady killer and I'm not interested in being your next victim.'

It was different with her, he protested.

'I'm sorry. Definitely no. All the same thank you for asking.'

She didn't want to be tied in a relationship—if John Nicholson was remotely interested. Perhaps it was a gamble but she was prepared to listen to her heart and hope.

As time dragged by, strange feelings came over Andrew Baker. Even though medication was necessary for pain it didn't help the mental anguish, it only transported him to a different plane where reason slept. Insidiously, daydream merged with nightmare; confusion and misery followed.

Looking inward he saw an uncertain conscience. Grief, his father told him, was a cleansing flame that must be endured and from some provisional outpost beyond space a mother called urgently, pleading in a language no longer clear. There were times when he wished darkness to go on 'til he could vanish and yet others, when infinite distance was nigh, he longed for a glorious transcendental joy, an immeasurable incomprehensible perfect peace.

John found him propped up on pillows, with a saline drip strapped to his arm. His face lit up at the sight of the white-coated visitor.

'How are you today Andrew?' John sat on the bed studying reports.

'Worse doctor.' He was as blunt as he could be. There was no other way.

'Would you like me to leave?' Diane asked drawing the curtains for privacy so that they would not be overheard.

'I'd prefer if you stayed.' He turned to Andrew. 'What's on your mind?'

Andrew tried to sit up. It was an effort so they helped him.

'Thank you.' He began, finding it difficult to talk. 'I've been thinking about lots of things since we spoke. There's little else to do. I've only a short time left.'

John's voice was not convincing. 'There's a possibility of remission.'

Andrew nodded. 'Although the chances are remote. And even if a remission does occur it doesn't mean a cure.'

John went directly to the point.

'Correct.'

'In that case, doctor, I'll come straight out with it. I want you to use your new drug on me.'

John stared in disbelief. There was anger in his next words.

'That's impossible! Out of the question!'

He stood up immediately looking at his watch.

'I realize it hasn't been tested fully.' Andrew continued, 'and the results are unpredictable.'

'It could be fatal,' John said in a shocked voice.

There was a murmur of assent from Andrew. 'Don't you think I've considered that? And it terrifies me! Whichever way I look at it—drug therapy or not—the result will be the same. There's no alternative but to ask you, to beg you.'

John didn't reply immediately and he put himself in Andrew's position admiring his courage—but courage must have hope to survive. He waited a few moments, watching Andrew with detached pity. He then said gently.

'Professor Wainwright would never approve.' His voice faltered as he thought, this could be a way out!

Again, Andrew had an answer.

'You don't have to tell him.'

For a few moments John said nothing. You're quite right Andrew there's nothing we can do now. You're dying and dying quickly! All the signs are written loud and clear.

'Nurse Sutton told me you've tested the drug on my cells,' Andrew said slowly, 'and you were delighted with the results.'

He groaned inwardly. Oh, Diane, how could you put your foot in it?

'Doctor,' Andrew said, not looking at him, but his eyes brightened, he straightened in his bed and a small touch of colour came into his cheeks, 'to go on I must have something—something to lean on, to cling to.'

Was this total madness or could it be an answer? John was

trained not to get emotionally involved.

'We'll see Andrew. We'll see what can be done,' he said standing up.

Andrew smiled faintly and closed his eyes. He was glad he'd this open discussion with Dr Nicholson. In recent days he felt there was an answer — his premonition—and things could, just could turn out well. There was nothing more precious than time, nothing dearer than life, nothing more wonderful than the appreciation of things he took for granted. But time was running out and each day it ran a little faster.

John returned to his room. He wished to be alone, to sort things out. He thought of Baker, his short unhappy life, cruel childhood, escape to America where there could be a better existence but something mysterious seemed to happen. Then his inexplicable illness. Essentially a good person he'd never been given the right breaks, neglected and ignored, he was left to tremble in the harsh wind of life. Then admission to hospital, now dying and leaving nothing to show. A brief unproductive life that could easily have been otherwise with caring and devoted parents. What a waste!

Andrew said little enough; what was asked put John in an almost impossible position. Two options, one to refuse outright, the other to agree; both loaded with potential trouble. His better judgement was to say no, to refuse completely. This was selfish. He lacked the brutality to give a frank snub. Andrew was a pathetic picture, transparent skin, wasting limbs, lines of pain drawn deep on his face, injected eyes, clouded with tiredness, which lost silent tears and slept too little.

Stress and pain can cause different responses. Andrew fought both with courage, but what was really happening inside? He must have some hope to go on.

Had John given him hope, inadvertently? His words were intended to give hope as he would routinely to any patient, but he knew they didn't carry conviction. Although they might have fooled some people.

Andrew was different. Intelligent, with an inquiring mind, he'd thought deeply about his condition and was confused. So also was the medical team right up to Wainwright. What he was suffering from was a mystery that didn't fit neatly into textbook descriptions of any recognized disease. What he was told was true; there was an abnormality of the white blood cells, which suggested a strange type of leukaemia. That was all that was needed for most patients.

Andrew, however, wished to know more and was so desperate to survive he asked to be part of an immature research plan; a plan with limited evidence that a chemical agent seemed to have a target effect on abnormal or malignant cells and, fortunately leave healthy ones alone—a type of selective destruction. This finding was something extraordinary in the field of cancer research at that time. But the drug was not ready for human administration.

What on earth was John Nicholson to do?

Chapter 15

John Nicholson had to get away, to be alone. He trudged across Heuston Bridge, up Parkgate Street towards the Phoenix Park. The sky was torn and haggard. Movement of taxis, rolling buses and shouting figures on footpaths caused irritating noise, which rose like clouds of dust. On towards the Furry Glen he sat beside the lake watching the dying day mirrored in water. Grey turned to yellow in the west. As darkness percolated through the air, stars came alive; he could almost hear them quivering. Suddenly, one fell from the sky. It sped away and was gone—leaving a gap. Not for long! Others watched and then came together. It was now finished, forgotten, forever.

At three-thirty next morning Andrew Baker had a relapse. He vomited blood and night sister sent for Dr Pickford who was on call. Intravenous drips were set up for shock and drugs prescribed to help raise blood pressure.

'I've done what I can sister,' Pickford said with little hope in his voice, 'he won't last the night. There's no use phoning Wainwright—he knows it's hopeless.'

Sister shrugged. 'There's no point doctor. He's in Cambridge. We'll do what we can now.' And she meant it. They all liked this lonely young patient who had few complaints.

Picking up his stethoscope and notebook he prepared to leave.

'All right then. Good-night.'

'Oh doctor,' sister sounded apologetic, 'I see on the chart that Dr Nicholson wants to be called if there's any deterioration.'

Simon was cold and unyielding. 'Then you'd better call him sister.'

And he left as if he hadn't a care in the world.

John looked at the patient's pupils, which slowly reacted to light. Andrew was still conscious although badly shocked only managing to whisper.

'Hello doctor. I hoped you'd come. You know what to do.' Desperately he pleaded with his eyes.

'Andrew. I know.' He touched him reassuringly on the shoulder. 'I'll be back in ten minutes.'

He rushed to the lab, opened the fridge and returned to the ward.

'It's all right sister. I'll stay for a while. We want to talk privately.'

'Very good doctor.' She turned away and made for her office.

He drew the clear fluid into a syringe. 'There's sufficient to last twenty-four hours.' His voice was a whisper but still reassuring. 'It'll have to be repeated on three successive nights. Then the same course a week later.'

Andrew closed his eyes and tried to smile. 'I understand. Please go ahead.'

The fluid was injected into the plastic transfusion bottle and slowly gained access to the blood stream. An hour passed before John felt he could leave.

'It seems to be going satisfactorily. Feel all right?' He looked straight at Andrew feeling complete trust.

'Yes. I'll do my best from here.' Andrew smiled again and raised a hand.

'I know you will.' John answered with infinite patience.

John told sister the patient was comfortable and left the ward. He felt like someone who'd placed his entire capital in the final throw of the dice. Why did it bother him so much? On a daily basis he dealt with life and death and there was no pang of conscience; it was the job to be done.

Now conscience had wakened into a disturbing bedfellow. It was the realization of what he'd done and there was the terrible wait. He was searching for the truth; it can lie deep in a pool and one has to disturb the mud to find it. If he'd refused Andrew Baker it would still be hidden and uncertain. Now he was going to find out, one way or another.

Sweat gathered on his forehead, his hands were unsteady and muscle tension rising. He ran a hot bath and lay in it soaking the tension out of him; he couldn't shake off the uncertainty. He went to bed fatigued, listening to night noises and tried to determine his destiny in the shadows of the long night-light. Sluggishly time flowed! Perhaps this is the way—elation then despair. To suffer the swings of the pendulum. It remained so for a further hour or two until sleep claimed him.

Andrew Baker not only survived until morning, he continued to improve over the next week. The procedure was repeated. Then a slight rash appeared.

'Have you noticed any sensation on the skin Andrew?' He rolled up Andrew's pyjamas' sleeve.

'None at all. It's nothing.' Again he smiled and dismissed it as trivial. He was feeling so happy and relieved now. On the road to recovery.

'That's good. Tomorrow's dose should be the last for a while. We'll see how you progress from there.'

A voice came from behind John, alarming him. It was sister.

'Dr Nicholson I'm sorry to disturb you but there's a phone call. You can take it in my office if you like.'

He made straight for the office and lifted the receiver.

'Nicholson here.' He was abrupt at being interrupted in the clinic.

'John. At last!' Diane said. 'Professor Wainwright was looking for you today. He came up to the ward and spoke to sister. He wanted to see you.'

'But I'm on night-duty all this week.'

'And John,' she seemed not to have heard, 'he spent ages talking to Andrew Baker. It was most unlike him—as you know. Andrew seemed much better although he noticed a rash around the transfusion needle. He made a note in the chart.'

'Thanks for letting me know Diane,' he replied a little breathlessly. 'I'll see him tomorrow.'

Diane remembered that would not be possible.

'No, the earliest will be the day after. He has committee meetings and will be out most of the day. And John,' she hesitated. She hadn't seen him for a few days.

'Never mind. It can wait.' She replaced the receiver at her bedside.

John read the entry: 'Diffuse popular rash on the right forearm—more intense around venepuncture. Skin elsewhere normal. Patient no complaints. Query toxic eruption. No treatment advised for forty-eight hours. W.W.'

He went back to the patient. The rash had not changed from Wainwright's description. He sat with Andrew for about thirty minutes quite content to let Andrew rattle on. He seemed on some kind of high and it wasn't due to any prescription medicine. Internal mechanisms such as endorphins and encephalins were known to enhance mood at times of stress.

Andrew sat up unaided. 'Dr Nicholson thank you for everything, your kindness, your humanity and most of all for your courage. I've imposed a great burden on you. Perhaps it was selfish of me, I don't know.'

'No,' John protested with awkward modesty. 'Whatever the outcome it was you, Andrew, that was the brave one. I won't forget that.'

'Doctor you look tired. I won't detain you.' He hesitated and then added deliberately. 'Always remember—I think you're a wonderful doctor. I'll tell all my friends how kind you are.'

Slowly John returned to his room with a mixture of flattery, confusion and anxiety. He realized Andrew's treatment was an apparent success—an amazing success. He understood the scientific mechanisms involved but the proof had to be when the drug was used clinically. This he'd now done and was able to demonstrate that, in the short term at least, it did produce remarkable results.

Yet success was tinged with apprehension. Baker would probably require several courses of treatment to maintain a remission. John would have to report to his superiors, in the first instance Professor Wainwright. Trouble enough there and more trouble, maybe from sources that took a delight in causing trouble—the kind of situation in academic life where success was seen as unpardonable.

But no! He was becoming cynical and paranoiac. An overriding sense of elation and achievement was the last thing he could remember before the telephone rang.

Andrew Baker gradually felt consciousness grow colder and expand effortlessly. Out of a diminishing darkness something unseen, above intelligence, relentlessly moulded a continuous present. His awareness travelled to the edge of the unknown and beyond and recognized a dominion dimly experienced before, a blazing endless horizon, which sentences all that is known to complete and utter insignificance.

Again John returned to his room in the early hours of the next morning. Again he was greatly confused. With Andrew's sudden death he was shocked and thrown into deep sadness. Shock he could deal with as he'd seen so much misery and death around him. The dilemma he faced was part guilt, part grief, and part despair. Guilt because he'd yielded to the patient's request. A grave error of judgement and disciplinary action would inevitably follow if the news got out.

Yes, if the news got out. Was there a way out—to cover up? Probably a worse dilemma if Andrew had lived. In the background was despair. He was alone, lying in the dark unable to sleep, unable to rest. Hours were spent worrying about the future.

Would he be ruined disgraced and asked to leave?

CHAPTER 16

'Come in,' Wainwright shouted and John entered looking exhausted.

'You wished to see to me professor?'

'I did,' he replied with calm formality. 'Help yourself to coffee. Many good papers in Cambridge. Pity you weren't there. Don't stand there, Nicholson, pull up a chair. How've things been while I was away?' John hesitated. 'Come on man, how's your research proceeding?'

He was becoming impatient.

John sat, crossed his legs and took a sip of coffee. 'Not much progress since we last spoke.'

'Perhaps you'd be interested in this.' He handed John a manuscript, with a flourish. 'Maybe the answer you've been looking for.'

He was still perplexed at John's indifference.

'I'll look forward to reading it.' John placed the manuscript on his lap not bothering to read the title or the author's name.

'Are you feeling all right Nicholson?' Wainwright's irritation rose.

'Fine.' John nodded vaguely.

'You look awful this morning,' he said with asperity, his eyes challenging. 'Didn't you sleep?'

'I was on night-duty and on a case most of the time.'

He became more attentive to John's woes. 'Anything interesting?'

John's reaction was strange. He was hesitant, not knowing how to proceed. Then his face hardened. 'I'm afraid Baker in ward 4 died early yesterday. I transferred him to intensive care after he went into shock. It was useless.'

Wainwright was horrified.

'I remember him.' He shrugged. 'Andrew Baker, isn't that right? I examined him recently. He was doing very well except for a strange rash that looked like a toxic eruption. Goodness knows to what.'

Again, John slow to reply hoped he need only give the bare essentials. 'The rash got worse before he died. In fact, it covered his whole body.'

'How remarkable,' Wainwright said looking surprised. 'It sounds like toxic necrodermolysis bullosa. We'll have to do a post mortem. Will you arrange it?'

'Of course. What do you expect to find?'

'I don't know. The results may be worth publishing. It certainly is a rare condition. What do you think?'

John ignored the question and moved uneasily in his chair.

'I'll see to the post mortem.'

'Don't go Nicholson!' He held a hand up and took a gulp of coffee. 'I really wanted to see you about Isselherg's manuscript. I explained how far we'd progressed and the problems you're having with chlor 10-6A were—damn it, Nicholson, are you sure you're feeling all right?'

John appeared not to be listening.

'A little groggy after last night. I'll be fine after breakfast and a couple of hours rest.'

Wainwright picked up the manuscript, ignoring the comments. 'Isselherg would like you to work with him on the conjugation technique. He has a wonderful research set up in Stockholm. Only the best of everything and he's a world leader in his field. I can make the arrangements. What do you think Nicholson?'

'It would be a great honour,' was the numb response, with no enthusiasm, 'although I'll have to think about it.'

Wainwright was surprised and disgusted. Most would welcome such an opportunity. What's eating Nicholson this morning? He's damned contrary.

'You do that Nicholson,' he said with sarcasm throwing his copy of Isselherg's paper on his desk. 'I believe you get a few days off after night duty so you'll have time to consider. Quite frankly, I can't see what you've to think about.' He handed John the manuscript again.

'It makes good reading. Study it well. You may go now, don't forget the pm.'

Instinctively he felt there was something wrong. He didn't want to press it at present but would watch out for an opportunity to find out more. He'd like to help, if that were required; Nicholson deserved it on his work so far. He'd already made good strides in the treatment of leukaemia. But there were many things yet to be done.

John phoned Diane for another evening out and requested a walk in Trinity before eating. She accepted gracefully and suggested they meet at the usual place.

'I expect you've heard about Andrew Baker.' He said with an air of dejection.

'Yes. I'm sorry.'

He put his head down. 'Not as sorry as I am.'

'What do you mean John?' She was a little troubled.

Impulsively the words flooded out. 'I did as he requested.' He turned away not bearing to look at her.

'I see. He was making a good recovery.' She sat beside him and touched his hand. 'Could it have been the drug?'

'Seems most likely. His cells were definitely sensitive.' He was emphatic. 'But what went wrong?'

'Have you spoken to Wainwright?' She felt more anxious.

Evading her eyes again he looked into the distance. 'He suspects a toxic reaction but, of course, doesn't know about chlor 10-6A. He's ordered a post mortem though.'

'Will that show what caused the rash?' She persisted.

'I wouldn't think so. Not unless someone was looking for it.'

'I see,' she said quietly, 'let's go and eat.'

They walked the length of Dame Street. Everybody was in his way, especially those who walked slowly, forcing him to weave in and out. The world was full of slow coaches and jaywalkers, and all of them were in Dame Street with the intention of blocking his way. Diane followed meekly behind.

At last they arrived at the recommended restaurant; neither had been there before. The name was discrete above the door and a sign read 'please ring and wait.' He stabbed his finger on the bell and held it for five seconds. No response. He repeated the stabs, twice. On the third, a burly, tuxedoed gentleman with black hair and reluctant smile opened the door.

'Good evening sir. You have a booking, please?'

'We do.' John didn't want anymore hassle. 'Nicholson's the name. We booked a table for two.'

The gentleman disappeared, leaving them on the pathway.

Eventually, he returned, grinning broadly and waved a hand of welcome.

'Please come in. We've been expecting you. Hope you'll enjoy your visit.'

John gestured to Diane to enter, and followed, keeping his silence. He'd misgivings on first impressions. A stranger entering the room could feel at a loss because of the gloom and darkness. He was leaning forward slightly, as if carrying a burden. Diane noticed immediately.

'May we take your coats? The main restaurant's through the archway.'

The gentleman pointed the way.

They were expertly relieved of their coats and led through an archway into a larger room with candles lighting on each table. Several people were seated and talking to each other. The patron asked the new guests if they'd like to be near the log fire or in a quiet corner.

'Well Diane?' John turned to her. 'What would you like?'

'I'd love to be near the fire. It's so inviting on an evening like this.'

'Very good madam. Please come this way.'

They settled at a round table beside the fire; the glow from it bounced off Diane's face. She loved the red designed carpet with stained oak showing at the edge.

On the walls were hand painted scenes of ancient Rome, each discretely lit from below giving a warm effect. The curtains were luxuriously thick and drawn closed against the noise. The atmosphere was cosy comfortable and romantic. For a while they looked at the menu, not reading.

He came straight to the point.

'I'll have to tell Wainwright.' He said with infinite pathos.

'You're too hard on yourself,' she pleaded, leaning towards him, eyes fixed on his. 'You only tried to help.'

'It was not enough. I defied the rulebook. And that's the greatest crime!'

She shook her head slowly fighting back tears. 'Please don't talk like that John. It upsets me.'

The whole revelation was a shock and she didn't know how to take it. Telling Wainwright. She sensed trouble. Was there an alternative? Why not let things be? It was most unlikely anyone would suspect. John could be impetuous and do more harm than good. She desperately wanted to help because, well because she felt even closer to him, whether he knew it or not.

'I won't mention it again,' he said blankly, a little hurt. 'Thanks for listening. Just had to talk to someone.'

Later as they walked across the square of St Mary's he asked would she like coffee in his apartment.

She smiled.

'That would be lovely.'

It was a large room, warm in purpose, cool in colour with a predominance of blue. The walls were pale, floors wooden, chairs deep, and an immense mirror hung over the mantelpiece. A glass-encased Victorian clock sat below it occupying the room with fragile sound.

He lit the gas fire and watched her reflection. As he turned, their eyes met. In their lives they shared the same atmosphere of thought and feeling, the same storms of indecision, but now a new awareness entwined them.

With an inrush of light she saw how blue his eyes were; blue is the colour of air, sky and all ethereal things, always far-off. The more it is approached, the further it recedes, always moving, changing, elusive—unattainable! Melting under his gaze she looked into his deepest self.

Exhaustion had become a permanent illness but now he felt life returning. His will abandoned him and a power gripped his whole being.

Impulsively, he embraced her and she surrendered like a flower blossoming.

'Diane I've longed for this moment,' he said breathlessly.

'I've dreamed of nothing else.' She meant it and closed her eyes.

'Diane,' his eyes were dark and dilated, 'I'm afraid. Desperately afraid.'

'John?'

Behind the grey and green of her eyes, beyond the tears, there was an enormous calm acceptance of him.

He held her closer.

'Yes?'

'Would you like me to stay?'

The street lamp grew brighter in the mirror and an all-pervading penetrating warmth from the fire enveloped the colour of the room.

CHAPTER 17

'Come in.' Wainwright waved John Nicholson to a seat. 'I'll only be a minute.'

John watched the professor signing reports and felt his mind slowly drowning. Inside something kept saying—why the hell do you have to say anything? It's pretty certain no one will find out. Yet, he was plagued with by a potent conscience; it rarely left him alone.

'That's interesting.' Wainwright said with a flourish as he signed another document and threw it on the desk.

'What's that?' He asked looking startled.

'It says here Baker had a rising eosinophil count days before he died. I thought the skin eruption was toxic necrodermolysis bullosa. Dr Kelly found a subepithelial bulla and now this. Points to some toxicity but damned if I know what … '

' … Probably a reaction to chlor 10-6A,' John said trying to keep calm.

'I beg your pardon Nicholson?' Wainwright looked at him in complete shock.

'A reaction to chlor 10-6A.'

'Please explain yourself Nicholson!' Wainwright exploded

He cleared his throat. 'It's difficult to know where to begin.'

Wainwright fumed as he fiddled with his dagger-like letter opener.

'A request came from Baker to go and see him.' John's words stumbled out. 'I was told it was important.'

'Who told you?'

'One of the nurses on the ward. Before this—about three weeks ago I think—he asked questions about his condition such as diagnosis, complications and he wanted to know the outlook. I usually find that a difficult one.'

'Go on.' Wainwright's gaze was fixed on him.

'I said there was always hope of a remission and … '

'… And you knew he wouldn't believe you?'

John nodded. 'I decided to be as honest as I could.'

'Who mentioned your research?' Was the inquisitional question, which could be important in any future investigation.

'He did. There was a lot yet to be done. Anyway, I did my best to encourage him and repeated the possibility of a remission. Then I left him.'

'You mean you left him to think about chlor 10-6A,' Wainwright said angrily.

'I'd no intention of that.'

Wainwright was silent but eventually spoke. 'The trouble with you Nicholson is you're too damned honest and you've a lot to learn. Anyway what happened then?'

'The next time I saw him he'd a severe relapse,' John said with great sympathy. 'It was soon after vomiting and he was badly shocked. It was then he asked me to give the drug.'

Wainwright snapped. 'He knew the possible consequences?'

'Fully. We discussed them at length.'

'Nicholson,' Wainwright shouted, 'why on earth didn't you tell me?'

John's voice faltered; he couldn't bear this much longer.

'You were in Cambridge.'

Wainwright paused, trying to find the right words.

'I see.' He conceded with a gesture. 'Unfortunate. What did you actually do?'

'I gave the drug intravenously—six divided doses over two weeks.'

'Yes.' Wainwright's expression was stamped with weary patience. 'He seemed to be making progress. That might be explained on psychological grounds.'

'Maybe it could. But his blood picture improved after the first week.' John stated trying to prove a point.

'And you attribute that to the drug?' Wainwright asked irritably.

'It has to be,' John admitted quietly. 'It could not be psychological.'

Wainwright nodded. He put his glasses on and looked straight at John. 'All right. You seem to have told me everything. The question remains—what do we do now? You realize this is a serious matter.'

John bowed his head and studied the back of his hands.

'Of course I do.'

Wainwright was insistent.

'You do now but did you at the time?'

'I'm sure I did.'

John still had his head down as he handed Wainwright an envelope.

'I want you to have this professor.'

Slowly Wainwright read the contents. Carefully he replaced the letter in the envelope. When he spoke his voice was tinged with sadness. He was surprised at this development.

'Do you have to go this far Nicholson?'

'Peace of mind can only be achieved by a clear conscience—or none at all,' he said feeling as if a load had been lifted off his shoulders. 'At present I feel I cannot continue.'

'I repeat, Nicholson, you've a lot to learn. I don't know what to make of you and what made you do it. I can only guess. Maybe, it was pity, but I really don't think it was that alone. Pity is a convenient sentiment, which can easily turn into contempt. No, I suspect it was something deeper, even admirable. I think it was compassion, true compassion, which is rare nowadays.'

For the first time that morning Wainwright smiled indulgently.

'It's a quality I admire in you John. In one way I hope you won't lose it, but, at the same time, I hope it will not land you in deeper trouble sometime in the future.'

He stood up and held his hand out to John who smiled uneasily and murmured a bland remark.

Wainwright nodded.

'All right then. In the meantime, don't worry. Leave the matter with me.'

So I was right, Wainwright thought, my premonition. This was a serious matter, an awful dilemma. Why didn't Nicholson just keep quiet—say nothing until, or unless, he had to? My God, he'd seen far worse scenarios in hospital practice.

This Nicholson affair was very different; it certainly was not negligence. The opposite, too much care! Ideally, the patient would have died quietly with ineffective treatment. The only thing that might have worked was the new experimental medicine. And the patient had given informed consent, indeed had asked for the drug. It was a gamble that could have paid off.

Nicholson deserved a second chance, and would be advised he should carry on regardless, and his Head of Department would support him. The matter was now closed as far as Wainwright was concerned. Relieved he'd come to this conclusion and looked forward to telling Nicholson. So that's that! That's final!

Simon Pickford entered Biochemistry making for the secretary, Miss Telford.

'Good-morning,' he said with his most friendly smile.

No response.

'What's wrong with everyone?' He looked around the room.

Again no response.

'Look Telly, it's not the end of the world.'

He knocked on the office door. There was no answer, so he knocked harder. An unintelligible yell came from inside. Winking at Miss Telford he walked straight in. His father was angry.

'I could not find you yesterday even though everyone was looking for you.'

'Look father I'm not a child.' He was defensive. 'I've my own life to lead.'

Professor Pickford's distress was evident. 'Wainwright is trying to get an extension for Nicholson. He made a strong recommendation at the last Committee of Management meeting.'

Simon shrugged his shoulders. 'What's all the fuss?'

'Well.' He looked at Simon. 'To the best of my knowledge and belief the next thing Wainwright will be angling for is to transfer your contract to Nicholson.'

Simon gaped at him in disbelief. 'They couldn't do that?'

Pickford put his pen down, leaned back in his chair and stared at his son with unblinking eyes. 'Indeed, I have seen it happen. I would like to suggest you find out what Nicholson is doing and how far he is progressing. Can you obtain this information?'

'I suppose,' he said absently, 'I still don't see the point.'

Pickford didn't answer. Instead he got up slowly and walked to the window.

When he turned, his face was in shadow. 'When you have lived as long as I have in the academic rate race there would be little doubt that you would know the reason. You may go now.'

Simon put his head around the staff room door beside ward 4.

'Ah, sister! I'm looking for Dr Nicholson. Do you know where he is?'

No she hadn't seen him recently.

'Any news?' He asked.

'We've lost Andrew Baker. He died yesterday in intensive care.'

'Really? I heard he was going into remission. Who was looking after him?'

She searched through various charts looking for Baker's.

'I can tell you who it was Dr Pickford.' Diane was standing behind them. 'It was Dr Nicholson. Night staff called him. When things got out of hand he transferred the patient to intensive care.'

'I see.' Simon was intrigued. He then said amiably. 'You seem to know all the answers. Where can I find Dr Nicholson?'

'He's on a week's holiday.'

She looked at sister. 'Please excuse me. There are patients to be admitted.'

'You may go.' Diane was dismissed with a gesture.

Sister started to write in the charts again.

'I'll be off too,' he said, 'I'll look for it in Pathology. Back for tea later.'

He asked in Pathology where he could find Baker's chart. It wasn't there so it was suggested he try Professor Wainwright. He knocked on Wainwright's door. There was no reply. The door was slightly ajar, however, so he quietly let himself into the room and went over to the crowded desk.

There was an envelope addressed to Wainwright in John's handwriting. It was open. He looked around and listened. No one was coming. Quickly he picked it up, removed the letter and read it. His eyes widened and he read it again more carefully. Putting it back in the envelope he replaced it on the desk.

He then went straight to Biochemistry to see his father.

CHAPTER 18

John Nicholson gazed over grey buildings and images of childhood awakened. He saw again heather, rock and bogland, mountains, lakes and skies that spoke eloquently—if one listened—of things beyond themselves. Indeed, there was nowhere that could heal hurt minds like the west of Ireland where he was born and spent his early years.

He'd asked for a week of his annual leave and Wainwright agreed; in fact, he'd put the idea in John's head saying it would do him good to get a change from the hospital, to switch-off for a while. John looked forward to it if only to get away from Wainwright's anger. He was also glad to escape the paper work generated by the bureaucratic machine now running hospital affairs, and the patient workload was increasing. Most importantly, however, was his sense of remorse, and guilt, over the Baker affair. There was no doubt that Andrew would still be alive if it were not for John's interference. Why did he ever agree to it? The drug had not been completely tested. All right, he had jumped the gun! Yet this was the only option open to the patient. They both had discussed its use, possible side effects, and each agreed that the risks did not out rule the potential benefit it could bring. Andrew had not only accepted them but had requested the treatment.

The drive to Galway took four hours and he checked into a modest lodging. Later that afternoon in the main street he saw girls lingering at shop windows choosing their trousseaus. They also inspected jewellers' wares selecting rings, necklaces and watches and on to mink and mahogany all the while digesting fish and chips.

He decided to seek sanctuary in a pub, large and ornate near the River Corrib. It had an ecclesiastical look; the windows were open and beams of light dragged up dust from carpets and customers. It was one of those places where a lot of drinking was done, although, no great quantities were consumed. He ordered a drink and made his way to a corner. The room was half-full of locals, some whispering secrets, some talking with relish about lives, deaths and departures and others still in a lofty manner about nothing at all.

His gaze rested on a man who was determined to get himself outside as many pints as quickly as possible. When he came in, his hands trembled so much it took three attempts to light a cigarette. The man battered at his neighbour's reluctance to listen and during the next half-hour only succeeded in getting two responses. 'I'm sure 'tis' and 'tis to be sure' to everything he said.

Presently, his glance fell on John. Here was a more appreciative audience so he levered his large frame off the stool and invited himself over—not forgetting to order another round on his new friend.

'De problem is,' he started without introduction, 'when ah'm sober ah don't wan' to talk to anywan an' when ah'm tight no wan wants to talk to meself.'

'That could be a problem,' John said, becoming aware of an odour less of labour's sweat more an ammoniacal reminder of the eternity of the soil. The man sat for a moment, nodding thoughtfully. He then gave a sigh like a child after crying and his eyes leaked. 'By Jasus, do you know, mister, solitude is de mudder of grief and sorrow.'

'I'd say you discover in it only what you take to it. Why are you lonely?'

The man described his wife's recent death that left him alone, completely alone—with eight children. Sure, 'twas no wander he'd to seek comp'ny somewhere! There can be a strange respect for a man drunk to a degree, John thought, similar to that of primitive people for the demented. There were many occasions he'd come close to and had to deal with a man who was drunk. Initially, this had upset him but, as time went on, this changed to compassion. He realized this is what happens to some people when the dreaded things of life confront them. Some are strong, others not so; they try to runaway, drink helping them to do so. Also, when age weakened the faculties, it can be harder to keep a grip on things, to be in control. Who could love this muddled, bitter old man? Perhaps his children could, if only he would let them. John was about to offer some advice but the man, excusing himself with perfect manners, rejoined his friends who continued to drink one another's health and ruined their own. This time, the man tried to interrupt but it was like shaking hands with an empty glove. Eventually, he became quiet, abandoned his efforts and directed his attention to his glass. For ages he sat thus, content to live in the past. The drink made his memories merge with the present and the future and stopped him listening to an endless cacophony of old sins.

Next morning the sky was pale and worn. John took the coast road, stopped beyond Costelloe and parked the car beside a stretch of water. There were no trees but the gorse dazzled. A mongrel dog greeted him as a long lost friend. Chatting away they selected comfortable rocks to sit on near the water. The sun was warm, the beach was empty, the company was good and so they were happy doing nothing in this dream-like place—even when they ran out of things to say. An hour crept by. They must have dozed for children returning from school woke them; their voices wandered down the lane from the road. His friend perked up his ears and struggled with indecision—to go and investigate or stay awhile? His mind was made up when John produced a basket. Together they shared lunch and he knew he had a friend for life. More's the pity because it was time to move on. Farewells said he drove north to Maam Cross with its lakes overflowing with light and reflecting mountain granite.

The road through the Inagh Valley was superb with Ben Corr towering over its lesser subjects and Mweelrea Mountain, floating in fog, was magnificent guarding the entrance to Killary Harbour. He drove along the south side of the fjord drinking in a vision of grey and green rising almost vertically out of the fathomless water. Acres of sky appeared between leaden clouds and lofty Mweelrea wore robes of vivid purple.

Next day he visited Cleggan—a lonely place beside the ever-changing ocean. It was lunchtime when he reached the village. He stopped for a meal and then went out to Rossadillisk about three miles further west. He got out of the car and walked to the beach. It was deserted. An isolated wind sent a shiver through the long grass.

' 'Tis a bit cold and blowy today sir.' A voice came from behind. He turned but could see no one. Then he looked into a ditch. There sat a man, motionless, holding a stick and gazing into the distance. By his side an alert collie dog sat staring at John.

'It's cold all right,' John said, relieved. 'I suppose we'll have rain soon.'

'Aye. Looks dat way. But won't last.'

John studied the man. He was tall and thin with deep-set eyes and cadaverous cheeks. A cap that was probably removed once a week sat on his head and he wore a coat held together with string. Torn trousers disappeared into ancient rubber boots. The man stood up aching with age. He was a kind being, perhaps a little simple in his ways—his job was to mind the cows—yet there was shrewdness in his face that only comes to those who've survived winters of wild solitude. Beyond the beach, on elevated ground some cottages stood. Now, only wind and weeds inhabited them. John asked about them.

'A tragedy sir. A great tragedy,' said the man apparently bearing a lonely grief, 'we call it de Cleggan disaster.'

'Can you tell me about it?' The man did. One calm October evening most of the men folk of the village went out fishing in their currachs as they had done for generations. A few miles out the finger of calamity pointed at them as one of the most fearsome storms descended and their fragile boats were easy pickings.

All were lost.

And as their souls were torn from the sea they left behind those who normally sweeten labour—the wives and children.

'A long time ago?'

'I remember it as a young man.'

John noticed a tear travel through the salt-sprayed cheeks. Thanking his companion he climbed over washed stones to the village with the sea heaving and dropping behind. The collie, called

Lad, decided to accompany him, perhaps, even show him around. He came upon skeletons of cottages and cabins—he counted twelve—standing vacant and roofless. They were festooned with creeping plants making them more a hedge than a house and windows peered through leaves like distrustful eyes of some shaggy beast. The houses, their hearthstones choked with nettles, huddled together like old folk forgotten by the living without care or thought or love. Something seemed to hang about them as a pervading presence. A breeze, moaning through the empty spaces, whispered to him. It told a wordless story of the sea and its human wreckage; the women and children chained to life, locked in its embrace for a while by poverty, illness and decay. He could almost feel their shadows as they hurried about their work and smell the burning turf. He imagined the air full of voices as a dream that damages sleep. A vision of his ancestors, struggling to survive, distilled in him the essence of the Great Famine when thousands were allowed to die of starvation and oppressed into the anonymous dust of time. And all the while, Lad sat beside him still staring at him. He almost felt that there was a person inside the lovely creature and would love to tell him further stories. As he walked though the deserted village with Lad he came across places where melancholy seemed to ooze out of the very soil. He felt a sadness and disenchantment in the air and rain seemed to weep rather than fall. Yet, there is a self-evident truth that every age will be nostalgic about the one before it. There can be a kind of sadness, a loss for the happy, leisurely days that are now gone forever. Those times when our forefathers, with their faults and doubtless hypocrisies, were probably closer to the eternity of the soil. But these people were different.

Later that afternoon work was finished for the old man with the torn trousers; he had gathered his few cows together with the help of Lad, the collie, and the animals knew exactly where they had to go for the evening's milking. As the party slowly walked back to the cottage and cowshed there was a great peace everywhere under the light coming from the spring's full moon. In the east the jagged outline of the Connemara hills was blurred in a blue haze. In the west the deserted village stood dark and naked against the glowing sky over Inishbofin. The water changed from a light azure to an antique silver grey, and the air was crisp, clean and pure.

The old man was a stranger to all this beauty around him, blind and deaf to Nature's music. He was a local peasant farmer, who had grown up here and had known nothing else. He was just rooted in this small piece of countryside as a willow tree is planted, to stay, to grow and then to die. This was only a place where he lived. The single beauty he enjoyed was to be found in the people, his neighbours and their children. The ever-changing growth rates of these children seemed to amaze him constantly.

When John had finished his tour he took one final look around the Cleggan area; the land was now grey; with small twisting roads and intensely blue hills—as blue as the Mediterranean and they were hallowed by the most golden clouds on earth.

The old man spotted him on his return and invited him back to the cottage for a cup of tea. He was delighted to accept. As they walked slowly together

John realized these people had to live in a cruel beauty. The desolation and barrenness around them was never meant to give food and shelter to man or beast; thin cows could only scavenge through the rocks in search of nourishment. And the small potato patches, no larger than a small carpet, were pathetic looking but essential to sustain some form of life.

John had never seen a more ragged man before; his trousers were mended with enormous patches taken from previous pairs. But, the man himself was really a gentle soul, well mannered with eyes that were dark and thoughtful and the nose was straight and thin. There was a hint of withered aristocracy about him, and the most ardent social reformer could not make any headway with these people. There happens to be no class barrier to deal with. No doubt there was poverty of a kind, but not the kind found in an urban slum. It was not poverty full of pity, because these people felt no self-pity. They reached the cottage and a glorious turf fire was lit in seconds. John knew of no heat that could be more sociable, gentle and appealing to the imagination. It permeated the house, and around and about its scent would invite weary travellers to come and rest awhile. The pungency of the smoke on one's clothes could be a reminder for days to come of the hospitality and kindness of a local's home.

And in the old man's house there was not a book to be seen but John discovered there was a whole library at the tip of his tongue.

For the next few days he travelled up the coast of Mayo, through Killadoon, Louisburgh and visited his old school in Westport. He stayed in Yeats' country in Sligo and finally went to Achill Island.

Achill was a distant memory with its two silent mountains, its cathedral cliffs formed, God only knows when, by a convulsive shiver of the earth and, its sea thrashing wild and unhindered. This was his last day.

Then over the bridge at Achill Sound, he turned left and parked the car at Cloghmore in the south. Passing the little harbour he walked westwards on the Atlantic road. The enormous ocean appeared and he felt the thrill of a new discovery. Waves were being torn apart by jagged rocks and froth unravelled into white ribbons in the blue beyond. And they came back for more and more. Masses of cloud came rolling in from the southwest like huge ships spilling their cargo and leaving trails of water in their wake; they were squalling raiders chopping the sea to pieces and then leaving it alive with sunshine.

With the taste of salt on his lips he sat on the grass facing Croaghaun. He closed his eyes and a feeling of aloneness came over him. In a place like this, days could slide into months and years without notice.

Hours later, the sun sank into a flaming sea. He was glad he had come back for now the life and love of these places, and their people—his parents, now gone, and childhood friends—spoke silently of being and what shall be. When weary hours weigh heavily what could be better than to think of the deserted village where the weather only happens and the shuffling old man lives apart from the world in dreams of his own, and to wander in spirit through greenwoods splashed with sunshine, in the shadow of bare mountains, on the shores of lakes full of light and to marvel at the joy that grips the mind at seeing them. And to wonder at the meaning of it all.

To wonder whether the longing we have for that elusive peace that evades us so effectively in this existence has a home in some remote and distant land.

Chapter 19

John returned from the West late on a Saturday evening, tired but happy. Work started on Monday, so tomorrow was a day of rest. It would be an idea to see his aunt again, perhaps take her for a drive. He telephoned. She was delighted to accept.

'Anywhere special Auntie?' He asked kindly.

'Love to see Howth again John.' She sounded excited. 'I used to take the electric tram to Howth Head and views of the Bay were marvellous. And, John, I had many friends then. Admirers too, you know.'

'I'm sure you had. Suppose they weren't good enough for you.'

'John.' She demurred. 'That's another story. I may tell you about it.'

They arrived in Howth, strolled along the harbour walk, she linking him, and watched fishermen at the end of the pier. In warm sunshine they made for the Clarence Hotel for afternoon tea, settling at a table in the lounge near the window. Tea, sandwiches and cakes were brought and both set out to demolish them quickly yet, trying to stay within the bounds of decorum. Appetites were sharp from sea breezes.

'John, may I tell you of a young man who was crazy about me, and wanted to marry me? ' She asked timidly. 'I really did love him too.'

Her eyes brightened as she looked into the distance.

'So why didn't you get married? What stopped you?'

'Things are different today, John. When I told my parents, and of course, showed them the ring, the first question mother asked was his name and family. "And what religion is he?" She asked me. "Church of Ireland I think." I said. My mother thereupon threw a fit and shouted. "You'll not go through with this. My daughter. You cannot. It will bring shame on our family and we'll be outcasts." I told her he was a lovely kind person and I loved him dearly. "Stop there. The answer is no. You must give back the ring." '

John was horrified. A young girl's happiness was destroyed in one sentence.

He was devastated for her missing a fulfilling family life. Surely, God would also be ashamed if he was held responsible for this tragedy—all done in his name. Something was drastically wrong. And he told her so.

On the journey home the pain returned, reliving what took place decades ago. She'd become reconciled and accepted her lot graciously. John was seething at such injustice in the name of religion. It sickened him and he felt it couldn't happen in these more enlightened times. People now had more generosity of spirit.

A message waited for John on his return to hospital; it was from Wainwright and marked 'urgent'.

'I hope you had a good rest,' Wainwright said as he entered the office.

John nodded with satisfaction. 'I did. Most enjoyable.'

'Please sit down.' Wainwright looked straight at him. 'Remember I advised you to think about your resignation and we'd talk about it after your holiday?'

'Yes,' John said relaxing. 'It was an emotional decision and you've given me time to think. I've now decided to reconsider … '

Wainwright raised a hand. 'I must interrupt. Unfortunately, the matter has been overtaken by circumstances. The day after you left, Professor Pickford came to talk about the renewal of Simon's contract. The Institute is desperately short of funds and the University has been asked to cut back.' Wainwright explained. 'What's more to the point is Simon Pickford's been wasting time—to put it mildly. Because of this I was going to propose that funds be transferred from Pickford's appointment to you. It's to be renewed annually.'

'That's right.' John nodded again, but did not enlarge; he felt uneasy.

'Well, Pickford must have been worried about Simon's chances. So he came to ask my support.' Wainwright looked intently at John. 'Of course I refused.'

He went to the window and looked out. 'He said if I did not support him, he would expose you by reporting the Baker affair to the Board and beyond if necessary.'

'No!' John gasped his face pale.

'My hands were tied.' Wainwright said slowly turning to face him. 'Call it blackmail if you like but I had to agree. For the life of me I don't know how he found out. He was certain of his facts and emphasized no one else knew and as long as he got his way nothing would be said.'

Wainwright went on to explain if the circumstances were made public it could be the end of John's academic career or worse. Pickford knew that and it was agreed Simon would continue for another year.

John stared at him in shocked surprise. 'What can I say Professor Wainwright except I'm shattered.'

Wainwright smiled gently, and his eyes challenged him. 'How would you like to work in Stockholm for a while?'

'With Isselherg?' A new interest quickened in John's voice.

'Yes.'

'That would be wonderful. Is it possible?'

Wainwright said it would. 'I made tentative arrangements before the last Heads of Departments' meeting. I'm sure things will work out for you.'

John got up to go, wondering who'd told Pickford. It was probably Simon, but how did he find out?

Then he thought of Diane. She was the only person besides Wainwright that knew. It must have been her. There was no one else. How could she?

'Incidentally John.' Without lifting his eyes Wainwright said quietly. 'I made sure of destroying your letter of resignation the same day you gave it to me. I could never have accepted it.'

Ward 4 was busy when Simon Pickford walked in. Diane was writing reports and looked up as he entered.

'Will you help me celebrate the renewal of my appointment, Diane?'

'Simon.' There was pity in her intelligent eyes and she shook her head. 'I've told you many times my answer is ... '

' ... Please excuse me.' John Nicholson suddenly rushed into the room. 'I'm looking for Mr Kelly's chart. Do you know where it is Diane?'

'It's here. I'll get it for you.' A faint blush came to her cheeks. Simon gazed at the floor; obviously he didn't want to talk to John.

'Thanks. Sorry for disturbing you,' John said slowly without smiling.

'Not at all. Had a good holiday?' A smile lightened her face.

'Yes. I must hurry.'

He left the room without looking at Simon. A few moments of silence. She had detected coldness in John and felt hurt. Very hurt.

The end of the academic year approached slowly and nothing seemed right for John Nicholson. He'd an air of despondency. He'd been offered a wonderful opportunity to work in one of the leading research centres in the world. Still, this was going to make demands on his emotional, intellectual and deep seated affection for his own country. Going to miss it, miss it terribly. Things had been arranged, almost above his head and it would be foolish to turn down the offer.

If he did, what options were open? His contract with Trinity would be finished shortly; no longer could he have any research opportunities in Ireland. The UK could have vacancies but that was not a choice he would easily take to at present. What was he hesitating about, he asked himself? And yet. And yet. Oh hell! Let's get out of all this indecision. It can only make one sick if one dwells on it too long.

Only a few days were left in the hospital. He made a list of people he'd like to visit and say farewell, and, hopefully, to meet again. Sister Agnes who'd returned on duty after three weeks sick leave was first. He didn't know the details, except she'd a fall at home and rushed to hospital as a suspected spinal injury. He'd developed a quiet and healthy respect for her in recent times. If there was trouble in the ward, everyone knew it would be resolved, quickly and fairly, and would not occur again.

He made for the ward and knocked on her door.

'May I come in for a few minutes sister?'

'By all means.' She was delighted to see him. 'Please come in Dr Nicholson and be seated. You'd like a cup of tea?'

He was miserable and tired.

'That would be lovely.'

She prepared tea and biscuits and had them ready in a jiffy.

'Now, here we are, Dr Nicholson.' She placed cups, saucers and a large plate of biscuits on the table.

She sat opposite. This was the sister who'd a reputation for discipline and even aloofness. What he now saw was a strongly attractive face with fine features, dark dramatic brows, large expressive grey eyes, a little rimmed in red, suggesting long nights. Her complexion was clear and sallow, almost too pale against her dark hair.

The eyes were her most striking feature; they looked straight at him with a certain unyielding quality.

She took a sip of tea and came straight to the point.

'Is it true you are going to leave us?' She seemed genuinely upset. 'I mean going to Sweden to continue research?'

'I'm afraid it's true.' He said precisely. 'I go at the end of the academic year. Now that the decision is made I hope it'll come quickly.'

'Why doctor?' Again she gave him her straight penetrating look. 'You are very popular here, all the patients and, even the nurses—bless them—they all love you. You probably don't realize that.'

What she didn't add, however, was she found him charming, courteous, with perfect manners, which could cool any troubled water with his hushed voice. It would be useless to be cross with him. He'd open his blue eyes wider and maintain a silent dignity. Times he was in a world of his own, where many things passed him by.

'There are great opportunities in Sweden. And,' he hesitated a moment uncertain on how to proceed, 'and, well, I don't seem to get much thanks here for the work I've put in. At this time many others have had to go abroad to get on.'

She listened carefully. Always a good listener she knew there was a sense of frustration, even bitterness, but dare not ask. She was also aware of that savage modesty in such men.

Too much focus was on him and his woes, so he tried to change the subject.

'Sister, can you tell me what happened in the Catherine Kennedy case; the one brought by the father for negligence?'

'Certainly. As you know it was due to go to court. Apparently, the prosecution made it so obvious that compensation was really their prime concern. But when all the evidence was heard there was no case to answer. I think that Kennedy guy had more money than sense and had taken bad advice.'

'Stupid man. How did he think he could win?'

'He must have some expert lawyers advising him,' she said sardonically.

He hesitated before his next question.

'One other thing sister. If it's not too painful what happened the night you fell at home and ended up in hospital with concussion. Hope I'm not too inquisitive.'

'Not at all doctor. I don't mind telling you,' she replied slowly, looking away for the first time, giving no sign how the question troubled her.

As she began she was outwardly calm, even indifferent, and covered up her sadness. She mentioned her brief marriage, Bill waking out, Stephen's accident and her pseudo invalid mother—bedridden for no known medical reason. There was a row and she fell down the stairs. She couldn't remember anything more until she woke up in hospital. Her crippled son, Stephen, managed to save her life by forcing himself to use the telephone.

John was stunned, many emotions in his face, surprise, wonder and horror.

'What's the current domestic situation?'

'Stephen is back home with me.' She gave a sigh. 'Mother, unfortunately, has been admitted to a home with special care facilities. It was getting impossible to control her at home.' She didn't wish to elaborate further. Her bright eyes, with sudden passions of unshed tears, told the rest of the story.

'I'm sorry you've had so many problems. You have my deepest sympathy.' After that neither said a word and understood what was not said. Eventually, he stood up. He put a hand on her shoulder, turned to go and raised the same hand in farewell as if to say he would see her again, sometime.

And he had forgotten he was tired.

Professor Wainwright told John he'd never regret the move and to follow Isselherg's advice. He was to do nothing wrong, to keep to the rules and regulations, which were very strong in Sweden. To keep on the straight and narrow!

'I know you, John Nicholson, you are a bit of a rebel, a free thinker, even the word iconoclast comes to mind. So be warned!'

This came with a healthy handshake and a broad smile.

Then he met Diane in a corridor.

'Hello.' She smiled innocently. 'I haven't seen you in ages. You've not forgotten where ward 4 is, have you?'

'No Diane. I still remember—but I'm trying to forget.'

She objected mildly.

'Only meant you haven't come for tea recently.'

'I'm sorry.' He evaded her eyes. 'I thought you meant something else.'

He glanced at his watch. She sensed his uneasiness.

'John.' Her eyes questioned his with a hesitant smile, intensifying the perpetual ache in his heart. 'Please let there be no misunderstanding between us. Please!'

As they stood together, apart, he felt two strangers could not have been more separate. 'No misunderstanding, Diane.' A pulse was beating in her throat above the buttoned collar of her uniform. 'I must hurry. I've an appointment. See you again.'

'Yes John, see you again.' She sighed as he walked away.

Over the next few hours she kept repeating his last words. See you again. Was this a simple way of saying goodbye for the time being—but we'll see each other again? Or was it a type of wishful thinking—maybe, maybe not, or worse, could it be a coded message that really implied the opposite?

Maybe she was reading his body language rather than his words. A saying of his came back. He'd used it after the discussion with Andrew Baker. 'It's half a truth—which is always more than half a lie.' He was speaking of the difficulty of telling patients the truth, the entire truth. Do you tell them everything, gory details and all, or be compassionate and tell half the truth? Truth was such a difficult thing to dispense.

Yes John, see you again, she repeated.

Her green eyes clouded over as tears blurred vision and expressed so eloquently that fragile desire and sad frustration of life.

Part Two

Chapter 1

Autumn came gently at first. With cooler nights and moist dawns it appealed for sympathy in its decay and evening mists weaved a veil across the countryside. The university was set in the heart of the city where the activity of the nation's capital, its pleasures and cares, surrounded this haven where one could live a life of gentle thought and quiet persuasion. Moving to Stockholm was a watershed in John Nicholson's career. The Hall of Residence, mellowed with age, was close to the Helmuth Institute and King Stefan Cancer Hospital. His room, on the third floor, was large and bright and overlooked a carpet of smooth velvet turf framed with flowers. The air of solemn pomp was only the body of the place; its soul, its inner spirit, was everywhere and stared down from portraits of past dons that spoke of lives lived in stately simplicity and of respect for the dignity of intellect. What impressed most was the tide of youthful life that flooded all places; its enthusiasm, energy and hope, not yet overshadowed by disillusionment, rekindled in him a sense of purpose and direction.

During weeks of settling in, he was searching for a sexual identity outside working hours. Back home he was told things would be different in Sweden. Different in what way, he'd asked but got no answers. Most women he'd meet were either married, divorced or devoted to the idea of a permanent arrangement as soon as possible; in other words, not suitable for inclusion in a bachelor's diary for ready reference.

The Annual Reception of the Medical School was one of the grandest occasions in the university calendar. Professor Isselherg was Dean this year and he made it his duty to welcome everyone, along with his lovely wife Rachel. The event was important in introducing strangers to one another.

The Great College Hall, panelled in oak was impressive, where wall lights competed with vibrations from red carpets. Well crowded when John arrived and conversation, born of sparkling burgundy, greeted him.

'Good evening Dr Nicholson.' Professor Isselherg greeted him with a beaming smile and outstretched hand. 'May I introduce my wife, Rachel and some committee members and new residents?'

He followed Isselherg to the end of the Hall. 'Firstly I would like you to meet Dr Lindstrom, secretary of our musical and dramatic society.'

Dr Lindstrom was tall with straight blonde hair and china-blue eyes.

'Dr Nicholson. Have you long been in Sweden?' She inquired in an accented voice moving closer to him.

'A few weeks,' he replied in a slow, hesitant manner.

'And how you like it?' She sounded genuinely interested.

He wondered at her persistence with no time for small talk.

Unusual in a stranger! 'Very much.'

That did not tell her a great deal, so she tried again. 'What kind of work you are doing?'

'Chemotherapy with Professor Isselherg.' He said eventually. This woman doesn't waste any time.

Immediately she smiled and eyes sparkled. 'Underbar. I am studying radiotherapy in the Helmuth.' She replied modestly. 'Strange we have not met. I qualified in medicine three years since.'

She stood there, unflinching, eager to talk, eyes swift and searching. Luxuriant blonde hair flowed back in waves over the ears and halfway down the neck. Exquisite gold earrings dangled provocatively from a small circular chain. Width of brow and tilt of chin suggested a wild energy and a reckless nature. Indeed, the whole effect highlighted the sparkling, sultry eyes, as she appeared to look down on everything—except John, towering over her by three or four inches. She wore a straight burgundy dress without plunging neckline, and sleeves extending to the wrists and dress to the ankles. A slit raced excitedly upwards above the knees exposing slim legs and high-heeled shoes supporting the feet. Eventually, she was captured by other friends and had to excuse herself.

Other people he met that evening included an American teacher, who spoke in glorious Technicolor, had plenty of views on himself, on education, medicine and the world. In fact, there were so many things that left him speechless it took him almost an hour to say so.

Some weeks later Dr Lindstrom organized the first term concert in the Great Hall and sent an invitation to John Nicholson.

'*Hej*. Dr Nicholson,' she greeted him pleasantly. 'Again it is nice to see you.'

He extended his hand.

'Thanks for inviting me. Incidentally the name's John!'

'Jag heter Linda.' She admitted quietly. 'We are near the front. Hope that will be satisfactory.'

A large crowd arrived and the hum of conversation grew. She loved Schubert's music and they were playing his Octet.

'The music is like a conversation between friends,' she whispered as the applause died down. 'Do you understand?'

'Although there are times when a terrible argument breaks out!' He laughed as he settled in his chair.

For the next hour he went into a dream world. What music could give if only we'd let it; it had the power to express our strongest emotions—an ability far greater than words—from quiet contemplation to roaring excesses, from basest instincts to noblest thoughts.

After the concert they walked over *Helgeasndsholmen* by way of *Borrbro* and around *Gustav Adolfs Torg*. She pointed out the swans on the Strommen and looked across the river to the Royal Palace.

'Stockholm is beautiful especially at night,' he said suddenly serious.

'Well tell me, what you like best?' She was proud of her city and was thrilled to hear his praise.

'That's difficult,' he replied in his soft voice.

She looked at him inquiringly. *'Jag forstar inte.* I do not understand.' He didn't reply immediately. Instead they walked slowly along the embankment. It was a clear evening and the streets were deserted. 'Linda how about something to eat? It's not too late and I know a good place in *Vasterlanggatan.*'

The café was not crowded. They found a corner overlooking the street and she ordered smorgasbord and coffee.

'I think music is one of the most wonderful gifts,' she said settling in her seat, 'life would be awful without it.'

'Do you play an instrument?' He asked.

'*Ja*. Piano, although I do not get enough time to practise.'

He grinned and raised his mug. 'Still I'd love a recital sometime.'

'We will see.' She wished to keep him guessing. 'Tell me your favourite works.'

He thought for a moment. 'Let's see. Bach and Beethoven were great masters.'

'Bach was terribly religious. Do you like Bruckner?'

He shrugged. 'Yes, although he never finished his ninth symphony—ideas for ending it went into eternity.'

She gave a sigh and looked straight at him.

'Jag forstar inte. I do not understand,' she repeated sounding a little annoyed. Most people she could size up in no time, identifying them as a complete unit, as a figure in fiction or painting, fitting them into a category, seeing their qualities and failings, their family status. Everyone was processed and filed and finished, and marked as clearly as one's signature. Then on to the next. Now for some reason her way was challenged.

She was confused and even a little piqued.

'You do feel things deeply. Do you not John? Even though my second language is English I find what you say a little disturbing. Are you religious?'

Here she was again, with her probing questions.

'Yes although I keep it to myself.'

Carefully he watched as she held the brown mug in both hands and lowered her head, letting the aroma and stream waft about her. She lifted the mug, still in both hands, moving forward to meet it, mouth touching the edge in a sensuous way. It was tilted towards her parted lips, allowing sweet liquid into her impatient throat.

He suggested they finish with a nightcap. Two brandies arrived and she raised her glass in a toast with an elegant smile.

'To your conquest of Stockholm Dr Nicholson!'

He smiled and drank to that guardedly. There was no overt flirtation in her remark, only a timid, coy smile. Women with a sense of humour were hard to come by in his experience, and the more intelligent were either boring or unattractive or worse. Here were all three qualities, intelligence, looks and good humour and he played with the idea he could possibly take a chance, or risk confidence, closeness and perhaps something deeper still.

She put her glass down carefully. Her tone was mild and respectful.

'My parents are religious. Perhaps I got too much as a child and turned me against it. Now I am agnostic.'

She cupped her chin in her hands and looked at him.

'Let us not be serious. You will come to my recital, nar? When?'

He asked on the off chance.

'How about tomorrow evening?'

She thought for a moment. Yes, John seemed a nice guy, a little slow but sincere, with a certain hard to define charm. Quite a mystery man, she would just love to explore!

'*Ja. Varfor inte?* Why not? That would be fine.'

CHAPTER 2

Linda welcomed John to the apartment located on the top floor of a building overlooking the Strommen. The ceiling in the large sitting room curved down to handsome windows framed by russet curtains. He could see the miracle above the city; the air still and silent, stars near and houses bristled visibly.

She watched him return to the sofa, and felt his eyes, wondering what he saw and aware of the tenseness of one who tries too hard. She offered a drink. His was an unusual way of answering with a soft caress in his voice; she thrilled at how it could envelop her so she could not think or act clearly—a feeling new and strange to her.

Then the music. She became immersed in interpretation. As her hands moved rapidly across the keyboard, the sound echoed her emotions; the sadness of music was it had to end, if only moments could be frozen yet, of course, that's what memory was for.

While sound flowed over him he studied the bone structure of a chair. The rest of the room had a sofa, a fern sleeping in a window space, a grandfather clock, and a remarkable mahogany desk that must have been very old. The fire cast moving shadows and an elegant table lamp enhanced the redness of Linda's dress.

'Sorry. I had not much time to practise the Schubert. You like it?'

'It was beautiful, really beautiful,' he chuckled happily. 'Who's your favourite composer?'

'I love Chopin,' she answered enthusiastically.

'Will—will you play some more?' He was insistent not really knowing why.

She played Chopin waltzes. Fire and mind danced in unison. It was exquisite wrapping him in emotional pleasure—an experience he'd rarely had before.

A nocturne and prelude followed. She played with sympathy; her notes loving and gentle and as pure as water drops. The phrasing was assured with no attempt at false sentimentality but true to the art of interpretation—the subjugation of the player to the composer's wishes and genius. She played Chopin as if she understood the frustration of unrequited love. An emotional minefield seemed to be attached to the music she played so well and he was dying to ask about her reactions to music, but held back. It was too soon. Discretion was called for.

The music sighed to a close along a path of silence, leaving the room empty—except for the ticking of the clock. A spasm went through him as he gazed at her gold and ivory beauty with its power to inflict pain. A feeling of déjà vu. He remembered! Catherine Kennedy, the lovely ten-year old girl in St Mary's. The likeness was remarkable.

The spasm turned to a cold moist shiver.

Weeks passed but the institute, hospital and city didn't change—for John. Initially, strangeness, almost aloofness lurked everywhere he turned. His work progressed—he was familiar with procedures and techniques—it was the outside world that grated. In the normal commerce of daily life there was something that was hard to define. Was it hostility? A lot of people were trapped against friendship by their own egotism—or maybe that was unfair.

Maybe the fault lay within. A greater effort should be made to mingle, to give and not expect too much. People had their own lives and problems; they were occupied and not like him in background. His mood was gloomy indeed. A disease affecting migrants and travellers must exist, whose symptoms may include dejection, out of one's depth and of being unable to cope.

After all, this was one of the world's most beautiful cities and he still felt oppressed by old traditions and disliked the modern. Conscious of being alone and exacerbated by having to communicate in a foreign tongue. Even food itself was alien.

The smell of bracken and burning turf he longed for. There was no real cure. He'd to put up with it, to endure it like an attack of influenza. Eventually he'd recover. He'd go through the motions of daily activity. The person who had shown real interest was Linda Lindstrom. They'd meet in hospital discussing patient management, new scientific papers and occasionally the weather. Now weary and irritable, he wanted more than this, so on an impulse he went to the Radiology Department and came straight out with a request.

'Linda would you be kind enough to lend me your company for a while?'

She looked at him in a puzzled manner and then gave a smile of approval.

'That is a strange way to ask a girl. I am not sure I understand.' She dismissed her own misgivings with a gesture and a laugh. 'Of course John. I will be delighted to take you for a drive after work. See you at the entrance at six o'clock.'

She had agreed calmly. There was something about him she could trust. In her old Volvo they drove northwards through the city to an isolated place beside a wonderful stretch of water, the eastern shores of the third largest inland sea in Europe, she proudly informed him.

'That's amazing. Now I've seen quite something.'

'My father used to take mamma and me to this spot from Mora, our home town.'

'It's familiar to you?'

She looked across the water at the slowly sinking sun, putting on a pyrotechnic display. 'Yes I do love it.'

He was completely comfortable with this woman. She made no objection, and no excuses when he asked for her company. He was grateful and felt she was pleased he'd asked. Perhaps, what made her so confident was her medical background and especially having to treat cancer patients every day.

'You know Linda. I admire those who accept their fate—good or bad. We're usually the last hope they have in a long and miserable journey.'

'I have seen it in their faces so often,' she said thoughtfully, 'usually, they do not have to speak.'

'What do you see?'

'Fear is what I see. Fear of the unknown. You, John, are looking for a cure.'

'What if there is no cure? Then it's a matter of facing it squarely. To help, support, encourage. If not they'll reach a stage of negation, where dignity is lost and even the capacity to love. Sometimes, I feel I'm losing those same qualities I am trying to give to others. Especially true when I try to instil the benefits of false hope.'

'Poor John. Are you unhappy?' The warmth in her voice amazed him. 'You have the same look I saw on the night of the Dean's party. You were lonely then. You were like a bird high up in the trees looking down on all of us, and yet you were lonely.'

He gestured with a hand, suggesting helplessness. 'But how does one rebuild what one's constantly giving to others? It's very draining.'

She gave a laugh. 'If I knew the answer to that I could write a bestseller.'

She remained silent thinking about his question. Then she placed a hand tightly over his and he could feel her warmth suffuse through him. She continued softly.

'Maybe the process of giving is all entwined with the process of growing, so that eventually one becomes stronger.'

She smiled, removed her hand and reached for her keys.

'That is enough. It is getting late. The sun is gone and I am a little sentimental. You should go home now. I think you are a complicated man.'

They drove back to the city. Before dropping him off at his apartment she turned and kissed him on one cheek and then pressed him away.

'Sweet and pleasant dreams John. And keep out of mischief!'

CHAPTER 3

Gustav Isselherg owed much to his manner and appearance. Courteous yet outspoken he had the gift of complete attention to someone, anyone. His bearded face had pale features and the remarkable eyes were open doorways to the very keystone of his character. Most in evidence was a sense of humour, using it as a declaration of his superiority over misfortune. Since integrity without knowledge is frail and knowledge without integrity is dangerous he fortunately possessed both in full measure. In matters scientific his was a mind some found terrifying—and he was fanatically honest.

One morning he met John in a corridor of the hospital. He raised a hand.

'And how is the bright young man this morning?' He said with a hearty laugh.

John pushed back some hair with his free hand. 'I'm fine professor. Just finishing up for the present.'

'Good.' Isselherg looked down and then straight at him. 'John I would love you to come and meet my wife, Rachel, and family sometime. Would you ever agree?'

'That would be delightful,' and then he hesitated, 'but not really necessary.'

'Of course it is,' Isselherg beamed putting a hand on John's shoulder. 'You are now living and working with us and we like to make our guests as welcome as possible. It is a well established Swedish custom.'

'I see. Well when … ' He began, but Isselherg interrupted.

' … We plan to have some friends over next Saturday evening and we'd be thrilled if you would join us for a light meal and informal chat. Do not worry we can all speak reasonable English. You will not be sitting there in silence. I can promise.'

John smiled. 'Sounds great.'

'That's fine. I will pick you up from your apartment about five-thirty. And Eriksson will leave you home later in the evening. Will that be suitable?'

'Of course it will,' he replied enthusiastically. 'I'll look forward to it.'

Sharp at five-thirty on Saturday afternoon the doorbell rang. It was a chauffeur dressed immaculately in uniform, polished boots and impressive hat. Isselherg waved from the back of the Mercedes.

'Dr Nicholson your car awaits you when you are ready,' the chauffeur said deferentially, bowing his head.

'I'm ready. We can go immediately.' He put his long coat on, closed the door and locked it.

He sat beside Isselherg, who shook hands and smiled broadly. Seat belts were fastened and Isselherg tapped the partition. 'All right Eriksson. We'll be off.'

He was confident the evening would be enjoyable for everyone.

'How many people are coming?' John asked.

'About fourteen to sixteen, that includes you and our family of five.'

John looked surprised.

'That's a big number just for an informal chat!'

'Please do not worry. I am sure you will find a quiet corner to chat to someone and let the others entertain themselves.'

The car crept forward, its movement almost unnoticeable.

Isselherg gave a cough to break the silence.

'We live about ten miles outside Stockholm on an estate near one of the lakes. Hope you'll like it. We've been there twelve years and done a lot to it.'

'I'm sure it was hard work but well worth it.'

'We think so.' Isselherg stared straight out of the windscreen. 'You know, John, my father was a major industrialist and a successful businessman. He had two sons, Jan my older brother and myself. Well, Jan runs the business now. I went into medicine and academic life. He left both of us comfortable when he died. And for that we are very grateful.'

'That's wonderful for you and your family.' John remembered the scholarship that helped put him through medicine.

Eriksson left the motorway and crept along a side road for about two miles. He slowed further and turned right. The lights caught the outline of two towers, rather than pillars, and massive electric gates gradually opened. The car twisted and turned for another mile along the avenue and ended at the front door of a truly massive house with lights blazing in almost every room.

Chapter 4

An elderly gentleman dressed in black descended the steps and opened the car door.

'Welcome to Kungsangen House Dr Nicholson,' the man in black said, 'please come this way.'

They climbed twenty granite steps to the hall door closely followed by Isselherg and Eriksson. As John entered the hall he blinked at the array of walled lights and massive chandelier. Its beauty took his breath away. The man in black relieved them of their topcoats and disappeared into the drawing room. Then Rachel Isselherg and daughters came out to greet them.

She extended her hand, heavily covered in rings.

'Welcome to our home Dr Nicholson. Gustav has told us good things about you. We said,' she turned to the girls, 'we all said we would love to meet this bright young doctor. So it took little to persuade Gustav to ask you to join us in one of our informal gatherings. I do hope you will enjoy the evening.'

The three murmured approval, almost in unison. The formal introduction to an informal gathering was embarrassing. He was overwhelmed by the surroundings—and this was only the hall—where marble statues abounded, large gilt mirrors helped a sense of space and the sidelights along the walls mimicked candles.

He shook hands with Rachel Isselherg. She was an elegant commanding figure of a women who seemed completely in control of herself and, indeed, of those around her. She was in her late forties. Her hair, a mixture of grey and gold, was swept into a large bun at the back of the head. The facial bone structure was exquisite, complexion smooth and well preserved. She wore an exquisite evening dress. Her bearing and presence knew the finer points of protocol and impressed most.

'And now Dr Nicholson allow me introduce our daughters. This is Sara, our youngest, and this is Ingrid. Both are finishing school. And finally, Karita, our eldest, who is studying in the University.'

Karita was tall, an endowment from her mother, with short blonde hair, almost boyish, and carefully swept back behind the ears. The skin was tanned, and she wore an off the shoulder pink dress of pure silk. It was body clinging and descended by diamond shaped squares to ankle length. The sparkling face was so attractive, especially the eyes, a mixture of blue, grey and green; hints of green made the pink dress sing in harmony. And the fabulous necklace was astonishing.

She extended a hand; he was uncertain what was required. For a reckless moment, he grasped it raising it to his lips. The gesture gave him a thrill, although it was accepted as routine.

Gustav Isselherg, standing behind him, raised his hands.

'Come ladies, let us go into the drawing room.'

They moved across the great hall to a large room on the left of the hall door. About six people stood in two groups, glasses in hand. They stopped talking as Rachel introduced John with details of his work and where he was from. Some nodded, some smiled and continued talking. Two young girls carried trays of drinks. He accepted a glass and the girl, inclining her head, murmured thanks. Portraits in oils of Karita, Ingrid and Sara, as children, hung on the walls. He was undecided as to which group he would join. Karita noticed and came to him.

'I've come to rescue you,' she announced brightly.

'Thanks,' he replied.

'Dr Nicholson,' she continued, 'we are so glad you accepted our father's invitation to join us this evening.'

He smiled thinking he'd been thanked enough already. He noticed the diamond encrusted gold necklace again. One couldn't but notice.

'It's my pleasure. I'm delighted to be here.'

'My father has spoken well of you and your work.'

'I'm flattered.'

'He says you are so hard working and are getting valuable results.'

'Karita it's teamwork really. Everybody deserves credit.'

'You are right Dr Nicholson. Yet there must be someone able to lead.'

'I suppose you're right.' He conceded. 'Incidentally the name is John.'

Karita thought for a moment.

'Well in that case I have decided to call you Dr John. Will that be all right?'

'If you say so.'

The man in black appeared clapping his hands.

There was a sudden hush.

'Attention please, ladies and gentlemen. I wish to announce dinner is served in the dining room. Would you kindly make your way across the hall? Also please note places have been reserved for each guest by name on the table. Thank you.'

He bowed and withdrew.

Guests ambled across the hall. A long table welcomed them with a display of flowers, candelabra, silver and the finest china. A string quartet played soft silky music in a corner of the room. The scene was a revelation; he'd never witnessed the likes. Karita guided him to his place. She on his left and Rachel Isselherg on his right. Everyone was seated quickly. Gustav Isselherg stood up beside his wife saying a few words of welcome to everyone by name. He left John to the last.

'And now we have the honour to welcome Dr John Nicholson. John is a doctor and research scientist who has been sent to us, for a while, and if providence would allow for a long while, to carry out work into the scourge of cancer.' He turned directly to John. 'Let us all welcome you John and wish you well during your stay. And also wish you well in your personal life now and in the future.'

They raised glasses.

'To John.'

He had a sense of excess blood going to the head and a sickness in the stomach. The atmosphere was heavy with compliments and too much attention. He merely raised a hand and smiled.

'Good,' shouted Isselherg, and waved to the man in black to start serving.

Her husband on her right, Rachel Isselherg was well versed in attention to detail. She helped him select choices of food, and laughed softly at his jokes. She was also a brilliant storyteller and many flowed from sharp observations of politicians, friends and acquaintances. She had another approach to John, a light inquisitiveness about interests, girlfriends and impressions of Sweden, a skilful method of extracting information quickly, but done in a manner that was both painless and even pleasurable.

John was an exemplary guest; experience making him an attentive listener and skilled storyteller. His magic pot of memories he opened—adventures in the West of Ireland with his father, and accounts of life and the living of it in a remote and haunted land. He was under strict observation by an able and expert jury. Karita fielded awkward questions making fluent translations when necessary.

'Dr John,' Karita said when questions subsided. 'I want you to know that I am studying Swedish and English literature in the University. I have already completed one year.'

'That's wonderful,' he said enthusiastically.

'Karita dear,' her mother interrupted, 'please do not embarrass John. I am sure he would prefer to talk about other things.' She turned to him. 'John dear. Have you any hobbies to occupy you in your time off.'

'Hobbies?' This was unexpected and he was taken aback. Yes he'd a few hobbies. Nearly all his waking hours were devoted to work. 'I like reading and travelling to see new places.'

'Tell me about your favourite authors.' It was Karita again. 'I love poetry and I have written some although it is in Swedish so far.'

'Fascinating,' he replied with a warm glance.

'I love your Wordsworth very much. He is so true to the landscape.'

This stung him and he replied somewhat sternly. 'Karita he's not my Wordsworth. He was English.'

'I am so sorry.' Instantly apologetic. 'I have made a mistake?'

He nodded and relented.

'Please don't be sorry. It happens all the time.'

'What happens?' She asked rather awkwardly.

'I am mistaken for being English.'

'And does that upset you?' She spoke softly although with emphasis.

'Yes. Would you like to be called Norwegian?'

'Well, no but … '

' … I'm proud to be Irish.' Time to change subject. 'Karita, that's a lovely name.'

'Well Dr John. It is actually Finnish.'

'I see. I didn't know. As I was saying, Karita, I'm proud to be Irish,' he said softly, his eyes full of memories. 'We have a great tradition in literature and poetry.'

'You must tell me about that sometime. I'd love to learn about it and it would help my studies.'

'A lot of academics like their literature plain and aloof and very dead.'

She laughed, then leant towards him and whispered with a sudden impulse of naïve recklessness. 'Dr John would you like to visit us again?'

'I would be delighted of course.' This girl sure is full of surprises.

'That is splendid. Then I can show you my poetry. And, maybe, you could help translate it into English. Oh I am sorry. I should have said Irish.'

'Not Irish. That would be difficult. Let's compromise and say Anglo-Irish.'

She looked puzzled. 'Ja. Irish-English whatever that means.'

There was silence for a while and he was able to listen to the conversation going on around. A heated discussion was taking place on at the opposite side of the table and Rachel Isselherg was dragged into it. At this point Karita turned to John and said.

'May I ask, Dr John, and do not be offended.'

'It takes a lot to offend me.'

'Good. Well, I wondered if you are married,' she asked simply, with a little nervous laugh.

He had a feeling of discomfort again.

'No. I'm afraid I'm not.'

'But why are you afraid Dr John? Are you afraid of women?'

This was difficult for him.

'No. No. I'm not afraid. I rather like women—if the truth were to be told.'

Karita smiled a gorgeous melting smile.

'I am so glad to hear that. It makes me so happy.'

CHAPTER 5

Weeks passed, winter came with late dawns moving through streets closely followed by dark evenings. A paralysis crept over the land and exposed the skeleton of nature. Then snow, a sudden great fall, transformed all things; a white carpet weighed heavily on trees and grass and stamped buildings with sombre significance. Blinding blizzards came from the west sweeping down from hills across the water to the city. No escaping it.

Snow piled high in valleys, on exposed roads, in drifts across fields, seeking out those areas where it could almost get shelter from itself. It heaped in nooks and crannies where it could accumulate, such as doorways, garage fronts and sheltered corners of gardens. First deposits froze over like hard granite and superficial snow was lashed away by winds.

Then a lull. A beautiful starry night. Not for long. Raging torrents of white reappeared producing new downfalls. A softer layer was deposited on the foundation of ice. The winter was harder than locals could remember and was the first for John

Nicholson in Stockholm. He dreaded long nights, penetrating cold and high boots that groaned at every step.

A time for introspection. The axe had fallen, cutting him off from all he'd known and loved—friends, landscape, familiar vital things and a way of life. The land was alien in winter, the language foreign and life strange. A numbness froze his feelings and he longed to retreat to where the rock and heather, the sea and sky went on forever. The door was closed concealing the ache and emptiness.

Isolation lasted months. Then a strange thing happened, winter grew in sympathy and almost became a friend. By a slow catharsis it supported and strengthened him. He was wiser now. Gradually it weakened its grasp on the land and an ill-defined feeling quickened in him. Solitude had been a companion helping him survive life and living. Now it was challenged by a stirring sentiment that whispered softly with unalterable obstinacy.

Late one afternoon he sat at an open window with a medical journal on his lap. Green was returning to the velvet gardens below, yellow crocuses appeared, a fragrance rose from purple shadows and great oaks sent branches stretching and yawning upwards. Far away a train announced distant places had arrived.

For some time he'd intended calling Linda. It still wasn't too late. And tomorrow was Sunday. He telephoned to see if she'd be free. She was. Would she like to do anything special?

Ja. She'd love to take him to the *Moderna Musect* on *Skeppsholman*, Stockholm's museum of modern art. So that was settled. He'd call about ten-thirty. The museum opened at eleven. He woke early and minutes gathered pace. He caught the underground to *Gamla Stan* and walked to the apartment.

Linda put finishing touches to freesias—her favourite—and

stepped back to admire them. A silk neck scarf hung over her shoulders; a white belt gripped her thin waist and patent high-heels made her taller than usual. She stood, caught in a contradiction. Her hand looked for reassurance as it drifted to the gold necklace—a gift from her mother—the fingers trembling as they fondled it. It was given to her on the day of graduation, a time of joy and happiness.

When she started university she enjoyed every moment. Freedom was wonderful; it intrigued her. Freedom to explore her wonderful city alone, not to do others' biding. She could have her own way in everything, able to put herself together, a new self-confidence emerging. Her family were still concerned, from a distance. She moved to the window as the doorbell rang.

They crossed the *Strombron*, passed the Opera House and towards the *Skeppsholmsbron*—a bridge that impressively strode over an inlet of sea. Morning thrilled at the prospect of summer and water dazzled as it reflected the marvellous light.

Then the *Moderna Musect*. As they moved around the exhibits she enjoyed herself immensely. He became increasingly irritated.

She looked at him in surprise.

'*Vanligen*, please what is wrong? Do you not like the paintings?'

A dark puzzled expression appeared on his face.

'I don't. Most of it is rubbish. Someone once said that abstract art is. "A product of the untalented, sold by the unprincipled to the utterly bewildered." '

She turned on him with a hint of anger. '*Jag forstar inte*. I do not understand, how could you say such a thing?'

'Linda, I'm not only bewildered I'm intensely annoyed.'

She shrugged and demanded. '*Hur kommer det sig?* Why is that?'

At that moment an elderly man entered the room unnoticed and gazed at one of the pictures.

'If you were to ask any of these so-called artists who produced this stuff,' he pointed contemptuously at a blank canvas with an old boot tied to it, 'he'd probably say the past's a junk heap. This is wrong because we're all the result of the past.'

'These are sincere expressions of human feeling,' she replied with rising tension. The excitement, the new and the experimental she loved—all meant to provoke.

He looked at the old boot again. 'It's simple and it's original I'll admit. But—but Linda, it's not beautiful, is it?'

'To the artist it may possess a certain beauty.' Her voice was defiant.

He tried to find words to answer, but not to hurt.

'Then I wonder what he'd call ugly.'

The stranger walked over to them.

'Forgive me my dear,' he said with a slight bow. 'I didn't mean to alarm you though I couldn't help overhearing. It seems you're rather annoyed.'

He looked at John.

'That's an understatement.' John was emphatic.

He gave a gentle cough. 'Permit me to introduce myself. I'm Neville Chance from the Tate in London. I've been invited to lecture at the Academy tomorrow evening and I thought a little peace and quiet would help collect my thoughts.'

'*Forlat mig!* Excuse me. You are going to speak about what?' She enquired.

'Some reflections on how the development of society in Europe has been influenced by art and science over the last four hundred years. It's quite a task as you can imagine.'

'I cannot imagine,' she said firmly.

He looked at the two of them inquiringly.

'Why not come along and find out?'

She answered for both of them.

'*Tack*, well thank you, yet we could not do that. The Academy has a strictly limited membership.'

The man put his hand in his pocket and produced two cards.

'Nonsense. Take these and give it a try. I can't promise to supply all the answers. At least you'll get a different point of view.'

CHAPTER 6

It was too early to go to the Academy when John finished his afternoon walk, and he didn't feel like returning to the apartment. They planned to meet at seven-thirty. Company he wanted, yet remain anonymous discussing ordinary things like the cost of living, price of food and how women were so different to those back home. Sometimes, he liked a taste of low life—especially now faced with the Academy—it was easy to find people to share it with. The nearby bar was just the place and he knew it well. He ordered a Scotch, treated the barman to a beer, settled on a high stool at the counter and discussed local and major issues. When resolved, he left looking for a flower shop.

He found one easily. Inside a tall girl, with big scissors, ribbons and clear plastic was making a presentation and an excited young man was loading several orders into a van. A substantial madam, with enormous decorative glasses and a voracious smile appeared desiring to know his pleasure.

The audience gathering in the foyer was typical of such events the world over. John was aware of those who turned up to be seen, and was thrilled when recognized by someone of substance. Some were formal and punctilious, others oozed money making no attempt to hide it. Conversation was clubby with members standing in exclusive sets. The main focus of attention was nearly always over the shoulder of one's partner. Even though it was an interesting lesson in human behaviour he had little time for such displays of self-importance. An air of insincerity was everywhere; he didn't wish to be part it.

Linda was upset with John's intransigence in not accepting progress, as she saw it. How could he be so rigid? She needed to calm down and spend some time in the nearby park. Slowly she walked to the water's edge where it flowed into a stream at the end of the lake. A ripple of pleasure went through her as goslings, trembling in the wind of new life, bravely followed their mother into the lake and together set sail to conquer the world.

Running water always made her happy; identify with it, dancing over stones or gliding smoothly onwards. It reminded her of *Velkonstad*, deep in the country, where long maned winds came down from mountains and where she would sit below the old bridge watching images floating in the stream.

John was waiting when she arrived and handed her flowers as a peace offering.

They'd no trouble at Reception as the invitation signed by Sir Neville Chance was accepted immediately. Through a dimmed auditorium they found their seats near the front. Above the lectern *The Pursuit of Knowledge* glared from the screen. The President introduced the speaker as a leading art historian and philosopher and said how pleased the Academy was he had accepted their invitation. Applause greeted Sir Neville whose flowing academic robes contrasted with white hair and short beard. Michelangelo's Pieta appeared on the screen.

'Richie, in his Scientific Method said. "The pursuit of knowledge consciously and for its own sake is a thing of yesterday; it is almost the last product of civilization." ' Not all would agree.'

Rembrandt's disturbing picture of the Anatomy Lesson came next and brought back memories for some.

'When mediaeval methods,' continued Sir Neville, 'were being applied to the treatment of disease other great pioneers were sowing the seeds of theoretical knowledge of biology bordering on medical science. Today we are still benefiting from their work.'

Sir Neville went on to describe how modern philosophy was born, how the foundations of modern medicine, geometry and chemistry were laid and our concept of the universe was revolutionized. The seventeenth century was pulsating with new life; new systems, theories and science flooded humanity's vision with a light of brilliance never before imagined.

'The modern consciousness was evolving.' Then a series of pictures appeared on the screen illustrating the catastrophe of the Great War.

'These speak for themselves,' he said as the lights came on again. 'Then science lost confidence. In medicine and psychoanalysis, Pavlov, Freud and the behaviourists used in their work, theories that made chivalry, nobility, love—all the gloriously hazy and evocative emotions of the romantic poets—look vapid and silly.'

Lights suddenly went down and a picture of an old boot tied to a canvas appeared on the screen.

'Perhaps, today we are caught between two conflicting forces, our reason and our imagination. Some of you will remember this.' A ripple went through the audience. 'It is, of course, in your collection of modern art here in Stockholm. It may help to illustrate my remaining comments. This confusion extended itself into the arts—if, in fact, it had not originated there. The result of all this change, often brought about in a storm of violent and public controversy, was to create doubt and bewilderment. For some, the atmosphere was infinitely exhilarating but for others, probably the majority, there was only a vacuum—which, according to a belief that is doubtless outmoded—Nature abhors.' The audience laughed.

'There was a craving for new beliefs and certainties. The intellectuals of the twenties and thirties felt the surrounding confusion keenly. Yeats, an eminent Irishman and a great genius, summed up the dominant mood as follows.

"Things fall apart; the centre cannot hold;
Mere anarchy is loosed upon the world,
The blood-dimmed tide is loosed, and everywhere
The ceremony of innocence is drowned;
The best lack all conviction, while the worst
Are full of passionate intensity." '

Lights came on and the illustration of the old boot disappeared.

'Today a living organism, animal or human, is considered by many as a mere physical and chemical machine,' he continued with a sweeping glance around the auditorium. 'I think this is an oversimplification of the essential nature of life itself. Through the process of evolution primordial life contributes in direct lineal descent to every living being. Our present state of knowledge—cosmic and biological—can be considered an evolutionary process. Previously, we have been mainly satisfied with the limitations of mathematical logic and ignored the relation of scientific achievements to be a relevant development of our order of thought. A more profound enlightenment is required today to apply the experience gained from natural sciences including the controversial but essential issue of animal research to human life and disease if the pursuit of knowledge is to fulfil man's ultimate concern.'

A moment's silence followed his last remark and a burst of applause occurred. Everyone in the hall stood up, continued to clap and shout 'Bravo, Bravo.'

Sir Neville remained erect in front of them and gave a gentle nod. He then sat down and appeared exhausted.

As they left the auditorium John turned to Linda.

'Would you like a bite to eat? It's quite early.'

'That would be lovely. How about the same place in Gamla Stan?'

'Fine. Let's go.'

Settling into a corner table with a candle between them he was full of questions.

'What did you think of the lecture?'

'Interesting but a little too technical for me.'

'Really?' He was surprised. 'It was supposed to be about science and medicine. Surely, it has to be a bit technical!'

'I'd have preferred a little creativity, perhaps a little romance.'

'I wonder how you can get romantic about science.'

'Oh John.' She was irritated. 'Use your imagination for a change.'

'I liked the illustrations, except the last one.

'Deliberately put in to provoke.'

'Not again!' He gave a sigh. 'This modern art business. I can't stomach it.'

'On that we agree to differ. Incidentally I am sorry if I upset you yesterday.'

'Don't worry. You didn't upset me. It was the awful boot contraption on the wall that made me angry. Looking at it wouldn't inspire me to pursue knowledge. What did you think about the ending?'

She had forgotten.

'Remind me John.' She said absently.

'Those bits about we need more enlightenment into the relationship between animal research, human life and disease.'

She looked a little puzzled.

'What more enlightenment do we need?'

'I don't really know. Although it set me thinking about what I'm trying to do.'

'Gain more knowledge about human diseases,' she interrupted, 'and curing them by using animal models. It is simple!'

She opened both hands in a gesture of certainty.

'Exactly. That's it, for obvious reasons,' he said, 'at least they were obvious to me. Now I'm a little uncertain. I still don't know what he was trying to get at.'

'Well I do not know.' She said simply.

'The last thing he said was really a loaded question—a greater enlightenment, whatever that means—will lead to the correct pursuit of knowledge and fulfil man's ultimate concern.'

'That is a bit heavy for me John. Please explain.'

'He was trying to invite us no matter who we are, and what we're doing, to ask ourselves some questions. Then honestly answer them, and finally to put those answers into practice almost as a life's goal—if we are to fulfil man's ultimate concern.'

'It is a little clearer. But what is man's ultimate concern?'

'That's precisely the whole point of the lecture,' he said, 'each of us has an ultimate concern. If not, we should have. Identify it, journey towards it and finally achieve it.'

She felt comfortable, relaxed and a little sleepy.

That curious affection in his voice, which produced a glow in her, was back. Captivating! She yielded to it as she responded with a smile.

'Again, a bit above my head. My ultimate concern is to be warm, eat well, wear lovely clothes, be happy and love somebody that I can trust. That is mine. What is yours John?'

'I've never thought about it in such a clear way. He's telling me to look closely at life, work, and existence and live it not just for myself but also for everyone else. If so. Fine. End of story.'

One thing he did not mention. 'If not, I could be heading for trouble. You know, Linda, I've had premonitions and having running battles with just one word.'

A new interest quickened in her and she sat up.

'What word?'

'Cruelty. Sometimes I can't get away from it, lurking in the back of my mind. When I'm not too busy it'll attack me, producing a guilty conscience. Even had some unpleasant nightmares. Trying to tell me something and I don't want to listen.'

'John. Drink up your wine. You are too serious. Try and look on the bright side of things. Everyone knows you are doing great things and getting some good results. And that is all that counts.'

'I don't know if that's all. But thanks, Linda, anyway.'

'All I can say Sir Neville is a clever man, brilliant speaker and his learning comes through including an appeal for compassion. Then he leaves it up to us. But John, did you notice that he is a little old fashioned? Perhaps, he should have said people's ultimate concern!'

Both laughed heartily.

After delivering her to the apartment, he made his way home wondering, behind her confidence, was there a certain inflexibility, even arrogance hidden under her modesty. Maybe, that's the way most Swedish girls are made.

CHAPTER 7

Back in Dublin a stranger could feel unwelcome entering Tom Nolan's studio. The walls were plain and pale; other items included an ancient radio, large easel, stacked canvases and little furniture except an old rocking chair. The acrid smell of oil paint was evident and could arouse emotions in people. Bay windows allowed good light in, which could be controlled with screens and an open fire with a dog sleeping in front of it, completed the picture.

This morning nothing could be seen through the windows because of fog. At regular intervals a booming sound, like a great sea monster, vibrated through the room. Tom Nolan leaned forward in his chair reading a letter. His eyes were dark and troubled—those remarkable eyes that transmitted life directly, usually not for reflective thought, more for instinctive and immediate action. Normally, he would speak openly about his feelings and his art; and always his best listener was Patsie, his wonderful dog, with her eyes of liquid gold. Indeed, he loved all animals dearly and believed they could give consolation beyond measure.

This morning was not unlike others as he worked hard for his second one-man exhibition in a leading city gallery. He'd achieved considerable success in the art world and shown regularly at the Academy. But this project was his burning ambition for years, the result of a journey on the western seaboard from Malin to Mizan. Malin Head—the northern tip of Ireland—was an obvious place to start.

Some people said to him that landscape painting had run out of things to say. This could not be true, he argued fiercely, because—never before—had nature been under such attack and the landscape spoke to him of this threat. Painting it had an urgency and could impart a sense of atmosphere, of place, which was not possible with words. In him, there was a 'last chance' feeling that artists had not experienced before.

In the western landscape, he told everyone, we still had a unique wilderness but the enemy was at the gate. Humans, by their reckless abuse of nature, now contributed the latest and, perhaps, the most dangerous of all threats. Extensive new forests of Sitka spruce were alien to it and its wildlife. He deplored careless farming, fish farms, wind farms in scenic areas, uglification by developers and the greed of the JCB. Then there was mining caused by the scent of gold, hideous power lines everywhere, sheep stripping mountainsides, the ubiquitous barbed wire, and 'Private' signs and gravel extraction scarring the countryside. In addition to polluting the air, land, lakes, rivers and bogs, we were conveying more people on more roads and airports to have this very landscape explained to them in unsightly interpretative centres.

All this made him angry, very angry. He'd said many things, harm may have been done, but 'twas never intended. We may travel far and wide, he said, searching for something and then come home to find it.

Examining the completed canvases, time melted, and his eyes moistened; this seemed to sharpen his vision as he looked back on his first day on Malin Head. He remembered that bright morning when spring was clothing a naked world in preparation for better things. The smell of flowers that came up to greet him, the sight of crocuses and daisies—white as angels—and the silence of rising sap gave an expectancy to everything, everywhere. The sound of waves breaking on rocks below was like a living pulse. And the sense of place was deeply moving; he was aware of other journeys here, including Columbkille's life-long exile, the tragic Flight of the Earls, the Spanish Armada and the naval convoys in the Great Wars. But it was not so much time measured on calendars; it was more the character of seasons he wished to record. Round and round went his thoughts like a treadmill and now this letter. What was he to do?

'Come on Patsie. It's time for lunch. I hear Ruth ringing the bell.'

He needn't have spoken. Patsie was already standing at the door.

He sighed as he sat at the kitchen table, his face rigid and remote. Something was stuck in his mind like a barb, something he was trying to resolve. He looked at Ruth.

'That letter has upset me.'

'What letter?'

'It came this morning.'

He handed it to her and she read carefully. 'It's wonderful in one way,' she said at last, 'but what about your lovely work for the exhibition. What will you do?'

'I don't know.'

'Let's eat. We can talk about it this evening.'

Ruth was practical and didn't like anything to upset her peaceful domesticity. She was also beautiful, tall, and proud. Her skin was olive and unblemished with a delicate arch to the nose. She tossed her thick gold hair about impatiently and her lustrous grey–green eyes shone daringly.

Twelve years ago she met Tom Nolan in art school where she was busily murdering her talent, and he innocently accepting prizes. They married in their first year and things were not easy. Still she knew people who had everything but contentment and this consoled her. She was an optimist hearing the bright notes in everything—the chuckling of rushing water, and the song of the blackbird could move her to tears. She knew there could be no shadow without the sun, her husband adored her, she felt it and knew it. Then baby Annette came along—a perfect gift—and completed her happiness.

Years passed peacefully as the Nolans lived in a little coastal town south of Dublin. The house was small but comfortable near the sea and harbour. Nearby Ruth's father lived alone—but not lonely—and was always willing to further reduce his small income to help. It was a struggling but happy family. Annette Nolan, now ten-years old, attended the local school about a mile from the house. Her mother, and Patsie, always waited at the gate to escort her home, and today was no exception. She was a graceful girl who walked with a confident air, her gold-brown hair swept back in a long pigtail and she had wide, knowing blue eyes. She'd many of her mother's features whose love she returned in her own thoughtful way. Occasionally, her father's quick temper flared in her.

She bent down to hug Patsie who responded with delight. All three then set out for home along the sandy beach towards the harbour. They had to hurry when rain clouds appeared from nowhere.

CHAPTER 8

Daffodils were the first thing Tom Nolan noticed that evening when he entered the sitting room. A vase held them beside the violin stand. They glowed and he could almost feel their light—yellow was his favourite colour.

Everything else was just the same, the warm rug framed by stained wood, the black fireplace and open fire burning brightly with Patsie asleep, and curtains closed against the gales outside. On the mantelpiece the ornate clock filled the room with its elegant sound. It was all secure, comfortable and nice.

He stared into the flames.

He'd always loved these moments of quiet reflection; himself and Patsie sitting together while noisy preparations for tomorrow were taking place in the kitchen. Painting had always been his first love and went back as far as he could remember. In secondary school he enrolled in evening classes in the College of Art in Kildare Street behind the National Library. These were invaluable because he was immersed in the traditional approach to representational art, which was under attack. His dogged adherence to these principles won him recognition from a number of patrons but not the Arts Council. He continued school studies and obtained a good Leaving Certificate. Then there was no alternative but the National College of Art.

Ruth and Annette entered in a bluster and he was abruptly brought back to the present.

'You can do your homework at the table,' she said to her daughter before sitting opposite her husband.

They sat together neither speaking, yet they communicated. She appreciated him every bit, his broad forehead, his thick black hair, expressive mouth and bearded chin. And she was always captivated by his unpredictability; his dark eyes could be harsh and stubborn, and they were full of intensity and affection, and so blue.

She loved his hands, warm, nervous and aesthetic. When he was away all the protective sparkle, glow and warmth were taken away from her, only then she'd feel the cold, harsh daylight. She also shared a critical understanding, an implied antagonism to the conventional, to authority and its inept bureaucrats.

Although praise has its true value only in its scarcity she now felt it was needed.

'I love your new paintings of Donegal Tom.'

He'd just returned from the northwest—on location he called it—and welcomed any chance to talk about it.

'The atmosphere at Marble Strand was extraordinary,' he began enthusiastically, 'the hill was so dark under the shrouded sky, the clouds were almost too oppressive for this world. And yet the trembling light on the brow of the hill redeemed the scene. I think I've captured it'.

'Brilliantly,' she said.

He described his few days in Dunlewy near Errigal. The first morning was warm and the air was full of expectancy. At early breakfast in the cosy little kitchen, the fire in the hearth was warm on his stocking feet, and the scent of the burning logs and freshly made porridge was a delight. At the time he was happy to be starting off on exploration of what was reputed to be the most beautiful areas around—those regions around the conical quartzite mountain of Errigal. Outside a wind was running, making it seem that a flame had gone through the few small bushes. The sky was broken and promised splashes of blue, which meant a changing landscape—ideal for him. Just the way he loved it! Patches of sunshine moved across the bog and lower mountain slopes. It was going to be a day of challenges and discoveries.

The desolation around Errigal, caused mainly by that awesome figure—the Great Hunger—standing outside doors and gradually inhabiting entire houses; its work effectively completed by rents and evictions, profoundly affected him.

Tom's mind was never quiet or serene. Turmoil raged beneath the surface and like a volcano he could erupt at any time. Demonstrating this to Ruth he continued. Around Errigal Mountain, with its harsh-edge, glittering granite cone, he felt an intense sorrow. For miles around no dwellings could be seen, not even deserted villages, yet, it was recorded that hundreds of families once lived at the mountain base. Before the terrible evictions. As he walked he imagined the screams of women and crash of battering rams echoing across the glens. In one day alone two hundred and forty-four people were made homeless and became beggars on the open road in winter.

A river of sorrows drove the entire population on to the roadside to wither and die or emigrate, and to by replaced by sheep.

Before eviction, existence must have been a great struggle with winter cold, gales and unending poverty. But, at least one earthly solace was the warmth, companionship, and shelter around the lighted hearth, which comforted children and old alike. The growth of families in such a close and intimate way is not easy to understand today. It was their way of life, their only way of life. Any interference was a catastrophe beyond measure; there was no fall back, no alternative.

Orders came to clear these families, burn down all dwellings and leave no trace behind. The outrage was the most heinous crime to humanity recorded in these islands. The ultimate catastrophe to befall an indigenous population. There was no mercy or kindness shown—even the kindness of an instant death for example. No, just a cruel destruction of the hearth and all that it meant. Families thrown on the roadside were sent wandering through history.

Tom found it difficult to settle on a suitable composition of this remote and poisoned land. Its physical beauty was undoubted, ruined for him by the knowledge of the suffering endured and the final calamity—and all for the sake of a few sheep. Where was the justice in it?

As evening approached he hadn't done any decent work. No work in such glorious surroundings! This was unusual for him.

The air was powerfully scented as he walled back to his lodgings. The lush green vegetation was running to sap. Breezes rolling down from the hills carried a perfume of clover and honeysuckle, perfect for honey and bees but there were no bees. He noticed a faint acrid smell. Then a challenging sound came from around the corner carrying its hideous smell; a flock of sheep was passing.

Immediately on reaching his room he lay down, emotionally exhausted. Consciousness raced ahead. His pulse beat rapidly and seemed to throb through the whole earth. Must be a touch of heat stroke. His skin was burnt and dry and he felt hot all over. His mind was preoccupied, in a kind of delirium to notice anything else. And he was so tired! Instead of reading, he turned out the light.

Nothing else to focus on, it became dark inside as well as out. It was his genetic make-up, his collective memory, which stirred, unknown instincts suffocated, and he found it difficult to bear it, shut as he was in this dark building. A low ceiling pressed down, and dark unknown demons lurked in the gloom. They heaved and raged and stormed at him. It was terrifying. He'd give up anything for easy everyday things, just to be left in peace and quiet.

He suffered enormously that night, almost all subconscious. It was his life, guilt, passions and raging storms. Next morning his body was drained and hollow yet, he'd a clear head with only little after effect.

Next he spoke about the walk on Rossbeg Strand as one long lingering with moving reflections for company.

'Then Glencolumbkille, where the sea was blazing white behind Glen Head.'

He told her with a far away look. 'When civilization and learning were being extinguished throughout Europe and vandals were massing like vultures over the corpse of Rome it was then that we experienced our golden age.'

'Now what about O'Neill's letter?' She threw another log on the fire.

'I'm reluctant to see him, although tempted,' he said evading her eyes.

'Tom love,' she whispered, 'we need the money.'

This stung him.

'You should talk to him and hear his side. He didn't say much in the letter.'

Feeling, perhaps, she'd said enough she turned to Annette and noticed rapt attention on the girl's face. What could she be thinking?

'Best come along to bed, darling,' she said gently, getting up to go.

Just then they heard a familiar noise at the door. Patsie was in trouble again. And the clock ticked nervously into the night on the mantelpiece.

CHAPTER 9

Tom Nolan's mind raced ahead that night. He recalled Ruth's words; before leaving the sitting room she took his hand and gazed with large understanding eyes that could make a man master of the world. Next morning as the sun crept into the room he reached for his watch. It was seven-thirty. Downstairs Ruth was already fussing with Annette. Yes, he would go through with it and telephone Mark O'Neill. It was agreed Nolan would travel to Mangerton House, the O'Neill estate near Ashbourne, County Meath, about fifteen miles north-west of Dublin. Could Nolan make it about seven o'clock that evening?

Even though he left in good time in the yellow van there were delays as he crossed the city. Traffic was heavy in Stephen's Green and around St Patrick's Cathedral. Passing the building he sensed a foreboding; the stone structure looked down like an ancient, silent beast, waiting. Then across the river, through Phibsborough and passed Glasnevin cemetery, its monuments proclaiming victory over defeated beings in its mortal domain. Evening was settling down for its own stage-show as he drove up the avenue to the house and the sun wrestled to free itself from clouds hanging on like unwelcome guests. He parked the car near an extension that was designed to blend with the elegance of the Georgian Mansion. A pretty red-haired girl, with a melting smile answered the door. She'd the bearing of that age when, with gracious pride, she had discovered a wonderful inheritance. She ushered him into one of the reception rooms that was large lofty and richly coloured. He strolled uneasily into the empty room. The carpet Donegal, thick and soft and the oak panelling added a sense of opulence. Several striking paintings of animals, mainly horses, hung from the walls; the one above the marble fireplace was a Munnings. Nolan knew little of Mark O'Neill; he'd been a successful businessman in America and had returned to Ireland to continue his enterprises. O'Neill was now a wealthy man, by all accounts, and that was as far as it went. But why was he sitting in this gracious room—way, way out of his depth? He looked around and was aware of a figure standing at the door.

A woman appeared as if from nowhere. Although beautiful in an ageless way her expression was aloof with a face like a mask of chronic passive anger. He stood up and immediately felt small and shabby. Awkwardly, he offered his hand, which was ignored.

'I'm Charlotte O'Neill,' she said flatly as she walked to a table lamp to switch it on. 'Mark will be along shortly. He's finishing in the stables.'

He tried to tell a little about his work, his travels but she wasn't interested. She stood keeping her distance, affectedly formal with strange unyielding eyes. She gave the impression of someone who has had the satisfaction of revenge and, yet, was still stranded where she'd destroyed her adversary.

He gave up and shrugged his shoulders.

'That's all right I'll wait.'

'Good.' She left the room.

With a sigh he walked to the window. Five minutes later O'Neill rushed in and shook his hand warmly.

'Thanks for coming. I've been looking forward to meeting you.'

Nolan relaxed at last. This was a man he could talk to.

'Would you like a drink Tom?'

'Thank you. No. Never touch it,' he replied but gestured towards the tray on the table, 'but please don't let me … '

' … No. Won't bother. Have a good journey down?'

'Very pleasant. Thank you!'

'Now Tom. Down to business.' O'Neill looked straight at him with clear brown eyes. 'I'd like to talk about painting. I'm one of your admirers and I was greatly taken with your animal pictures in the Academy this year. Superb work.'

'Thank you Mr O'Neill.'

'Oh Mark please.'

'All right Mark then. I'm glad you liked them.'

Mark leaned back in the sofa and crossed his legs.

'Tell me something about your work. What are you doing at present?'

Tom studied the man. He presented the image of the perfect country gentleman; tall thin with straight fair hair pushed back behind the ears, a fresh complexion and an obvious delight for bright coloured waistcoats and tweeds. One could imagine him with a roving eye for glamorous women with his good humour and witty speech. He spoke with a cultured voice and air of authority and said things as if they should be listened to. More importantly, it was the character breathing through the words that mattered to Tom; he was still cautious and uncertain. However, here was an opportunity he couldn't miss. He outlined his epic journey where he searched for mindscapes that no one had seen in landscapes everyone had seen.

Mark laughed. 'Well said Tom! But why do it?'

'What a question!' Tom exclaimed. 'I think we're all aware of, and understand, far more than we can ever express in words.'

Mark leaned forward placing his elbows on his knees; he made a pyramid of his hands and examined his visitor. What he saw he liked; a striking dark haired middle-aged man, well groomed, and meticulous in dress, even smaller details were examined closely. All seemed to fit the picture of a man who was proud of his appearance and confidant to put his views forward in a convincing way.

'Go on,' he said listening carefully.

'Art is a means of expression and I think its purpose must be to remind us of our humanity, to achieve a stillness in the midst of chaos … '

' … Like music?'

'Exactly. And it should not be a mirror to the world or merely reproduce the visible; it should make visible things that are important to our instinct for beauty. It can be complex, mysterious and thrilling, in which only one element counts and that element is the most difficult to explain.'

'I don't understand.'

Tom nodded. 'No one has yet solved the question of beauty. It's like a form of energy, or electricity, that we're able to utilize but do not understand. Great art is without ostentation yet the grandeur of the idea can be sublime.'

'The subject and content you mean?'

'An artist's experience takes hold of his mind without intervention of numbers or words.' He tapped his chair for emphasis. 'And demands an answer.'

'And?'

'If the response is superficial the result will be shallow and indifferent; if it's false the outcome is obvious for all to see, but if it's genuine and involves almost reaching beyond one's grasp, then the reward can be great. Art has become a fundamental means of interpreting nature.'

Mark frowned. 'You certainly take your work seriously. However I wonder if the response is false is it obvious for all to see? I mean in so-called modern art.'

For a moment the question hung in the air, a suspended chord of confusion. Tom shivered involuntarily; he became stiff with anger, his eyes blazing.

'Today, some forms of experimental art are incomprehensible, so complex as to seem untouchable by reason. Good art cannot be produced when the artist is only intent on expressing himself with no interest in the subject. A mannered abstraction will become an empty creation lacking conviction. The artist must have something to say.'

Mark raised his hand and smiled. 'Hold it there Tom. That's precisely why I asked you to come here this evening. To discuss subject matter.'

Tom appeared not to have heard. 'Most people can see but are blind to perception. That awe and wonder in a child's mind, or the thoughts of one looking on the world for the last time, is the kind of insight required for convincing work.'

Mark had been sitting back listening patiently. He'd always been used to holding his own. For the present he was perplexed and lost for words. He could only smile and gently nod, as Tom would not be put off. 'For years an epidemic of ugliness has infected our world leaving some with an attitude of defeatist awe. Not me. No.'

'Agreed', Mark managed to interrupt sounding a little frustrated, 'again, Tom, why do artists paint?'

'Beautiful landscapes possess, not just geological forces beyond understanding, but something more sublime, an inner power that can, if we let them, have a profound influence on our lives. In the process we become aware of an essential reality, of the universal in the particular, of that which lies behind the surface of things.'

'That's a little deep for me but I'm coming round to your point of view?'

Tom felt he'd impressed the importance of his work, his dedication. His eyes were clouded with fatigue and furrows appeared across his brow when, with a sigh, he concluded.

'You know, Mark, great works of art don't easily reveal their secrets; we just surrender to their magic without question. The formal mechanisms are lost in the statement, in the effect. It's probably true to say that no activity reflects more accurately the mind of a person as painting. Some would call this inspiration, a state which probably belongs to a world outside common time when, for a while, something extraordinary is drawn out of us by the sheer grandeur of the subject matter.'

Mark was instantly alert.

'The subject matter,' he echoed with a disarming smile, 'you also love animals?'

'Enormously.'

'It certainly shows in your work.'

Tom was thoughtful for a moment.

'They can be difficult subjects.'

Mark looked at the painter with detached approval.

'Well Tom,' he said hesitantly, 'the main reason I asked you here is to offer you an important commission, more correctly a number of commissions.'

Tom's heart missed a beat. This could be a breakthrough in his professional career, if he handled it well. Ruth would be proud and Annette. Perhaps, they could afford those luxuries they had to constantly do without. Perhaps, a better life, leave the daily struggle behind.

'We're in the process of building a west wing on to the main house.'

It was now Tom's turn to listen, and carefully he did—like a lawyer hearing details of a new brief.

'The house is mid-Georgian and the new wing will blend completely in every detail. There'll be four additional reception rooms, a ballroom and music room for occasional concerts. We'll leave the present building as it is. Enough done already.'

'Sounds wonderful.'

'Now Tom,' Mark went on with enthusiasm, 'for a long time I've admired your work. And after talking to you tonight I'm convinced you've the ability and commitment to undertake what I've in mind.'

'Yes?'

'I want you to do some mural paintings and one large-scale work in the new wing. The main structures are complete and the internal fittings are installed. And while your work is progressing you and your family can stay in the old Dowager house over at the lake, our guesthouse.'

'Really? Sounds great.'

'It's very peaceful there and one of the Range Rovers will be put at your disposal. I don't know how long you'll need, a year or more. Not important. And, of course, Tom, money's no problem. Just name your price. If you accept I'm sure you'll enjoy the project.'

'But may I ask what is the series to depict? I mean what's the subject matter?'

'The subject matter is to be about the glory of the hunt. You see, next year I'll be President of the Meath and Kildare Blazers and I'd love to have the entire wing known as The Hunters' Gallery. I've already built up a collection of animal pictures which will be included along with yours.'

'The glory of the hunt.' The words went through him clean as a bullet.

'Yes,' said Mark his fine features bright with excitement, 'the damned fox is everywhere around here. One can see the flash of him from dawn to dusk.'

A silence followed, each pulling a different way. O'Neill, always the gentleman, charming and courteous, became self-conscious sensing there was something amiss. He tried to be helpful. 'Tom is something wrong?'

A storm of agitation was forming in the painter's mind as he looked at his hands trying to find words to frame his thoughts.

Without lifting his eyes he said gently, 'I cannot do it. Sorry I can't.'

'Pardon?'

'It's against my principles.'

Mark stared in shocked surprise. 'What on earth has that to do with it?'

'You haven't listened to anything I've said,' Tom answered despairingly. 'The subject matter is of supreme importance. I cannot prostitute my art to portray the cruelty of a pack of bloodthirsty animals incited by sadistic humans to seek out and destroy a single, pathetic creature, no matter what its faults may be. Blood sports must be banned not glorified in art galleries.'

Mark sat erect with an air of helpless disbelief. He then stood up and drew the curtains to shut out the withering sun.

'There are no innocent victims,' he said his voice touched with compassion.

'I'm sorry,' was the weak reply.

He turned from the curtains and saw Tom slumped forward, his face buried in his hands. He shook his head slowly, extended his hand and said gently. 'I'm also sorry you feel like that. There's no point in discussing the matter any further.'

The day was dying rapidly as Tom Nolan drove south through Dublin. The street lamps trembled as they sprang alight in a blaze against the darkness. St Patrick's area was deserted and the cathedral, looking like some ghost from the past pointed a finger skywards. The car crept home to the little house beside the harbour and surrounded by fog-dripping trees. The rest of the night slipped away like sorrow on a wreath.

Next morning he sat in his studio unable to work. The flow of life in him had ebbed away. He was lost and bewildered. With clenched hands, a letter resting on his lap, he desperately tried to keep some composure, some balance as he endured something he knew not what.

Meanwhile, Ruth Annette and Patsie walked slowly along the beach to school.

Chapter 10

John Nicholson worked hard on the manuscript for days. Problems arose where he least expected and the more he persisted the more intractable they became. Dizzy with fatigue he threw papers on his desk, leaned back and Linda came to mind. She was attractive and she'd been warm and welcoming. Yet, was he ready, or risk a polite rejection? Maybe he was. Not the whole truth, however; with regret he remembered Diane Sutton and was wary of no repetition. Besides, other things were on his mind.

Back to the paper work. After some minutes it was more complicated than ever. Perhaps, it was the way he was feeling.

He then tried to work out the best way to invite Linda for a weekend in the country. Where to go was no problem; comfortable hotels were within reach of Stockholm with galleries, potteries, workshops and an innocent type of nightlife she'd probably enjoy. And the weather was good just now. Phone calls were made and rooms with views of the lakes provisionally booked. That was one hurdle.

The next was bigger. How did he want the break to develop? Would it simply be a tourist trip to see the sights, a brief, pleasant affair, or a deeper thing altogether? In hospital they'd performed a ritual of advancing and retreating, of joking and arguing, all in the same environment and nearly always with others present. This would be different and the next move was up to him. His father's advice came back. 'You can amuse yourself with women in many innocent ways. And that's fine. It'll always be appreciated by those who agree with you, but don't ever treat love as a temporary amusement. It's too serious a subject for that because people get hurt and sometimes badly. Don't play games with fire. You will only get burned.'

The phone interrupted his thoughts. It was Linda inquiring about a hospital problem. When that was resolved, he took his chance and invited her for a weekend in the country—somewhere not too far, perhaps around Karlstad.

She was taken aback yet thrilled at the suggestion.

'It is most thoughtful of you John,' her voice was firm, 'but perhaps it would not be the right thing to do at present.'

'Why?' He asked abruptly.

'Well do not you think it is a little premature?' Her tone was hesitant.

'Please listen to me.' He was impatient and brusque. 'I've booked in a lovely place and the scenery is splendid there.'

She wanted to dig her heels in, yet was unsure.

'John you did not hear me. I will not be coming.'

'Linda you're not a child anymore.' He spoke meaning to be heard—clearly. 'You're grown up. A woman of the world and able to make up your own mind. Nobody can force you to do anything you do not want to do. So, live a little and don't have so many hang-ups. Life's for enjoying and not being perpetually afraid of doing anything. Where's the adventure in you?'

She was silent for a long moment, sizing up the situation. She liked his attitude and wanted to be told what to do. Then her voice was calm and deliberate.

'You are right Dr Nicholson. I will expect you at ten-thirty tomorrow morning.' She laughed and replaced the receiver.

Next morning he arrived in good time. She had her overnight bag packed, was dressed in casuals and ready for the road. There was a sense of excitement as they headed out of the city and joined the E 18 going northwest. The day was bright and warm, which helped expectations—at least the sun gave its blessing. They talked awkwardly about hospital matters, research work, clashes of personalities amongst colleagues, and then, settled into more intimate exchanges.

She was an only child. Her mother would have preferred a bigger family. It was unfair to have only one child; where is the companionship, the growing up together, the chumminess large families have? It never happened, so a closeness developed with her parents. It meant her childhood was shortened and she had to become an adult before her time.

He was in the same boat. She did not understand. An only child, he meant. This lead to bullying in school. He'd been able for it because of his height, which seemed to command respect from his tormentors. It was one of the evils among young people and didn't appear to be recognized by authorities, or perhaps ignored by them for their own reasons.

'What do you think Linda?' He asked as he manipulated a difficult roundabout on the E 18. 'Do you think it has anything positive to contribute?'

'Oh John. Here we go again.' She was perplexed. 'You presenting little me with difficult questions, which I do not think even you have the answers.'

'I'm sorry Linda,' he replied, 'I didn't mean to confuse you. They were rhetorical questions.'

'John you are a mischief-maker. You create mysteries where there are none.'

Suddenly a suicidal maniac tried to overtake them, going out into the oncoming traffic, which swerved to avoid him. John turned the steering wheel towards the hard shoulder to make room for the vehicle from hell. The maniac must have had someone praying for him because the combined actions of John and the slamming of brakes by the juggernaut behind prevented a multiple pile up and many deaths—all because this lone madman wanted to save a few minutes on his journey.

On a mortuary slab courtesy of some fool trying to save five minutes, they thought.

John's immediate response was a stream of obscenities.

Fortunately, they were near the junction for *Karlstad*, so they turned off to allow the maniac continue dicing with death, and with a little luck he might even make it home in one piece for his favourite sports programme, only to have the same minute performance the next day.

They reached their destination on the shores of Lake Vanern and checked into their adjacent rooms, which Linda thought a quaint arrangement. He could not understand the true meaning of her remarks in Swedish, or perhaps he pretended not to understand.

The hotel, on the waterfront, was splendidly appointed with a Swedish flavour. She expected something old fashioned and heavy downstairs like oak panelling; period antiques, matching chairs and a lot of clutter. Instead there was a sense of light and space and little intrusive furniture; the pieces on display were minimal and made for relaxing. Effort had been made to interconnect all rooms easily without loosing privacy in each room.

John thought it wise to book for dinner in the famous Skoghall Restaurant across the lake. This was confirmed for eight o'clock so she asked for an hour or two to rest. At seven-thirty he waited in the lobby. She turned up in a figure hugging pink dress that almost took his breath away. She reached up and kissed him with agreeable intensity. Helping her put on her coat and they made for the landing stage. They crossed the lake in an obtuse angle—the only means of battling the currents in the lake. Talking was not possible because of the roar of the engine and the hammering of water on the vessel. Minutes later they were decanted onto the small harbour and walked the fifty paces up to the restaurant.

She was goggle eyed at the exotic interior, oak panelling, rich tapestries, oil paintings by some recognizable old masters, and statues in Parian ware, probably dating from the great London Exhibition of 1851.

The table was placed well away from the band. Everything was going well for a while until a row brewed at the next table. Two young men sat there, with their partners, and the consumption of spirit was fast and furious. He couldn't follow the conversation so she translated as the action took place. Apparently, the argument concerned an alleged insult to one of the women. Glasses were smashed and blows were struck.

Then one of the belligerents looked across at them. He shouted something, pointing at Linda and the others laughed. She turned away. John asked her to translate but she refused. He guessed it was another insult, directed at her. With the speed of lightning he landed a blow on the side of the face of the speaker who fell to the ground. John stamped on his hand when he spotted the knife to lock it out of commission.

He began to speak in his most courteous, most sympathetic Swedish he could muster up and apologized for intervening. Although his Swedish was understandable to most people, it was obvious he was not one of their own; he was an outsider and, perhaps, someone to be respected, someone in authority. John continued that, of course, everyone should settle their own quarrels as best they can, but this one seemed to be getting dangerous. They must agree that somebody, especially the ladies they were there to protect, just might get hurt. He then reached for the knife and handed it back to the owner, placing money on the table to cover the costs of damage.

He asked Linda to go with him. Applause broke out from guests and staff in appreciation.

Back to the ferry the captain pointed to another restaurant, which was almost beside their hotel and said they should be well looked after there. She crossed her fingers at the reception desk. Although they were busy they could manage another two guests. Would they prefer the main restaurant, or the barbeque on the other side of the swimming poll? They opted for a dark corner on the main floor and glad to be seated in a place that, hopefully, was geared to entertain and feed their guests. Long boats with noisy engines roared on the lake outside, propellers frothing the thick brown water with dancing lights reflected on its surface. The sound combined with the music of the band went in some way to hypnotize the fatigued mind.

An hour passed over the meal. Both were tired and the wine had a greater effect than expected. Fragmented memories with interruptions were dragged up; old stories had unsatisfactory endings or none at all.

'I think we're both great talkers,' he volunteered, 'but not good listeners.'

'I am trying to listen but you keep interrupting me,' she protested.

He chuckled happily. 'I'm listening now Linda and what you've just said doesn't make much sense. Does it?'

She looked confused.

'Please could you repeat the question John?'

He thought for a moment. Then he admitted. 'I can't remember what it was.'

'Well that does it.' She perked up. 'We both have had enough excitement for one day. Please can we go back to the hotel?'

'Of course.'

On the balcony they took a last look at the silver reflections and heard the night music of the water. It was a short walk back to the hotel. Strolling towards it they mixed with the nightclub crowd, half listening to the slow music that came from the clubs and cafes. Young faces flashed by, looking strange in the glare of streets lights. Some were celebrating events and telling strangers about it; others were pale and tired, yet, forcing themselves to participate in weary excitement. He watched them with fascination. Was he missing anything in this continuous struggle to find happiness on the dance floor fuelled by an endless flow of cocktails?

They went straight to their rooms. The instructions the porter had given them, how the rooms were interconnected focused his mind. He knew he could just slip into her room on a pretext of inquiring if she was all right after the awful episode in the restaurant. It would be easy to drop in. The third option he'd quietly discussed with himself; option one and two, at the moment were so weak as to not hold him. But option three? He sat back on the bed. He was torn yet again between temptation or bide his time.

Suddenly Linda appeared as if from nowhere.

'Oh John.' She approached for an embrace. She had been crying.

'I never thought our evening could have been spoiled by such events.'

'Don't worry Linda,' he reassured, 'these things are happening all the time.'

'But John. My dear John.' She held her hands. 'You were wonderful in protecting me. I have to thank you. Remember I was the one who first heard the terrible insults directed at us.'

'I know. You knew exactly what they were saying.'

'And it was awful.' She still looked unhappy and shocked.

He stared open mouthed. 'Could you translate for me now?'

She shook her head. 'No John. I could never do that. Never.'

'Why not? I'm a big boy.' A puzzled smile dawned on his face.

'No.' She insisted. 'I do not want anything like that to come between us. Ever.'

He was intrigued, yet did not want to upset her. At that moment he knew he truly loved her. All the things he'd ever wished for in a woman seemed to have blossomed in her, naturalness, affection and compassion. She did not possess an iota of the capriciousness of other women, who could easily arouse tenderness and not return it, making a mockery of the other. What she had she would give freely with no expectation of reward. For once, indecision deserted him.

'Linda thanks for coming. I have to tell you that I love you.'

She looked at him surprised and overjoyed.

'I love you too John.'

She held him closely, tightly and let go.

She then sat on an easy chair evading his eyes.

'Now we have admitted it, John, let us go along with it for a while. No firm commitments. No promises. We can wait and enjoy what we have between us. If it develops, it would be wonderful. If not, so be it.'

'I can only hope it grows Linda.'

They embraced again, this time for longer. She could feel his heart beating and trembling arms and was quick to notice the sincere, but patient love for her in his appealing eyes, and the insistent but quiet central desire. She had heard and read about these exciting situations, and even friends had hinted around them with obscure words, but it was the first time she'd experienced that quiet, yet powerful, central desire of a young man who had suppressed and suffered during his youth. She was faint hearted and confused as a warm glow went through her and she felt herself yielding to him.

She pushed him away gently.

'You must not rush me, John, please. You must promise not to rush me.' She touched him on the cheek and looked straight into his eyes. 'You realize we are rational adults and we both know where this can lead.'

'Of course, and I want it to go in the right direction.'

'And I do too. But I need time. So do not pressurize me. Please.'

She sounded desperate. She had to make the request on this occasion; she could draw him to her again, and next time it could be stronger. Then a sharp pang of jealousy alarmed her—unless there was someone else to take him.

For the present she was flattered.

She was aware that love was a war where victory went to those who knew how to walk the fine line between giving and guile, between tantalizing and torment. She also recognized that a man, once kissed, was half conquered.

She asked him not to rush her. She'd always accepted life, for the moment, and cherished it, but also had an unreasonable attitude of not asking too much from the future.

'John, I do not want to make promises neither of us can keep. I live only for today and accept what it gives. That way I feel safe. Not constantly looking to the great maybe.'

'What do you mean maybe?'

'To come together, bound in a kind of cruelty we see all around us. I am not strong enough for that. I would not last. I want to love you, so you would have a lasting contentment. The love I offer is I would allow you to leave without recrimination, if you were not happy.'

'Linda dear. You've thought deeply about us I can see that.' He kissed her lightly on the forehead. 'Are there any more maybes?'

She lowered her head and placed it on his shoulder.

'Maybe something terrible could happen.' Her voice was almost a whisper. 'Maybe you could die. Maybe I could die. Maybe.'

'Linda. Stop that. It's silly and absurd. And I won't hear any more of it.'

'Yes John.'

'Someone has to think of the future. Without planning we'd drift aimlessly.'

'Yes John. I am listening.'

'Linda I want to take care of you.' Her forehead remained on his shoulder. 'I've always tried to be independent, self-reliant. I was a loner, and full of ambition, a person they'd love to catch out, to trick into some folly, but couldn't because I'd no feelings. Now I know what I want. And it is you.'

Leaning towards him a shiver went through her as his warmth invaded her. The embrace was delicious and she appreciated his closeness now, almost in slow motion; his clear smooth forehead with thick black hair straggling down, his strong chin and full passionate mouth. She loved his strong hands all over her; she loved his hypnotic voice and enveloping arms.

When she drew away she was completely drained. Perhaps, she was one of those fantasy women whose desire exhausts itself at the mouth.

They remained thus, not speaking until she drew further away, and held his hands.

'I understand you better now,' she said, 'I have told you before, you are a very complicated man.' Her look was simple and giving. 'All I want is for you to love me, John. Just love me. Now I must leave.'

Quietly she let his hands slip away, turned around, closed the connecting door and returned to her room. Tomorrow was another day.

He slept deeply and awoke strangely refreshed. Early sunshine was welcome in the room. Through the dew of a sleep-drenched night he looked at his watch. It was six-thirty.

Linda still slept easily in the next room, contentedly and inviolate.

CHAPTER 11

Next day was dry bright and warm. They decided to see as much of Varmland and Dalarna as possible, two provinces the cradle and soul of the nation. Lake Siljan lies in Dalarna and is regarded by many as the most beautiful lake anywhere. Further south is Varmland, which opens onto Lake Vanern, the third largest inland sea in Europe. The surrounding area is rolling countryside, mountains, lakes and islands.

After seeing a number of craft centres in *Karlstad* they moved north into the Dalarna district where Linda was born, bred and educated. She was anxious for him to see it especially between *Vadstena* and *Jonkoping* where the road snakes along the eastern shore of Lake Vattern.

Then Alfred Nobel's Bjorkborn about thirty-five miles east of *Karlstad* on the edge of Lake Mockeln. It was a white-sided manor house, the home of the inventor of explosives and who later became a famous philanthropist establishing the Nobel Prize. Even though he made a fortune it was to implode on him as an enormous sense of guilt.

Linda was nervous as they drove through beautiful countryside. Great efforts were made to emphasize the good points in this, that and the other—her way of apologizing. Occasional tears surfaced, which John wasn't supposed to notice. The previous night could affect the future. How secure was it?

With a chill in the air and wind racing through trees they started on the journey home. Linda sat quietly not wishing to talk only to soak up the scenery. It was useless. Still tense, nervous and confused she was afraid of something, but did not know what. Maybe, it was a fear of losing him even before it started. What a dilemma. Not recovered from the incident in the restaurant and the hurtful remarks afterwards she was ashamed of the horrible people, their behaviour unforgivable. Perhaps it was delayed shock. She was prone to it. How could she make it up to him? What must he think of Sweden and the people? He was too polite to say anything.

In spite of their love—with no promises—they could not communicate their reassurance as they drove back to Stockholm. Each was withdrawn. The E 18 motorway was packed with commuter traffic and approaches to the city were even worse; noise, rain and lights turning red deliberately combined to increase the level of frayed nerves.

After he left her at the apartment he returned home feeling like an alien from another planet who'd landed in bedlam. He unpacked, shaved and showered and was gradually restored to normal. His thoughts rambled. Well, that was a bright idea to have a pleasant weekend in the country! It turned out to be a disaster, certainly for him. He didn't know what Linda thought of it. All through the second day she was apprehensive, overactive in her speech and followed by silences, not her usual happy, good-humoured self. For the present, he would be discrete; use small endearments, perhaps kiss cheeks without emotion and not delay when parting. He should still adhere to all the courtesies, and step back from incipient quarrels. That way lay peace, but what way progress? He had no answer except to play it cool. There are times in every love affair no matter how sudden, when the close, intimate link is shattered, when each is thrown back into that isolation and solitude from whence it started. In that state, each would have a too perfect view of the other, where each could do no wrong. Yielding together is a blinding admission of this; their joy is so complete neither can believe the existence of prejudice or intolerance. The slightest upset in this balance may cause over reactions, which seem out of all proportion. Quarrels and rows cause the pendulum to swing violently between withdrawal and rushing back with greater passion.

The story of love through the ages; the more true the more intense, and is known to those who've experienced and survived it. For him and Linda, at this time, it was a confusing and painful process. She longed for reassurance, to be indulged, and spoilt. She'd many needs, as women do, which she couldn't plainly ask for. He should know what they were. He'd so much to learn.

They had yet to realize life is too short to squander on fruitless resentment and pique. A lot of things concerning love can be irrational and they went their separate ways without reconciliation.

And Linda heard about the forthcoming Isselherg's Easter party.

CHAPTER 12

An early spring accompanied a late Easter and Linda decided for good reasons to spend the holiday in Velkonstad, a small district north of Mora in the Dalarna district where folk-culture permeates the Siljan hills and lakes, the red cottages and woods and where God, and the devil, saints and prophets often dominate the lives of people. The train journey home was marred by heavy rain.

Still shocked and she should be happy, looking forward to a new life. Now where was she? In the wilderness getting nowhere. Was she wrong asking for more time, not to be pushed, not to be pressurized? Certainly, John had not intended it that way—according to his words. When she said they should drift along and see what happens he seemed taken aback. He'd done his best to convince her she was someone special, someone he wanted to care for. He'd never felt this way about anyone before.

All she could say.

'Please do not push me!'

She should only have hinted at these things because he did let her go, let her go too quickly! Another would have grabbed her, accepted no nonsense, and perhaps demanded his due reward for all the grandeur in the expensive hotel. But not John, although, maybe, he felt it. Something inside stopped him; maybe something called respect, let her go, let her escape back into her lonely bedroom. He made no objection to her closing the adjoining doors, letting her disappear into the enchantless night, a night of opportunity to disappear forever. Even though she was the first to leave after their passionate words, she felt she had blown it! Why was she in a hurry when he was poised on the edge of something, something that could be life long lasting? The way things finished up were her fault, she had made mistakes, but in the end if his strength of character were to match his words, then sooner or later, he would return. All she had to do was wait. And wait patiently.

The Lindstrom home, almost two hundred years old, is situated on the northern shore of Lake Velkon. It's a rambling comfortable house made from local wood with large windows that view the scenery to maximum advantage. Linda had grown up there and knew her ancestors, knew them as friendly beings that still, somehow, liked to keep her company in the old place.

Her mother also welcomed her eagerly that Easter—her farther was delayed on business. Mrs Lindstrom was a harmless soul of medium height and an unrestrained manner gave her a lively warmth. The passing years had been kind and she allowed them to do their work unhindered. Her figure was still trim and well preserved, her hair abundant, straight and streaked with grey.

The lines on her face were drawn and fashioned by smiles and laughter. Her eyes kept their youthful exuberance, the sparkle, and the magnetism she had transmitted to her daughter; eyes that could instil unbroken admiration, adoration even, or inflict pain. No wonder her husband, Jens, would always defer to her better judgement and treat her with great respect.

Linda loved the physical glow that enlarged her mother's words but it was the laughter, infectious sparkling laughter, which impressed most and lingered in the air long after the sound had ceased. She also loved her father, who'd built a successful business in Mora on the highest moral principles, and who could never let go of his rigidity in spite of the laughter; he was completely unaffected by it. Life was not meant to be laughed away, he would say—rather often—it was a serious matter and had to be taken seriously. There was no time for laughter, one must strive to get on, be good at what one does, do it to the best of one's ability and only then will one get a reward, if not here, then in a far better place. Mrs Lindstrom, being independent, only laughed all the more, not at him—of course—it has to be said, but with her daughter resulting in both having confident, well-rounded personalities.

The smell and taste of freshly baked muffins her mother would have waiting for her when she returned from school, Linda remembered. The horrible taste of wine one Christmas, long ago. Why the fuss? Eventually she would find out. The thrill of dressing in her mother's clothes and clomping in high-heels over wooden boards and the kind uncle who always gave her money to spend on herself. There was little of it about at the time. Bits of conversation came floating to the surface—and of no consequence—but usually words of happiness.

They were a happy family. She remembered images and occasions that were beautiful but would never be repeated, the visits to the zoo when animals came forward for the children's offerings, but smelling of incarceration rather than wide open spaces. They seemed depressed dejected and hard done by. Birthday parties in the big wooden house; the children were expected to stay in the garden but many with paper hats made their way elsewhere seeking adventure in forbidden rooms.

She remembered windows open on summer evenings when the sun refused to go asleep, and laughter coming from her mother's friends downstairs late into the bright night, and dreaming about the hunting prints hanging in the landing outside her bedroom, trying to visualize the stories behind them. Various people had told them to her and each was different, which puzzled her immensely.

Happy times came flooding back this bright Easter evening; she glowed with the pleasure they gave. She was at home and at peace.

Next morning was also a journey into the past.

'Everything is lovely this time of year mother.' She said as she passed through the kitchen to the garden.

Daffodils along the wall leading into the orchard were resplendent in the sun; pigeons cooed in trees and the air was full of birdsong. This was her past, and it thrilled her to see it again after the noise and bustle of Stockholm.

Its attraction had not diminished, hills circling the lake, with stretches of wood worn like a garment on their shoulders, little red painted farm houses interspersed in clearings, and the blue streak of river flowing past the church towards the lake. She loved this place extraordinarily and would probably do so to her last day. It featured many times in her dreams. It was almost irrelevant if the sun shone on her face, or she saw the delicate patterns of frost on glass, or snow along the naked branches of her favourite trees. The sights and smells of spring were waiting around the corner.

This was home and always had been. No matter what fate had in store, it would always be a place to come back to, perhaps, in her hour of need.

She made her way across the lawn and sat dreaming as clouds drifted from the southeast scattering shadows on their way to the mountains and an immense destiny beyond. The sun grew stronger, its marvellous clarity penetrating the woods. The lake mirrored Mount Velkon and the sky. As the air sighed, it touched the tranquil image that shimmered; then was gone. Mount Velkon reposed in brown, its shoulders capped in green, and above, snow glowing pink on its brow seemed to belong to the sky. That is where earth and heaven meet, she thought, and the blue is so wonderful. She walked along the shore to where branches tunnel daylight, stopped at the old bridge and listened to the stream, now an excited flood flowing past snowdrops and primroses. The birds, water and leaves formed music of intangible potency that stirred something deep inside. Spring is here unashamed in its nakedness and summer the consummate reward.

Later on the evening was cool and seductive as she gazed at the dying sunset. Slowly, colour was replaced by a speckled darkness as stars came alive. Gradually the vast dome became a glittering profusion; the place was content and at peace, her ancestors well pleased as she imagined they carried the warm breezes and sparkling dust in handfuls about the old house.

Before retiring she loved to have a long, lingering bath. She filled the large, circular tub with streaming hot water, lay back and submerged her body giving a quick intake of air to counteract the enveloping heat. It was delicious and she thrilled at the soft, soapy water moving over her. So sensuous. Scented steam rose up and blurred everything, wrapping her in a euphoric haze. She melted deeper into the water, and had an unearthly feeling of being suspended in a void, protecting her from all that's nasty in the world. Here she could drift, float, self-absorbed and begin to dream dreams of all nature of pleasantries.

She stepped out of the bath, wrapped herself in a pink towel, dried and applied fragrance. Then she slipped into bed between fresh linen sheets and let herself drift into a gradual sleep; this was the part of giving up she enjoyed most. She could fantasize; she could dream lovely thoughts, feeding on memory. Tonight, as she lay, tired and relaxed, she thought up a dream of a dark, smiling stranger holding her hand as they walked around the lake. Then as he changed from man to passionate lover, she was raised to another plane of consciousness. Nevertheless, this was only a delusion and there could be no wrong attached to it at all.

She slept soundly that night.

Chapter 13

Linda woke early next morning. No work today, and not for a few days. Not having to rush anywhere was a great feeling and she luxuriated in the security of home. She lay on the bed gazing at the ceiling. The events of the weekend with John came back. He had left her home when they reached the city and did not linger. He was distant as he carried her suitcase up to the front door. Her invitation for coffee was refused. He preferred to be off home to get his papers in order for next week. Just an excuse? Trying to escape and was she going to lose him?

Poor tormented John! He was established in society here and had friends. The evening with the Isselherg family was common knowledge. He was more confident and seemed to cherish his way of life—and his freedom. If she was going to hold him—she was not sure if she wanted to—she'd have to make up her mind, go and capture him, snap him up before another grabbed him, like Karita Isselherg or someone else who was given the opportunity.

Well maybe she did not want anyone at present. She had work to do, she was young and, besides, there were plenty of others. So why hurry? She was ambitious and wanted to succeed. Such efforts used up a lot of adrenaline and, thereby, not leaving much to spend on love and passion. Yet she missed him.

Linda dressed and went down to breakfast; her mother was fussing around the kitchen while she ate. Many searching questions were directed at her, discrete of course, but also inquisitive. Mrs Lindstrom had a shrewd knack of extracting information from anyone in an innocent and delicate way.

'Well Linda.' She faced her daughter head-on. 'Any new boyfriends yet?'

'No mama,' she replied looking away unsure of herself.

'Are you sure Linda pet?' Again extracting something she knows is there.

' I met a nice Irish doctor and we went to a lecture in the Academy.'

'How did you manage that? The Academy is exclusive.'

Linda told how Sir Neville Chance found them arguing in the museum and invited them to his lecture.

'What were you arguing about Linda?'

'Oh that is too complicated to go into.'

'And the lecture?'

'It was wonderful although a bit heavy. A lot of philosophy and stuff.'

'Did your young doctor like it?'

'Yes he did, ' she replied eagerly and added, 'he enjoyed it more than I did.'

'How do you know?'

'We went for a meal afterwards and we had a post mortem on the lecture.'

'John is doing research into cancer chemotherapy in the Helmuth. I think he is rather nice.'

'But is he interested in you?'

'That I do not know. In a funny way, I do not think so.'

She did not give many details. 'He left me home recently and I invited him into the apartment for coffee. He refused saying he had a lot of important things to do.'

'Sounds like the cold shoulder Linda,' her mother warned, 'I would be careful there. Do not be too eager to accept any more invitations to lectures, or other events, unless he can give a good reason for doing so. And Linda there are reasons, and reasons.'

'I know what you mean mama,' she said knowingly, 'I have a good teacher in these things.'

'Good. Then we know where we stand. You must be careful of someone who does not appreciate small courtesies like coffee in your room at night, which of course to any gentleman, is not a small courtesy. It is much more. And one thing can lead to another.'

Linda saw her mother was getting a little agitated, so she decided to draw a close to the matter.

'Nothing happened. He left me and walked away without byes your leave.'

Her mother was fishing again. 'Then you are free at present?'

'I suppose I must answer a guarded yes to that.'

'Why guarded?'

'Because I have many admirers in the college and hospital, although I have not yet exploited any of them, but they would appear to be easy picking but not really desirable.'

'Linda darling. The man who gets you must be the best, the very best, and successful; not really in money, although that would be a bonus, but someone who knows what he is doing and knows the reasons why he is doing it.'

'Mama, that sounds like a speech in a presidential election! Instead, I have just to think of this John Nicholson. He is a dynamo in many ways in his work, even brilliant according to Professor Isselherg, although I would suspect a vested interest in Isselherg because of his three eligible daughters. What finer catch for one of them could be a brilliant research worker, under the guidance of her father? That would be a first class fairy story.'

'I see,' her mother said as if she already knew all the facts. 'Then it would appear that you, Linda, have two options. Firstly, if you really feel for this John, then go all out for him, grab him, ensnare him by gentle means, of course. Nothing underhand, because he would never forgive you if you trapped him.'

'Yes mama,' she replied, 'at least I know the folly of shotgun marriages. It never works in the long term.'

'What if this academic person decides to dump you, what then?'

'I will continue to work,' she said proudly. 'I will survive. I know I will.'

'I seem to have developed a soft spot for this doctor fellow Linda. I think I would love to meet him.'

This was a rare compliment in the Lindstrom household.

CHAPTER 14

John Nicholson went over recent events. He was uncertain how to proceed; Linda asked not to be rushed, to be given time. That must be respected. He'd do precisely that. He wouldn't telephone her and allow her to recover whatever she needed. He'd told her his feelings and she shied away. What path led to the future? If things could be so tense early in a relationship, what stormy waters lay ahead? Better be resigned to a world of contentment and not seek the torment of happiness.

No, it was not worth it! A night on the town and enjoy himself. He visited his favourite restaurant and took in a concert in Symphony Hall. Love sickness was an extraordinary state, similar to agony, and no substitute could take away the bitter yearning.

Next morning he went straight to Radiology to speak to her.

The secretary informed him.

'Dr Nicholson. I am sorry, Dr Lindstrom left for Velkonstad. She decided to take a week's leave over the Easter vacation. That's where the family lives.'

'I see.' John was disappointed. 'Then I'll call back on her return.'

'I will tell her you were looking for her.'

'Please don't. Just leave things be.'

As he was returning to his department Gustav Isselherg called after him.

'John you were not in the laboratory,' he said a little breathless.

'I was in Radiology.'

'What I wanted to ask you, are you doing anything special over the Easter vacation?' He said regaining his composure.

'Not particularly. I've no plans.'

'Splendid.' Isselherg seemed pleased. 'Then would you like to spend a few days at our country estate? It is a lovely place and there is so much to do I can guarantee you will not be bored. Now what do you say?'

In John's state this was manna from heaven.

'That'd be wonderful. I'd be thrilled to accept.'

'Splendid. Splendid.' Isselherg patted him on the shoulder as if he had won a prize. 'Eriksson will call on Thursday morning. He will drive you to our house and we can all go to the country from there. I hope you can stay for three or four days.'

'I'm sure I can. Sounds wonderful. I'll look forward to that immensely.'

Eriksson called the following Thursday and drove him to Kungsangen House. Excitement was palpable as he shook hands and received several powerful embraces from the family. He felt like a returning son or a celebrity. Two cars were prepared. Gustav, John and Eriksson went in one, Rachel, Sara, Ingrid and Karita in the other. The convoy headed north. The country estate was about twenty-five miles north of Karlstad and was situated beside a river flowing into a lake surrounded by forests; a medieval scene in a motion picture setting.

The two cars were unpacked by household staff. The gentleman in black showed him to his room.

Over the next four days they kept their promise that he would not be bored, even though he'd brought reading material. They had evolved a highly sophisticated system of part-games, lone-games, leisure games, horse riding and boating and fishing—if in season. He'd the impression everything would be provided, immediately, with the click of a finger or the push of a bell. Rachel explained the bones of the organization to him soon after arrival.

'My dear lovely John.' She sat him down in the morning room. 'Please make this your home for the time being. Come and go as you please, anytime. But one thing we would ask you to adhere to is mealtimes, and, if possible, if you could join us. Everything is at your disposal. Really, John I hope you will have a great time here. There is no excuse not to.'

Karita insisted on walking him through the flower gardens near the house. They strolled together in the gently weakening sun. Almost unnoticeably she slipped her hand into his and felt it was the most natural thing in the world to do, in this cold climate. Yet the weather was fine, the winds were light, and there was nobody about.

The moist air encouraged delicate scents to rise and mesmerise. Karita was full of talk and proud of her families' achievement in building up such a magnificent retreat.

They sat on one of the garden chairs beside a wooden table used for picnics.

She wanted to share secrets with him; after all he was a doctor and would keep confidences. He decided to be light hearted.

'What would you like to be when you grow up Karita?'

'But I am grown up now, Dr John! I am a university student in the middle of the course. And looking forward to getting my full qualification in the near future.'

'I know. I was only joking. If you wish to talk about anything at all, that's all right by me. And I can lend you a handkerchief if necessary.'

She stared at him not knowing how to proceed.

'You do mean it Dr John? Do you not?'

'Of course. People come when they are sick, and sometimes they don't know it. However, sadly there're times when they come and it's too late; and, so far, we've no means of getting rid of it, although your father and I are working on that.'

'I have heard so much about it. It is truly wonderful. But, one thing upsets me, Dr John, and that is using animals to test the medicines. I think it is cruel.'

'It upsets me too Karita,' he said wistfully, 'someday we may be able to change our approach. For the present we've to work with what we've got.'

'I hope so. I hate to think of any creature suffering unnecessarily.'

Her indictment goaded him and he reacted quickly.

'Karita, don't use the word unnecessarily. I cannot accept it is unnecessary.'

She squeezed his hand, left it resting on his and then looked away.

'Dr John now we are going to change the subject, if you do not mind. I would like to talk about other things.'

He nodded. 'Such as?'

'Well, about me for instance,' she laughed gently. 'Dr John, I am now coming close to my twenty-first birthday and I have not yet had a true love in my life. Someone I can give my heart to.'

He was surprised. 'That's hard to believe. An attractive young girl like you would surely be the life and soul of any party. To me you'd be the belle of the ball.'

Her face lit up. 'Really Dr John? Do you really think so?'

She moved closer, still holding his hand.

She was her dada's favourite, the first-born. He wanted to inculcate principles, moral standards and beliefs, the ways of a good life as an example for others. As she grew up he told her stories that gave her a vivid imagination and a longing to write.

Karita was brought up in the principles of the Church. She believed in God and knew eternal ruin hung over everyone, like the sword of Damocles. The catechism forbad all never to stray, but to keep to the straight and narrow. But, increasingly, she was facing a dilemma. Her friends told her she was plain old fashioned and was missing a lot of innocent fun; and life was too short to be afraid all the time.

'What do you think Dr John?' She asked innocently. 'Am I being silly and missing out on a lot of fun?'

'Karita I've never met anyone like you before!' A gentle smile would hide his embarrassment. 'To ask me, above all people, to answer such a question is both a compliment but also a risky business.'

'Dr John I do not understand what you are saying. I asked a simple question.'

'No Karita. It is not simple.' He looked away and removed his hand. 'You will gradually learn to answer that question with experience.'

'But how do I get experience?'

'By living life as best you can.'

She interrupted him. 'Now you sound like my father.'

'I was going to say, and enjoying it alone or with someone who enjoys the same things as you do. I mean, if you'd someone you respected and admired, note I didn't say love, these feelings would probably grow and lead to greater things.'

'Like love?'

'Yes. Love and marriage. Even marriage can be a precarious agreement at the best of times, and cold, inflexible virtue could do more damage than a little forgiveness and compassion. After all you only get back what you give.'

She held his hand again and smiled.

'You are so wise. I think I understand you better now.' She hesitated for a while thinking about what he said. 'Whatever it is, I seem to frighten off boys. Maybe, it is because of my father and who he is and I am the eldest. He has given me everything and more. Do not think I am not grateful but what he cannot give me is my independence, my freedom and myself. My parents always want to know what

I am doing. Where I am going, what I am going to do next. It can be maddening!'

'Poor little rich girl I suppose.'

'I suppose. But it is suffocating.'

'Well you're alone with me this evening.'

'Of course. They know that and in a way I suspect they wish it that way. They trust you. My father said you are so dependable and straight and upright.'

He began to get uncomfortable again. All this plain speaking was new to him.

Karita comes out with everything she thinks of, almost without thinking. It was unusual, refreshing but it could get her into trouble someday.

'I feel so happy and relaxed with you Dr John. Will you let me take you horse riding tomorrow? It is a great way to see around the lakes and there are wonderful, secret places to explore in the great forest. Will you come with me, please? Please say you will?'

'I'd love to.' he said hesitatingly, 'provided your parents have no objection.'

'No. They would be delighted. I have already asked them, and they are having a packed lunch prepared for us. So there! You will come. Oh I am so happy.'

Indeed, she had it all worked out.

She then told him about her studies in the university. Words fascinated her and how they could express things so well especially poetry; magical images to feed the mind with descriptions never seen before thrilled her. And her own work she would show him, and, perhaps, he would allow her to read some examples. Yes, he is lovely, considerate and makes her feel safe and secure.

CHAPTER 15

Horse riding, walks, meals and plenty of talking occupied Saturday. Everyone joined in and John learned about local history both ancient and modern.

It was just before dusk when Gustav Isselherg invited him into the large conservatory. He was proud of his collection of rare and exotic plants whose care was becoming more than a hobby. His knowledge was extensive and John was impressed.

'Please sit for a while John.'

He pointed to a couple of easy chairs beside a large window overlooking fields, lakes and countryside leading to purple hills. A breeze brushed a scent of roses and cut grass towards them.

'You must be tired after all that horse riding this afternoon.'

'A little,' John replied. 'And a bit stiff in places I didn't expect to be, especially when one is not used to it.'

'I am past that kind of thing.' He smiled and crossed his legs. 'I'd prefer to talk to my favourite pets in here, and leave the horses to the girls. They really love it.'

John laughed. 'Don't I know?'

'My favourite time of day.' Gustav's eyes rested on the display of warm colours. 'And this is my favourite place to sit and think.'

'I can see I'm in good company.'

'The day is not yet over, but one's work is done. Eyes are rested from the harshness of a dazzling sun—and those dazzling papers you keep sending me—yet we have all this drama of farewell. You know, John. I have been a lucky man.' Gustav gazed thoughtfully over the rose garden.

Many colleagues had suffered serious illnesses, some long drawn out with permanent disability. Others died before their time. Yet others sank into bitterness and senility. Here one was surrounded by comfort and beauty. He had no regrets, no resentments. They were foreign to his nature and a waste of time. Although he had some years left in academia he looked forward to retirement and, if things were right, perhaps early retirement. He could afford it. Certainly. No problems there. But having worked so hard, and loved it, he was anxious to leave it in capable hands. He could spend time in horticulture with friends and other interests.

'Although, I should tell you,' he looked straight at John, 'there are times when sleep is slow in coming. I think of poverty around us and a disturbing thought recurs: Why me, why all this? Why not others? There is no answer I therefore wonder if it will only be revealed to me on the other side of eternity.'

John sat through this in silence, listening attentively. Isselherg never had the time or inclination to confide in hospital. There, it was a different world. Why was he being frank and open, even sentimental, now?

'You know, my dear John, this is a wonderful place to unwind, see the world from a different perspective and get the dust and grime of the laboratory and library out of your lungs. I think I know what you are wondering,' Gustav continued quietly, 'why am I telling you all this? I do not really know myself. Maybe, it is an attempt to give advice to a young man that I, and my family, want to give. Even though it may not have been asked for.'

He uncrossed his legs and bent forward, as if he did not wish any one else to hear him.

'The greatest blessing in my life has been Rachel. She has stood by me, supported me and, indeed, rescued me from some awful experiences. What I am saying, John, is a good woman in one's life is the greatest gift a man could ever have.'

'And your daughters are a credit to you both. Each one is charming and has inherited beauty from her mother.'

'And some of my faults too. Outspoken I mean.' He gave a short laugh.

'No. I didn't say that.'

A bell sounded in the distance. It was time for dinner, and they'd have to appear at their places soon or there would be trouble.

Chapter 16

Gustav Isselherg was master of ceremonies on Easter Sunday. He decided John was a Catholic, being from Ireland and all that. The household, dressed in superb refinement, paraded to the front of the local church for morning mass. Heads turned and whispers spread when John was seen.

After lunch Karita invited him to the library. Tomorrow was his last day and she wanted to show him her writings.

'Dr John thanks for sparing your time,' she said as they entered the library.

The table was covered with books, manuscripts and a large ancient hourglass, which measured time with golden sand. He was intrigued.

'I have always been fascinated by time,' she said.

She watched him handle the instrument. 'I love to stare at the sand, as it flows it sets off my imagination; sometimes the grains move slowly, especially at the beginning and then miraculously they gain speed flowing faster and faster.'

He smiled. 'A lovely way to express it. You could write a poem about it.'

'I already have,' she said impatiently as she rummaged through papers. 'Perhaps later. What I want to show you is this.'

Sitting with the sunrays coming in great bright flares behind her, he realized how beautiful she was. A bacchanal with lustrous golden hair, which she tossed exaggeratedly when she wished to emphasise a point, her black eyes shining daringly at him, her white teeth, perfect and glistening with laughter and rimmed by attractive lips.

He only stopped staring when she handed him a ten-paged manuscript with the title '*The Journey*' written in Swedish at the top.

'I wrote this before you came and will try to finish it this weekend.'

Flicking through the pages he felt overcome.

'Karita. It's all in Swedish. I'd be lost. You'll have to explain it to me.'

'That is what I want to do,' she announced calmly, 'and please, please tell me if there are any mistakes or blunders in it. Promise?'

A smile dawned on his face. 'Why me?'

'Because it concerns a different time. As a teenager I became obsessed with the idea of time, extending out to it was like reaching to gather freedom. Future and freedom were the same to me. I suppose it was a longing to grow up, to mature, to be self-reliant and independent.'

She turned the hourglass upside down so that time with him would flow slowly to begin with; and then speed up.

'I hate it when the sand stops flowing. It is horrible. It's like an end to something, a passing even a death.' There was an air of sadness, of longing.

'You surely have a vivid imagination.' He looked at the crude instrument and tried to reassure her. 'It's flowing very nicely at present.'

'It is. If only it would stay like that forever. This would be my wish.'

He coughed gently and pointed to the manuscript.

'And now for your new poem.'

Her thoughts jerked back to the present.

'I nearly forgot.'

The emptiness in the room was all too apparent.

'It takes the form of an epic story in the western part of your country. The time is long ago when wild animals roamed through forests and around lakes. People lived in groups for protection and there was a powerful leader who lived in a great castle. He had a daughter who was imprisoned in the castle and she was very unhappy.'

'Stop there Karita. Why was she unhappy?'

She looked into the distance. 'Because she had no one to love her, and time was flowing past with ever increasing speed. Time was her enemy. She wanted to change it; make it faster or to stop it altogether; either would be less painful than the torment of static time—everything remaining the same forever.'

'How did she cope then?'

'She escaped into a kind of illness where the future was no longer acceptable, to recoil into a dark world of nothing and nobody. This state of suspended animation seemed to last an eternity. The sand had stopped for her, there was no meaning or purpose left.'

'Oh dear,' John sighed, 'this is all very sad. How did it end?'

Impulsively she put the manuscript down and appealed to him

for help.

'That is just the problem Dr John. The story has not yet finished. And I do not know where it will go from here.' She hesitated and looked at him with bright shining eyes. 'Any suggestions?'

He tried to think of an answer. 'It strikes me this poor girl needs to be rescued by somebody, preferably a strong young man, her own age of course, and she should be taken away, cared for and cherished because time is so precious. It's been terribly wasted so far. After all time is life, without it we don't exist. Now what does that really mean? I'm beginning to get confused.'

He hesitated and broke off, difficult in finding the right words.

'We, ourselves, are just like your character,' he said. 'You and I know people, some we've loved, and others we've despised. But we should not live in the past only. The present is always important and, from a solid base, we can plan the future.'

'My father was right. You are so intelligent.'

He shook his head, worried by factors, and a sense of guilt, he dare not reveal.

'Karita don't expect too much. There are times when I feel useless.'

She looked at him with tenderness and shuddered.

'That is untrue. I am sure you give far more than you are aware. I just feel it. A woman knows these things instinctively. That is why you are so precious to me. And you have given me the perfect ending to my story.'

Karita had been sheltered and protected all her young life, by a stream of caring and careful nannies, tutors, guardians, nuns and above all, loving and wealthy parents; and she shared in the privileges and traditions of her class. But, there was a price to pay, that price was a sense of responsibility.

He felt she hadn't achieved it fully; perhaps, the privileges may have prevented her reaching maturity, of being able to stand on her own two feet and make up her mind on matters important to her. She was still a girl-women, still vulnerable, still suggestible, and still searching for her prince who would appear from nowhere. Then there would be no more striving, no more elation born of expectancy. Girls like her were on this roller coaster of high tension, plunging down to despair, all the time.

Perhaps, the solution lay in the ending of the epic poem.

Her own salvation, he told her, in all this confusion and indecision, would be to make a good marriage with a compatible young man of her own background, whose prime concern would be her happiness, which she could and must return in full. She should also remember the final account of love was not always settled in the gift and giving of the flesh. There was far more to be jealously guarded and treasured.

She looked at the hourglass. It had stopped flowing. He watched as she gently stroked the smooth glass of the instrument with discovering fingers, in the same way she might fondle a pet. She took pleasure in the intimacy of things. How caring and loving she must be with living creatures.

She bent and gently kissed him on the cheek.

He spoke with difficulty and mumbled some regrets. She'd finished her story and it was hard for him to find the words to say goodbye. There had been a thrill, an electricity in the air that was both challenging and exhilarating.

She was determined to leave him alone now. Maybe, women know when enough is enough, so a certain longing, if that is there at all, be magnified by a sudden absence. Maybe, it was a trick that women learn to play when they're young to keep a man dangling, and hopefully hungry for more of the same or something more intense.

'I must go now. But you have made me so happy, now that I know where the story goes,' she said seriously, almost as if she believed it to be true. 'I must go to my room and finish writing. Please excuse me.' As she turned to go she blew him another kiss from the palm of her hand and he pretended to catch it in both hands.

As she left him sitting in the library, she wore a gentle smile and her eyes were sparkling. He had just solved her problems; he was so clever, and so attentive to her requirements. This was wonderful, she never had experienced anyone like this before, exciting her, arousing her, helping her on the next stage of expectation. He must continue, if life is to go on, if time is to go on and allow the sand to flow forever.

The last day came and Karita made herself chief coordinator of John's movements. Yet he appeared to be unaware of this. She had decided they would go on horse back to a remote area beside the lake. He was a little more worried when he discovered that it had already been decided, *en famile*, that Karita and John would spend the day together around the forests and lakes on their own. They also had the rowing boats available if necessary. What could be more natural?

As planned they set out on their daylong adventure. Soon his fate would be sealed; the time was fast approaching for this to happen. Today, all he wanted was to enjoy himself, and especially enjoy the exquisite company of Karita, who seemed so eager to respond to his every whim.

So Karita and John went out riding for the remainder of the day.

CHAPTER 17

John Nicholson's work flourished. A significant number of tests showed no adverse response to chlor 10-6A; however a few reacted to small amounts and no explanation was found. He discussed the problems with Isselherg one evening.

'You have to find out why,' Isselherg insisted. 'How about the conjugate?'

'We're trying but—but we're faced with the same problem,' he answered flatly. 'Anaphylactic shock occurs with the smallest dose and cannot be controlled.'

Isselherg's face brightened. 'Have you discussed the situation with the radiotherapists? Radiotherapy can be a very useful adjunct.'

'I have at length. Why do you ask?'

'I understand you are a frequent visitor.'

John was embarrassed.

'Please do not worry, my friend,' Isselherg said putting his hand on his shoulder and smiling benevolently. 'Dr Lindstrom is a delightful person and has the makings of a brilliant scientist.'

John accepted Linda's invitation to visit the Lindstrom home. With uneasiness he travelled to Velkonstad by train and arrived in the early evening. She waited at the station and threw her arms around him as he stepped down to the platform.

'How was your journey?' She asked eventually releasing him.

'Fine.' He was a little guarded. 'Lovely scenery around here.'

'I think it is.'

They drove directly back to the Lindstrom residence on the northern shores of Lake Velkon—a glorious location on the edge of the water. Mrs Lindstrom, eager to welcome him, walked to the car dressed in a brocaded house gown. Abundant hair, gold streaked with grey, was swept back and held with a metal clip. Her hands, adorned with rings, were held out to him. Unsure how to proceed he bent down, took one hand and kissed it, then looked up for approval. This was becoming a habit.

'Perfect. Young man,' she laughed heartily, 'you are just perfect.'

She gave him a bear hug, which broke the ice immediately. A log fire burned in the lounge and he was relieved of coat and case.

'Please be seated John,' Mrs Lindstrom said gesturing towards an armchair. 'My husband is working late tonight and sends his apologies.'

'I look forward to meeting him,' he replied settling in the chair.

'Perhaps you would like to eat when you are ready. Linda has prepared something simple, which we can all have in here.'

'That'd be most welcome.'

'Linda will show you to your room and when you're ready we will return here.'

Linda brought him upstairs to a large bedroom with French doors leading to a balcony. The room was clean and sparkling, and the furniture traditional and comfortable. A medium sized bookcase containing many titles in English that he recognized was placed against a wall. A white door opened into a cream-coloured *en suite*, which was the height of luxury.

As he bathed, washed and shaved his tiredness wore off and replaced by exhilaration. There was so much to explore. He had a short rest before dressing and going downstairs. The talk that went with the meal was like a fencing match between experts. He'd two adversaries to contend with, which was a little unfair.

The meal was an understatement. He counted at least four courses and was beginning to struggle over coffee and cheese. The conversation was more hectic than the meal, a mixture of too much talking, little listening and much laughter. He laughed but was not sure why.

The hall door opened and closed loudly. It was Jens Lindstrom, home at last. He entered the lounge and John attempted to get up,

'Please stay seated and please continue talking,' Mr Lindstrom said solemnly, 'I do not mean to interrupt anything. I just wanted to pour myself a drink.'

They looked at the father with relief on their faces. John sensed a powerful presence even though little was said. When the man entered there was a change in the room. Here was the master of the house and his word reigned supreme. It seemed as if some lights had been reduced by some magical rheostat making everything glow a rosy pink. Mrs Lindstrom's bright humour and frivolity disappeared and Linda took on an aura of guarded correctness. Talk lost its banter and was transformed into a pseudo intellectual mode. John suspected this was a kind of plot practised on the old man, a vague euphoria spoken by them to soften the impact of *Anno Domini.*

That night John read a disturbing story Karita had recommended in a book about traditions and folklore in the Dalarna district. An emphasis on the rights and ceremonies of a people who lived hundreds of years ago. Certain things went on that would make hairs stand on the back of the neck.

He read chapter after chapter and went deeper into the meaning of things, good things, bad things, mischievous things and lots nobody could understand. It was fascinating because it bore a striking relationship to traditions active in the West of Ireland—traditions he was well versed in.

In the small hours he put the book down and sank into a dream sleep. First to come in view was a vast landscape, flat with little vegetation. It looked eerie, cold and uninviting. It was dusk. A full moon and starry sky glowed all around. His vision swept across the plain, as if he was flying in a machine. Some activity was taking place in the centre of the plain; something strange was happening. A small, trim figure was present but he could not make out any details. Moving closer he realized it was Linda, gently swaying and dancing. She was unaware that hooded men were approaching on horseback; they were armed with swords and looked as if they were about to attack. He tried to shout, to warn her of the danger, but his voice was paralysed. At this point he woke in a panic. He stared at the ceiling with the bedside light on for comfort. An exhausted black sleep claimed him for the remaining three hours.

Later, when consciousness returned, he was momentarily puzzled by his surroundings. It was six-thirty—too early to get up. Dawn was breaking with shimmering fingers on the lake and touching a mist on the far shore.

As he lay on the bed, gazing into the past his old friend, self-doubt, came back. Life stretched before him with its ineptitudes and feeble strivings. He realized what was happening between Linda and him. His was no flash in the pan, no road to Damascus. Instead a slow process of a maturing love was developing that he hadn't known before and demands from her that no one had ever made of him. The kissing and embracing were expected of course.

But that was not sufficient; apparently, she was delving deeper, searching for ways to have and hold his heart and inner being. A new and exciting consciousness dictated he must protect this woman and resent the attention others gave her. Determination to succeed in her career and an ability and level headedness to challenge anything that got in her way appealed to him.

She conjured up images he could never dream of—perhaps it was her Dalarna upbringing—and she was like an open fire, which could light up the faces and minds of all present. Yet, there was one wish he had—if only she'd relent on her obvious, controlled scale of affection, and give in to the surge of passion that was beyond it.

There were times when bed was a waste of time. This was one of them. He'd rested enough and there was so much to discover here in Velkonstad, so much that Linda had told him and, he suspected much more she didn't tell him. He crept downstairs and went into the huge lounge, well lit by daylight. Mist on the lake was lifting, unveiling the majesty of Mount Velkon.

He sat in what he guessed was her father's chair and found the surroundings comfortable and peaceful. A noise came from the kitchen. Linda was preparing breakfast. He'd leave her be for the moment.

He was delighted to see her last night, but it was only for a short time and they were not alone, polite conversation was expected, given and adhered to. Now she was in the kitchen, alone. Alone at last. This love business was a complete distraction. He'd no fine words like Karita Isselherg to describe it; hers were exquisite but tortured and difficult to understand in a foreign language. Now he must forget about Karita. That was a folly, and a mistake, and difficult to extract himself from. There was even a time he felt he'd go along and see what was on offer. But that was too much of a temptation, which in turn leads to guilt, remorse and sometimes worse. Now, he was back with Linda, in her house as guest of the family who'd welcomed him openly.

A romantic, who had a way with words, could make it a moment of spiritual renewal, made stronger in its resolution by absence. But not trained in noble words he'd no easy way between tongue's tip and pen's tip. He let his pounding heart and trembling hands settle before he knocked on the kitchen door.

'John darling. Nice to see you again.' She rushed over and hugged him tightly. 'We did not get a chance to talk last night. We were both tired. I hope you had a good sleep.'

'It was great. And what made it more enjoyable I dreamed of you.'

'Lovely. I hope we both had a good time.'

'I must tell you about it sometime.'

'I missed you. I thought you were cross about something, although I can guess what it might be. So I left you alone, because, you see, I was almost afraid of you. I felt you were disappointed in me. If so I am sorry and I do mean it.'

'Linda. Please don't ever be afraid of me. I am not like that. If I'm angry I withdraw, and stay silent hoping the storm will blow over. I hate confrontation; it's not the best way to resolve problems. It always makes them worse.'

'I know. You are so kind and understanding. Now, tell me why did not you call me after we returned?'

'You wanted to be left alone, not rushed. Remember?'

'Oh, John. You must not believe everything a woman tells you.' She teased. 'I may have said something, but I did not mean it. I did not want you to ignore me. I telephoned several times but there was no reply. Nobody knew where you were. We should not do these things to each other. I find it upsetting, even hurtful.'

She noticed a strange look in his eyes. 'I get a feeling something has happened John.' She sounded anxious. 'Can you tell me what it is?'

His prevarication was easier than he thought.

'Nothing happened, Linda. Except that without you I have been a bit foolish. First, there was a night on the town.'

She persisted in asking. 'Alone, on the town?'

'Of course. A meal, a concert and a few drinks. It was only half enjoyable. I was angry and shouldn't have felt that way. Would you forgive me?'

He tried to embrace her, but she drew away. A hint of anger in her voice as she spoke.

'This is what I hoped would not happen John. There is a need for us to change, both of us. We must not let the past come back and threaten us. This is why I suggested we wait and give our affection a chance to grow into something and lasting.'

'You still have this fear of the future?'

'John, I do, provided you understand what makes me so. And another thing, darling John, you must not lie to me. That would introduce mistrust. If there happens to be something you do not want to reach my ears, then keep silent, but do not lie. You will have the same promise from me.'

'Is there anything else on your mind?'

She looked at him inquiringly.

'I still want some time, but not too much, and certainly not a blackout or complete breakdown in communication. I do not know where you were over the Easter vacation. And, in a strange way, I do not want to know. Wherever it was I hope you enjoyed yourself.'

'I certainly enjoyed it. But I am glad things have come back to normal again.'

She smiled, held her arms out for a long embrace. It was reassuring for him. Inside there was remorse, and guilt, but she didn't want to know about it, although she suspected there was something. To seal their commitment she kissed him passionately and he felt he'd been granted a silent absolution. She sent him back to the lounge so that he would not interfere with the preparation of breakfast.

Chapter 18

Everything was meticulous in the large kitchen. Flower prints and hunting scenes decorated the walls. Ropes descended from the ceiling to wooden laths operated by a pulley system and used to dry clothes. Curtains and cushions were yellow and a large pine table rested proudly in the centre of the room.

Linda prepared breakfast. From his position John had an opportunity to study his surroundings and was beginning to wake up. The room was the hub of the house where the action took place. Eye-level cabinets, with soft internal lighting and displaying prized china and rare glass, covered most walls between the pictures. Above, a Dutch dresser contained copper utensils. The cooker was log fired and looked similar to Aga Cookers back home. A gentle roar came from it giving a glow of heat. Two chandeliers, hanging from the ceiling, were the most striking objects. Swedes must love chandeliers. A multiplicity of red and white bulbs produced a sparkling effect.

Now he saw Linda as never before, in her home environment. He was beholden to a phenomenon. She was taller and blonder with a face used to seduce on Scandinavian cruises and her figure was enough to cause a riot.

She drew pictures on the table. 'Weather going to be good for days.'

'That's great. We deserve it after that winter.'

'Do not forget your boots. The going gets rough up there.'

He was puzzled. 'Up where?'

'Up the mountains of course,' she replied with a mischievous laugh. 'John I love climbing. I always have. There is something magical about it. When I was young my father and I climbed all the mountains within reach of Dalarna. And I have never forgotten them.'

'Why do you love them so much? I prefer to look at them.'

'You have not lived until you have conquered the next mountain.'

'Why?' He persisted

'It is difficult to say. But let me try,' she said as she looked across the lake to Mount Velkon. 'I suppose firstly it presents a challenge and I love a challenge. Can I do it or not? That requires judgement. It also requires the will and strength to do it and I am attracted by the magnetism of the highest point.'

'Sounds like a streak of ambition. That could apply to other forms of endeavour. You know to reach the top.'

'John this is a physical thing. The highest point is in front of you; instinctively it challenges you to reach a state of personal awareness, to be above as much space as possible, to see distant horizons invisible from below and not to go any further. You have reached the end of the journey or reached your goal. It is a wonderful feeling. '

'What a way to put it. A lovely concept. You've achieved it

whatever it happens to be. I like that. It must be an exhilarating feeling.'

She laughed with excitement because he understood.

'When you reach the top you know it is the most sensitive place on earth for you at that moment. I remember the last time I climbed Mount Velkon with dada—oh many years ago—he said to me. "Listen carefully Linda. It is only here that we are privileged to hear the huge slow heartbeat of this place." And you know, John, I think I did hear it because I wanted to hear it and I have carried it with me ever since. It has helped me to make a life when I hear it.'

'Today we're going to recapture that feeling and I hope I'll hear that great heartbeat,' he said, 'I'm looking forward to it. You've convinced me it's worthwhile.'

She smiled, linked him lightly and they set off across the lawn.

Outside shadows were shortening. The air was full of fragrance and a musk rose from delphiniums, drooping like hooded monks, on the terrace below the lounge. Dahlias, heavy with crimson, demanded to be seen. They preened themselves in obvious display for their journey though the day; and no matter how much we respect modesty it's completely out of place here!

'Aren't they beautiful?' He asked.

'My father's joy. They are named after Andrea Dahl, a Swedish botanist.'

They passed the honeysuckle, which stopped breathing in the heat and on to the road by the lake. The air sobbed in branches overhead; sunlight splashed through leaves and danced on roses making them flame like startled spectators. They reached the old bridge where water was calm and flowed like silk past yellow fleabane and purple loose strife. The road wound through leafy shade for three miles and gave way to open country. As the day grew, light dazzled from the south and they rested a while. Minutes later cattle appeared around a corner carrying their sound with them.

'There must have been a fair in the village,' she said.

He watched the soft faces, frightened eyes and jerking heads that only thought of wayside grass to the annoyance of the boy and his dog. The procession disappeared leaving a silence after it. The road became a path as they walked with their shadows following.

Then came the climb, gradual at first; the way became steeper, more precipitous. On they went, higher and higher. Streams became agitated and mountain avens huddled together in clumps for protection from the still remembered winter. Onwards and upwards. He was enjoying life as never before. Exhilaration was everywhere. The wind grew in strength, playing with sunshine and producing shadows from the next boulder, rock face and cliff. Up they climbed, to where everything was moulded by nature alone. As they climbed into a wilder solitude, cloud shadows raced downwards. They reached a pass, drenched in that mystery common to all high places where sky and earth almost touch each other.

Below pine trees bristled; in front earth and rock became exposed, more naked. He loved it; the light and unfolding earth revealing views invisible before, stupendous rocks and frenzied water falling downwards, with utter compulsion, never stopping. He was also aware of Linda's magnetism, her exquisite movements, her voice and outstretched hand whispering messages into the deepest parts of his being.

At last they reached the summit of Mount Velhon. It was here the eyes of fate gazed on them, a place where one could feel the interval between minutes. Almost out of breath he embraced her tightly and completely. With only the living rock as witness he poured out words.

'Linda. I love you.'

She moved closer. The swirl of her body scent and the closeness of her animal heat combined to form a heady, almost overpowering mixture.

'I wish this could last forever,' he continued.

She remained silent as the seconds throbbed. Waves of emotion gripped him, echoing and re-echoing. Minutes passed. She was silent, her face pressed hard against his shoulder.

Eventually obsession became too much.

'Linda will you marry me?'

She flung herself closer.

'Of course I will, slow coach,' she mumbled. 'I thought you would never ask.'

Overpowered by each other's presence they remained thus and he told her in many ways, most eloquently without words, how he felt.

When they returned to the old bridge the wind was tired and daylight dissolved into dusk, the lake prepared for darkness and small things of the wood crowded on the edge of night. They collapsed into the garden seat.

'This is a precious moment.' He said slowly.

All through dinner she was aware of his presence that was so attractive, so opposite; the gesture to the hair, the distant look, the sadness as he appeared not to listen to her words, only to her voice. Afterwards she suggested a stroll in the garden.

As they opened the lounge doors the night retreated and its coolness bathed their faces. They walked towards the water. She became aware in some deep well of folk memory that they had company not far away.

'This place is full of ghosts tonight,' she whispered, linking him tightly. 'And you can see their shapes all around if you look carefully.'

As their eyes adjusted to the dusk they saw blue shadows filling the hollows on the hills, similar to mountains in Kerry rushing down to the sea. As in all lonely places locals believe in ghosts and things not of this world that had a way of making one look backwards.

As they reached the water's edge, there was a silence, golden at sunset, a suspended elation in the air that was almost palpable. No bird song, no movement from small creatures; only clouds changing colour slowly, waiting for something extraordinary to happen, maybe a return of ancient gods.

Sadness grew in the silence around them, in the hills and sky, emanating from the roots of this land's consciousness. Strange stones, like sleeping men, were lying in the half-light, and at any moment they might move up, gather together and march towards them with some dreadful intent. Even trees sighed a message of warning as wind passed through their branches. A church bell rang out in a village. Standing close together, alone, they looked at the pagan symbols.

But not for long.

'Linda. Time to go inside. It's too dark and getting cold. We'll leave all these folk out here to get on with their business. We must have our rest because tomorrow is another day.'

She felt time belonged to her—inevitably. It was alive and rich with pageantry; the book of minor chords was modulating to a life of sensuous major harmonies.

Later, in bed she travelled again through her day; the sun-splashed lake, windswept trees, scented fields awash with colour—

all images she jealously guarded in her scrapbook of life. And John with her. How could she think of anything else or worry now as she floated on the fringe of time? Yes, pain, loneliness and sorrow do occur, but not in this place where the landscape was engraved in her forever. And even though her journey in this house was drawing to a close she had an overwhelming sense of coming home.

When glistening shadows changed places in the corridors of trees, as dew dripped from leaves and stars showed the memory of their time, she drifted into the arms of night.

CHAPTER 19

The Lounge was large and square and about sixteen-feet high, the wooden floor stained a dark oak, walls a pale ochre and woodwork a complementary green. Furniture included an eclectic mixture of sofa, easy chairs and remarkable marble heads, one on the mantelpiece, the other on a mahogany table. Windows extended from ceiling to floor and gave wonderful views of the garden and lake. Jens Lindstrom sat impassively in an armchair by the window.

It is strange how a room can easily assume the character of the person within. The man's brow was furrowed as he stared at the lake, mouth drawn and eyes rimmed in red overflowing with remoteness.

The whole demeanour radiated hostility.

John interrupted the silence. 'The dahlias are magnificent just now.'

The other only nodded acknowledgment.

He wondered how this could be Linda's father and came straight to the point. 'Mr Lindstrom I've asked Linda to marry me.'

Jens Lindstrom looked at him as if he were far away. John trembled under the glare. The old man struggled to quell emotion, crushing any appearance of disturbance, right down to the bare, cold barrenness of the human male, unyielding with nothing to give. Words were not necessary to convey his animosity; they could even be a hindrance.

Each sat, in the room, miles apart. A knot came into the older man's throat. His voice was slow and deliberate. 'I disapprove.'

'But why?'

'The reason is simple,' Mr Lindstrom said flatly, 'you are not of our religion.'

'I'm a Christian and always have been,' he said firmly chastened, though not silenced, determined to go on.

Jens Lindstrom turned on him angrily.

'Yes, but you are Catholic.'

John's calm exterior abandoned him and he blazed back. 'Is that really important? I love your daughter.'

Jens Lindstrom's voice was full of invective. 'It is important. Most important.' There was no flicker of emotion in the tired old eyes. 'One's religion is the most important thing in the world.'

'But.' John looked at the man in shocked surprise as he tried to object. His way was blocked.

'I have brought my daughter up in our religion,' the other interrupted, 'the religion I was brought up in and which I cherish above all else.'

John felt a rising passion and his head throbbed. Previously, he'd judged this man as living in a shadow, overcome by domestic worries, a man standing aside in a cold existence, almost haunting the house rather than living in it. Now suppression was swept aside, revealing an implacable being rigid with tradition and immediately Northern Ireland came to mind.

The difference between them was immeasurable. He'd thrust out his hand, only to have the gate of prejudice slammed against him. Religion could be a fog of misunderstanding in which everyone became separated in feeling and isolated in fear. Already it had strangled Jens Lindstrom, filling his mind yet emptying it. In spite of the man's enmity John had a sense of pity.

He struggled for words. 'I would argue.'

'I do not wish to argue,' the other interrupted, 'there is no argument. You will not have my blessing.'

The man was totally resistant. John couldn't understand the rejection, his whole future. Resentment welled up. 'I cannot accept what you say Mr Lindstrom.'

Jens Lindstrom raised a hand; then let it fall to his side. A long silence followed. Cold eyes surveyed John from head to toe as if viewing some lesser being. Thin lips parted and the words uttered were deliberate and meant to hurt.

'Then you must leave my house. Nothing would please me more.'

'If that's your wish. I will go.'

Torment was tearing John apart. Consternation in the kitchen. Everyone knew Jens Lindstrom's word was final. Tears, recriminations and denials flowed. There was a train for Stockholm later that day.

Linda said impulsively. 'Never mind. I come with you.'

'Perhaps in a day or two.'

'But, *alskling*, darling I will die without you.'

She collapsed into a chair.

'Don't worry, ' he said trying to soothe her. 'It'll be just a few days.'

Mrs Lindstrom silently put her arm around her daughter drawing her close, and stroking the blonde hair as she'd done many times.

Linda drove him to the station. Standing high above the church had a strange sinister appearance as it looked down from darkness on darkness. The dim and mysterious image brought back fears and recriminations. It rose like a silent monster made of stone, wondering when to point a finger at a passer by. A layer of reflecting cloud rolled back revealing a sharp narrow spire extending into the endless blackness.

John's mouth was closed and eyes watchful as he waved to Linda with a kindly gesture of parting and promise. Slowly the train moved forward, gathered speed and transported him from Mora scorning all stations—there was an urgency to escape from the incomprehensible.

Now things looked bad, very bad. Nothing could detract from the hurt and indignation Linda felt at her father's treatment of John. And so the emotion of his departure, mumbling assurances that things would eventually work out, was not realistic. He had no idea how iron fisted her father could be; and this caused the wound that had pierced her heart, to go deeper than ever. Liberty in the Lindstrom home was at a standstill and a mockery.

That night she was inconsolable and cried herself to sleep. She woke before dawn. It was very cold. She lay still, wrapped herself tightly in bedclothes, gradually dosed off again, and felt like a woman who had died and passed away. She was beyond hope. During the dark hours, she heard a great crash at the centre of things. Maybe, it was her future, or a crash nearby, which meant something ominous. She was afraid of the coming hours. Would she be able to cope?

Next day was empty. There was nothing and she did not want to do anything. She was even afraid of the coming night. Yet, she was a passionate being, someone to be afraid of, with a character far stronger than her mother. She was proud and inwardly violent.

Mrs Lindstrom tried to be optimistic, to look on the bright side. She prepared tea for Linda and sat quietly with her. Her daughter had a rare beauty and she was so proud of her. She admired the flawless complexion, delicate arched nose, rich golden hair, and the exquisite large china-blue eyes, now bloodshot from crying.

She tried to console her daughter. Both knew it was serious, very serious. Jens Lindstrom had been implacable in the past, and always it had been impossible to change his mind once made up.

Mrs Lindstrom did not know what was going to be the outcome, but she felt, deep down, there was something radical, something serious about to happen. But goodness knows what! Silently she looked at her daughter, her brilliant and determined daughter, who was at this moment so miserable, with a look of fatal despair.

CHAPTER 20

Blank pages stared at John Nicholson as a wintry day visited Stockholm in summer. Beside him a waste-bin overflowed and a microscope was empty of vision, a beta-counter trembled, an incubator slept cold and sterile and a clock ticked with unnatural tenseness.

Linda's photograph was the sole object of sympathy. She'd telephoned to say she could not get away as her father had suddenly been taken ill and there was no one to look after him. John would understand. She would certainly keep in touch and he was not to worry. Yet, her voice came over a distance not measured in miles.

He sat pretending to read. It was useless. Instead, with slow torture the interview in the lounge in Mora returned. Perhaps Jens Lindstrom was right, seeing him as a danger, a menace to his daughter and future generations.

How was she feeling at this moment? Always he'd been gentle and respectful with people, especially his superiors—that, of course, included Jens Lindstrom. Yet, he couldn't forget the silent hostility. Every word was meant to hurt and insult.

He'd never met such a negative person before; there seemed no way out. He couldn't forget the cold stare from those eyes that had the shrewdness of a thousand years in them. Jens Lindstrom was surely a man of the past, living in the present.

Spending a night with only rejection for company was unbearable. He sat in the laboratory motionless, unable to work, to think clearly, all drive and energy gone, drifting aimlessly in a becalmed sea. Jens Lindstrom's rejection was a blow to his confidence and could prevent him obtaining Linda's hand—ever. The rigid laws of parental control in this alien country were hard to understand and accept. It was characteristic of people living in rural areas for decades and city folk could be more tolerant.

Come evening he still felt abandoned; his present world was seen in the fragments of a broken mirror. There was no purpose, no future seen clearly, only confusion and negativity.

Rather than retire to his room, he got up, shaved, showered and dressed for a bachelor's evening. He knew several places in town and headed for one. As he was early he got a booth in a quiet corner of the club, away from the line of fire of the band and sheltered from the hallucinogenic flicker of strobe lights.

Champagne was delivered and one of the house girls asked if he needed company for a while. Perhaps later. Dark surroundings, music, the atmosphere and glamorous guests weaved their tenuous gossamer. Early on, they were background props that one could take or leave; but once the web was woven, in a place like this, he could be caught or seduced like a fly in a web.

After an hour, the old shop magic began to work especially when the same house girl returned and almost invited herself to sit with him in the shaded booth. It was make up your mind time. Was it to be an early night or, perhaps, a very late one? He remembered his father's saying nothing good ever happens after midnight and listened again.

He woke late next morning. It was Saturday and, thankfully no work today.

His head throbbed, mouth tasted like stale fish and eyes full of sand. There was nothing wrong with his hearing because a phone screamed beside him making his headache worse. When he found the instrument his answer was less than cordial. It was Isselherg. Could he see John for an emergency meeting that evening? Recent developments were of grave importance, and he wished to have discussions with members of staff, including John.

That evening, darkness rose from the earth clinging to trees standing like statues along the driveway from the Institute. He walked past them and into the busy street outside. It's remarkable what we don't see walking along the pavement. What one may read in a face, truth—if only we looked?

A swarm of girls passed carrying the excitement of the night, followed by a host of brollies taking some home to passion and struggle, still others clutching their collars reluctant to return. Then the underground where people in a jam of non-communication, glowed with importance and exuded a loathing of their neighbour. Approaching Isselherg's Department he sensed mood and doom mirrored one another.

And he was to discover that a new virus had been born into the world.

Chapter 21

Dawn threw itself across the lake and Mount Velhon; slowly dissolving shadows everywhere. A lonely cry came from the steamer as it cut its way to church leaving waves whispering to shore. This Sunday Jens Lindstrom was not on board, the first time for many years. He was too ill. Wreathed in silence he sat unaware of colours pouring into the lounge. Instead, he stared into empty space witnessing something drifting away, something deeply precious and was helpless to prevent it.

Doctors advised complete rest after his collapse. The old trouble had come back and tests confirmed it was serious, very serious. The pain had been getting worse, at times overpowering. Always lurking in darkness it would surface and fling itself at him. Then it would be quiet, always watching and waiting, but he knew it would return like a beast of prey. Gradually it absorbed him, twisting his body and his mind. He fought it in those secret places where he stored his strength, thoughts and fears. Eating was difficult and he became weaker. Surprisingly, his daughter knew what had to be done. She understood what he was going through and took charge.

He remembered her as a child, both shy and wild. Totally miserable she was, when people treated her with contempt. Console herself she would with music and became good at it. Few friends she had because, always, he had to censor and approve them. She had to be protected from the evil in the world—there was so much of it. And she was stubborn, which made it more difficult. Surprisingly, she was now proving herself a tower of strength. And he had never realized.

Visits from the lurking monster became more frequent, those of his wife less. Eve Lindstrom was overwhelmed by his dissolution; she could not bear the anguish tearing him apart and almost felt it happening to herself. She recoiled and lost her grip on daily life.

As for Linda she did her best. Each day she sat for hours seeing him get thinner and weaker. She suffered his pain and shared the torture that gnawed the life out of him, and she fought it with encouragement and painkillers. At times he rallied. For him she laughed and he heard the sound of tears. He pretended he was getting better and she went along with duplicity.

Also Linda had strange dreams during the times she was able to sleep while nursing him. One evening, before the end, she dreamed it was snowing, and for some illogical reason it was falling through the bedroom roof. It fell with great gentleness, but she was helpless to stop it. It was going to cover her all over; she was going to be buried alive under it and it was terrifying.

Then she woke shivering with cold.

The last time she spent with him he was exhausted. Consciousness was intermittent. The morning was grey and reflected the colour of his face. She sat erect, hand in hand, each on the edge of departure to different horizons.

He tried to speak. Then for no reason the sound of his voice cracked like melting ice. 'My blessing you have, Linda.'

And he was gone. She trembled as if a cold wind blew on her face. Then a collapse gripped her and she was afraid, totally afraid and alone.

She threw herself across her father and cried with complete abandon.

Autumn is a time of reckoning as nature takes stock; morning drags its heels, the land fades and mists linger in woods and hills. From a window of the train John saw how it had swept over the land blazing through valleys and mountains, stripping all that was perishable and uncovering the nakedness of winter. Awesome was this conflagration as he returned for the funeral of Jens Lindstrom. In places winter had almost arrived, adding to his uneasiness. Flat fields were ploughed with grey earth that looked as if they were full of the clay of dead men. Skeletal trees stood sentinel around fields and alongside the roads.

As the journey progressed thoughts revolved like a prayer wheel. After his ordeal with Jens Lindstrom it was difficult to think of anything more testing than sitting patiently in the train, waiting for an unknown reception, as the distance to Velkonstad lessened. With the heat of the train he dozed off, and experienced a strange unreality. The happiness with Linda was faded, and everything was artificial, insincere.

Linda was waiting as he stepped to the station platform. His face had conflicting emotions, delight, surprise and a touch of horror at how she had changed. She was thinner and paler and seemed to have lost something; there was pain in that crumpled face making it a mask. She'd suffered greatly and was now in the throws of delayed shock.

As they hugged she cried a little. They were two people alone together, who'd undergone dreadful uncertainties. She was first to break the silence and gave a odd smile. Her face was thin and sallow and her nose red from the cold. For a moment, her sad eyes softened with humility that makes a man feel on top of the world.

They stood on the platform for ages; almost all the other passengers had gone. Initially, she looked everywhere but at him. She then looked at him, and straight into his eyes, so that he'd to blink several times and turn away. She searched for something deep inside and her stare was too close for comfort. Then with enormous, trustful submission she stood on her toes and kissed him deeply. She liked what she saw.

They decided to bury Jens Lindstrom in the island graveyard overlooking the lake; it was his last wish and the service would be held in the thirteenth century church in Mora. As John entered the building he shuddered at the gloom. Stillness followed the clanging of the congregation and compelled him to think of the man who was no more. Although contempt still clung he was also ashamed.

The pastor's words began to take on meaning as they echoed through the silence. This man, Jens Lindstrom—he said in ringing tones—had started life here in Mora from humble beginnings. His dedication to the community was never exhausted and he had a complete conviction that what he did was right. He was an inspiration to others who may, at times, have doubted and was unlike many who only lived on the capital of their energy and drifted along, without aim or purpose, leading nowhere. Often he spoke about the cataclysmic wasteland of the world about him, much of which had proved correct. Those who did not listen or refused his advice were now reaping their reward. The pastor finished in a resonant voice.

'He brandished words to great effect which now cling to the hearts of many. We all know the stronger the light the clearer the shadow. His words shone with ultimate truth, and with surgical precision they laid bare the terrifying consequences of evil.'

He bowed his head. 'Now his shadow is no longer present. Now he lies in its place. But he is better off in that glorious world beyond the sun where he always was aware of his continuation with the utmost certainty.'

'Let us pray for him so that he may pray for us.'

Immediately everyone knelt.

These were inspiring words about a man John never knew and wished he had. He looked around. Eve Lindstrom, nodding several times during the eulogy, managed to whisper. 'He was so good.'

Linda was not weeping, only tears flowed unhindered as the cortege passed the old house and on to the steamer for the final journey to the island. Mourners, some standing others resting on wooden seats, were silent as they gazed at the moving water. The pastor sat reading in comfort and seclusion in the cabin, the space of his book warmer than the wintry outside. All were conscious of the homeward journey of a soul sliding away; now nothing to do but arrive.

Linda was entranced by the wake following the boat, slipping from white into distant green. Since our life and the living of it is as mysterious at its end as its beginning she was acutely aware of the occasion. There's nothing as awesome as the fire of autumn sweeping through the great forests, stripping trees until they stand abject and naked before the reckoning of the Swedish winter. The ancient ritual of fire removes all that is temporary and perishable from the spent life so that which is true and lasting will accompany the spirit on the journey to whatever might lie beyond the here and now.

The motion of the water disturbed her but as soon as they landed the feeling vanished and the solid earth calmed her. Here it was safe. Six men walked cautiously with their glistening burden and high on the hill an open grave waited. It had a fine view.

The whispering crowd collected around the lowered coffin. Wreaths, made from flowers the dead man loved, were placed beside it. All around the sun dripped like melting crystal from leaves whose agitation was growing in the breeze and the morning dazzle almost hurt.

The graveside ceremony, conducted by the pastor, was a sad one. The mourners, some silent and others quietly whispering, watched the final stages of this man's journey. He'd reached his resting place, a place chosen carefully for his own reasons. It was not hard to guess what they were.

John stood beside Linda, her mother and close relatives. The eulogy was just as inspiring as in the church and gave consolation to those who had loved him; it was also a strong panegyric for those who never knew him. John watched as events unfolded, his eyes hidden by sunglasses. Mrs Lindstrom wept quietly. As the ornate coffin slowly descended into earth his eyes closed holding back tears. He now belonged as he stood with Linda and her mother for the final prayers. Suddenly an overpowering fragrance rose from the flowers that rested on the filled grave.

Funerals are sad affairs and this brought back the death of his mother. She died unexpectedly two days before Christmas when he was twenty-four. Home for the holiday having attended a concert—a performance of The Messiah by Handel—in Galway he was late getting home. She waited up for him, most unusual as she normally retired early. She wanted to hear all about the concert, who was there, and did he meet anyone interesting? She would love to have been there, living up to her spirit of adventure. Perhaps, she suspected he'd an interesting companion. The audience was great, the concert was great, lots of people there; but that was all. Her questions got nowhere, so finally she agreed to retire and climbed the stairs with difficulty. He tried to help. She resisted.

'No John. I don't need help anymore. Your energy will be required elsewhere.'

At eight o'clock next morning she was found dead in bed.

A lump of earth hit the lid of the coffin. Then the quiet rumble of sound as the mourners moved away, coupled with the sharp scrape of shovels gathering clay.

That evening Linda spoke about her father. Around *Velkonstad* Jens Lindstrom always felt in the presence of a great mystery. Mountains, trees and flowers were not merely isolated signs to him, but were the purest expression of God's thoughts, the closest to his act of creation. More wonderful than anything man had ever achieved and could give a consolation beyond measure. Animals he also loved, but believed they were already one step away from that which made them, and one step towards the exile of man.

CHAPTER 22

Linda took John to see Pastor Jacobson, who lived in a rambling building beside the river and not far from the church in Mora. The pastor, in his mid-forties with hair the colour of ripe corn, was a good friend of the Lindstroms.

They were shown into a simply furnished room, yet with all the comforts a man would need. The pastor entered dressed in clerical regalia from thatch to toe. Confidence in himself was his main characteristic, which contrasted with a boredom of things around him. Also as a writer he had written three novels, but found it difficult to interest a publisher. His manner was ritualistic and dramatic; he was smitten with the idea of God, and in a condescending way, would even admit he rather liked his neighbour. The sequence of the marriage ceremony was no problem at all.

It rained with enthusiasm the day before the wedding; hour after hour it came down in sheets drenching towns, villages and farms making them look pathetic. Towards evening it eased, leaving an unearthly afterglow on lakes and hills and a vivid green on the landscape.

As light was drawn out of the sky stars appeared over the Lindstrom home where Linda, her mother and friends prepared for the big day. The traditions of Mora and Dalarna were rooted in her. A kinship, a sense of belonging to something infinitely good and lasting, of possessing and being possessed by Svealand where Sweden was born. Everything was about to change.

The following day was clear and full of expectation. The river went gossiping past meadowsweet on its banks, sun poured light through woods and caused cloud shadows over the hills. A breeze entered the church and touched the wooden rafters. Silken banners, flowers and ribbons decorated pews where guests were assembling, some talking, others gazing from the privileged harbour of old age. Organ music filled the air and the minds of those who let it, and on the alter masses of candles burned brightly.

The groom sat patiently on the first seat staring in front of him with many competing thoughts. He was instructed by the pastor with the corn coloured hair to sit, and wait, and do nothing else whatsoever. Days of worry, nights without sleep, irregular meals, culminating in an emotional crisis, left him a stranger to serenity. Yet, these arrangements helped shield him from stabs of memory.

Although not entirely. He remembered his aunt's rejection of marriage on religious grounds; she'd lived to regret it. Jens Lindstrom's word was all-powerful and when he said no, it meant no! Everyone would have to obey his command. If Linda had gone against his wishes she was sure to be an outcast and disinherited from the Lindstrom's business, which was not inconsiderable. What changed Jens' mind, when he relented and gave his blessing? Was it a deathbed conversion and hatred had no place in religion?

Perhaps, to clear the decks of all doubts. On his mind, not wanting to leave forgiveness unresolved. To do the right thing and die in peace.

The pastor stood at the alter watching, motionless. His personality compelled admiration. Garlanded in ribbons a white Rolls drove to the entrance and people whispered as the door opened. Linda's uncle, stern and upright, emerged first and extended a hand. A frothing of satin and lace preceded a blonde head crowned with flowers and a foot reached down to a red carpet. Commotion went through the crowd as the bride, veil trembling, climbed the steps. Suddenly music blared out commanding all to stand and Linda appeared before John more radiant than ever. As the pastor cleared his throat a silence moved swiftly through the congregation. Placing large hands on the lectern he steadied himself and started the sermon. Splendid words thundered forth as if the Almighty himself was speaking. Then a priest—a friend of John's—assisted in the ceremony itself.

Great jubilation there was afterwards and the air shook with ringing bells. Linda, complete on the arm of her husband, posed for photographs and more photographs. The hotel reception was packed with women wandering in happy confusion, the older living in memories, younger demurely hoping. Men discussed serious matters pretending not to notice. Groups assembled, waiters moved obsequiously forward with wine lists bound in red leather, women with hats and flowing gowns swept imperiously to their allotted places conscious they were been observed and glad of it. And children in enchanting clothes longing to runabout were nailed to their places by the eyes of watchful mothers. Afterwards friends went to Arlanda Airport to see the couple off.

CHAPTER 23

John and Linda hired a car in Majorca and drove to Valldemosa. Chopin came here in the late 1830's suffering from tuberculosis. The home he chose had previously been a Carthusian monastery. The musician could hardly have chosen a more beautiful place. A guide invited them into the house that was plainly furnished; one room was exactly as the composer left it. They looked at the piano. No one was allowed touch it but because they were the only visitors the guide said nothing as Linda sat down to play. The Fantasie Impromptu sounded exquisite and the guide kissed her hand as she stood up. He explained the composer had only used it a few times before returning to Paris—to die—as it happened.

They went into the sunlight. Stopping for a moment John took her hands and drew her round to face him. There was an answering pressure.

'I adore Chopin.'

'Do you know much about his life?' He prompted.

'A little. It was tragic.' They chose the shade of an olive tree. 'He was born near Warsaw. Poland was going through one of its periods of suppression. As his talent developed so did his love of country.' She picked up a handful of earth. 'Do you see this John? This could mean nothing or everything to a person. He was torn but was finally persuaded to leave Warsaw and Poland. As he did so his friends gave him a silver casket and he was never parted from it not even in death.'

'What was in it?' He said carefully

She looked down. 'A handful of Polish earth. He died in Paris when he was thirty-nine and his friends scattered the contents over his coffin. They also removed his heart and took it home to Poland. So it ended its long and difficult journey.'

'The passionate pilgrimage of a tormented soul can still be heard in his music.'

'You are being poetic,' she laughed happily. 'I talk too much. Your turn.'

'Don't worry.' He smiled. 'In fact I wrote a poem for you last night.'

'*Kan ni saga mig?* Can I hear it?'

'Let's stroll back along the shore. It's getting late.'

Next day they stopped at the 3000 year-old Bronze Age settlement at *Capocorp Vell* and he couldn't stop her crawling down the winding, pitch black tunnel to the base of the larger tower to see the burial chambers of his ancestors—as she put it—towers were built by North European Celts who were the first prehistoric settlers.

He turned to her. 'Talking about ancestors I think the family one's going to have is more important than the family one's come from.'

'*Alskling*. Darling! We are going to have a family?'

'Some day with the help of God.'

'I want your help John—not his!'

The glamour of evening lay over *Puerto Pollensa*. She wished to retire early and he suggested dinner in their room. Beforehand he insisted on visiting the town alone on a special errand.

Dawn arrived next morning in a noisy cart pulled by a dusty donkey. After breakfast they made for a road south of *Pollensa*. Soon it was siesta time, when heat poured like molten lava over the countryside, and locals disappeared under shelter. The air conditioning in the car was a blessing.

Eventually they reached the Monastery of *Lluch* that also belonged to the weather and sun. *Els Blavets*, the famous boys choir dressed in blue were rehearsing inside. The building was almost empty and Bach's Chorale *Wenn ich einmal soll scheiden* was performed. Sound caressed every corner of the building and sent a glow to the core of Linda's being. It was so beautiful she asked for the words.

'Bach could almost convince me.' She looked at him through moist eyes.

It was a place where an aesthetic could survive, and be happy as they looked forward to entering that other world with their credits for sacrifices, or whatever performance indicators Saint Peter used in assessing suitability of various applicants.

Unusually quiet they were that evening strolling along the beach at *Santa Ponsa*. Eventually he produced a silver pendant and handed it to her. 'Your present.'

With a smile she opened it slowly. Inside was a sheet of paper on which a poem was written in impeccable handwriting with the title:

'The Walk.'

Inside the lid in the same script was. Linda/John.

Chapter 24

The flight from Palma to Rome was at night, a bright starry night when the heavens vibrated with scattered diamonds too numerous to mention. When they struck ground with a thump things changed, stardust became ground dust, the air gritty and dry. John and Linda filed through passport control like lemmings, eventually reaching the central concourse where they were surrounded by a sea of noisy men, women and children.

Neither had been to Rome so the bus trip from the Airport was fascinating. At the station they hired a yellow taxi to the Marini Strand Hotel on the *Via del Tritione* and were shown to a bright pleasant room on the sixth floor.

'What are we going to do now?' She was eager to get going.

'We'll start with a coach tour this afternoon. We're only here for four days.'

The coach took them to the *Piazza Della Repubblica*. The first stop was at the church of St Peter in Chains with the statue of Moses by

Michelangelo. The Colosseum was next.

'*Fantastiskt*. It is huge. Is it not?' She said. 'It takes your breath away.'

'Sure does. Although it's more acceptable as a ruin than what it used to be.' Near the top she gasped at the expanse of the place.

'It must have held a lot of people.'

'Fifty thousand all screaming for blood.'

With instructions from the hotel porter, and a rough map, they made their way on foot that evening to the fabled Augustus Restaurant. Food, music and guests were the only evidence of the present. Everything else was antique: furniture, oil paintings, tapestries, cabinets, silver, stucco work, carpets so precious they hung on walls, great black sofas and armchairs, which would seduce any tired soul with their charms. Soft lights helped them view things in an unearthly glow and high ceilings absorbed the enthusiasm of musicians. In this oasis they could eat and share secrets away from the flurry of the city.

With great ceremony they were shown to their table. Slowly she moved her arms outwards.

'It is wonderful John. Is it not?'

'What do you mean?'

'I mean life. I do not want this moment to stop—ever.'

He looked surprised. 'You mean you wish you were immortal?'

'*Nej*. No. I did not say that.' She frowned in disagreement. 'I know what I want and I think I have found it. That makes me complete. There are many who do not know what to do with the life they have, and long for another, which will go on forever. Not me. I live for here and now and I have you, my *alskling*, all to myself.'

He grinned looking away again. 'You're so contradictory. One moment you want time to stand still and the next you deny immortality.'

She nodded. 'All right then. Can you prove that one is immortal?'

'Countless millions for centuries have believed it.'

'And they also believed the Earth was flat,' she said triumphantly. 'No John, I cannot accept immortality. There is much suffering here and we see more than most. It is better to alleviate misery in this life and not be obsessed with another. Religion is so unjust.'

He felt irritated. 'Why's it unjust?'

'Because it states that the Son of God, who is ultimate perfection, is sacrificed for the guilty. If that is not injustice I do not know what is!'

Next day the catacombs. Those of St Sebastian, which extended over eleven miles, were first and no one was allowed in alone. She asked how it was so many thousands were buried there in a time of terrible persecution and was told they were left alone because Roman law decreed all burial places sacred and inviolable. Pagans were normally cremated.

She felt enormous relief as they emerged into the sunlight.

'I think the worst thing about the catacombs is the darkness,' she said as they returned to the coach, 'I felt I was descending into hell. I was frightened. Terrified!' She trembled as he held her hand.

'Are you all right darling? Your hand's cold. And it's a warm day.'

She did not reply and remained silent on the return journey.

There was a commotion in the lounge when they arrived at the hotel. They sat down for coffee; he suggested she needed it. Beside them two large ladies were discussing in loud voices their day's events. One, known as Jane, was a big, sallow woman, who sported horn-rimmed glasses giving her an appearance of an aggressive cranky owl. Her voice was deep and gravelly and the waving hands revealed brown stained fingers. She continued telling her story to her friend and others felt it was also meant for them.

'Minding my own business I was and enjoying a wonderful lunch,' she said stridently, 'then some young punk shouted—"murderer"—at me and ran away.' She pulled her fur coat tighter around her shoulders. 'Would you believe it? Ran away the cowardly idiot.'

Her friend tried to soothe her. 'You poor thing Jane. I'm so sorry.'

'I've got every right to wear the coat as anyone.' Her voice was getting louder. 'I've worked bloody hard all my life and I deserve it. The punk yells the obscenity at me. Just imagine. And what have I done? Nothing. I tell you, God damn nothing.'

'It's all right Jane. Don't worry.' The companion's efforts made her worse.

Jane took another gulp of wine to calm her nerves. 'And she ran away. To hell with it. I tell you I was livid. No one is going to tell me what I can or cannot wear.'

'You're right,' Penny agreed embarrassed at other people's attention.

'These vegetarians and animal-do-gooders make me sick the way they carry on. They are the most vicious of all. If I could get my hands on that young skunk now, she wouldn't recognize herself for months. They're so vicious.' Another reinforcement of wine was taken to give her strength.

'I agree.' Penny's voice was getting softer.

'I'm normally a quiet person minding my own business but I'll tell you if that young pup comes up to me again, she's going to regret it for the rest of her life.'

John stood up and extended a hand to Linda. 'Come it's time to go.'

Then the lady, called Jane, turned on him still full of aggression.

'An' what are you looking at Buster?'

Her friend Penny tried to intervene. 'Stop Jane. You've said enough.'

'Be quiet Penny.' She glared at John through the horn-rimmed glasses. 'I just asked this guy a question.'

John stood erect staring back in disgust.

'I had my back to you for the last half-hour and was not looking at anything in particular.' He took Linda's hand and continued. 'But now you mention it I can see a lot from here.'

'Whatcha mean by that Buster?'

'Just listen to yourself once in a while.' His voice was slow and deliberate. 'I'm sure it would make a big change.'

'You know something Mister.' She spat out the words. 'You're crazy. Just crazy.'

As John and Linda left the room a loud scream split the air. They looked back to see bowls of mustard and salad cream falling from a passing waiter's tray right onto to the precious fur coat.

CHAPTER 25

On returning to Stockholm John's work made significant progress. Isselherg congratulated him warmly—being doubly pleased it was carried out in the Institute.

'Suppose I was lucky,' he said in spite of his misgivings.

'Nonsense my dear fellow. The more one tries the more one has. I'd like you to come to my office sometime, John. There are some matters I want to discuss with you. I'd like to get your views on future planning and strategies. Things are changing, and changing rapidly in the scientific world.'

'Don't I know! It's a problem keeping up with the literature—growing at an alarming rate.'

'When would suite you?

'Free in half an hour. Would that be all right?'

'Indeed. See you then.'

John headed for the library. Articles on molecular biology, genetics and DNA coding he wanted to get copies of before speaking to

Isselherg. His search, completed in record time, he headed straight for Isselherg's room.

'John. You are a good time keeper as well as everything else.'

Isselherg waved him to a chair beside the table used for seminars and tutorials.

'Would you like coffee to get the brain cells working?'

'Please. Great idea.'

They both grabbed coffee and spread themselves around the large table.

'Firstly John, how was the honeymoon?' Then he raised a hand. 'Before you answer, I want to congratulate you and Linda on making a splendid match. I hope you'll always be as happy as Rachel and me. One thing though, and hope you do not mind me saying this, there was some wishful thinking, even outspoken hopes, that you might fall for one of our girls.'

'Karita's a lovely girl in everyway. And very clever in her language studies. You must be proud of her.'

'Of course we are. She is like a coloured butterfly flitting around, here and there, and not making any real commitments.'

'A beautiful butterfly who should've no difficulty in getting a suitor.'

Gustav smiled at the compliment. 'She should not. But, you know John, she has such high standards and she had her heart set on you. She told us so!'

For a while John remained silent. He didn't have sufficient, or the right words to respond. He let things be.

'To answer your original question, the honeymoon was most enjoyable.'

He told Gustav about Majorca and Rome. He recalled the lady Jane, her fur coat and all the fuss and nonsense she created. It was not easy to forget because of the verbal attack on his person completely uncalled for.

'That was unfortunate for you and for Linda. It's awful if one is blamed for something one has nothing to do with. Done nothing wrong.' Gustav rubbed his chin. 'What do you think was wrong with her?'

'I don't know. I suspect part of her problem, which she'd never admit, is a guilty conscience. She must know there's a vociferous body of people, some well organized, who abhor killing animals just for cosmetic reasons.'

Gustav was inquisitive. 'Does it improve the image of the wearer John?'

He'd no hesitation in answering. 'Certainly don't think so. On the contrary, it displays an ignorance of a changing world, when compassion should be a top priority in those who care for the global environment and have some responsibility for it.'

'That is quite a speech John.' Gustav laughed. He took a long drink of coffee, reached for pen and paper. 'What you have said, John, brings me round to the subject of our research. As you know we use animal models, which have been very useful in testing chemicals and some dangerous ones too!'

'It's the accepted norm generally. And great progress has been made in the treatment of leukaemia in children.'

'We both agree on that.' Gustav hesitated, doodling with his pen. 'What I am going to say you might find upsetting. For sometime now I have had a distaste using toxic chemicals in animals hoping that one or two may pull through and indicate a good response. Others are rejected. Thrown away as useless. By products. It is not their fault the drug has failed. It is really our fault. Many of these animals have to be destroyed and sticks in my conscience, becoming a bigger issue than it used to be.'

John was amazed to hear this.

Gustav looked away as he continued. 'Science will probably go deeper into molecular biology, genetics and genetic disorders and the structure of nucleic acids, including DNA. This is already receiving attention in the States and Britain. We should be looking into genetic disorders. Maybe, look into a predisposition for cancer. Undoubtedly, some are transmitted genetically, but what are the mechanisms involved? If we could find the rogue gene, then sometime in the future we may be able to eliminate it and prevent cancer from developing in a family where the prevalence is high. This may only be a pipe dream to visualize the future but not to participate in it.'

He put the cup to his lips and took a long drink before continuing.

'So, if I am not going to be able to change direction completely, perhaps, it is up to you and people you train to reap the benefits. For example, would not it be wonderful to obtain a complete genetic print-out of a particular disease or condition? Then your problem is half solved. Go for the defective gene, eliminate it and replace it with a harmless one.'

'Sounds beautifully simple. But think of the technology involved.'

'Nothing is impossible in science John. That is my motto. Believe me I have seen a lot of so called miracles in my time.'

John produced several papers dealing with the subject matter.

'Professor, the future may be nearer than we think. I'd like to write to these people, with your permission, and get more information on setting up genetic experiments and gene probes. The whole world of molecular biology sounds fascinating and may reduce our dependency on animal testing or even eliminate it.'

'We can only hope. But we seem to be one of a kind, you and me. Cruelty is cruelty no matter where you find it.'

Finishing his coffee, he thumped John on the back.

'You know, my dear John, we may be on to something really worthwhile. I think the spur pushing us in this direction has to be a matter of conscience.'

'That's right professor,' John said tapping the table for emphasis. 'You've hit the nail on the head. It's a matter of conscience.'

Chapter 26

Linda was happy to take some weeks off to organize a home. The apartment in Vasterlanggaten would do until they found something bigger. The concept of home was important and she wished it could have been Velkonstad. She discussed her dreams with John.

'What is home Linda?' He asked in his soft voice.

She looked into the distance. 'We can travel far and discover wonders but it is always best to come home. The familiar house and surroundings give me a feeling of home.'

He tried to expand the concept. 'Maybe you're thinking of security instead of opportunity.'

She wished to be provocative. 'All right what about our future? Where will we settle? I suppose we should have discussed this before marriage.'

'I don't know, but we should distinguish between hope and expectation.'

'I do not understand! You speak in riddles.' She sounded

frustrated.

'And the future is obscure,' he said.

'Oh John! That's your pessimism coming out again. The future is always difficult.'

'Again what is home to you?' He persisted.

At last she relented. 'My home will be any four walls that include the right person. That is settled now—so how is the research?'

He evaded her eyes. 'Very well. I'm hoping to finish the thesis soon. It'll probably mean bringing work home. Better than staying late at the Institute.'

'Why not use the old desk.' She pointed to the corner of the room. 'There should be enough room for your papers and things.'

He walked over to it and sat down, trying to imagine a pile of papers on it. 'I've always liked it Linda. It's beautiful.'

'It was a present from my dear mother when I qualified.' She reminded him, her words full of feeling.

Two weeks later a letter arrived from Wainwright. It was hand written.

'My Dear John,

I'm writing to wish you well in your newfound happiness. Professor Isselherg told me of your forthcoming marriage. I was delighted. He told me your wife-to-be was a splendid girl and that you had made a wise match.

'The old fox!' She interrupted.

'Ssh Linda.' He put his finger to his lips.

'I would like to offer advice for what it's worth as one who has experience and trust you will take it in the spirit it is intended. It is this, the secret of a successful marriage is to avoid the unforgivable, and regard domestic crises as incidents and none of the incidents as crises.'

'Now Linda,' he said smiling, 'remember that the next time we have a row?'

'But alskling, darling, we have not had a row except perhaps over art.'

'Let me continue.'

'To change the subject. Since you left several changes have taken place that may surprise you. These were mainly in staff structure. However, it would be wise not to put my views in writing at this stage. What I would like to know is whether you would be interested in returning to Dublin. There is a possibility, and I emphasize only a possibility, I will have a Senior Lectureship position on our new staff establishment. I thought it only fair to let you know of the requirements—they normally include a higher academic qualification such as MD, PhD or equivalent.'

'Do you hear that Linda? And I'm almost finished my thesis. Isn't that great?'

'Ja. I am sure it is.' She was doubtful.

He remembered their earlier conversation.

'Are you not pleased?'

She threw herself on the sofa not looking at him. 'I do not know what to think. He sounds vague.'

'Wainwright has always been over cautious. He won't decide on anything unless he's certain of the result.'

'Is that so?' She said slowly with little feeling. Something was bothering her. 'You did not ask me if I would like to go to Dublin.'

'Well. Would you?'

She curled up in the sofa before laying down a challenge. 'You know, John, I am also entitled to be considered. English is only my second language, and I have worked hard, very hard. And this is my country and my home. And I have a lot of friends here.'

He remained silent.

Eventually, she asked in a low voice. 'What ever else does he say?'

He turned the letter over.

'Professor Isselherg speaks well of you and your work; in fact he has given me glowing accounts and so I am sure you are well on our way to completing your thesis. Is this not so? Please let me know of your progress and also if you will be coming to Dublin for the International Cancer Meeting. If you intend travelling I would appreciate if you would call on me before or after the meeting. I can then give you more details I referred to in this letter.

Finally let me renew my warmest congratulations on your marriage. A small gift will be forwarded under separate cover with fond wishes.

Until I see you again,
I remain your obstinate teacher,
Walter Wainwright.'

'*Tack*, thanks, John,' she cried, 'he sounds a pet. I'd love to meet him.'

'You will Linda. You will.'

Confusion came over her. Although she was happy and loved John—no language could express it—she also had her career to think of. Now things had changed. She was afraid of loneliness, the naked terror of isolation—if he left her!

Wainwright's letter disturbed her. Here was a challenge, something she had not envisaged, or planned for. Her whole world could be taken away. She had assumed, perhaps foolishly, life would go on here in Sweden, more or less indefinitely with a touch of " they lived happily ever after." And her mother still lived there, alone, in the beautiful house beside the lake. It was so easy to visit her every weekend, to keep an eye on her and enjoy the company of a being that was a credit to the human race.

Now the threat was real; she would have to leave the richness of family life, the glorious Siljan sunsets, and the friendly people of Dalarna who were her kith and kin. Also she would have to leave a career in radiotherapy in the hospital. A problem was looming. How was it going to be resolved and what were the long-term options?

He replied to Wainwright saying the thesis was nearing completion; also, he was going to Dublin for the meeting and would be delighted to discuss plans.

Several days later a parcel arrived by recorded delivery. Inside was an exquisite drawing of King's College, Cambridge. It was Wainwright's Alma Mater and it must have meant a lot to part with it. It was bought in Cambridge the year Wainwright met Isselherg. Linda loved it—their first original.

Then for some reason John's work had a setback. At least half of the animals died a month after chlor 10-6A was stopped. He couldn't understand it and post-mortems could find no clues. One evening as he worked alone—Linda was at a concert with friends—he took his notes out of the desk and spread them over the surface to check the work protocol. Suddenly he noticed dirt on those concerning the most recent procedures. He gently pushed it away and as he did so it marked the paper. He looked at other papers under the top copy. There was more. It looked like clay! Bending down he opened a lower drawer. At the back he found one of Linda's handkerchiefs that contained more of the clay. Some was scattered over the floor.

He sat back on the sofa. Alone he reassessed his approach to work and began to dread facing his experimental creatures everyday and administering chemicals.

Things were beginning to change.

Chapter 27

Peter Sutton strolled across Butt Bridge towards his hotel in O'Connell Street in Dublin. It was getting dark and there was a commotion near the Custom House where nourishment was being dispensed to those who could not take the world anymore. He moved nearer and saw a few poor souls covered with boxes and newspapers sleeping under the railway bridge. Motionless they lay like parcels embodying the floating underlay of human wreckage resting for the night before being posted on.

Rain started and the soup kitchen prepared to leave. He then noticed another bundle on the pavement beside the iron railings; it was a girl, hardly twenty years, asleep with water dripping from her hair. She was lying against the stone wall, one hand gripping the railings. Her face was ashen and skeletal, dark shadows ringed the eyes, streaks of wet black hair framed the small face. She was a woeful sight. He was moved beyond pity; this could've been his own daughter, Diane. Impulsively, he slipped a twenty-punt note into her hand. The skin was damp and cold, yet soft.

She looked at him with sad eyes in which hope was already dead. He could say nothing and hurried away. This encounter was the start of a premonition. A bitter wind gusted across O'Connell Street, rain turned to snow, his hands felt numb and he was wet all over. Approaching the hotel his awful sensation came back although he no longer cared.

Next day he reluctantly caught the train to Westport, his hometown, wishing he could've stayed longer in Dublin with Diane but the demands of a busy practice would not allow it and there were other demands.

Maud, his wife, told him long ago she always appreciated the finer things in life and thought herself—modestly—as one of them. It was her background, of course, her breeding. Mere nobodies, imbeciles who did not count surrounded her in this town, she told him repeatedly.

She never had the opportunity of meeting people of substance, solid genuine people—her own kind—who would listen, sympathize with her, understand her. It was a tragedy; and she blamed him—her husband—constantly. Only she knew how selfish, how cruel he was. After all, she was his wife, genteel, fragile and caring. Then hideous blinding headaches developed that could not be cured, not by anyone. Never! And the pain was terrible, she said. You only had to look at her to witness how dreadful it was—and how she suffered.

She would glare at him through tinted glasses perched on top of her stubby nose—herself now the antidote to desire. Then she turned on their eighteen-year old daughter, Diane, and accused her of deceit and hypocrisy. Peter knew Diane was deeply hurt and did not understand. She'd done nothing wrong. So when Diane left home the brightness went with her and a frozen wreath of respectability descended on the house. That was some years ago now yet Maud's voice continued to lacerate him as the train roared westwards.

That evening, time alone couldn't measure his pace as he slowly walked through Westport—it was about all he could manage. Yet, he loved this place dearly; the air was cool and the river fell open like a carpet cutting the town in two. Mist and space wrestled above tearing the sky to shreds over Clew Bay. Then voices of lives he'd touched echoed in his conscience and the premonition returned, although he couldn't put it into words.

CHAPTER 28

Back in Dublin, Diane, felt strangely cold as she climbed the stairs to her apartment—unusual because it had been a sunny day. She went to the window and saw the twin towers of Sandymount Power Station. Her father liked the apartment but thought it too far from the hospital where she worked as a staff nurse. She lit the gas fire then caught sight of herself in the mirror. Her face was pale, the eyes black pools and there was tightness in her throat.

She stood up and turned the radio on. After five or six stations nothing pleased her so she switched it off, went to the window again and even though she saw nothing she'd leave the curtains for the present.

She relived the previous day to Howth on the Dart, the slow walk along the harbour and the meal afterwards. They were surrounded by a world of characters; important people listening to very important people, elderly men and womenfolk gossiping about friends and others, middle-aged women in dresses that did not cover parts that should be and fought for room around small tables. Then there were parents who tempted the roving mouths of offspring with sweet concoctions and boys and girls, ignoring all around them, sipped coffee complete in each other's company.

The room glowed as the fire gave its colour to the walls and ceiling. She went into the adjacent room, switched on the light and opened the bed for the night. Returning to the fire she sat on the sofa with a silk nightdress across the seat beside her. Alone, she sat—motionless. Then a hand moved back and forth on the silk, slowly at first as if its smoothness would give some comfort. Her mind wandered over the day's events and a thrill went through her. Again she heard her father's voice and smiled. She knew how he'd suffered, silently, over the years and how he'd strived to keep things going. And yet he'd failed recently; she was sad as she thought of him and the future.

Always, we have this striving for something that might be, something beyond our reach. The more we try to grasp it the more it recedes, always beyond. Never near. If a tree is withering and its arms can no longer collect the sun's nourishment nature will help it with a breath of wind. That's good. That's as it should be and not have technology ventilating corpses as she was helping to do, again and again.

And her mother was still poorly.

She was unaware of her hand moving back and forth, persistently, almost pleadingly. John Nicholson came to mind, perhaps because of her father's questions yesterday. Although John had been her love, her complete love, his memory she'd tried to shut out. The last day in the ward, before he left for Sweden, was a wound that would not heal. Yet her mind persisted in going back, questioning those events that deprived her of the essential quality, which would've have brought him to her.

She blamed herself entirely. With it she'd taken her chance like anyone else. For her part she'd tried to analyse the circumstances that resulted in tears, and her heart never stopped crying for the life that was in her. Many times she sent unwritten letters saying in different ways—'the things we've done and said together, John, you've forgotten—yet, for long hours, I've remembered in the darkness of each night.' One can talk of healed wounds although she knew there was no such thing. They can vary, of course, and always they leave a mark of suffering—a scar. She was badly scarred yet there was nothing she could do—except hope. Someday, she hoped he'd return; she'd courage enough for that.

News of the wedding came and the wound was torn apart. Grief changed to despair. As time limped by she tried, with increasing difficulty, to cope and her tiredness became progressive. The ingenuity of fate is like the fiendish ability of water to leak through, over and around a dam. It takes many people to stop it. Diane had no one. Her mother was preoccupied with her headaches, her father old and exhausted, Simon a disaster and now—John lost to her forever. It was too much to struggle alone against the illness in her soul.

A shudder went through her and she began to cry. At first she resisted, only the tightness in her throat grew stronger. She sat there helpless, her thin shoulders trembling and hands clasped together, tightly. Then from within, she was beaten as a great wave came and she gave into the uncontrollable agony of weeping.

Eventually, she returned to the window and saw the Power Station with its erect chimneys penetrating the silent darkness.

It filled her with disgust. She hated it.

Diane's health worsened over the following months with weight loss, severe tiredness along with other mysterious symptoms and she began to know the meaning of long nights. Yet, nothing specific could be found in blood tests.

Then, an overwhelming storm descended, suffocating her and she had to be admitted to hospital for further investigations and treatment. A chaos of emotion went to the very core of her being the evening of admission.

Next morning a sound rang through the room. It was the phone—her doctor had the results of current tests and would like to come and talk to her.

The Sutton's also received a telephone call from the hospital informing them that their daughter, Diane, had been admitted to hospital with Pneumocystis carinii pneumonia. The consultant had a long and detailed discussion with Dr Peter Sutton. The news was like a door being slammed in his face. Of course, he would come immediately. However, his wife was unable to travel because of severe headaches and besides she told him it was inconsiderate of her daughter to need them especially this time of year. After all it was a mere chest infection she herself had many times.

'Peter, don't you know well I just hate hospitals.' She reminded him. 'Even to visit one would be a major ordeal.'

He knew this from experience.

'Anyway,' she concluded, 'I have enough problems of my own to contend with.'

CHAPTER 29

When Peter Sutton left the house next morning to drive to the station his wife, Maud, was fast asleep. Her room was dark because the long red curtains were, as yet, unopened. No hint of disturbance had yet penetrated the sedated cloud beyond which she drifted. She was a late riser and nothing, but nothing, was allowed to interfere with the final flourish of her somnolence. Pointless then of Peter saying goodbye before leaving for Dublin.

Much later—perhaps mid morning—activity began, and was as per instructions laid down by the mistress. A maidservant entered, silently as possible, crept towards the curtains; they were slowly and gently parted to let in whatever sort of light the wretched seaport town had to offer.

The movement reached an art form; the rate of progressive lighting was judged by the response of the individual returning from the twilight zone. No sudden movements or noise would be tolerated. Even when completed, the tentacles of light did not reach the bed and this was, indeed, a blessing because the incumbent at this time of morning was not a pretty sight.

The servant then left the room.

Minutes later Maud tried to shake off the hypnotic haze and facing such problems as puffy swollen eyelids, dry parched mouth and stiff joints. And, of course, she mustn't forget her headaches. That wouldn't do at all! Through squinting eyes she complained to herself about the day outside, whatever it happened to be. Several attempts were made to wake up properly, until, finally, she reached for the packet of unfiltered cigarettes, lit up in a great cloud of blue smoke and inhaled deeply. This always made her feel dizzy, but she knew it was good for her, as it cleared the head for new thinking and raise the blood pressure to normal levels.

The maidservant knew almost when the first cigarette was finished, because she appeared in anxious jocularity with a laden breakfast tray. Maud made a few sarcastic comments. There was a flow of invective about how run down the house and garden was and why wouldn't someone do something. When exhausted it was about time for the maidservant to remove the tray and herself for another day.

The lady had important business to attend to.

Maud felt a little more human after breakfast and her second cigarette so she slid out of bed and inspected the views of the back garden from her window. There was so much that wretched gardener had failed to do, although she'd given him strict instructions days ago.

He promised faithfully he would do all she wanted when he got time. Unfortunately, she changed her mind so often the poor man felt the effects of severe confusion, and didn't know what the hell she really wanted! Sometimes, he had started a job and she'd come running out in a rage saying she didn't want that job done at all, and that he never, ever listened to her.

The next chore in her ritual was in the ultra-luxurious bathroom. There she had have complete privacy amongst the gilt taps, Italian marble, French tiles, arrays of soaps, lotions, tonics and conditioners, which made the shelves look like the proverbial old fashioned chemist's shop. As she submerged into the strongly scented green water it seemed to alleviate, gently and tenderly, the remaining effects of her drugged sleep and now she was able to admire the still beautiful lines of her well preserved body. She had this illusion of youth still reluctant to leave her aging body. The illusion was real to her, it involved no one else to pass judgement, and it was her own private fantasy. She admired her still slim, body, good legs, flat stomach and moderate waist. She couldn't see the lines on the neck and facial wrinkles, easily camouflaged by those clever creams and potions she'd ordered in abundance.

After bathing, the luxury of massaging with soft warm towels came, and the sequence of lotions, creams and ointments were applied with great care. Glowing and almost naked she returned to the bedroom, made for her dressing table and unlocked a small drawer. A letter, wrapped in a pink ribbon, was removed together with a locket containing a cutting of human hair and both were placed on the working surface below the mirror. Then, slowly and provocatively, she dressed herself in front of them.

Applying make-up completed the ritual. Only now was she ready to brave another day and deal with all the problems awaiting her, and her alone. Maud had been Peter's wife for many years, and had done her best to keep up appearances, especially her own. She'd raised the final flourish of her make-up to perfection; things she had been taught on trips to health farms. All this preparation was time consuming.

Of course, she felt it was worthwhile as she gazed in the mirror. The brown hair was greying a little at the temples. She would be able to hide that quite easily. Her figure was slim although the waist was causing a little trouble recently, but the face somehow still gave the impression of a faded photograph. Others would probably just think she was tired or worried about something, or the headaches were bad again; yet this morning that faded photograph stared persistently out at her from the mirror. Maybe, she'd only lightly touched herself with lipstick and powder. Perhaps, they were not enough. She searched for a more dramatic skin colour scheme and had great trouble in finding it.

Something was bothering her, but couldn't remember what it was.

She decided to leave things be. She still had a comely figure and another lighted cigarette would be just the thing to improve her image amongst the staff and patients waiting downstairs.

Yes, the heavy burdens of running a busy doctor's practice fell on her. She remembered now, and was also reminded by the maidservant, that Dr Sutton had already left hours ago to catch the eight o'clock train to Dublin.

That's what it was!

'Why has he gone to Dublin?' She asked impatiently, and not a little annoyed. It would mean extra work, putting off all the patients and rebooking them for another time. How inconsiderate of him gallivanting around the country and not telling her where he was going.

The effrontery of it all!

'But madam he had to go to Dublin,' the maidservant gently reminded her, 'to see your daughter Diane. Apparently, she is not well, not well at all. He said he just had to go.'

'Nonsense! People get chest infections all the time and, in a few days, they get better, especially young ones like Diane. He's just wasting his time. I know the real reason and that's to get away from this wretched town and spend a day or two swanning around Dublin enjoying himself. That's what he's really up to. Mark my words. The selfish man!'

She gave a martyr's sigh and said loudly.

'I'm left to pick up the pieces, and try to think of some excuses why we should hang on to our patients.'

She cleared the waiting room in no time at all with new appointments and refused to answer any questions, even from some of the more sickly people. They would all have to wait the return of the doctor, and that's that!

Then exhausted from her clinical efforts, she began to feel all the good that her precious morning bath had given her was beginning to fade and, of course, the headaches were just lurking in the background waiting to return if they got a chance.

She had earned a rest in the garden, even though that wretched man had not done any of the things she'd asked him to do. She made for one of her favourite spots beside a statue of a Greek god, Apollo, who rippled in muscles and not much else, and a fountain of running water beside him added to the fanciful thoughts she could have, if so inclined.

She sat opposite the statue, and gazed at it, thinking her thoughts, then lit another cigarette and inhaled deeply. It made her relax and still a little dizzy. She still continued to stare at the Greek god.

She was aware that other feelings would take over her body, feelings that would be misunderstood by others, but lots of women arrived at the menopause not prepared and were in distress. There were many recommended methods of combating it, but she knew what suited her best. The small bottle of hypnotics and painkillers for her perpetual headaches were all that were needed. This system worked well and that was all that mattered, to cope with her suffering, her own life and besides there was nothing else she cared about, so why bother? Life was comfortable and sheltered and marvellously oblivious when she wanted it to be. She could avoid inconveniences and troublesome problems. They'd to be avoided and ignored to keep her headaches at bay.

Time for another cigarette.

She wondered what time Peter would be home this evening. But it didn't really matter; she'd probably be asleep when he arrived home, as usual.

CHAPTER 30

The journey from Westport was longer than ever and Peter Sutton's premonition was more real. On his lap was a recent copy of the British Medical Journal, dated 1983, and open at a page with the title *A New Virus Is Born Into The World.*

And there was no cure.

The ward sister spoke gently to him on arrival. Diane was on the critical list and required continuous monitoring. The single room was bright after the dismal railway carriage. She was alone surrounded by flowers and cards, her eyes were closed, oxygen leads for breathing and saline drips were running. He froze in silent torture as he looked at his sick daughter. Straight auburn hair framed the hollow cheeks; flawless skin was pale and the sharp edge of the jaw clearly defined. A feeling of *deja vu*. Yes! The scene near the Custom House.

Slowly he approached the bed, slowly she opened her eyes—now dilated and black—and she watched him from a great distance.

With an effort she smiled.

'Dad. I'm glad you came. How's mamma?'

'She sends her apologies and love.' He tried to change the subject. 'I brought you these flowers, your favourite.'

'They're lovely.'

She turned towards the window and the light. As he sat down he bowed his head not wanting to show tears. He reached out and clasped her hand, which was all that she needed. Time passed and she let it pass—silently. The present seemed simple, complete and inevitable just like resting after a long day's work.

And it was better to go now than outlive all that one cherished and loved.

'Dad. Thanks for the flowers,' she continued, 'now there's colour everywhere and it fills me with joy.'

He turned away again.

'Dad. Do not cry,' she whispered, 'there are no quarrels, no murmurs, and no doubts anymore. We are all friends and I have no pain.'

Then she told him she got this rare viral infection from a patient in the wards when helping with surgery. He knew it already, yet remained silent.

Again, she turned towards the window; the light was not like that before. It was different. She lapsed away from time with an exquisite sense of utter abandon, of flowing out into the harmony of things.

An alarm screamed beside the bed and noise and clamour surrounded him.

Medical staff rushed in to take control. It was useless. He stared at her with many emotions in his face, surprise horror and pain. She was so pretty, so intelligent, so innocent, so brave and so dead. He could only think that death—any death—was tragic, but having to die without having lived was appalling. Since our life and the living of it is as mysterious at its end he became acutely aware of his surroundings.

Suddenly, an overpowering fragrance rose from his flowers beside Diane and he'd a strong feeling, based on recent tests on his heart, that it might not be long before he met his beloved daughter again.

CHAPTER 31

John Nicholson travelled to Dublin for the Cancer Meeting in the Castle. The occasion was hailed as important because of recent developments. More scientists than ever were now working on chemicals to 'find a cure for cancer', as the media billed it. The search was on for chemicals that could be refined, almost targeted to seek out malignant cells and ignore healthy ones. Another aspect was sponsorship and support for research by multinational companies that were not altogether altruistic; the potential for financial gain was enormous. Contributors were specially asked for papers on alternative ways of testing.

Before attending, John went to see Professor Wainwright.

'John. Nice to see you again.' Wainwright waved him to a chair and sat beside him. 'And how've you been getting on? Incidentally thanks for your letter. You sounded pleased with your progress and I was delighted, of course.'

'Unfortunately there's been a setback that I find

incomprehensible.'

A delayed reaction occurred in some tests and no explanation could be found—this held back the thesis. Wainwright suggested he discuss the results at the meeting. With a sigh he left his chair and walked to the window.

'Would you like to continue your work here John? Before you answer, I should tell you things have changed. I couldn't say much in my letter. We've been having protest marches from animal liberation people. Nothing serious—yet! And we've a new Head of Biochemistry—a Professor Phillips. He's brilliant and very helpful. He seems to be liked by everyone.'

'What happened to Professor Pickford?' John looked surprised.

Wainwright's tone was dismissive. 'Early retirement. Due to ill health and other things.'

John leaned forward. 'Other things?'

'Domestic problems.' A mischievous smile formed at the corner of his mouth. 'His son turned out to be a great disappointment.'

'Simon?'

'You probably remember him,' he answered with a touch of bitterness, 'held a Research Fellowship for three years renewable annually.'

'Of course.' John nodded agreement.

Wainwright was sombre. 'It was terminated and he was asked to leave.'

John stared at his old friend. 'But why?'

It was a long story and Wainwright didn't know all the details. In fact he didn't want to know although as a member of the Board of Governors he'd no choice. Apparently money from the research fund had been misappropriated to finance gambling debts.

'Unfortunately that's not all.' He paused before continuing. 'We also had another tragedy. The first AIDS' death on our staff—one of our nurses. A sad business.'

John was suddenly alarmed. 'Do you remember who?'

Wainwright's voice was tinged with sadness. 'She was a good-looking girl—very attractive,' he said leaning back in his chair. 'She used to work in ward 4. Diane ... ' He broke off in mid sentence as John interrupted him.

' … Diane Sutton?'

'Nurse Sutton. That's right. She used to be our staff nurse.'

John was overcome. He stared at Wainwright in shocked amazement.

'She died remarkably quickly from Pneumocystis carinii pneumonia. She appeared to have little resistance—or the will—to fight it in spite of intravenous co-trimoxozole. It was thought she caught the virus accidentally in the ward from an infected needle. Quite extraordinary and a great tragedy.'

They were silent for a moment. With great effort John pulled himself together. His voice trembled. 'Would you excuse me professor?'

As Wainwright stood up stiffly and walked to the door to open it, he felt the cold chill of age in his bones. 'Of course John. Thank you for coming.'

Pain is usually more permanent than pleasure. Similarly, when we have to confront grief it's sometimes important to travel back along the path that brought us there. So it was with John as under a compulsion he returned to the Phoenix Park. Weather was grey and faded like an old photograph and, far off, a repetitive hammer demanded entry to nowhere. Bitterness flowed over him as the sound beat in sympathy with his head. He clenched a hand as if to seize a wisp of air from this place.

Diane had made it lovely. Words came back reminding him of days when he had another's trust; that time was golden. Then he'd listened to an inner voice, which could tell the cruellest lies urging him to do the sensible thing, to trade his deepest feelings for ambition and success. Now he realized that sometimes there could be few things so loathsome as the self one's left behind.

If he could have imagined that place, the time, Diane sitting in the refectory looking over the courtyard at an empty world, he might've understood. He hadn't said goodbye, there was no communication, no word, nothing. She must have suffered in her fight against infection and the development of full-blown AIDS. Little was known about the disease, the gradual loss of weight, poor energy, multiple infections and other complications let alone its treatment and management. Apparently she got it from an infected needle in the ward. Greater was his remorse when he recalled the incident; it was when she assisted him with Andrew Baker, who, in retrospect, was thought to have HIV infection. A ghastly tragedy for her who least deserved it.

Chapter 32

It was one of those drizzly mornings in Dublin when its citizens seemed sad, and a little pinched around the ears. Even the Gardai, patrolling the streets near the Castle, looked miserable. In a laneway off Dame Street a parade was gathering. Anger was palpable, fuelled by their leader in a grey duffle coat, who spoke about the importance of this march, about the opportunity to protest against these butchers, including governments, allowing them to continue with torture and murder. This was wrong, and could never be justified, no matter what. With his megaphone he warned them if these people succeeded, they would be able, by stealth, to experiment on humans and maybe without their consent. That meant we could be destined to become guinea pigs.

In his final rallying call, the duffle coated man, known as Tom, said if we don't stop this horrific exploitation, then he could see secret plans being drawn up to have us as the final court of appeal in testing drugs for use in future generations and some government departments were in the hands of gamblers and fanatics.

Someone shouted from the back of the crowd.

'And what's wrong with that?' And disappeared immediately.

Press and television people were there also along with Gardai. John walked from St Mary's to the Castle. At the entrance the bearded man tried to stop him and was restrained by two Garda officers. He arrived in the conference hall in time to hear a lecture by Dr Evans from the University of California. The title was. 'Hazards and Complications of Repeated Immunization in Experimental Animals.'

During the discussion he asked Dr Evans if he'd come across anaphylactic shock in animals a month or more after giving conjugated human gamma globulin. Evans had not, although he was interested to know why the question was asked. The chairman interrupted. 'I'm sorry, Ladies and Gentlemen,' he said emphatically, 'we must stop at this point. We've run out of time. May I suggest that Dr Evans and the speaker continue their discussion at the end of the session.'

'You're Dr Nicholson. It's a pleasure.' Evans said after the meeting as they shook hands, 'I'm Ted Evans. I've read your publications and I like your work.'

'Thanks Dr Evans.'

'Call me Ted.'

They found seats in the lounge near a window. Evans was tall, thin, and in his mid-thirties with dark brows and large eyes whose brown colour had a way of holding you—if you let them. John explained his recent problems.

'It sounds strange to me,' Ted said stroking his moustache. 'Obviously one thinks of an impure batch of globulin, contaminated chlor 10-6A, a supersensitive strain of animals. But you've considered these? Sorry. I've no solution for you.'

He paused for a moment. 'Or perhaps I have. Why not try it on a patient?'

'No thanks.' John was emphatic.

Ted tapped him on the knee. 'You're not ruthless enough pal. Believe me I've seen things in the States that would make your hair stand on end. I can see your work could've a bearing on AIDS research.'

'That's right. AIDS and some cancers are similar in many ways, as you know, especially the lymphomas and some forms of leukaemia.'

'The AIDS problem is becoming enormous in the States.' Ted's voice had a hint of bitterness. 'It's now pandemic and the tragedy is a lot of suffering could've been prevented.'

He went on with rising passion. Did John realize since the virus appeared a series of monumental blunders had allowed it to stampede through the nation? John said most progress seemed to be coming from London, Paris and Switzerland.

'And Sweden?'

'Possibly,' John replied, 'although this type of research is changing rapidly, bigger teams, high technology and invested interests of the pharmaceutical industry.'

'And not forgetting your problem—more sophisticated animal models.'

'You're right,' he sighed, 'AIDS research is becoming heavily dependent on primates. I suppose it's the price they have to pay for being so close to humans.'

'Some would argue they shouldn't have to pay the price.'

A chain reaction was set off in John. 'I'm sure you're right Ted.

They must not have to pay the price. For years I've used animal in developing drugs.'

'I know. And long may it last.' Eyes brightened, he straightened in his chair and smiled encouragement.

'Ted, I don't know.' John sounded upset. 'I just don't bloody-well know.'

'What do you mean?'

'For sometime I've had a blinkered approach to what I was doing. I only saw the end result, the final goal. We almost wrote the results before we started. I know that's wrong but you have to have confidence in what you are doing. Inside a time bomb was ticking away on two fronts. The animals themselves I completely ignored.'

Ted seemed genuinely puzzled.

'This is interesting stuff John, but what really started your initial conversion?'

'Believe it or not a fur coat in Rome. Commotion about it's display in public.'

He went on to describe the scene.

'I see,' Ted said sitting back with a broad grin.

'The word cruelty came back to haunt me,' John continued. 'And it's been getting worse. I felt like a chaperone of death.'

'That's a bit strong.' Ted looked straight at him. 'At times I've felt the same, but one has to develop a thick skin and ignore your conscience.'

'That's precisely the problem. I can't ignore it. It bothers me more and more.'

Ted decided some strategy; some planning was required.

'John come on cheer up. Remember Matthias Claudius. "Who loves not women, wine and song, remains a fool his whole life long." Although I don't quite agree with all of it, still it's a good principle to live by. Don't you agree?'

John gave him a searching look.

'I like it. There's a lot of sense in it.'

'John, my friend, today we're mere onlookers in a battle zone. All around us is death and everyone has become hardened to it. No, we do not ignore it, we encourage it in our children; in film and television it's glorified. Just like the plague, murder is endemic. After each overthrow of a regime, the assassins do their job, and the torturers do the rest. Sadly, only sometimes morality persists upholding the sacredness of life.'

'You present a horrifying picture. Surely that's not progress?'

'Progress or not, it is progress for some.' Ted bent forward and spoke in a deliberate tone picking words carefully. 'John, a word of advice, for what it's worth. When the time comes for a showdown with Wainwright don't let him push you around. He's the type who'd welcome a stiff fight. But I may be wrong. At the same time swallow every insult. Stay with him and don't let any argument come from your side. Only facts. Repeat, stick only to the facts.'

Chapter 33

Linda had been ill with and abdominal upset when John was away. But it was more the effects of stress. Milder attacks occurred in the past and were dismissed as the wear and tear of hospital life. This was more dramatic, and deeper, with a sense of loneliness and drifting towards a dark cloud on the horizon. Depression was the worst part of all. It could not be explained and would not go away, even after tears were exhausted. And she was gradually losing weight; her reflection in the mirror was thin and tired. She needed love and affection but John was away. Her friends, aware of her a coolness and even aloofness, avoided her. She was a contradiction, she wanted and yet she did not want.

She moved about in streets and shops, showing no interest in anything. Sleep came slowly at night, and when it did, it brought such disturbing images that she woke up sobbing. An inner stamina made her cling to hope; the demons would pass. And John would return soon.

He did return but dismissed it all too quickly, thinking it was a woman's privilege to be moody; besides, he now faced a bigger workload than ever. Research must be done during the day and study at night preparing protocols describing the use of tissue culture cells, such as HELA cells.

One evening she came home and banged the door.

'You have not time for me these days Dr Nicholson.' She flung herself on the couch. 'It is not fair!'

'What's not fair?' He sounded angry. 'I don't understand.'

She rounded on him with intense invective. 'That is it. You do not try to understand.'

'Understand what—for God's sake?'

'If you do not know what, I am not going to tell you.' Her voice was petulant.

He stared blankly at her. 'Linda you're not making sense. I'm trying to work.'

She went into the kitchen. After several minutes a lot of noise came from the room—unnecessary noise that irritated. Then she reappeared with a mug of coffee and a sandwich. The instant she entered a wave of terror came over her, almost as if a flame engulfed her.

Both sat in a blaze of silence, neither wanting to be first to speak.

'What's bothering you?' He asked when the silence became unbearable.

Sitting on the couch she began to eat slowly. Even though her heart was heavy she had a strange look of satisfaction.

'I feel as if I am being used because of what I am.' She stared into space.

What she was getting at? Threading lightly he lowered his voice and said gently. 'And what's that Linda?'

'A woman! Do I have to remind you?' She shouted at him.

This was unlike her. 'You don't have to remind me.'

'A woman is required to have twice the ability to go half as far as a man.'

He was losing patience. 'Are you worried about male domination and that nonsense?'

'It is not nonsense.'

This was nonsense especially in Sweden and he replied in no uncertain terms. 'Women could achieve equal rights today if they'd give up some of them.'

Anger flew through her like a flame. She stood up trembling and, because she loved him, searched for those words that would hurt most. At last with eyes blazing, she fumed. '*Forsvinn*! Go away. You are horrible. Just horrible. I hate you.'

And the battle raged. She shook her head heatedly, emphasizing the exasperation in her last words. And yet, the passion and love she had still gripped tightly. She stormed out.

He'd never known her to behave like this and the hostility upset him greatly. Perhaps, she couldn't help it; women's feelings were inexplicable, sometimes turning on themselves—they could be like that.

Finding it impossible to work he decided to get something to eat. As he passed the bedroom he heard her crying softly. He knocked. There was no reply. Slowly he opened the door. The room was in darkness but light from the lounge fell on the bed. She was face down on the duvet. With cheeks streaming she looked up.

'John.' She sobbed miserably; there was no anger left. 'I do not know what came over me. I am sorry.'

'That's all right,' he said going over to her, 'forget it. It's nothing.'

'But I can't forget it. It's the first time we have quarrelled. I feel awful.'

'I love you so much Linda.' He wiped her tears.

'John, *karlek*,' she whispered, 'please make love to me now. I need you.'

He kissed her 'til the lights appeared to fade. Their ecstasy knew no bounds, he'd never experienced a passion so exquisite and fulfilling, a losing of oneself completely to another. All senses were heightened and sharpened gradually to a point on summit where there was nothing left to do but automatically give, and give totally. A pervading calm, a sadness, and stillness of unspoken secrets followed the act of love.

When the loving was over Linda lay back giving a long, contented sigh, and in no time a restful sleep claimed her. It was as if she had been taken on a private and happy journey with no more stress or worry to bother her. He was different, sad yes, but solitary, and alone and awake in the darkness of a long night. Next morning she was the first to wake. She turned and gazed at him sleeping contentedly.

He then opened his eyes.

'You are not asleep at all.' A nervous laugh she gave and tapped him on the cheek. 'I am sorry about last night. You must think I am awful.'

'I think you're wonderful,' he drawled lazily. 'Making up afterwards is the best part of a row.'

'But not the reason for having one.'

'I don't know,' he said with a wry smile. 'Didn't Othello say. "If after every tempest comes such calms, may the winds blow 'til they have wakened death." '

Suddenly, she raised a hand and looked at him seriously.

'Do not talk about death John. It frightens me,' she said with a rush of emotion and jumped out of bed.

'Why?'

She ignored the question, walked to the window and drew back the curtains so that sunlight flooded the room, making the vibrant design on the carpet come to life.

'Let us have breakfast. It is getting late.'

CHAPTER 34

John Nicholson's application to Trinity was successful and fortunately Wainwright obtained an excellent position for Linda in St Mary's Radiology Department. Plans were made for the move to Dublin.

However, she had to remain in Stockholm for three months to work out her notice. Soon after returning John passed the MRCPI and telephoned her immediately with the news. He then went to see Wainwright.

'Congratulations.' Wainwright's craggy face was lit with a genuine smile. 'Of course you deserve it.'

He encouraged John to devote more time to research. The Stockholm procedures would have to be repeated and would take about twelve months.

'There aren't many around with your perseverance.'

'Some would call it obstinacy.'

'They're just cynics.'

John's worries faced him head on; his work from now on would gradually change and be unpredictable. He decided it would be an appropriate time to confront Wainwright. It was going to be difficult at any time because Wainwright was set in his ways and would speak his own mind. He chose to press ahead. Hesitatingly, he explained his approach using HELA cells.

Wainwright reached forward and picked up a paper knife resembling a small dagger examining the ivory handle. He wanted John to be seated so that they could face each other at eye level. John remained standing so he looked around the room and concentrated on the metal blade again.

'Why bother Nicholson,' he said with a gesture of dismissal, 'everyone knows animals models have been more satisfactory in yielding reliable information over all other methods. It's established practice.'

John felt uneasy. 'If there's a dependable alternative we should explore it.'

'That's nonsense Nicholson and you know it.' Wainwright shouted.

'I accept what you say about the past.'

This stung Wainwright and he moved uncomfortably in his chair.

'But,—but our knowledge is changing, and changing rapidly,' John continued, 'there's good evidence tissue cell culture may be more accurate in measuring the toxicity of some chemicals, although there're only a few centres involved in the work.'

Wainwright remained silent. He was always prepared to listen, always had been, that is only if there was something worth listening to.

'You see professor at present our knowledge about cell growth and gene technology is expanding so rapidly it beggars belief.'

Wainwright was cynical. 'I see. I suppose the next thing you'll tell me is that scientists will be experimenting with genetic material in nature, and perhaps, on humans hoping to change faulty genes. And perhaps even cloning!'

'Yes. I think I can see that happening sometime in the future.'

Slowly Wainwright digested these thoughts and shook his head. His life had been littered with battles and professional detachment had helped in conciliation talks. So his role in arbitration had the patina of long practice.

He was moved by Nicholson's predicament. Guilt was no stranger to Wainwright and he recognized the difficulties in purging it. It was a major affliction of the human condition.

It was easy to expiate minor faults, misgivings in oneself, but the consequences in others could spread outwards as ripples in a pool, and give rise to dangerous undercurrents in scientific research. If this kind of new thinking emanating from his department got widespread publicity a lot of damage could be done. It could be enormous. And it worried him.

He gave a cynical laugh.

'And pigs will fly, you'll tell me next!'

John was taken aback at the outburst. He couldn't understand why his old friend, and professor, should've adopted such an attitude. After all progress is progress.

'I'm sorry Nicholson,' Wainwright said slowly putting his arms behind his head. 'I suppose I should've asked you why you've really changed your approach. I do hope it's not all this humbug, liberation stuff and nonsense by anarchical groups.'

'No, Professor Wainwright,' John said looking directly at his old friend. 'It is certainly none of that. It is something deeper. It's difficult to explain, but having worked with animals for years you get to know them intimately, their personalities, and forgiving love for us beings and, if given the slightest kindness, their complete trust.'

Wainwright was furious.

'Look here Nicholson. This all sounds like sentimental balderdash. I've no time for it. No time at all.'

'But sir if only we could find another way.' He was almost pleading.

'Please stop there, Nicholson,' Wainwright said and pushed away a pile of papers. 'I've heard enough of all this—this—nonsense. It sickens me. I don't want to hear anymore. It must be stopped before it starts. Do you hear me Dr Nicholson?'

John was startled at his tone. 'Yes sir. I hear you.'

Wainwright had finished his admonition and then tried to salvage some of the old camaraderie; after all he had his say on the matter. He had to state his views in no uncertain manner but it was finished.

Now, like a chameleon, he reminisced about his young days. The narrative was vivid, with hints of sarcastic humour, and a touch of resentment about wasted youth, or was it simply a lost youth? By the time he'd covered most of his past John had the impression of someone who had achieved great things but, somewhere along the way, had lost out on happiness.

John left the room, not convinced.

Wainwright sat back in his chair breathing a sigh of relief. He was feeling old. Little things like walking were easier if he brought a stick and excessive reading made his eyes tired. He did not welcome long conversations and often wished the other talker would go away. He accepted changes reluctantly. Memories became increasingly important. He relished those parts of the past he enjoyed, and perhaps even embellished. In contrast there was no way he could pick and chose the present; and this Nicholson affair upset him more than he realized.

Shattered and confused, John decided to go somewhere, anywhere for an hour or longer. Wainwright's stinging words were not unexpected but they still hurt. He was off-duty so not in a hurry. No one required his company, no place would miss him. He walked aimlessly along streets viewing useless objects. A smell of food wafted from establishments but there was no temptation, and people who passed him looked like out of work actors wearing masks of anonymity.

He might welcome some company, but whose and for what reason? It would be useless anyway, because he'd have to walk away at the first greeting—so deep was his dejection. His mouth felt dry and a thirst came on; then he realized he'd probably choke on the first gulp.

His head began to hurt—a tension headache. And his feet. He decided to go home. A strong coffee revived him.

He wanted to forget about the encounter with Wainwright and pulled a book from the bookcase. Without looking at the title he went straight to the opening on the first page.

Down the page he focused on words of Kipling.

'If you can bear to hear the truth you've spoken
Twisted by knaves to make a trap for fools,
Or watch the things you gave your life to, broken,
And stoop and build 'em up with worn-out tools.'

CHAPTER 35

A culture shock awaited Linda in Dublin. The buildings, the people and the way of life were different. Stockholm was one of the loveliest cities in the world to her and her own people, although quiet and reserved, were efficient, reliable, and dependable. Now confusion reigned—even the weather was fickle with bluster and drizzle when everything was cold and grey. Then blue and gold were reflected everywhere with days in between full of indecision.

She imagined the city as an elegant lady shrouded in ragged shawls. Slum land was seen from the airport bus as a maze of television masts searching the sky for snippets of UTV and BBC. Alongside the beautiful Georgian houses framing green parks were ruins half hidden by gaudy billboards and garish neon lights. A grim façade that replaced a street of fine Georgian houses near Merrion Square and an ugly skyscraper with a green roof overshadowing the glorious Custom House shocked her.

Certain smells and sights identified its essential character; smoke and stale beer from pubs, how a gust of wind would blow plastic bags and papers across streets ending up in railings, bushes and trees. The city was also a very holy place indeed—as shown by the number of churches, convents, church schools, monasteries, missions and seminaries.

And the people themselves were unfathomable—perhaps it was her accent or looks—she could not easily make them out on many occasions in her work, during shopping or travelling around discovering places. The image of the typical Dubliner was difficult to describe yet she would not be put off.

The result was someone usually with a nasal voice and words containing random facts mixed with quackery and medicine and a determination not to be found wanting in any subject—whatsoever! Someone with a fund of good stories, which she found hard to understand, an open readiness to malicious gossip, an irritating attraction to circumlocution and deviousness and whose greatest ambition was to have the last word—always!

She discussed her feelings with John one evening. He knew many people who were wonderful at saving those they had drowned.

'I do not understand. You talk in riddles again.'

'Think about it.'

She laughed and protested at the same time.

'John they are to be found everywhere.'

'There are plenty in Dublin swathed in self-regard. Just look at some of our greatest writers entangled in ongoing quarrels and jealousies,' he replied and added thoughtfully, 'you know, Linda, in this town it is very hard to forgive success.'

'There you go, John, spoken just like a true Dubliner.'

Then she discovered others who had a more sensitive awareness than she had known elsewhere; the spontaneous chatter of strangers, the wordless communication and knowing look at some funny incident, people moving aside more quickly for one to pass, the odd smile and nod of the head. And she was particularly taken with the charm of conversation when thought and expression collided, with those who were continuously dazzled by their own brilliance—even laughing at their own jokes!

Yes, this city was different and would take a lot of getting used to. And she missed familiar things; the order and tidiness of life and of course her loving mother.

As she returned tired and exhausted one day and was about to open the front door a large, black cat rubbed against her legs. As the door opened the cat shot straight in and made for the sitting room with no hesitation whatsoever, as if she instinctively knew her bearings. Linda held the door open and gently told her to go home. She sat looking at her full of understanding but silently telling her who was boss. Linda ignored the visitor and unpacked the shopping in the kitchen. She returned to the sitting room and there beheld the black bundle on the sofa looking meaningfully at her. Linda read the medallion hanging from a neck strap.

'I am Tomassina. My mom is Bre.'

And the telephone number was printed.

'So you are Tomassina,' Linda said accepting the invitation to sit down.

Tomassina moved closer and sniffed her cardigan. Linda passed the inspection and so she moved elegantly on to her lap. Tomassina knew exactly how to position herself for maximum comfort. Linda gently tickled her between the ears and down the back. The fur was soft and smooth; the body warm and heavy like a child's.

She began to relax and felt a little drowsy; other things could wait, the unopened letters, the telephone calls, the preparation of supper; they were not important. This pleasant, innocent, communication between two beings was somehow right, somehow complete. And the gentle purring grew louder and more hypnotic.

One evening, Linda was reading quietly as John worked on papers. His mind drifted and casually he asked if she liked her book. She did not know really. He then wondered if she was feeling all right and was reassured except she tired easily.

'I had a blood test today and the results were normal except for a small drop in haemoglobin. It is probably "women's problem" as they say. Anyway I have started taking iron. What is new at the hospital?'

He handed her an invitation.

'We've been asked to a Christmas party. The staff are holding a musical evening and everyone's invited to take part. Would you like to contribute?'

'Fantastiskt! I could play something. How about you?'

He shook his head vigoursly.

'Why not?' She asked. 'You could sing something. And I will accompany you.'

The party was in the examination hall and Linda played magnificently. It was John's turn. The music started and he reluctantly launched into Annie Laurie. He sang with a defiance and determination that thrilled the audience. After the first verse his mind went blank. Linda commenced the lead in and he started again although this time it sounded strange; that is strange to everyone except Linda. She smiled and put her head down concentrating on the music. He sat down and refused to get up. The MC whispered to him, then announced that they'd had a special treat—the second verse was sung entirely in Swedish!

At this they clapped even harder.

Wainwright warmly congratulated Linda on her performance.

Her eyes brightened. 'Thank you professor. And what did you think of John?'

'Most unusual. I don't think I've heard Annie Laurie sung like that before.' 'And not ever likely again,' John interjected.

They arrived home.

'What happened to you?' She asked.

He grinned. 'How do you mean?'

'That was not Swedish. It was gobbledegook!'

'I know but you may have recognized a few words.'

'Very few.'

'I completely forgot the second verse.'

She laughed. It was infectious and so he laughed until tears ran down his cheeks. 'John what would you have done if there were six more verses to get through?'

Chapter 36

Professor Wainwright found it increasingly difficult to cope in the few months left in academic life. He'd always been a hard negotiator, a ruthless maker of bargains and left compromise to the last. Now his time was getting shorter, and his legacy would be judged not only on what he achieved but also on what he left behind.

He'd struggled with his own demons before, which could be traced to Gillian's illness and death. Early on no diagnosis was looked for, let alone made; he merely accepted mood swings as part of the tribulations of life. Most people in stressful jobs suffered similar experiences. Now he was aware of his moods as clinical depression, which was confirmed by a friend and colleague. When a label was put on it there was relief, the culprit forcing him to swing between hyperactivity—or crotchety intolerance—and a descent into dark depression. With an insight he was able to get by. Using psychotherapy, he was able to attack the swinging pendulum. Yet he was entering rough waters again, the beast raising its ugly head, his rationality more fragile.

He was guilty over the outburst with Nicholson, but there was difficulty in finding words or occasion to apologize. He'd never say sorry to anyone, no matter who that person might be. By way of compromise—to himself of course—he decided to ask John and Linda to dine in Trinity.

Both were invited to his house before going to College. When they arrived in Orwell Gardens, Rathgar, they found an elegant red-bricked detached house on considerable grounds. There wasn't much traffic and the sun shone to ease their way. John rang the bell and a young girl answered, in white hat, apron and black shoes.

With an inviting smile she showed them into the sitting room, bowed and disappeared. The room was well appointed, with a geometrical perfection and Spartanly attractive. If Wainwright liked an item it was unique and placed specifically to speak for itself. An austere atmosphere was present achieving a type of serenity.

'I'm not a collector.' Wainwright's voice came from behind and startled them. 'Good evening to you both. You're most welcome.'

'Thanks for inviting us,' Linda said extending her hand.

'As you can see,' he looked at John with a hesitant smile, 'collecting involves so much selection, reselection and, of course, rejection. It's a tiresome business. Please sit down for a few minutes.'

Wainwright was a good listener, which was important with Linda around. He was also more courteous than expected, although when questioned his answers could have a sharp penetrating quality. After half an hour they were taken by taxi to Trinity.

The great library with its cathedral-like ceiling, window embrasures forming side chapels, the oak panelled senior staff room full of ghostly atmosphere and a few Christmas decorations were shown to John and Linda. Candles flickering on the faces of other diners completed the feeling of times past.

A waiter appeared from nowhere and greeted Wainwright.

'Good evening professor.' Menus were distributed to all. 'Sir, would you like a drink to start with?'

Linda looked at the square commanding man standing above them. His almost completely bald head reflected the candlelight yet longish hair protruded abundantly well over the ears. He studied her sharply as Wainwright asked what she would like.

'I would love an Irish whiskey with a little water.'

'Very good. And you John?'

'Same, please.'

Wainwright turned to the waiter, named Carruthers, and gave the order, which was written down with an obvious tremor. When drinks arrived, the orders were again written down by Carruthers and a bottle of the best Burgundy was to be included.

'What's Christmas like in Sweden Linda?' Wainwright asked.

She hesitated with some nervous gestures.

'Well after the Reformation attempts were made to get rid of Saint Nicholas but they did not succeed although pagan gods such as Odin and Thor travelled across the sky with swords of lightning fighting the forces of ice and snow.'

'We could do with them in this country.' John looked at the ceiling.

'In the countryside around Dalarna, oats and porridge are left out for the birds and the occasional elf,' she continued, 'eventually our modern Santa Clause emerged from various traditions and now lives, we believe, in Kiruna just east of Kebnekaise—our highest mountain—in the Abisko National Park well north of the Arctic Circle.'

'I didn't know that.' He smiled. 'I must pay him a visit

sometime.'

'And what would you especially ask for professor?' She inquired with an impish grin. A silence occurred as Wainwright gathered his thoughts.

'To be able to play keyboard music like you my dear.'

She was at once taken aback. The unexpected compliment thrilled her.

Wainwright observed her with commanding eyes. 'My dear Linda could you tell us something of your musical background and development. I've a keen interest in chamber music, especially the late quartets of Beethoven. They're awe-inspiring. I first learned to appreciate them at Cambridge years ago when a lot was happening in my life.' He made a gesture of dismissal. 'Perhaps more of that later. Now how about you and your wonderful talent.'

The first bottle of Burgundy arrived and was tasted by Wainwright. He nodded to Carruthers who reverently poured for the others.

'Thank you sir.'

Carruthers bowed deferentially and withdrew.

Linda settled comfortably in her chair, looked around the room, then fixing her gaze on Wainwright.

'I do not really know when my interest began. Mother told me it started before I could walk. When music with rhythm was heard I would be transfixed and wave my arms trying to dance, sometimes successfully, but more often on the floor.'

Wainwright laughed and drank more Burgundy.

'Please go on Linda.'

'The first thing I can remember is when men in a big van arrived at our house. After a lot of talk and signing papers they lifted a new upright piano out of the van. That is the first I knew of it, although

I was only five at the time. It was pounded everyday not just by my mother. I spent hours playing tunes I heard on the radio. My parents must have realized this was unusual.'

'So they intervened?'

'Yes professor. They were wonderful to me. They found where I could get piano lessons and discovered a lady who worked part-time in the Academy in Stockholm who also lived in Mora and took a limited number of students.'

Wainwright finished more wine and listened carefully.

'I was accepted. This meant cycling to her house at the other end of the town once a week. I practised harder and harder. Eventually it paid off when I was entered for a teacher's Diploma in the Academy and obtained First Class Honours.'

Carruthers approached the table with a murmur, poured more wine for everyone, and Linda noticed his tremor was now gone. On withdrawing he gently smiled at her. The conversation became relaxed as the meal progressed. 'Music can exist without culture but culture cannot exist without music,' Wainwright announced as he put his glass down.

'Depends on what you mean by culture,' she said.

'Also what is music?' Wainwright asked. No one answered. The candles were burning low and some diners were getting ready to leave.

'Yes, Linda, life is full of sound, and sound originates in motion.' The burgundy was beginning to speak. 'And what do you think of the cult of dissonance?'

He looked at her intent eyes, anxious to get a response.

'We had two great wars this century that have changed the lives of millions,' she said looking into the distance. 'Everything had to be new, exciting, sensational because if it did not excite it had to die and be forgotten. Life and living were all important after so much dying. Music searched wildly for new themes heaping dissonance on dissonance.'

'But to what purpose?' Wainwright drank more wine. 'Where will it end?'

No one replied so he continued.

'Today's audiences have answered with their feet—they're against modern music if we look at concert programmes filled with products of the past. They've grown tired of the senseless noise and clamour, which will never satisfy. They can only take refuge in an older time with its order grace and discipline. Dissonance can tumble all over the place feeding our anxieties and neuroses. It rushes about in a frantic race with diminishing effect so that we now have a celebrity on stage sitting there in silence at a piano for over four minutes. Then standing up expecting applause for his non-existent composition. Where do you think the future lies John?'

John did not know what he should feel or say.

'A lot of today's music is a theoretical experiment coming from the brain, which may be interesting only to automatons pointing the way to a dismal future when computers will compose happy or sad music at the press of a button.'

'Terrible! How boring.' Linda looked shocked.

All three were thoughtful over coffee. Wainwright smiled at his two guests.

'I think we've solved it!' He tapped on the table.

'Solved what?' She looked puzzled.

Wainwright waved a hand in a dramatic gesture.

'The question—*what is music?* To the banal it's merely an acoustic happening, to the intelligentsia a matter of harmony and counterpoint and to those who really love music it's the magical unfolding and fulfilment of all our dreams and deepest longings.'

John felt a blush coming on. He was well aware of Wainwright's propensity for this type of decorative speech, but he wondered how Linda would handle it.

She put her hands on the table, fingers apart, and looked straight at Wainwright. A smile, suppressed for so long, suddenly burst forth.

'Perhaps someday, professor, Santa Clause will come to you and grant your wish. Who knows?'

'One can only hope. Now to finish I'd like to propose a toast to you both!'

They all raised their glasses as Wainwright continued.

'I would like to wish you both, Linda and John—my best student—health, wealth and love and the time to enjoy them.'

Then John mentioned that the brandy was of exceptional quality.

Chapter 37

Linda spoke to her neighbour soon after moving into their apartment. Her name was Brigid, but everyone called her Bre for short. She must have had a beautiful face, once. It was thin and fragile, with large blue eyes and full lips that were smiling in the sunshine. Linda guessed the hair would have been fair to blonde, but was turning a dramatic white. It hung neatly on either side of the face curling around it. It also glistened strongly indicating regular brushing.

Anyway, Bre she would prefer to be called. She didn't like having things formal, like you know, and if she were a member of some of the more talkative classes she would have been open and chatty. However, now she'd arrived, through circumstances, she had to be careful of her words, her cheerfulness and not let them run away with her. She often felt a sense of humour coming on, and quite often she would have to deliberately quench it just in time in order to contain her composure.

Linda was invited into her apartment for a chat. Comfortable chairs were placed in such a way to get direct access to the television in a corner of the room. Linda noticed the kitchen was impeccably clean and Tomassina, the cat, had a large basket filled with rugs. Everything was neat clean and nice.

'The first thing I want you to know about me,' Bre started as they sat down, 'is that I am a no nonsense person. I say what I like and I like what I say—usually, that is, but not always. And I'm very independent. I don't ask nobody for nothing. So don't worry. An' I know a lot of people around here, like, and I can tell you where to go to get the best of food and things like that. So, darling, don't hesitate if you want to find out anything. Just come and ask Bre. Always willing to help. You must remember that. An' you're always welcome to have a cup of coffee, but you may not be interested in doing that with an old lady. You're too young and busy to get lonely, I suspect. But, darling the invitation is always there. I'm sure you'll like this neighbourhood. The people are great, but be careful, some of them are terrible talkers. They'd keep you standing all day long discussing this, that and the other and you would never get anything done. I know. I've met them and they don't know when to stop, believe me. No names mentioned. I'm more careful than that. An' do you know I couldn't tell. I really could not tell you. An' another thing you should know is … '

Linda raised her hand and said she had to move on, to get some shopping done.

It happened three days later. John was working in the laboratory when the phone rang.

'Nicholson here.' He hoped it wasn't yet another call from administration.

The voice on the line was full of anxiety. 'Doctor Nicholson. This is sister in radiotherapy. Your wife has just collapsed. Dr Donaldson's looking after her.'

'I'll come immediately.'

He threw the papers on the desk, slammed the receiver down and rushed to Radiology. Linda was lying on a couch in the recovery room—pale but conscious. Donaldson was sitting beside her.

'I came as soon as I could. What happened?' He kissed her on the forehead.

'She fainted while doing an angiogram,' Donaldson said guardedly. 'We took her in here and she's coming round nicely. Her blood pressure's still low but I'm sure she'll be all right. Isn't that so Linda?'

He put a hand on her shoulder.

'I feel much better now. Thank you,' she said with effort, 'I am sorry for giving you a fright.'

'Don't be silly.' His face brightened immediately. 'As long as you're all right.'

Donaldson made a sign for John to follow him into a side room. When they were seated he asked had this happened before.

'No. Although she gets tired easily.'

'Has anyone examined her?'

'No, except she'd a blood count. She's a little anaemic so she started on iron.'

'What was the cause?' He asked awkwardly.

'I don't know. I wanted her to have a check-up but she dismissed it.'

Donaldson's voice was hard. 'I'd advise her to see a surgeon. She told me she'd been having some abdominal symptoms that seem to be getting worse.'

John asked Colm Murphy to see her the same day as a matter of urgency.

Linda was deep in thought as she sat waiting, hands resting on her lap. Fingers were long thin and graceful; nails short and manicured and had a light covering of clear varnish. The skin was smooth and pale. Now and again she moved her hands to straighten part of her clothing, or even search for non-existent flaws. A slight tremor was present. With no work, her hands settled back on her lap. Not for long as they were not used to idleness. Normally they were occupied with radiological calculations; at home they were restless and found work constantly because she was a tidy and clear-headed person. They were most active, of course, when music was played, coming into their own with startling and magical effect.

Now she was waiting. Being a special room there was nothing to do except wait; not for long, she hoped. This gave her some insight into the feelings of patients. Reaching for a magazine she flicked through the pages pretending to read. Putting it down again, she looked at the back of her hands and turned her wedding ring round and round. Mr Murphy appeared. Afterwards she was admitted for tests.

Next day Murphy invited John into his office.

'Please sit down,' he said quietly.

He stood with his back to the window, his face in shadow looking at John for a long moment. This was going to be difficult, even for a hardened Cork man. Many times, he'd to break news to patients and relatives. It was a horrible business and the more he did, the harder it got. Now he was to confront a young colleague and his wife; and he'd to choose the right words.

Walking to the desk he placed reports in front of him, leant forward and began to speak slowly, as if each sentence was dragged from some deep recess.

'I'm afraid I've bad news. The tests show a carcinoma in the large bowel. It's probably an adenocarcinoma.'

The word crushed John like a vice. He stared at Murphy—stricken, utter confusion! A silence filled his entire being, a crushing silence of the grave; suspended from all normality as he sat there motionless. Then shock set in gripping him totally. Linda has cancer was all he could grasp. He couldn't believe it.

'There's no doubt Mr Murphy?'

He could hear himself groping for words.

'None whatever. As for prognosis—I cannot say. There are many variables.'

John put his head in his hands.

'You'll operate as soon as you can?'

'As soon as preparations are complete.'

'Will you be as radical as possible?' John asked.

'I'll do whatever's necessary.'

He paused.

'Mr Murphy. I can't believe it. It must've started some time ago?'

'Perhaps nine months, twelve or longer. No one can tell precisely.'

'There's been no warning,' John said.

'Probably there were things you both ignored. Has she been depressed recently?'

'Yes and it was most unlike her. What should we tell her?'

Murphy advised she shouldn't be told the diagnosis—not yet anyway. He'd just say there was a polyp that needed surgery—it would help her to recover more quickly.

Here was the classic situation John faced repeatedly, what to tell the patient, and how much? He remembered Andrew Baker. Unfortunately, he'd told Baker too much and was in big trouble, which eventually led to his own transfer to Stockholm. Results were far reaching and now the same matter had come home to roost.

If Linda was told, Murphy said, being a doctor every ache and pain could be a secondary, and everyone would be made to suffer. As it was she could drift along in the happy knowledge the operation was a complete success.

Only John would have to carry the burden, the real fact of life and he knew the statistics on recurrence and complications. The risk factor was high and he'd to be eternally vigilant. Responsibility placed a heavy hand on his shoulders, which he'd have to bear with an appearance of indifference.

Almost in anger he asked himself. How can you keep a joie de vivre when you know that your closest is suffering? Yes, one should be told the truth and to hell with the consequences! If he was ever struck with a fatal illness he'd want to be told, told just once with no ceremony or false expressions of sympathy, and then allowed to get on with fighting the internal enemy as best he could.

But no! He had his instructions to remain silent.

He could not, must not break that trust.

Chapter 38

The news was like a bolt out of the blue for John. Then silence; a shocked silence that sank into his bones, followed by anguish —an anguish that had been easy to cope with in others as he'd dispensed pain and loneliness with his medication. Now, it was different. One hideous thought became mitotic and spread to another, and another. Round and round they went in ceaseless motion, suffocating him.

That night he lay beside the sleeping Linda, who was sedated, and tried to unwind. Physical fear took over—the restless breathing, the trembling, the swallowing. A fist gripped his stomach and a headache crushed him like a sledgehammer. He got up, struggled to the bathroom and was violently sick. This gave some relief but the headache persisted. He took three aspirin and returned to bed.

Linda gave a sigh. If he kept still with eyes closed the headache was less. His skin began to crawl with drops of sweat—like teaming insects. Unbearable. It disgusted him. Yet, he almost felt a perverse pleasure in it all. Something whispered to him, reassuring him. He'd ample reserves anyway. People do get over these things and, after all, there's nothing one can do with grief but suffer it.

The following days were an agony of waiting, and a time to watch the translation of himself through the mill wheel of his mind. If only he could breathe words into his feelings, but he couldn't talk to anyone—it would be almost indecent. He could think about them though, and go on thinking; then his grief took over so completely he became apathetic. The slightest exertion was too much. Reading and writing were an effort—even talking. And he found it hard to listen. To take it in. It was meaningless. Still, it was worse when the talking stopped. Everything irritated.

He walked slowly back to the apartment after Linda was taken to theatre that wet morning in June. The operation would take about three hours—three hours of eternity. Strange, he thought, how fate requires us to suffer our profoundest experiences alone and the most moving moments in life will probably find us unable to express them, in spite of the writings of frail and fallible men. Then, for a while, his mind went blank.

Steady rain had been falling since dawn and the room seemed damp and oddly naked. His legs turned weak and he flung himself on the unmade bed. Unaware of his sodden clothes he stared at the ceiling conscious only of the writhing passion in his breast. An enormous fear flowed through him; many times he'd known fear. It now returned in a wave like never before, devastating—a fear of the unknown. In vain he longed for release, for peace, for—surely this was the moment of truth—truth always lags last in the remorseless working of things.

He wondered about guilt—Linda's or his own—by neglect. No

answer. First truths are discovered after all others—and he'd not yet discovered. Perhaps this tragedy was the first step. Even punishment he questioned—but for what? All punishment must be evil. His love for Linda, in which eternity was in a moment, now turned to pain as his mind felt every moment as eternity.

His gaze moved from the ceiling to the world outside; the sky was dark and brooding. His eyes closed and the stillness of the room scratched at his senses with its claws. Drugged with exhaustion, its gaunt figure grew in his imaginings and confused images crossed his consciousness.

Surely, the hardest death to bear is that seen ahead. He felt this final horror, which comes too early or too late, carried with it a supreme, an ultimate terror. It had no tomorrow! His anxiety was compounded by the fear of Linda being eternally forgotten. As her mortal flame burned low he came face to face with death; its steely hand gripped his and lead him slowly, reluctantly, with inarticulate speech to the edge of the infinite and, for a moment, let him gaze into depth beyond depth the unending now.

At this thought, an uncontrollable rage came over him; it rose chokingly in his throat as he got to his feet, his face white his eyes blazing. Its realization broke through the deeper mists into his mind and produced a reaction of haggard disbelief. He wanted with all his might to hit out, to break something, anything, everything! But he was completely powerless.

He could not help Linda any way; there was nothing, absolutely nothing. Tears gushed from his eyes.

Suddenly a tremor spread through his body, in the anguish of re-birth he came back to reality, to reason, to himself. The catharsis had induced a clear, calm logic. Slowly the veil parted and he'd a surge of lucid power. He was fully awake. He would now try to turn that key—he would try to pray. No words came forth. It didn't matter—his soul was on its knees!

A sound rang through the room like a crack of doom. It was the phone.

'John. Colm Murphy here. We've just finished and I'm glad to tell you the growth seemed to be well localized. A resection and end-to-end anastomosis has been carried out. Linda was taken back to the ward ten minutes ago.'

'When can I see her?'

'Come later this evening about seven o'clock. She'll be asleep most of the day.'

'Mr Murphy.' He hesitated. 'Was there evidence of spread?'

'None that we could see,' said the other cautiously, 'but nobody can tell what's happened at microscopic level. I only wish it could have been otherwise,' he gave a sigh as he added. 'I've done all I can—it's up to Linda now.'

She would be asleep for several hours after the anaesthetic. It was a Tuesday and work had to go on so he kept busy with ward rounds and in the laboratory. About seven o'clock he went to see her. She was in a three-bed unit on the ground floor; two middle-aged women occupied the other beds near the window. Curtains were drawn around the third bed. Staff nurse was attending to Linda and checking all the intravenous leads were correct. She sensed John's presence and peeped around the curtains.

'I'll only be a couple of minutes Dr Nicholson,' she said loudly, 'just seeing that everything's all right.'

'Of course', he said calmly, 'take your time. I'll wait.'

Minutes passed filled with whispers and movement around the bed. Then she appeared and triumphantly drew the curtains back. It was almost a theatrical gesture because the scene revealed an impressive spectacle of patient linked to various drips, elevated back supports and an electronic console wired to essential functions.

Linda was awake and alert.

'What kept you? I thought you would be here before this.'

He felt aggrieved. 'Mr Murphy told me not to come before seven o'clock.'

Typical of her—she looked at her watch.

After the chaos and turmoil of the first few days she began to settle into a situation where she drifted in and out of sleeping, but mostly sleeping. She only half remembered groups of visitors, mainly friends and colleagues from the hospital, murmuring pleasantries and bearing flowers.

Then she had broken nights when she'd to call for medication for pain relief. Gradually, the realization of the procedure she'd gone through threw a great emotional strain on her. And John seemed to be always there, day and night.

Each new day was a bonus, a gift; every short walk in the corridor an enormous thrill, every conversation a fresh achievement. Emotional storms led to strange feelings never experienced before, and she wanted to share them.

Then, for some reason the pain became worse, much worse.

'Have they not given you something for it?'

'Yes but it is completely useless.' Her gaze roamed around the room.

'Do you know the name of it?'

'No John. No. I do not. Please do not upset me.'

He went straight for sister's office.

'Sorry to intrude sister, but Linda is still in bad pain.'

'We gave her the recommended dose of pentazocine an hour ago.'

He looked exasperated. 'Well it's had no effect.'

'Mr Murphy prescribed it four hourly. I can't do anything further.'

He went back to Linda who appeared to be a little easier.

Late next afternoon he returned to her.

'No. No. It is useless.' She was speaking to the house surgeon.

Sitting on the edge of the bed he felt devastated. 'Oh Linda what's wrong?'

'I cannot stand the pain and the hallucinations make it worse.'

'Are you still on pentazocine?'

'Yes I think so.'

'This is no good,' he said angrily, 'I'll speak to Mr Murphy.'

He telephoned Murphy and explained Linda's intolerance to the medication.

'Oh dear, this is most unfortunate. We're doing a trial on post-operative pain and she's not responding. Let me have a word with sister.'

'Fine. I'll transfer you now.'

He continued with routine work as best he could, although with great difficulty.

Next evening he saw Linda again.

He asked with trepidation.

'How are you tonight?'

'A lot better now that I have been changed to omnopon and scopolamine. I have no pain now,' she smiled and then asked,' John why do they have to experiment on us? That pentazocine was useless,'

He relaxed and held her hand. 'All right you have proved a

point.'

He left her sleeping quietly and made his way back to the apartment. The city streets were isolated and eerie. Everyone had gone home; there were only a few stragglers here and there and an occasional dog. As he walked the narrow streets the alleys were silent, and his footsteps were louder than usual on the pavement. Under one of the old-fashioned street lamps he stopped and was flooded with shimmering gold light.

Suddenly, he was gripped with a sickening sense of loneliness and panic. Everything he held sacred and dependable was now like ice cracking under his feet. An immediate threat to his well being, his security and his sanity. Could he get through the next few days and weeks?

The lesion was graded as Dukes' C on biopsy and the cells were poorly differentiated suggesting a possibility of distal spread. Four weeks later Linda was allowed home. She was determined to make a full recovery.

And her relief was enormous.

CHAPTER 39

Months dragged for John and raced for Linda who seemed to regain her strength. The experience reminded her how fast life had flown; everything was deeper more exquisite. Beauty of thought, sound and sight was precious, and held a hope that stretched beyond understanding.

A letter with a Swedish stamp arrived on John's desk in the hospital. *Private* was written in red on the top. He slit it open and read.

'My Dear John,

My friend Walter Wainwright wrote to me about your wife Linda with some of the background to her recent illness. We were all dismayed and shocked to hear the news. The letter was brief so we did not get a full picture. We can only imagine how you and Linda are suffering at this moment and our hearts go out to you. Needless to say our prayers are also with you.'

'I understand the future is uncertain. It is at times like this you will become aware of your true friends and you will probably find there are few of them left and this can give an insight into the quality of human relationships. You must be numb and heartbroken at this time. Please let me say, we are here, and if there is anything we can do, anything at all; please just ask. We are thinking of you at this time and wish it were not so. We remember Linda as a truly wonderful person. She had the makings of a brilliant scientist.'

'Finally, we are all agreed that if you both, or one of you, ever want a vacation in Stockholm or in the country estate you would be more than welcome. We would do our best to make your time here enjoyable.'

'John, think about it. Please ask Linda first. Obviously, it would have to be her decision.'

'Allow me to offer our every good wish. And, you John please do not neglect yourself. You are equally precious in the whole equation.

Yours sincerely,

Gustav and Rachel.

P.S. Karita has asked me to tell you she has not finished her epic poem yet. She feels she needs more help to draw it to a successful conclusion. I do not know what she is getting at. Perhaps you do?

G.'

John would keep the letter to himself—for the present.

On a weekend break they went touring in Wicklow. Driving out of Dublin the sky was dark and later sunshine fell. They discovered a laneway; to him it was just a dreary, out of the way track protected by fragments of fence and hedges from the desolation of bog and field where unopposed wind and rain held sway and even rushes bent to one another indifferent to a passing world. The remains of a cottage crouched beside the clearing.

'*Alskling*, darling, let us rest here,' she said as she removed her cardigan.

After lunch she continued to drink in the peace of the place.

'You're very quiet, Linda. Is anything wrong?'

'On the contrary everything is right.' She smiled. 'This is a wonderful spot and it is a wonderful day. *Underbar*!'

'Is everything still wonderful for you Linda?'

There was no reply.

And there was Linda's flower. They found it and the bush on which it flourished behind a wall. The bush was sprawling among garden flowers. It then discovered a larger place and ran riot, sparkling everywhere, well washed by sun and rain. Near her it was sleeping and only appeared as carefully folded crimson tufts. Then a cluster that could no longer resist temptation gladly yielded up. A host of blossoms swayed in front of their new visitors. Suddenly, she cried uncontrollably.

And her relief was immense.

Why, and from what, was obscure.

Autumn came and she began to develop back pain. It was not much—only an odd attack but it gradually got worse. John discussed it with Colm Murphy.

'I'll have to see her again,' Murphy told him.

Blood tests and more X-rays were done. Murphy presented the results to him. Linda had multiple carcinomatosis. Deposits in the spinal column were the most likely cause of pain and she'd now have to be told.

'We've no choice now,' Murphy said as he replaced reports in the folder. 'I'm afraid we must face facts. The prognosis is not good, not good at all.'

John fought bitterness welling up. His control cracked like breaking glass; eyes filled and lips trembled. 'And I'd hoped against hope. Is there anything that can be done?'

'If you weren't a doctor I could tell you half-truths. But you know surgery is no longer feasible and radiotherapy is too dangerous. You have my fullest sympathy, but I must remind you that you're a doctor … '

' … And a husband.' His voice was full of angry despair.

'A loving one too, but also a doctor. So to answer your question—chemotherapy today apparently still has some way to go in bowel cancer.'

John was stung by this remark. He should have made better progress but he was dragging his feet. With Linda's illness it could be a remote option.

'Then there seems to be nothing further.'

Murphy tried to be positive—there were things that could be done to make her comfortable. John asked how long she had left—that was difficult to predict but because of the bone deposits it probably meant no more than eight or nine months.

'I see.' He bowed his head. 'Will you tell her?'

'I will. Although you should be present.' Murphy stood up. 'We'll go and speak to her now.'

They both walked briskly and in silence to Linda's room. Before going in Murphy stopped and put a hand on his shoulder, as if to say: I'm completely behind you. What he did say was. 'God give us both strength at this difficult time.'

'Thanks,' was all John could say.

They both entered. When John saw Linda his heart sank. She was sitting on the bed in silk pyjamas and matching dressing gown. Her skin was as pale as alabaster. When he took her hand it was cold and trembled slightly. Her smile, however, had not changed, still welcoming with a hint of mischief.

She sat quietly while Murphy talked. Her only question was the same—how long? Murphy attempted to comfort her. It was unnecessary.

When alone, John went over to her and, for several minutes, they said nothing. He sat on the bed and put his head down. His heart was breaking. Putting her hand on his chin she raised his head—a moment he'd never forget. She had an aura of extraordinary calm, beyond the reach of rage or malice.

'When can I go home?' She said softly.

'I've come to collect you.'

For Linda the worst had come to the worst—suddenly. The shock was fresh; it was hideous and horrible, it dominated, filled and emptied her. The word 'cancer' clung cruelly; it prowled through the house, the streets and roamed through her mind and very existence. It emphasized the struggle of that enormity between birth and death and she keenly felt the days allotted to her. Unreasoning dread could only be exorcised by understanding—cancer and courage go together not grow together. At first, the torment robbed her of speech and her silences became eloquent. She lived days of quiet turmoil; occasionally mere words did come but it was like talking across a chasm.

There is no tomorrow, there is only the present—what remains will be an exquisite jewel. The gift of memory dazzled and brought tears. She searched his mind, sometimes looking too far, seeking those places where he stored his strength.

'*Tack*, thank you, John, for not running away,' she'd said at last.

In the sitting room one evening she arranged freesias with discovering hands like a mother loving a child and the flowers appeared to yield as to the sun. In the same way her hands touched his face with an innocence that rarely flowers. He noticed her paleness.

'How are you feeling Linda?' He knew it was a silly question.

'As all right as I ever will be darling. I have been thinking a lot recently. Thinking about us.' There was not much time left to settle things; she asked if he'd marry again when she was gone. When Linda was gone—it sounded incredible.

'There could never be anyone like you,' was all he could say.

'Thank you.' Her eyes were intensely on him again. 'We have always had a special thing between us, so complete and fulfilling. But I would like you to marry because you have much to give and you cannot keep it all to yourself.'

'Let's say no more—we still have each other and that's what matters.'

'All right darling,' she mumbled an apology. 'I did not mean to upset you. I also wanted to discuss something else. Recently the pain has got worse.' First time she'd complained.

'It was bad today but I don't want to take medication unless I have to. I must enjoy every moment while I can.'

'I understand.'

'Do you really? Since Mr Murphy told me the prognosis I have developed an appreciation of things—the colour of flowers, marvelling at how a writer can unfold a story and, of course, music. Above all being in your company.'

'How do you really feel?' He was probing.

She gave a nervous laugh. 'I have just told you.'

'Really?'

'You do not believe me?'

'I do believe what you've said. It's what you've left unsaid that worries me.'

'Now you are confusing me,' she said and then her laughter sounded like a death knell.

'I'm sorry Linda.'

She bowed her head. Tears rolled down her cheeks and she made no attempt to stop them. Eventually she spoke. 'I do know what you mean and I am frightened.'

He said nothing. There was a lump in his throat.

'I will tell you how I feel. Sometime ago I read a book by Nevil Shute called "On The Beach" which made a lasting impression. It describes the lives of people who survive a nuclear war but their days are limited because of global spread of radiation. I feel like them John and I am frightened of what is to come. Nobody can help me now. Nobody.'

She cried bitterly and was inconsolable. He was helpless, unable to comfort her. He merely drew her close, embraced her tenderly and she nestled her face on his shoulder. Tears reached his chest and as he continued to talk each sentence caused an involuntary tremor in her as she listened, almost like a defeated boxer reeling to the onslaught of winning blows in a contest. When the clouds of emotion were more controlled, she lay huddled against him, terrified to move.

Autumn darkened to a white winter and she tried to keep things as normal as possible. She tidied the apartment everyday although it was an effort. One morning as she cleaned the mahogany desk she ran her finger lovingly over the inlay and spent an hour polishing. When finished she opened the drawers one by one sorting out his papers. The rest of the morning was spent on the telephone.

She slept for several hours that afternoon and woke noticing a strange, black statue sitting on the windowsill that overlooked the street.

'Oh, Tomassina. It is you again,' she said sitting up and resting on one elbow.

'How did you get in? I will never know. Anyway it is nice to see you again.'

For a minute or so Tomassina looked at her benignly and then turned to face the window. A meticulous grooming took place, which fascinated Linda. Tomassina turned her head into strange angles so that she could lick her back, her paws and her tail; all the while the head moved up and down like one of those plastic toys in cars.

At intervals she stopped and inspected the street below. She groomed the white patch of fur on her chest. When finished the street was inspected again and suddenly, with a rush of excitement, she shot out of the room and stood inside the front door to welcome John home.

That evening Linda asked did John notice anything different. At first, he couldn't see any change then it came to him. 'The desk. Your beautiful desk. Where's it gone?'

'To an antique dealer,' she said triumphantly.

'You sold it?' He couldn't believe it. It was so beautiful.

'Yes.'

'Why? It was a family heirloom.'

'I know darling. I never really liked it.'

'I didn't know that.' He wondered if he could believe it.

'Now you know. And I got a good price for it too.' She looked at him pleadingly, and made a play of fumbling for words. 'John *alskling*, what is happening must be causing you a lot of suffering. If there is anything that … '

' … Stop Linda.' He put up a hand as he interrupted. 'I'm not important. You're the one who must have everything—every consideration. Not me.'

She seized her opportunity and faced him directly.

'Would you take me back to Rome?'

He'd no hesitation whatsoever. 'Of course.'

'*Underbar*! Wonderful! We could use the money I got for the desk.'

'I'd have got it together anyway,' he assured her.

'I wanted to do it this way, John. Believe me it is important.'

They stayed in the Marini Plaza Hotel in the *Via del Tritione*. The weather was cold yet she was determined to do exactly as previously. He advised against it; she insisted. And there was an urgency about everything, although they spoke little.

The last day included a visit to the catacombs. At one point she slowed down—they were at the back of the coach party. They'd better not delay, easy to get lost.

'Do not worry John. I will be all right. You first go down the steps.'

'Please be careful.'

The passage narrowed at this point and the burial shelves were close. He went ahead. A white handkerchief was taken from her pocket. It was full of clay. She gently kissed it and concealed it in the loose earth.

'Come on,' he said as he turned around. 'You're holding everyone up.'

'Do not fuss, *alskling*. I am coming.' She walked towards him.

It stopped raining when they entered the coach and the sun was bright on the Appian Way. She had a heated discussion with an elderly American on the relative merits of early Roman civilization. At the *Piazza della Republica* she got off the coach first. Before descending John felt a tap on his shoulder.

'You know, young man, you've got a remarkable wife.' It was the American. 'I thoroughly enjoyed her company. Take my advice. Look after her well. Hope you realize how lucky you are.'

'Don't worry,' he replied stepping down, 'I do. Thanks for the compliment.'

The American added with a sigh. 'It must be great to be young.'

He shook hands and walked away.

PART THREE

CHAPTER 1

Tom Nolan travels to Sligo as he continues his journey from Malin to Mizen. He's put the affair with Mark O'Neill behind him and is full of exhilaration—he's on location again! Here is a land of enchantment legend and antiquity. Streams cascading over Benbulben's cliffs thrill him, especially when wind causes them to flow upwards and Drumcliff River is liquid gold in fading light. He has eerie experiences at Eagle's Rock in Glenade and among megalithic stones in Carrowmore Cemetery, which are like sleeping beings in the half-light and—with imagination—they could move.

Waves on Portacarn Beach in Belmullet are remarkable. Their grace and rhythm make eloquent the surrounding silence; here the Children of Lir heard the bell, which restored humanity to them, a story his daughter Annette loved to hear. Another is dawn over Croagh Patrick, full of drama, when the black mountain has its edge eaten away by light, as the sun lifts itself, naked and molten, across the glassy waters of Clew Bay. Mweelrea Mountain impresses especially from Moyard where its profile has a touch of God on its brow and the misery of Doolough, Killadoon and Ballinakill, in rain, touches something deep inside. Near Doolough he discovers a whitethorn tree in bloom, a branch reaching into an overcast sky with dark mountains, including the Devil's Mother behind it. The outstretched hand is like a cry for help, gentle rain like tears of exiles and wind—whispering in a voice soft as glowing candles—the weeping of those forced to die in foreign lands.

The walk in the Inagh Valley is a narrow path leading off the main road at the north end. The countryside is morning still. White rocks shine beside their shadows and hills give off a strong silent heat.

Gorse stands out against the undergrowth and is exciting in the glare of sunshine. Across the valley are yellow patches of wheat, green pastures and woodland descending to the edge of the lake. He walks towards Letterbreckan Mountain, where he hopes to capture a unique image. He discovers a field with bundles of barley standing in rows. Streaming to the ground are untidy stresses and stubble glares white.

The road from Ballinaboy to Toombeola is sheer enchantment in the evening when the light comes in low from the west. It runs through Roundstone Bog, which hasn't yet been inflicted with Sitka pine or commercial development and is unique. The joy of travelling this road is a flickering of nows, each as transient as a melting snowflake. He walks it with Patsie letting tomorrow's work soak in and pass an extraordinary tree. A handsome hawthorn it is nearly twenty feet high but broader as it grows away from it tormentor—the wind from the west. It seems determined to go on, not for an age, but forever and forms a willing subject for a painting. The scene is a page from the book of life; fortitude, tenacity, even courage are qualities that come to mind and, like a living document it has endured to tell its story.

Light effects sweeping over structures remind him of waves on rocks or a veil gently drawn across a face. They fascinate him and prevent his paintings becoming static as vision percolates to the brush.

On his last day he paints a scene looking west to Rosmuck. The sun melts the clouds and a sweet perfume forecasts its sad transience. There is sorrow in it too—the sorrow of parting. Sometimes music can move us so much it becomes almost unbearable. The scene becomes so intense he has to turn away. Hills around remain hushed as the harmony drops an octave and colour is dragged into the earth. The sky grows pale, hills go dark, water is at peace and that wonderful light of the west is gone.

Some say that time goes by, but there are places like Connemara where time stays and we must go. Tom Nolan has to return to Dublin, to his family and to his studio. The journey is half-over; it is time to take stock. Meanwhile, the blue expanse of Mayo Mountains, Croagh Patrick at dawn, the Twelve Bens—his abiding subject matter—grow, not dimmer, but more distinct with memory.

And there is work to be done, plans to be made.

CHAPTER 2

Plans take time and months go by. One day the sky darkens and snow falls in the breathless air, swirling and dancing in a frenzy. Whiteness covers everything. Towards evening all is quiet again. Trees are black under their shroud and the church kneels in prayer, its spire rising in silent authority. Out of the shadows a car emerges and stops at the church.

Tom Nolan and two colleagues have waited for this moment like opportunist pathogens. Time and place were planned with great care; a St Mary's employee, and sympathizer, would unlock a side entrance to the research wing.

Anger creeps over Tom's face as he looks across the scene—the Institute is hideous and malignant. In the distance a dog moans as masked men defect from the car. They stagger through the snow shivering with the devilish cold. The side door is open and they slide inside. Tom knows what to do and others follow. He easily overcomes the security arrangements and the alarm system is inactivated.

Having cut an entrance to the first hut they exterminate all the rabbits and cats, in the second the guinea pigs and dogs. The third, marked *ISOLATION UNIT* is more difficult. Previous experience, however, proves invaluable.

'Poor creatures,' he whispers to his friends 'must be really precious to the bloody torturers. Gone to great lengths to protect their victims.'

Once inside they find about two-dozen animals in separate units. There are chimpanzees and monkeys of the African Green Species. Quickly, and out of compassion, they systematically shoot them with silencers. All except one chimpanzee.

Their ammunition has run out.

'Blast!' Tom cries putting his gun away. 'We'll finish this one by hand.'

The others open the cage door for him. Suddenly the demented animal rushes out in a frenzy. It springs at Tom seizing him by the neck, its heart at breaking point. It hangs on, tearing and beating with all its God-given might. They fall to the floor gasping for air. The little savage is trying to strangle him! With wild fury the creature fights for its dear life. Tom overcomes it with the others help. He kneels on it, crushing and strangling it, his eyes wild and strange. Before the animal is struck the fatal blow it bites hard into his left arm. It then goes limp and lifeless. Blood is everywhere.

Tom Nolan rises slowly ragged and dazed. In a confused state he scribbles a message on a sheet of paper and addresses the envelope to Dr Nicholson. Then something snaps inside him.

'Let's finish the bloody place off once and for all,' he says to the others.

The research wing is set alight.

The three men stop some distance from the buildings and look back. They've already removed their hoods and anyone would take them as innocent bystanders at this stage. They witness the fruits of their evening's work. The fire starts in unit one and because the structure is mainly wooden flames take hold and spread quickly. Initially, there are tears in Tom's eyes; what the emotion is would be difficult to define. They soon dry up as adrenaline levels increase.

There's little smoke to be seen because of the darkness. As appetite feeds on eating, flames roar upwards engulfing the fabric of the building; their greed seems boundless as the steel structure becomes alive, a mass of torture among the showers of sparks.

The ever-increasing fire is a hypnotic spectacle the likes of which they have never seen before. Flames grow higher and spread horizontally with equal speed. Inflammable liquids and chemicals are stored in the huts causing loud explosions followed by mighty bursts of flame from the source of the noise. As each roof implodes into a blazing cauldron, fire splashes outwards in all directions, and the crowd moves back. The steel framework becomes white-hot and twists into indescribable shapes as if in agony. Around the inferno air becomes unbreathable. Several units of the fire brigade arrive and start the battle for control but too late to save the little souls inside and the valuable research.

Everything has been destroyed. The full horror is soon apparent. The Fire Brigade establishes the cause is the work of arsonists.

Crucial research work has been done in St Mary's and the Cancer Institute by John Nicholson and his dedicated team. Until this fire. He walks over to a badly burned survivor; it can hardly whimper. He speaks softly and it goes limp. There is another that has escaped the flames. It lies still, looks at him and closes its eyes. He feels for the carotid. Nothing. It has died from sheer terror and the remainder are in deep shock.

A rage grips him as he walks among the ashes, staring at the smouldering obscenity—it yells back at him. It's a murder that shrieks to high heaven, a murder of the most odious kind, a murder of countless beings not yet born. It is the slaughter of knowledge. Why did this fire have to happen? What is the reason?

Some weeks later he goes through his files relating to the fire and finds a copy of his letter to the President of the Animal Liberation Front. He reads.

'Dear Ms Thorndyke-Smythe,

Your secretary, Tom Nolan, came to discuss certain matters this afternoon. He told me he had been sent by your committee to ask us to stop our current research. He put forward some arguments to convince me what we are doing is wrong. However, I have yet to be convinced and this is the reason why I am writing to you.'

'Everyone is entitled to his or her opinion on any subject whatsoever. Mine was conveyed to Mr Nolan today. I must say here that I will listen to, and respect, your committee's views provided you and your members will give a written undertaking to abide by the following criteria.

(1)That if you become ill for any reason whatsoever you will not consult a member of the medical profession for help during the illness.

(2)That if any member of your immediate family for whom you have responsibility becomes ill you will not allow that person to

consult a member of the medical profession.

(3)That you refuse to allow yourself, or a member of your family, to be vaccinated against any of the major diseases such as tuberculosis, typhoid cholera, that are still killing millions of people throughout the world.

(4)That if you, or your family, keep animals as domestic pets and if these animals become ill you will not seek the help of the veterinary profession.'

'The reason why I put these points before you to answer is because it is generally known that practically all major advances in finding the cause of human diseases and in developing medicines to control and cure them have come from knowledge gained from animal research. Should you and your colleagues achieve your stated aims you will, in my opinion, succeed in putting the scientific clock back into the dark ages and this would mean an intolerable increase in the sum total of human misery and suffering.

Do you really wish to do this? You cannot have it both ways.

I look forward to your committee's response to this letter. I may yet be convinced.

Yours sincerely,

John Nicholson, MSc, MB, MRCPI, FRCSI'

He sits down slowly, totally shocked. Nausea comes over him as the pages fall to the ground. How could he have thought of, have said such things and committed them to paper? What arrogance!

Most people are kind and compassionate and avoid causing pain. However, when confronted by cruel individuals they shrink from speaking out. The episode of the woman, called Jane and her fur coat comes back; how self-righteous she was. Others could compare him to Jane! Two of a kind, inflicting pain. Every exquisite fur could tell a story, a hideous and bloody story.

His thoughts are confused.

Blind neutrality was his attitude; he realizes neutrality is contemptible. A study of animals' behaviour shows their ultimate concern is to enjoy life and to communicate joy to others. Even domestic pets will adore the vilest among us, supporting vanity with unflinching respect.

And they called Jane a murderer!

He picks up the letter again. Bloody hell! If we stop loving animals we cannot be far from hating humans. We cannot have it both ways—anymore! Those who battle with monsters must be careful lest they become monstrous themselves. There has to be another way. A crisis of conscience plagues him and John Gay's saying comes back to him. *'He best can pity who has felt the woe.'*

CHAPTER 3

Linda's illness constantly darkens her inner landscape with nauseating stillness followed by needle-hot attacks that overwhelm her. Only then she agrees to medication, obtaining relief and remaining safe from living—for a while. Eventually, the mist breaks and lets the world in again. I do not want to lose contact, she tells him; I would prefer my time capsules—her comfort blanket of memories.

However, pain insists on attention; it screams, it gnaws spreading a desert in front of her and becomes wedged into her brow. It cannot be shared; it is her burden and she carries it alone. Through suffering a strange end-of-experience looms, with a feeling of home. Hers is a different road and she is in urgent need of provision.

'Alone into the alone.' She quotes several times.

As for John, if ever there's a time for thinking, it is now. Her suffering consumes him and pierces him to the last fibre. If she's to be shattered, he must remain unbroken and elevated views are useless. Such imaginings as 'the sum total of human suffering' come to him. Linda is that, in front of his eyes. It's now reached—maximum for the whole universe. Add another thousand, another million suffering beings and it adds not one jot. It's here now. All of it.

And it hurts like hell.

It's also an effort to keep associates away—those who collect around tragedy not merely to sympathize, more to gloat, those who wander through life scattering secrets like confetti and come together at inquests to relish the murdered reputations of poor dear friends. Linda had become a dear friend. An inquiring infliction would arrive, spilling over with affection and leaves dear Linda exhausted with concerned compassion.

Except Professor Wainwright. He'd written a short note to John expressing his sorrow immediately he heard the news. He telephones one evening to ask if it would be an impertinence to pay a short visit.

'Of course not,' John says, 'we'd welcome a visit anytime.'

'Good. Would tomorrow at three o'clock be acceptable.'

'We'll expect you then.'

Wainwright arrives precisely on time. Linda sits upright on a high chair, her hands holding the armrests. John gestures to the sofa facing her and he takes the stool.

'And how's Linda today?'

'Quite well although tired at times.'

'That's good. I spoke to Colm Murphy yesterday and he said you came through the operation extremely well, although there were a few hitches afterwards.'

'Oh the pentazocine. Do not remind me. That was awful. It was a nightmare.'

'I'm sorry you'd to go through that. Some kind of clinical trial was going on.'

'We didn't know that,' John interrupts. 'We should have been informed.'

'Look here both of you,' Wainwright says forcefully, 'this is only the beginning of such trials on patients, and of course pentazocine is an acceptable drug in others. You know that. Previously, we've had little feedback clinically and had to depend on results from animals. Now we hope to use clinical trials.'

'An alternative!' Linda explodes. 'Why experiment on us?'

He sits back on the sofa and plays with the frills of a cushion.

'Please Linda don't say experimenting on you,' he's trying to be conciliatory, 'we're now facing a greater challenge than ever in testing drugs. What better material could there be than human subjects?'

'But professor that is frightening.' She looks alarmed. 'What would happen if something went wrong?'

He hesitates. There's no quick answer. 'We can cope with most eventualities.'

She remains silent gathering her thoughts.

'Perhaps informed written consent is a way forward,' she suggests. 'So unfair on us, speaking as a patient. Like treating us as guinea pigs.'

Wainwright feels uncomfortable, not just because of Linda's illness—after all he had to go through Gillian's death—but also because his department is geared to achieving results in drug protocols by whatever method possible. Any attempt to interfere would be a threat to his authority in the university.

However, this is not the real reason for his visit, so he changes the subject.

'You know something Linda,' he says reaching for her hand, 'I lost my own dear wife, Gillian, from leukaemia when she was about your age.'

'How dreadful. I never realized that. Tell us what happened?'

He unfolds the saga of falling in love with the most gorgeous Irish postgraduate student in Cambridge, his marriage, which lasted a few years, and her gradual descent into the final stages of the illness. He is just about to describe the last few weeks but holds back. After all, his feelings are less important than this young couple's sensitivities.

There is an awkward silence.

CHAPTER 4

The Nicholsons are reading in the lounge. Linda puts her book on her lap and places a bookmark inside.

'John, *alskling,* how is your work progressing?' She asks calmly.

'Slowly in spite of the fire.' He shouldn't say too much. 'Tissue cultures are sensitive but the drug is too toxic for humans.'

'And you are making it really safe?'

'That's right.' He avoids her gaze.

She looks at him unblinking. 'And it is powerful stuff!'

He nods and smiles. 'Yes darling. Just too powerful. We're trying to make it safe by conjugation and using combination therapies.'

She remains silent, struggling. She looks straight into his eyes. This time he cannot escape.

'If I could have one wish—it would be to have my next birthday.'

No reply. There's sweat on his brow and upper lip. It's removed quickly.

'I want to ask,' she hesitates, handling her book nervously she goes on, 'to ask if chlor 10-6A would be effective in my condition?'

The question he most dreaded, although not completely unexpected.

'Linda it would be too dangerous.' His protest is too quick. And he has a feeling of *déjà vu*. 'Anything could happen and … '

' … And?'

He stares at her open mouthed.

'And it's only meant to be used where we know chemotherapy is effective.'

'Where we know,' she echoes looking down at her book and turning the pages. Even though she speaks slowly her stress levels rise.

'We know your condition wouldn't respond to chemotherapy.'

There is a moment of painful silence.

'John, do you realize I am dying!' She shouts.

Reason, distilled from experience, tells him the answer. His reply is immediate.

'And it could kill you prematurely.'

'How do you know?' She challenges him.

Words are hard to find yet harder to say.

'I don't know.' His voice is pure logic. 'We need time to test and refine it.'

'I have not much time left.'

Nausea comes over him and he wipes his brow again.

'You've given me a Hobson's choice Linda.'

A silence and then she relaxes, staring ahead but not at him.

She is almost smiling now.

'John I really did not want to say this but I think the time has come.'

'What is it?' He's desperate. 'You know I'd do anything.'

'Anything at all?' She hopes he will understand without the necessity of words.

He'd like to smile but cannot.

'Yes—as long as it's sane.'

'What is sanity?' She gives a gesture of helplessness knowing she will not get an answer.

She stands up slowly, kisses him on the forehead as he writes at his desk.

'I am tired John,' she announces all agitation gone. 'Please excuse me. I will go to bed.'

'Fine. I'll be up soon. I want to finish this section of the manuscript.'

She goes to the bottom of the stairs and remains there. She has to. Her head throbs, hands tremble and there's pain in her back on inhalation. Slowly she mounts the stairs, one at a time. The effort tells her more clearly than any specialist how advanced the illness is. Pain is like a knife as she reaches the top. Avoiding deep breathing she prepares for bed and tries to relax. With the side light on she closes her eyes and waits. But waits for what? It would be so easy to slip into the final stages of despair—a lot is there already. Many things were on in her mind that evening which she did not say. She wanted to spare John, but they bore down heavily. Nothing mattered anymore. He could ask questions, yet, there is the inner turmoil, and the terror she alone has to cope with. In recent days—and nights—she felt how easy it would be to have a warm bath, retire to bed and be within reach of the small bottle of oblivion, lie back, sleep and not to wake again—ever. It would be simple. And yet…

Time cannot measure John Nicholson's pace as he trudges the city streets later that evening. The air is cool over Heuston Bridge.

Towards the west, a fiery globe emerges and light spills on water setting it ablaze. Colours grow intense as the sun throws handfuls of it into space. Purple follows, shadows rise and night urges stars to invade his vision with yesterday's light. A figure, caped in green and black, stands on the slender Halfpenny Bridge. A single white freesia is clasped in her hand as she stares into the dying sunset.

The same regimen as for Andrew Baker is used, followed by a low maintenance dose. Days become weeks and there's no change in Linda's condition, at least no deterioration. She seems confident. And there's the waiting that lingers at home, in streets and follows them everywhere.

She longs to get away, to escape now that spring is here.

A week in Cornwall is planned renting a cottage within sight of curved Whitsand Bay. The visit excites her; she has read about it, knows the works of Daphne du Maurier but had never been to England. This is probably a good place to start—at Land's End. It is easy to reach and spring comes early.

He admires her enthusiasm although riddled with lots of what ifs. Her progress could be monitored in Dublin but this trip to a remote part of England is not the same. He'll be able to continue the maintenance dose. She argues they are not going far and it is only a week. Anyway she feels able for the adventure.

After a long boat journey the car races down the final road and comes to rest outside a shaded door. Travellers' Joy hangs from the entrance carrying wisteria and clematis over the walls and roof.

Next day the weather is bad tempered, so they travel north past Newquay and on to Treyarnon Bay where Atlantic breakers roll incessantly and trail long ribbons of spray. They stop at New Polzeath and she marvels at the surfers standing on water. Then it's time for home past horizontal grass, cottages creaking with arthritis and trees pointing the way before dissolving in dusk.

A major storm moving up from the Bay of Biscay is mentioned on television that evening. The forecaster warns that winds could reach storm force ten or worse and would hit the southeast coast of England around midnight. It would probably be safe in the southwest only getting the edge of the storm. They light the fire in the quaint open hearth as darkness falls.

It is magical and hypnotic.

Linda sits on one side and stares into the dancing flames, apparently deep in thought. Needing to relax she welcomes a period of silence.

John thinks this would be an opportunity to write, in draft form, about his feelings and inner turmoil, not for specific publication, more an exercise in analysing his own conflicts. For now he's content to make a modest start.

He moves about the little room while she sleeps and his thoughts start going round and round like an oxen circulating a threshing machine, releasing the grain. Slowly, husks fly away and seeds of information collect on the floor.

All he has to do is sort them out. When he sees enough, he moves to the table and spreads his writing material before him, opens the A 4 size notebook at the first page. He looks over at Linda. The fire has done its magic—she's now sleeping peacefully.

Blank pages stare at him, inviting and challenging. A surge of energy rises, images role back and change vividly like the leaping flames in the fire. Words flow from his pen; the first in the title, come out of nowhere.

He writes. *The Burden of Guilt.*

CHAPTER 5

At eleven thirty everything is calm and the effort of writing tires John. He takes his glasses off and rubs his eyes. His thoughts are written in coherent order, although some will have to be added, especially the growth of bureaucracy.

Sounds simple! And it used to be. Sadly regulations and red tape, mostly written in gobbledegook, were getting in the way.

A shiver takes hold of him. Shadows move about in the room. Some are accusing ghosts. Recently, prayer had not come easy. He feels the need, but words of childhood are useless. Different words are called for and are not there.

Linda said to him on the way home.

'If you live your life waiting for the storm, you will never enjoy in the sun.'

He must rest now.

At one o'clock a screaming noise wakes them; a noise so powerful and eerie it terrifies. And it goes on and on. She is fully awake. Behind the curtains comes a brilliant flash, then complete black again. Not for long. Another flash flutters like a moth outside covering the window in white. Several storms are overhead. Almighty explosions closely follow more flashes as battles are fought in the sky, and nothing is going to get in their way. Nature has let loose a colossal force and is flattening all in its path. In addition to the screaming there are crashes of trees and buildings. The storm, better classified as a hurricane, lasts four to five hours and leaves them exhausted. Next morning all is calm as they wander about to inspect the damage.

The final day arrives. She is first to wake after a sleep-soaked night. She feels well and strangely new. It is wonderful to be awake again. Her gaze drifts to the diamond leaded window as she hears a creeper tapping on the glass. She slips out of bed and opens the latch.

A sudden fluttering occurs among the shadows.

'You rascals,' she whispers to the house sparrows.

Leaning forward she breathes in warm air and hears the cawing of rooks high in the trees. Beyond, a yellow light shimmers on the sea, inviting. Impulsively she accepts.

John is not disturbed by the click of the bedroom door. She goes down the stairs as quietly as she can. Walking boots are put on and a warm half-coat. Even though it is bright and sunny there is a sharp bite in the air.

John's notebook lies face open on the kitchen table. She glances at his scribbling thinking it is more scientific data to be worked on, and dismisses it crossly. How could he bring work on holidays? Now she is going to enjoy herself with a pleasant walk to the sea with only spring flowers and babbling brooks for company. Paradise! Then the title on the page catches her eye. The Burden of Guilt. What on earth is all this about? What guilt? And whose burden? She reads:

... All of us have a need to communicate; some do it by talking, by performing poetry, by reading the works of others. For me, the written word now seems appropriate. A burden has been with me for months and probably started when I struggled through the ashes of the Institute for Cancer Research. Here the major conflict probably started. The big question then was: Why? Not only why the fire? In some way I felt I too was to blame ...

... I have tried to understand why strong-minded people would go to such lengths to stop the work we are doing. I now have a clearer view of their side of the story and it hurts me that I could have been so blind. What opened my eyes was reading my letter to the Animal Liberation Front and reliving the anger I must have felt when writing it ...

John never showed me the letter, she says to herself. She reads on, even though the writing rambles in places.

... The blinkers have been removed. All fellow creatures should have a happy, contented, pain-free life. It is not a privilege; it is a right. When one is close to the problem for so long one can develop a rigid point of view, almost a one track mind. To get results at all costs, even cost to others, human or animal. Humans can object, animals cannot ...

... I felt jealous of the layman who is not directly involved in research, does not know about it and probably does not want to know. In so doing, he is protected; yet, his is the one most likely to benefit from the knowledge gained …

She finds it difficult to read the next section but struggles on. There was no simple answer. He had never opened his heart to her about his misgivings. Everything did seem to be going smoothly. He appeared to have no worries, no guilty conscience, and no problems, until the day of the fire. This was a watershed in his research.

She makes a cup of tea, goes back to the table and tries to put her thoughts in order. Is she supposed to see this document? Is it a mistake? Well, it is right there on the table, open and for all to see. So she is really not to blame. She cannot help seeing it. Does he expect otherwise? Or maybe, it is left open deliberately. It saddens her to think her husband is now in the eye of the storm. She continues to read.

… When I forsook surgery to go into research there was zeal and enthusiasm for work. Only the job in hand. It was all that mattered, to solve the chemical equations, to modify and prepare new products in cell lines, in tissue cultures, refining them, testing them on rodents, calculating the good and bad results and measuring benefits against damage. No other thought, only the result ...

… The perfect drug has never existed, and I wonder if it ever will. All had drawbacks but we accepted them, studied them, subjected them to fine-tuning and tried again, and again. Occasionally, there was a breakthrough and these drugs were developed assiduously ...

... Greater demands were creeping into the research world where higher mammals, including primates, would be better models, more dependable and quicker to get results. The main reason was their make up; their physiology was almost identical to humans …

… A crisis of conscience was developing. Could I continue to use these intelligent, but pathetic, creatures purely as a death machine to get a few more points to prove than chemical X was slightly better than chemical Y? …

… Was it worth finding out? Pharmaceutical companies were constantly promising the wonder drug, the elixir of life supported by extensive advertising campaigns. Knowledge should be shared; otherwise a monopoly is created and the only reason is greed …

… Then a tragedy slips in blocking the system—a phial of poison not properly tested and released before its time, such as antibiotics that killed bacteria and brains at the same time. The global tragedy of Thalidomide that sedated mothers and allowed monsters develop in their wombs. More cases could be quoted, and greater secrecy has been demanded to protect companies. As a result more rigid testing has become so important today to protect the legal interest of companies …

She takes a long drink of tea and sits down.

… The obnoxious woman in Rome must have lit the spark for change. She was certain only she was right, no one else could have a view at all. We had to sit listening to her account of being insulted by a teenager and blamed the young girl for everything …

… There was no thought for the death and destruction unleashed on her behalf, the suffering entailed in getting a precious fur to its present owner so that she could show it off—more correctly show herself off. She only wanted to be seen, to be noticed. A status symbol to improve her image …

… Her behaviour did exactly the opposite …

Linda finishes her tea and looks into the empty fire grate. It was so warm and cosy last night falling asleep beside it. This must have been when John was busy writing. The fire is out and things look cold and grey. She turns the page.

… Many times I have tried to analyse my conscience. It was a gradual process. Something inside seemed to be awaiting another sign, another excuse, questioning the wisdom of our work. It started small, perhaps in microcosm on the battleground of a changing consciousness. To start with there were desperate attempts to keep patients alive and well—no matter what the costs …

… To cling to the spark of life, in a child or adult, was my prime and only concern. Once that spark was lost, as in Catherine Kennedy, it could never be relit. Any attempt to prevent the loss of life by blocking that magical infusion in a drug had to be resisted …

… Yet, wider issues kept intruding. It is our greatest instinct, the instinct to survive. Anything that threatens it from within or without I resisted. Every animal, including us, has this instinct, but there are arguments about other's right to survive. A corrupting concept. Debates have been going on for centuries, and conflicts test the arguments …

… Perhaps, the issues will never be resolved and others' rights to survive question our own arrogant monopoly on life …

… Each working day I noticed a small tally of defects. Early on, they didn't affect me. Now they do, and Isselherg's views were a major influence. I realize, and it pains me grievously, that I cannot stop others from using animal models. Some have used the expression: *The Tools of the Healers*. It has a ring of truth about it, but the tools themselves won't be healed—only us. That is for others now …

… There is a scent of power about the whole issue. No one is left unchanged by power. Some will use it for egotistical reasons, including self-aggrandizement and revel in the accompanying flattery. Others will go down the paths of cruelty and abuse, the hallmarks of the true bully …

… Others will be disposed to enlightenment and wisdom to do the right thing. The storm that has been raging inside is abating because a narrow line of research will occupy me. The whole field of exploring the cellular universe is opening up. Now to salvage as much dignity as possible and then walk away is my one wish. If I do not choose this fork in the road, I can visualize the storm getting worse, until perhaps no vestige of sanity is left. For me, and perhaps for me only, there is no place for a conscience while working with the *Tools of the Healers* …

… More, lots more, could be said before assuaging the guilt of the past. There is only one purpose of our being here, that is to placate our internal being—call it conscience—or what you will. It leads to the ultimate convergence of all things …

… We are all destined to pass this way but once, and deep inside there is a longing for unity and purpose in all things. Each has a journey to travel, which is shown by unaided reason and in the process we discover a personal conscience. It allows us choose the final pathway, to accept or reject it with our own free wills. If we fail to recognize, or knowingly abandon it, the way ahead is strewn with chaos, pain and madness …

Linda sees he has written more, a lot more, but does not read on.

She has seen enough.

It is time for that walk.

CHAPTER 6

Outside the air is calm and light. Linda steps into the morning sunshine passing between cliffs topped by swards of thrift and follows a path to the sea with a ribbon of water trickling alongside. She marvels at a spider's web glistening in the sun. Bindweed flowers open pink and white for the morning and are protected by their leaves.

'Are not you clever, growing anticlockwise,' she says, 'as if you want to turn back time?' Rosettes of daisies, brave on long stems, their white petals trimmed in red, radiate from yellow hearts. Their larger cousins, colonies of marguerites, sway to and fro like angels and wild fuchsia joins the pleasure of the occasion. She could never know all their names. Flowers, wild flowers and weeds. Who is to name them?

The beach comes alive with a shimmering sea. At one end, cliffs arrogantly stride out, only to be submerged. A sandy clearing welcomes her. She sits to watch, listen and dream. Waves come close, gentle waves, regular and hypnotic.

They glide, stagger and fall with a rattling sound.

She gazes inwards to another landscape. Calm clear ripples remain. The common thread of gold she can now see in all things. It embodies something mysterious, which at times she has come close to, almost discovered, yet elusive. Subconsciously, she has been watching and listening for it. The sea morning is a tantalizing glimpse, an echo and the very air throbs with its secret.

The light and heat become uncomfortable and she feels faint. Everything is like a dream that comes awake.

'That is it,' she quotes from John's poem. '*A dream that comes awake.*' This is a dream and I am going to wake up. But when?'

With a smile she sees his face and again reads the words written in her mind.

Many a time I have walked this way
And know the sound of sea on sand,
And listened to Nature quietly say:
'Come, let me gently take your hand.'
I then have walked with her amazed,
And wondered at the magic of her power.
In dizzy rapture I have gazed
And gazed, hour after hour,
At her beauty in the sky and sea,
And in the glory of the setting sun;
And with her I have longed to be
As close as could be one.
In the music of her voice
I found a calm so deep and pure
That banished all such hidden vice,

For thus, she can so peacefully lure.
'Tis like a dream that comes awake
When I behold these lovely forms,
Which I adore for thine own sake
To give me shelter from life's storms.

To give me shelter from life's storms, she repeats several times.

CHAPTER 7

Late morning finds John as sunlight enters the room. Outside sparrows are at their mischief. Passing swifts scream as they sieve the air. Screeching gulls disturb most; they're everywhere, struggling in the wind, fighting on the roof, asking, arguing. He cannot bear it.

Black cliffs retreat into a reproachful distance as he closes the window. How satisfied, how smug, how final is the complete cottage resting in its years of peace. Impatiently, he sets out to search for Linda. On higher ground a breeze pushes him towards the winding path and sun glares and dazzles. He approaches the sea and feels insignificant, a mere shadow. Far away lichen covered rocks stand guard over her. His sudden presence frightens her.

'Oh John you are out of nowhere.' She sighs standing up. 'I was miles away.'

'Sorry.' He offers a hand. 'Looks like another batch of showers later.'

She dismisses the idea.

'Let us go to Lake Trereen for a picnic.'

Provisions are prepared in the cottage and winged lodgers have theirs early. Then off in the car to Trereen several miles inland.

'Look John.' She points at two magpies perched on a wooden gate. 'Are not they lovely? And they are the same colour as the cows beyond.'

Fields smothered with oil-seed rape dazzle; their colour is magnified to a painful glare and is a vibrant reminder of change. The lights are red at the railway crossing. For several minutes they sit quietly and impatiently at the gates.

Tapping the steering wheel he asks. 'Where's that damned train?'

'Relax John. We are not catching it.'

Another silence. Then a steel monster roars by in a deafening clappity clap, clappity clap, clappity clap. Will it ever end? It does—just as quickly as it started, leaving a silence trailing behind.

They cannot drive directly to the lake; there's a walk over a hill rich in ferns and full of the scent of sea. A brook appears from a weedy pond and directs them sliding around stepping-stones and disappearing under the bones of a hawthorn bush. She notices how full of promise it is, this laughing infant falling over itself. The mere slip of a thing will grow to form a generous artery and become the life-blood of the land. She imagines how the character of the stream would change with the seasons.

Today, the stream is boisterous and happy as, in its bubbling voice, it points the way to the lake. More elder, bramble and ash form corridors along the velvety slope. One leads to a grassy clearing on the north side of the lake. Here they choose to rest.

The lake is a fine stretch of water about a mile long and half as wide. Opposite, Morvah Hill is partly covered in woodland, struggling half way up and rushing down to willows moving like seaweed. At the eastern end aspen shiver and tremble.

After lunch he stretches out and closes his eyes. Strange how he feels, near her—like this. Gradually the ache lessens. The sun pours with powerful persistence; then a shadow plays with it and touches the reflection of trees. The lapping water grows in strength and he's first to be awakened by the clattering on the shingle.

'Excuse me! What is happening?' She asks looking around.

He points at the clouds rolling in over the hill.

'It was forecast.'

'Oh dear. Time flies. Let us go home the long way.'

They hurry along the shoreline beside bracken whose wild beauty witnesses the contempt of humans for the untouched land that nourishes it. A path takes them to another clearing covered in a carpet of bluebells.

'Are not they beautiful?' She bends down to touch them. 'And they are still alive. Darling. They have waited for us.'

Light pours excitedly over the clearing; she's drenched in its brilliance. The blue tide ebbs and flows at her feet and he feels a shudder as the air tangles in branches, complaining.

They drive back to Whitsand Bay and park the car overlooking the lovely beach as it runs westwards. Heaviness hangs in the air. This is their last day. They sit in silence for a while, lost in their own thoughts, and looking out on the waves and still grass. Anxiety returns as he looks to the future.

'Penny for your thoughts,' she asks gently.

'Just work problems.' His tone is almost dismissive. 'I shouldn't carry them around on holidays, but, they seem to be getting worse. And, of course, your own welfare and future.'

She smiles knowingly at him and then looks out to sea. She, too, has had time to think.

A mischievous smile.

'You know what I think John?'

He keeps his silence.

'Well it is this,' she continues, 'there is no tomorrow. The only thing we have is now. And yet the remains of our yesterdays are still with us; it is up to us to magnify them or to reject them by selection, and mind you wilful selection, which can even destroy the present. Does that make sense? Or is it too complicated?'

'It makes great sense. In other words life is what you make it—and one should not blame anyone else for our own predicaments.'

'That is right John.' She teasingly pushes him on the shoulder as if she is pleased with him. 'You have put it much better than I have.'

He doesn't want to burden her with the future, the objections and obstructions that will be placed before him.

She senses his mood and tells him about Tomassina, her new friend who has adopted her. Tomassina knew Linda had suffered and was there to console her, to understand her. They were two of a kind, feline, feminine, devious in their demands, but direct in their affections. There was no nonsense. They communicated so well that a wonderful bond had developed.

They sit quietly with their thoughts. Again, she sees the notebook on the kitchen table with its outpouring of anguish. John had changed in the last year. Grey streaks at the temples; face thinner with a sallow complexion and eyes deep set serious and meditative. His speech was slower and more deliberate like someone carrying a weight on his shoulders. Some time back she noticed these changes, but dismissed them as stresses everyone had in hospital life.

She'd read the writings gaining an insight into his torment. It occupied her and worried her. How can she best help? Dare she even attempt to? He could close up like a clam refusing to talk. She knew him well. She decides this is an opportunity to raise the issue; after all, talk is better than no talk.

She reaches into the back of the car for the thermos flask.

'John I think there is some coffee left. Like some?' She asks pleasantly.

'Please. That'll warm us up.' He's feeling tired.

She pours the liquid into cups with her best evening smile.

'Feeling grumpy today. Are we?'

He shrugs off the question. 'As I said before, just work problems.'

'Is that all, John? Just work problems.' She persists.

He hesitates and nods agreement.

'Yes.'

'Do not we all have work problems?' She asks gently. There is a moment of silence and then she lays down a challenge. 'That does not mean a lot. Could you explain further.'

He decides to come clean.

'They're more than just work problems. It's really about a whole change of ethics and moral code on my part.'

'Does it mean you are going to give up work into cancer research?'

'No. Heaven forbid.' His tone is insistent, even shocked. 'It means changing methods. Last night when you went to bed I stayed up another two hours writing. It may be therapeutic, a type of confession or a catharsis. I was looking for absolution, from whom I don't know.'

He stopped there. She waited and then prompted.

'Go on John. Did it do any good?'

He sips his coffee. 'I think so. I might develop it further.'

'Glad to hear you have started it. You must continue. You could be entering unchartered waters, developing a new approach in chemotherapy.'

He looks at her in amazement.

'Did you read it Linda?'

She is taken aback at his abruptness. She gropes for words. Then what the hell. She laughs openly and happily.

'I did first thing this morning when I came downstairs. I could not but notice it. There it was open and for all to see.'

'That's all right. There are no secrets in it.'

She notices a fleeting smile.

He looks out to sea. 'It's only a start. There are more points I've to expand.'

'That is good John.' She is relaxing now. 'You must get it out of you. You are full of fears and contradictions that will have to be exorcised. Someday you may even have the courage to write a book about these conflicts. It would be fascinating reading and all you need do is change names but stick to facts. Fact always makes greater fiction. Maybe, now is your chance.'

'I know. And it sounds exciting. Imagine a whole book! But these fears could make me careless and lead to mistakes. Then I'd be in worse trouble.'

She laughs again. 'Do not be ridiculous John. You must have the courage of your convictions. I cannot imagine you being careless. I have lived with you, watched you, perhaps more than you think, and even when you are happy I can still hear the machinery clicking away inside your brain.'

'It's still a big problem with me, this burden thing,'

She begins to feel a little impatient but dare not show it—yet. His feeling of guilt is not logical. He should focus on his own place in the movement of things.

Then she has a brainwave. Some of the lines of a poem called Sussex by Rudyard Kipling come back. The metaphor could be applied to John.

'They may help you resolve things in your own mind.'

'Great. I'd love to hear it.' He says enthusiastically grasping at any straw.

'All right. Now listen carefully. "God gives all men all earth to love, / But since man's heart is small, / Ordains for each one spot shall prove / Beloved over all." That is it John. Think about it. Kipling has a message. You do not need to carry everyone's burdens, only your own. Forget the others.'

He stares at her. Of all the women in his life, she's the most straightforward, clear-minded and levelheaded. He loves her all the more dearly today and not as much as tomorrow and tells her so.

The tide is almost out in Whitsand Bay. Surrounding the curved bay he can see the formless shadows, some jutting out to sea, others pushing back against the land. All are sap green in colour and getting darker. In contrast, the silver sand glows against the hills, and parts still wet reflect gold, orange and red from the sky.

They drive back to the cottage, park the car and stroll the rest of the way to the cottage. Pink convolvuli are thickly woven around the grassy margin and the small hedge lining the path. This is their last walk together, here.

A lonely house a mile away, shines with importance on the night, while the sea becomes a dark space with tiny moving lights, and an occasional sweeping beam stationed in the middle of nowhere.

This time will live in their memories, the moment when the sun is drowned in water ending the day and night has not yet spread her wings; this strange limbo when there are no shadows and one could almost imagine the soil draining the light and expecting a message from above.

CHAPTER 8

It's time for Linda's check-up. Colm Murphy greets them with his usual courtesy.

'How's my favourite patient today?'

'I am fine thank you.' She sits down and smiles pleasantly.

Murphy glances at John and starts writing in the folder. After a moment's hesitation he says how pleased he is and continues writing. He inquires about the back pain. It is gone. The tiredness? That is gone too. And abdominal discomfort? None. His expression deepens and he recommends further tests. The results are available next day. All are negative.

'It's incredible,' he says looking at the radiographs. Previous films are compared, blood tests scrutinized. He's at a loss for words, a rare event.

At last she breaks the silence. 'You are pleased Mr Murphy?'

He's delighted and dumbfounded. If he hadn't known the background he'd say she's a hundred per cent fit.

'Why not do so anyway?' She hopes he will agree.

There's no answer so John inquires about previous cases. Murphy has never seen such a remission in anyone although, rarely, one comes across reports that made him wonder about the original diagnosis.

'And there was no doubt about Linda's?' John asks seriously.

'None whatsoever.' He's emphatic as he points at the previous radiographs.

The three in the consulting room have witnessed an extraordinary event. Murphy is filled with consternation, even bewilderment. He looks closely at each of them and tries to figure things out. He goes over details of the operation, the high optimism he had afterwards and the shock on receiving Professor Wainwright's report: 'This tumour is fairly well advanced, and should be staged as Grade C indicating some distal spread.' Then, months later there was radiological evidence of some, although slight, bony deposits especially in the ribs. Without treatment, this had to be progressive. Yet what have we today? We've evidence of regression—an almost unbelievable result. Something unusual going on.

It would be unwise to convey his thoughts and Murphy decides not to give in to speculation, because, at best, it's just guesswork and, at worst, it could give rise to opinions and suggestions that could do damage.

John's mood is one of elation. It means his beloved wife, companion and friend has a chance of staying with him for some time more. The chemotherapy probably played a role in her apparent recovery.

As for Linda, there is no problem. She is happy. Fate has smiled on her. There was a time when her future was bleak. The surgeon had done all he could, the radiotherapists said they could not help;

there was no evidence that X ray treatment would work and it was too dangerous on bowel cancer. Also, routine chemotherapy in the mid-nineteen eighties was only effective in a limited number of cancers. There was no known chemotherapy for adenocarcinoma of the bowel at that time, but perhaps in ten or twenty years there could be.

She had been left on her own and knew better than most what lay ahead—a slow decline to the inevitable. It was frightening. She had asked John was there anything left, any options. He had said no.

She felt there was. His work was progressing, getting some good results—and she also knew there were bad ones, which upset him terribly. No wonder he was terrified of using it on humans until the major hurdles were overcome. She helped him prepare scientific reports, with all their complicated statistics. Such inclusions as 'measurable and remarkable shrinkage of the primary tumour occurred using Chor 10-6A conjugated with gamma globulin in the majority of test procedures. There remained a minority where a striking rejection occurred. The reasons are unclear but are being vigorously followed up.'

This was her dilemma, but a human's greatest instinct came to her rescue.

Self-preservation. There was only one way out for her—chemotherapy—exactly what her husband was doing. And she had asked: If there was good evidence of its effectiveness, why could not she give it a try? Now she was living on borrowed time, meaning she had already lived her intended life, completely. She should not be here. She had been dragged back from the edge; gone right up to death's door and knocked. The knock was loud and clear, but no one answered.

CHAPTER 9

This is June, a period of perfect young summer keeping its promise with no sign its glamorous youth will ever fade. Also it is the anniversary of Linda's operation.

'Let us go to the Valley of the Two Lakes,' she says to John on the way home. 'You know in Wicklow.'

At first he is puzzled and then remembers.

'Oh Glendalough you mean?'

'That is right. It is my Shangri-La. It is a marvellous day and I am so happy.'

'All right then. I'll get someone to cover for me.'

The journey through Enniskerry with its three-sided square, past elegant Powerscourt, the Wicklow hills lying fold on fold, through Roundwood, is glorious; and Glendalough with lakes like fragments of fallen sky awaits them. Being a weekday adds to the remoteness. Strolling beside the upper lake the air is filled with small sounds and wonderful scents.

'You know John,' she says holding his hand, 'this place reminds me of Velkonstad. It is like going home.'

He smiles at her lovingly. Velkonstad seems far away now and so much has happened. 'No wonder people come here with their worries, frustrations and coronaries. Someone once said the bitterest tears shed over graves are for words left unsaid and deeds left undone.'

'Oh John please stop.'

There he goes again, trying to put on a philosophical slant on everything.

She adds. 'Too much thinking can make you ill.'

'Don't I know,' he sighs looking into the distance, 'don't I know only too well. Linda, I've been so disturbed in the last few weeks I thought I was going crazy. For years I've been a cruel monster, but I didn't realize it or maybe didn't want to. I can forgive others their mistakes but it's not easy to forgive my own.'

'Do not accuse yourself John.' Her eyes are bright with encouragement. 'It will do no one any good.'

'Linda. I've only one life. Any good I can do, any kindness I want to do it now. No excuses, no deferment, no neglect. I won't pass this way again.'

'Of course you will do what you want and I will back you completely.'

They reach the end of the valley and stretch out near a stream in the still heat. She draws an imaginary circle around it, shutting out other times. So, for a while they are silent; she prepares the meal while he imagines conflict between the grass and trees at the edge of the lake. Her work complete she strokes the rug beside her and looks up.

'Now let us make our own memories.' She invites him to sit

beside her and adds. 'In those we love we live on.'

Today there is colour everywhere and through it they can feel joy; for her it is the colour of flowers—especially wild flowers—that expresses it supremely. With their feet in earth and faces to the sun—something we cannot do—they shield us from a brightness that is too bright, and as glorious reflections they link earth and sun.

Eventually she looks around. The wind has eased and strips of dying light paint the leaves gold. She closes her eyes and understands that before we can see beyond the sunset and the beauty of a simple flower, we have to truly love this world.

She is thankful for life, for John and for everything.

In these sublime surroundings she is mildly hyper manic. But surely she is entitled to be a little hyper manic, when she was dragged back from extinction, and especially by her brilliant, non-demonstrative husband. But he is so tense. This cannot be good for him. If he could only let go and talk about his problems. Even when he married he was shy and reluctant to share secrets. Must he be so?

It's getting late when they arrive back in Dublin. He suggests a good restaurant. She insists on preparing a meal at home. 'Nonsense! We do not have to go out. It is getting late, John, and you are probably tired.'

He protests but she is adamant.

'All right.' He gives in reluctantly. 'Although there's one thing I have to do first. A new patient of Wainwright's is coming into ward 4 and he's asked me to see her. It's urgent.'

'Cannot it wait until tomorrow?' She asks anxiously. 'Well maybe not. The trials of being a doctor's wife.' She sighs, although she would not have it any other way. Incidentally, she has to visit the grocer's shop around the corner for a few things.

He stands up and looks for his keys. 'I'll go and get them for you.'

'Do not be silly John. I know exactly what to get and you do not.'

'Well you could make a list.' He puts on his coat and pockets the keys. 'Besides you must be really tired. You've had a long day.'

'Please John. Let me do this my way.' She opens both hands in a pleading gesture and feels a little irritated. 'I am not that helpless. And it was my idea to celebrate our great news at home. And please, it is what I want. Is it not? Please understand John. Please understand.'

He'd to smile at her turn of phrase, words refusing to flow into each other.

'Of course it was your idea. Fine. I'll see you later.'

She puts out her arms and he responds immediately.

'Alskling, beloved. I want to thank you with all my heart and soul for—for giving me shelter from life's storms.'

She rushes downstairs still feeling agitated. Why does John treat her like a child? She is a fully mature person that knows her own mind. Well, she would make an extra special effort to impress him this evening with something really grand. Yes, that is exactly what she will do. Surprise him! She will surprise him with something he will never forget.

'Hello Linda.' Bre, the neighbour, stops her in the lobby and is prepared for a chat.

'Bre. I cannot talk now.' She gasps as she rushes past. 'I have lots to do. I will tell you all later perhaps.'

And she disappears out the door in a great rush.

'She never looked—poor thing. The car went straight into her,' an old lady says to a friend standing at the corner of the street.

'I saw it happen Brigid. She was in such a hurry. '

The ambulance screams down the road heading for St Mary's and items of grocery lie scattered about.

John walks into ward 4 with a folder in his hand. The patient is an eleven-year old girl who has been referred with acute leukaemia that is not responding to routine chemotherapy. Staff nurse rushes in, as he is about to examine the girl.

'Dr Nicholson?'

John turns around to face her. 'That's me.'

'Sister's on the phone,' she says breathlessly, 'she's been looking for you urgently.'

'I'm sorry. I left my bleep with the switchboard because I'm off duty.'

'She wants you to go to casualty as soon as possible. It's your wife!'

Two minutes it takes to get there. When he arrives sister comes straight to him.

'Dr Nicholson.' She holds out a hand. 'At last. I'm afraid your wife has had an accident. The consultant is with her now.'

John's voice is strained and muffled. 'I must see her. Where is she?'

'In here doctor.' She leads him into the examination room. Linda is lying on a couch surrounded by resuscitation equipment.

The doctor-in-charge recognizes him. 'I'm glad you were able to make it,' he whispers. 'She's far gone but we'll do our best.'

'Is she conscious?' He can hardly get the words out.

'I think so.'

John kisses her on the forehead. Slowly she opens her eyes and recognizes him. She tries to respond but is unable. She then raises her hand and touches his cheek. The others stop what they are doing and the room becomes still. He takes her hand and feels the fingers tighten. He knows what she wants; he puts his ear close to her lips. With an enormous effort she says. 'John I will always love you.'

'Linda, Linda,' are his only words.

'I am sorry I will have to leave you now,' she continues in a slow fading voice.

He can say nothing. She then looks straight ahead and closes her eyes saying. *'Wenn ich einmal soll scheiden.'*

She smiles, but not at him.

The pressure in his hand gradually disappears and her arm falls away. There only remains a silence. A terrible silence.

Linda Lindstrom dies late in the evening. Her husband's outbreak of grief is terrible to witness. Suddenly, he appears to lose all control, as he throws himself across her, weeping bitterly and uttering incoherent words. He slides gently down and kneels on the floor, his head pressed to her side. Sister moves forward to console him, but Dr Donaldson raises a hand to stop her.

'Let them be,' he whispers. 'It would be best.'

After several minutes John stands up. All grief has drained away. He settles Linda in the most appropriate position, kisses her on the lips and draws the white sheet over her. He goes into sister's room, dazed and shocked, unable to talk. There he remains alone. Ten minutes later he emerges, calm, composed and hair in place. It is only the eyes that give him away; they are bloodshot and staring into a deep abyss. There remains a silence, a terrible silence in the room. Sister comes over to him and hands him a silver pendant.

'We found this doctor. We were able to identify her from what's inside.'

He opens it. A neatly folded sheet of paper is there. On one side Linda had written: 'I am Doctor John Nicholson's wife —Linda.'

On the other side is a poem with the title. 'The Walk.'

He stands up, leaves the room and goes to the laboratory. He sits in the place where he sat many times. He bows his head and weeps bitterly, asking himself. Why?—so many times. Why? Why did this have to happen—why did he ever become a doctor? Is there no end? The paper falls to the ground.

That night his mind plays havoc. At first a drugged sleep overcomes him while the grandfather clock, full of the dust of another time, ticks quietly outside the room. After midnight he wakes with an involuntary movement and stares into the veils of somnolence draped about. Then for a second, as the moon soaks his clothes on the floor, he hears a sound through the open window, a voice, faint and far away that dies gently on a bed of wind. Is it Linda?

A steel fist grips his stomach like a vice. He lies back again rigidly and listens. The clock strikes two and at that moment something collapses inside him. He turns over, his face contracts, eyes fill and his hands clench in the darkness. A breeze stirs the curtains, twisting them like sails towards the ceiling. It moves over his naked arm, caressing it, and goes through the closed door.

Perhaps Linda can also see the setting sun and rising moon and pause, for an instant, remembering, before she sinks into a timeless present. Or better still, perhaps she can now see beyond the summer lightning, the rainbow, beyond pain and grief. For him the sun and flowers and laughter of their world will never fade.

As dawn coagulates into a stormy sky a fretful dream descends on him. He returns to consciousness about six-thirty, still exhausted, and stares at the ceiling with a blue veined arm hanging helplessly over the edge of the bed.

Later when he returns to ward 4 to see the new patient he recognizes the address on the hospital folder.

And the girl's name is Annette Nolan.

ISBN 142516095-6

9 781425 160951